ELECTRICLAND

J. M. Abrahams

authorHOUSE®

AuthorHouse™
1663 Liberty Drive
Bloomington, IN 47403
www.authorhouse.com
Phone: 1 (800) 839-8640

Published by AuthorHouse   06/14/2017

ISBN: 978-1-5246-8714-4 (sc)
ISBN: 978-1-5246-8713-7 (e)

Library of Congress Control Number: 2017905471

Print information available on the last page.

This story is dedicated to my family, whose unconditional love has guided me through the roller coaster of my life and grounded me safely in this complex and challenging world.

I would also like to thank all the artists who have inspired my imagination, enabling me to pen this epic tale, which hopefully honors their own dedication to the arts and the sacrifices they made to tell their own stories.

To Stephen King, Jimmy Page, Lou Gehrig, Vincent Van Gogh and Robin Williams. You are all geniuses who have made an indelible impact in my life with your immense passion and talent.

Thank you all again, for inspiring me to be the best that I can be.

CONTENTS

PART 1

A jolt of lightning set's me back a pace
Feel like a visitor from outer space
Please excuse me if I don't quite understand
I'm just a stranger in Electric Land

-Paul Rodgers, Bad Company

PART 1

CHAPTER 1

THE LIVE WIRE

Friday, October 13

Jack Banks gripped the handle of his pool stick case like a vise. And though the night air was cool, his body still throbbed with tension and heat. It was an unfamiliar feeling, this kind of uncertainty before a game. But for some reason, maybe many this time, his body was telling him to stay away.

Even as the day had worn on, he had begun to feel more and more unsettled. Not only had his stomach slowly twisted into a knot, but it seemed as if as if a rock had somehow lodged itself in his throat. Now he was starting to sweat and it was beginning to annoy him. Without realizing it, his right hand had balled into a fist, sending pins and needles up his arm. His fist was so tight, the whites of his knuckles were gleaming in the street lights. He rolled his hazel eyes and reflexively jerked his head, flipping his soft, blond hair away from his face. He then put the cue case down between his legs and began rubbing his hands together. He couldn't afford for them to cramp up. It would ruin his game.

He kneaded his fingers, working the blood back into them while contemplating where he was headed. And he wasn't thrilled with the idea. The Live Wire was the last place on earth he wanted to be.

What a dive.

Junkies shooting up in the bathroom? Fights almost every night? Who needed that?

But Mickey needed him to win the prize money, and Jack had understood. Even if it meant risking his neck in the process. No doubt, Mickey would have done the same for him.

Winning the tournament would be easy for Jack. He was that good. Up until the finals, he had disposed of his opponents with little problem. Now all he had to do was win two out of three games of eight ball. Then they were home free.

The only problem was he had to face Sticks Favors, which was, in no uncertain terms, a clusterfuck.

Fighting his reluctance, Jack forced his legs to walk the final few blocks to the bar. When he finally arrived, the door stood there, like the mouth of some brooding beast waiting to swallow him whole. The bar pulsed with hostility, its lights flickering against the insides of the sooty windows as curses and threats rumbled like growls from within. And it dared him to enter.

All he could do was bend forward, put his arm on the door and lean his forehead against it. He closed his eyes, furrowed his brow and rubbed his forehead upon his sleeve, wiping off the sweat that had accumulated there.

Finally, after a few moments, he took a deep breath and stood back. He looked at his watch. Ten minutes to ten. It was time.

Fuck it.

He pushed his way inside.

Instantly, he was hit with a wall of chaos. "Got Me Under Pressure" by ZZ Top blasted out of the jukebox, its power rock rifts bouncing off the walls, the mirrors, and the neon beer signs. Volatile thugs were everywhere, smoking cigarettes, laughing, and guzzling beer. Most were bearded and tattooed, with facial scars and missing teeth. They were getting loud and boisterous already and Jack knew why.

They were there to see the tournament. Or more likely, what happened *after* the tournament.

Jack wound his way through the crowd to the bar and ordered a beer. He searched the place for Mickey but he was nowhere in sight. He continued to scan around until caught a glimpse of his opponent, back by the pool area. Enshrouded by smoke, Sticks Favors' rickety silhouette moved in fits and starts as he warmed up for the match. Like some giant insect, he crept around the room, his pool cue seeming to extend from his body like some freakish appendage, as his shiny, bald head jerked in spasm, as if being hit by some invisible club. In quick, erratic motions, he flung his spindly limbs around haphazardly, cursing himself with every missed shot.

Jack glanced around and realized people were amused. They looked back and forth between him and Favors, their eyes wide with excitement. Some even came by to wish him good luck, snickering as they walked away.

Gee, thanks for the encouragement.

Jack searched around for Mickey again. *Where the hell was he?* He hoped he wasn't doing coke in the bathroom again. The last thing Jack needed was Mickey all jerked up.

With a sigh, Jack jumped off the bar stool and headed toward the pool table. When he got close, he heard Mickey call and began to turn toward his voice. But just as he did, Sticks suddenly shot forward and grabbed him by the hand. He moved his face to within inches of Jack's, the sour vapors of whisky and nicotine on his breath. Grinding his knuckles, he grinned menacingly and said, "Don't even think about it," then withdrew as if on a treadmill accelerating backwards. He spun toward the pool table, jammed some quarters into the slot with a shunk-SHUNK!, and the multi-colored balls came rumbling out. He then smirked as he racked the balls, his emerald eyes squinting from the twisted Marlboro in his mouth. A chalky cackle emanated from his throat.

Jack felt like he was at a circus side-show. He watched incredulously as Favors busied himself arranging the rack. Everything about him was weird. *And what was he wearing?* It looked like a jacket made of green felt! It was all too much. It was as if some freaked out cartoon had come to life just to torment him.

Unbelievable.

It took another call by Mickey to break his spell. He turned toward the sound of Mickey's voice and finally saw him at the bar throwing back a shot. He watched as Mickey shuddered and waved him over.

"Be right back," Jack said to Favors and started off.

"Where you going, sissy boy?" Sticks taunted. "Giving up already?"

Jack just ignored him and walked away.

"We gotta play sometime, dipshit!" Sticks called to him. "Can't stall forever!"

Jack shook his head and fought the urge to simply walk out the door. He was so pissed at Mickey for getting them into this mess.

Trying to hide his frayed nerves, Jack stiffly made his way over to the bar. There, with a huge grin on his face was his partner in crime, Mickey O'Leary, the second biggest fuck-up he had ever known.

Jack, himself, was the first.

It was alarming that despite everything they'd been through, Mickey's decision making seemed to be getting worse. It was as if he had learned nothing over the years. This latest incident was particularly a concern. Mickey would never have fallen for anything like that in the past. Something was wrong and though Mickey tried to hide it, Jack could sense him falling apart.

Even now, as Jack approached Mickey, he was shocked by his appearance. He seemed to be deteriorating by the moment. With paranoid eyes and in desperate need of a shave, Mickey had begun to resemble a strung out junkie spiraling desperately out of control. Jack knew they were going to have to deal with Mickey's drug problem sooner or later, but at that moment there were more important things at hand.

Jack was so stressed out, all he could manage was a shaky "Hey."

Mickey was smiling so broadly, his cheeks and eyelids were quivering. He took Jack's hand, leaned into him and slapped him on the back. "Hey, Man!" he exclaimed, "You ready to kick some ass?"

Jack was less enthusiastic. "Easy for you to say. You don't have to face this lunatic."

Mickey glanced over Jack's shoulder to see Favors guzzle an entire beer and let out a huge belch. He looked back at Jack and said, "You may have a point."

"I don't need this shit, dude."

A hint of humor found Mickey's eyes. "Stop worrying, Bro. The way you shoot? This thing will be over before it begins."

"I'm not worried about the pool."

"Come on, Jack. Lighten up. This guy's a clown. My granma's poodle's got more brains in its ass. Just run the table so we can get outa here."

Jack glanced warily back at Favors. "You sure there's no other way? Seriously."

A hint of desperation found Mickey's voice. "No, Man. I told you before. I'm broke. And there's no way I'm asking my folks for more money. They'd start asking questions and I'd never hear the end of it."

"I know but…"

Mickey sighed and put a hand on his shoulder. "Look, if he gives you any shit, I'll take care of him myself, okay?"

He searched Jack's eyes until he was satisfied with what he saw. And then he smiled. "That's the Jack I know! Now go do your magic!" He shoved him back towards the pool table.

As Jack reached it, the emcee began his introductions over the PA. Favors was announced first. Immediately people began to boo and hiss. Jack thought he even heard a few raspberries. When Favors heard it, he took it as a complement. He strode around the table like a villain in a professional wrestling match, his arms flailing in the air and his chin jutting out with pride.

Jack got a more favorable reception. People cheered and squeezed his shoulders, patted him on the back and wished him well. Seeing this, Favors just glowered, clasping his hands together on his stick and waiting impatiently for the game to begin.

Jack, a little abashed, fought back a smile and began screwing his stick together. But before he could finish, Favors came over and slapped the cue ball in his hand. "C'mon Shit-fer-Brains," he said. "You break."

The ball hit Jack's hand pretty hard, sending pain up his arm. That was enough to set him off. In a rare, instinctive reflex, Jack thrust his face within inches of Favors' and glared deeply into his eyes. Then, in an even and threatening voice, he said, "Back....the fuck...off."

The bouncers immediately moved in.

Favors' face froze. He wasn't expecting that reaction. His arrogant sneer slowly faded and was replaced by uncertainty. He glanced at the bouncers and nervously chuckled. Then stepping aside, he spread his arms wide in a mock bow and swaggered stupidly all the way back to his seat. He began to laugh, a loud, irritating cackle that became louder and louder until his head began vibrating out of control.

It was getting ridiculous.

Once more Jack glanced at Mickey, who simply shrugged his shoulders.

Whatever. It was time to play. Without any time left to worry, Jack's confidence returned. Anger began to dominate his fear. He tossed the cue ball in the air several times and then placed it gently on the table. He then chalked his stick and centered the ball with it carefully, as he had done countless times before.

Everything depended on the break. It was the key to the game. The right break could start him on a run that could finish it all before Favors even had a chance to shoot. But he had to hit it just right. With a critical eye, he repositioned the ball, placing it exactly where it would receive the precise amount of force. Then, like a predator, he poised for the attack. Crouching slightly, left foot forward, right foot back, he slowly drew back the stick.

Then he felt it. The energy. It flickered deep inside him like a spark and ignited, sending an undeniable impulse surging through his arms. In a silent rage, he thrust the cue stick forward like a sword, firing the white ball across the table and smashing it into the others with a CRACK! The rack of balls exploded, propelling them into a dizzying flight. Like prey fleeing from a predator, the balls frantically sought refuge in the holes of the table. They careened about in a dizzying chaos until they could roll no more, helplessly laying vulnerable to yet another attack. Only the cowardly yellow ball had found the far left corner pocket.

Jack liked what he saw. He surveyed the configuration on

the table and immediately began to calculate. Methodically, he began making his shots in a predetermined angular sequence, sinking each ball and leaving the cue ball in a perfect spot for his next shot. He conducted the game like a maestro, making every shot he needed, until all that was left was the final shot.

The deciding shot of the game.

As Jack lined it up, his adversary moved out of the shadows. Like an apparition, Sticks Favors hovered behind the pocket where Jack was about to shoot, with wild-looking eyes. He leaned over the table, his green felt jacket blending with its surface, giving him the appearance of a levitating, decapitated head. He then drew back his lips in a chilling grimace and growled, "I wouldn't if I were you."

Jack stood up and met his menace, glaring back with a growing defiance. He was about to say something when he caught sight of Mickey, who was leaning back against one of the tables. Dressed in denim and Converse high tops, he looked like a gaunt, jittery kid who had trouble standing still. He was watching Favors, ready to jump in at a moment's notice, but his right arm was clearly shaking. Jack saw him grab it with his left hand in order to steady it. When he realized Jack was looking at him, Mickey relaxed, and a wordless communication passed between them. Slowly he closed his right hand into a fist and raised it in a gesture of faith so moving, that Jack never loved him more than he did in that moment.

Jack nodded, then refocused on the game. *Time to end it.*

As he shifted his gaze back to the table and realigned his shot, Favors' imposing figure drew near.

Jack simply peered up, raised an eyebrow and said, "Fuck off, you freak!" and slammed the eight ball home.

The place went berserk.

Despite the fact that Jack was a better player, many people still thought he would throw the game, so bets had been placed on either side of the contest. As Jack raised his arms in victory, the bar was swarmed with both fury and adulation. A week's worth of wages had just been won or lost. One guy could only turn to the bar, hang his head and pound the surface with his fist.

Sticks had to be restrained in a fit of rage. Before he had a chance to jump on Jack, and delight all those who had come to see the fight, the two bouncers had stepped in to hold him back. This disappointed many, but Jack, once relieved there was no longer need to defend himself, looked on somewhat bemused as Favors tried to struggle free. Once satisfied the danger was gone, Jack walked over to Mickey on air. An ocean of salutes and cheers guided him along the way. People slapped him on the back and thanked him for their newfound unearned income. All Mickey could do was simply beam with pride. He looked as if he were holding back tears, and when he grabbed Jack in a bear hug, it was both awkward, yet genuine. For a moment they savored the victory. When they pulled back, they pumped their fists in glory.

They decided on celebratory drinks and headed for the bar when suddenly they heard a commotion from behind. They turned just in time to see Sticks Favors break free from the crowd. Wielding his pool stick like a baseball bat, he lunged toward them.

"You little *shit!*" he bellowed, "I'm gonna rip out

your lungs!" and then swung the stick forward with a WHOOOSH!

It was a dangerous moment, but Jack anticipated it well and ducked just in time. Unfortunately, not everyone was as quick. Just as the stick swung over Jack's head, the momentum carried it into a girl to his right, and the tapered end of the stick clipped her just over her left eye, opening up a half-inch bleeding gash.

A collective gasp rose up from the crowd, and everyone just stood there stunned. The girl touched her forehead and looked at her hand. It was covered with blood. She rolled her eyes in exasperation and turned to her girlfriend. Calmly, she asked, "Is it bad?"

"Oh my God!" her friend cried and quickly pulled out some tissues from her bag. "Jesus, Tess. Are you okay?"

The girl nodded and winced in pain as she tilted down her head to press the tissues into the wound. After a moment, she glared at Sticks and said, "Idiot."

Everyone waited and watched. The girl turned to Jack and her expression lightened. She was about five foot tall, with short, black hair, and the palest blue eyes Jack had ever seen. "Nice shooting," she said, "Pretty impressive." She then said to her friend, "Come on, Ash. Let's go. Probably gonna need stitches."

Ash had fierce green eyes and dirty blonde curls that cascaded over her shoulders. She was about to take Tess to the hospital, but for the moment she had other ideas. "Hold on a sec," she said and suddenly began lashing out at Favors, knocking his ill-conceived weapon to the floor. "You fucking asshole!" she shrieked. "You could have killed her you mother fucker!"

Sticks, now dismembered without his pool cue, whimpered, "No!" and desperately groped for it on the floor. He cringed and winced from the girl's attack until the bouncers finally managed to regain order. A massive forearm grabbed the blonde by the waist and effortlessly lifted her in the air. She continued to kick and flail at Favors, screaming "Let me go, you bastard! I'm gonna kill that motherfucker!" until she was carried back into the crowd.

As she was pulled away, Favors was left cowering on the floor, his arms and hands protecting his head with the palms facing up. He was still cringing when he finally realized the girl was gone. As he peeked up, he could see the crowd looking on with disgust. Someone said, "Asshole." and a bottle cap landed with a clink next to his head. He was about to get up when a pair of heavily muscled legs straddled his face. "Wait, I didn't mean—" he started to say but was jerked up by the neck in a suffocating stranglehold. He made a strange squawking sound as he was pulled off the floor as another bouncer grabbed his legs. Despite his protests, they began carrying him out of the bar over their heads. He roared obscenities in the direction of Jack, his head swinging back and forth and his eyes clenched tight. Spittle flew from his lips as he raged like a madman. The last thing Jack heard was, "You're a dead man, Banks!" before Sticks Favors was flung out into the night.

* * *

"Wonderful," Jack said, looking at the doors. The fact that Favors' head had just been used as a battering ram brought him no comfort. Instead, the idea that their battle had only just begun was gnawing at him.

He was turning towards to Mickey to complain, when he noticed the girl holding the bloody wad of tissues to her forehead. The girl with the pale blue eyes. He wanted to somehow make her feel better, but he wasn't sure what to do. She had been jostled and shoved around by everyone straining to see Favors get thrown out, and she now looked lost, trying to find her friend Ash again.

Jack moved towards her, ready to offer consolation, when her friend suddenly reappeared and took her by the hand. For a moment, he stood there awkwardly, with his hand reaching out; kind, nervous words left unspoken on his lips. Then an uncomfortable heat filled his chest as he watched them walk away huddled in each other's arms.

He sighed, suddenly alone with his thoughts of Sticks Favors, and the dangers the lunatic now posed. He grimly contemplated the situation and moved to unload on Mickey, who was now in the midst of animatedly telling a joke to a group of drinkers. When they started roaring at the punch line, Jack discreetly pulled him away.

Mickey was still laughing as they sat down at a table.

Jack glowered at him. "Will you get serious?"

"What?" He tried unsuccessfully to suppress his merriment. Finally he wiped the tears from his eyes and said, "What's the problem?"

Jack pointed toward the doors. "*He's* the problem."

Mickey frowned as if his time was being wasted. "Who, Favors?" His dismissed the notion with a wave of his hand.

"Mick, you know he'll be back. He's crazy. Once he's got it in for someone he won't stop until he's in jail or dead."

"He's a numb nuts."

Jack sat back, exasperated. "You know, Mick, I was

afraid something like this was gonna happen. I just wish….I just wanted to beat him fair and square, you know? Just win a normal game and get outta here. With no blow-up."

"Look, dude," Mickey said. "He's a pain in the ass. Anyone else would have slugged him."

"Mick, don't you get it? He's not normal. This fucking guy *lives* for revenge."

"I wouldn't worry about it."

"Yeah, well you're not the one he's coming for."

Mickey shrugged. "I don't know. To tell you the truth, I think he's full of shit."

"Yeah, but you don't know what I know."

"What do you know?"

"I know he once waited two years to settle a score."

"What are you talking about?"

"It was weird. Like he sat down, thought about it and came up with some psycho scheme."

"What happened?"

"Remember Phil Kawalsky? He was in my auto mechanics class in high school. A real screw up, but the guy knew cars. A few years back, he and some degenerates formed some kind of half-assed auto theft ring. They stole a bunch of cars, stripped them down, and sold them for parts. And well, let's just say, one time Kawalsky stole himself the wrong car."

"Favors' car?"

"Yep. It was a souped-up 1965 Ford Mustang. Cherry red, like the one in that movie *Christine*? He had saved up for it a long time and rebuilt it from scratch. Just like that geek Arnie did in the movie. From what I understand it was a real hot car. He *lived* for that car. And when he found it missing one morning, he absolutely *freaked*. He went up and down the block, ranting and raving, threatening to kill all his neighbors. But when he finally found out who did it, it was too late. Kawalsky had already been busted and was doing two years at Rikers."

"So he waited for him to get out?"

"Yep, just like I said. He waited. And plotted. And finally he came up with some demented revenge."

"What?"

Jack leaned forward and said in a low voice, "He had him ripped apart by dogs." He nodded and sat back, pounding his fist on the table for dramatic effect.

Mickey just stared at him. After a long moment he said, "Ripped apart by dogs."

"He went out and got himself a couple of pit bulls, and trained them to go for the jugular."

"The jugular. And where'd you hear this?"

"I don't know, from a lot of people. Surprised you never heard it."

"I hear a lot of things, Jack. People spout crap all the time. And you know what it is mostly? Rumors. Bullshit."

Jack thought about this for a moment. "But Kawalsky *was* killed. They found him in an alley with his throat torn out. Right after he made parole. It was in the all the papers. How do you explain that?"

"I don't know. I'm sure Kawalsky pissed off a *lot* of people. Someone probably cut his throat and tossed him into an alley. Rats did the rest."

"But they found the dogs by his body."

"What were they doing there? Wait. Let me guess. They were eating him, right?"

"Um no, that's gross. But they were dead too. Poisoned."

"*Poisoned*?"

"Yeah, Favors probably didn't want them leading the cops to him, so he poisoned them. Chopped meat with strychnine or somethin' like that."

Mickey paused and frowned again. "Chopped meat with strychnine. That's the most ridiculous thing I've ever heard. Come on, Jack. You gotta stop believing every story you hear. Sounds like some kind of half-assed made up horror story to me. You're nuts, dude. Really. You gotta relax. Come on, let's have a drink."

They sat down at the bar, and with a wink a middle-aged barmaid gave them a couple of crisp, cold drafts on the house. For the next few minutes, Mickey went on abusing Jack until the pool player finally cracked a smile. Seeing Mickey in good spirits again was a relief to Jack, and the idea of having won a contested pool tournament felt pretty good. Even if the money he had won was going to pay a debt.

Mickey finished his beer and said, "I gotta take a leak."

Jack took a handful of pretzels out of a basket on the bar and tossed one into his mouth. His attention turned to a TV that was mounted on the wall above the bar. The Atlanta Braves were pummeling the Philadelphia Phillies in the third game of the baseball playoffs. Without taking his eyes off the TV, he said, "Try not to use the sink this time."

"You're a real funny guy," Mickey said and disappeared into the crowd.

Jack watched as Greg Maddox made a batter look silly with a ridiculous knuckle curve, leaving the bases loaded. The broadcast then slipped into commercial, leaving Jack to study the surface of the bar. It was scarred with years of knife carvings, with one particularly artistic illustration catching his eye. It was the hideous grimace of a mortally wounded man, a dagger protruding grotesquely from his neck. Blood was spraying from wound like water from a garden hose. The caption underneath read, "IF YOU EVEN LOOK AT MY GIRL THIS WILL BE YOU." It was signed " RAZOR" in thick, angry slashes. Jack searched his memory for a Razor and recalled a vague image of some dude with a crooked eye and rotten teeth. He made a mental note not to look at his girl.

Jack glanced across the bar and spotted Joe Garrett, the longtime owner of The Live Wire. He was a large, beefy man in his mid-fifties with the worst hairpiece Jack had ever seen. Sometimes when he was drunk, Garrett would doff it to the ladies like a hat, prompting either surprised gasps or light-hearted giggles. He loved shocking them. It always got a big laugh. But despite his sense of humor, it was best not to underestimate him. He always kept a bat within reach and, though he had more than enough bouncers to keep things in order, more often than not he would find his way into the fray of many a brawl.

Mickey called him the Thug with a Rug.

Jack caught Garrett's eye and waved him over. The bar owner finished hand washing a few glasses and approached in three long strides. Tucked into his belt, (which was pulled a little too tight) was a T-shirt depicting a fallen power line, writhing like a snake and showering sparks into the sky. Underneath the picture,were the words THE LIVE WIRE. "Nice game, pal!" he acknowledged as he hastily dried off with a rag. When they shook hands Jack noted Garrett's was cold, fat and still wet. "I can't believe you ran the table!

Favors didn't even get to shoot!" He leaned back against the back wall and folded his arms with the rag in between them.

"Yeah," Jack said, "I think he was a little pissed."

Garrett smirked. "Ya think?" His expression then switched from admiration to caution. "Just watch your back, kid. That guy don't forget nothin'." He then pointed at his head for emphasis. "He's a few donuts short of a dozen, if you know what I mean.'"

Jack new what he meant.

Mickey returned and Garrett gave him a wink. He then leaned in close to them both. In a voice barely above a whisper he said, "Guess you guys want the money. I can give you about a grand from the drawer, but the rest is in the back. Can't keep too much cash out here with all these derelicts around." He stood back and searched both their eyes for understanding. "You know how it is." They both nodded. They knew how it was.

Once in agreement, Garrett spun toward the till and danced his fingers on the keys. There was a loud cha-CHING! and the register stuck out its cash-laden tongue. Reaching into the drawer, he removed stacks of beer soaked bills and then motioned them back toward his office. They followed him and recognized the two heavily muscled bouncers who were guarding the door. Garret needed three keys to open it. Once inside, he told Jack and Mickey to sit down while he got the rest of the money from his safe. He returned with a handful of twenties and a large manila envelope. He licked his filthy thumb and made a ceremony out of counting the money. Jack couldn't help but be a little anxious. Too many crooks were in the bar. And junkies as well. Desperate junkies.

Garrett counted out the last few hundred dollars and placed them in the envelope. He then handed it to Jack. "I suggest you two get out of here ASAP."

Jack couldn't help himself from peeking inside the envelope. He took out a hundred dollar bill and looked at the print of Ben Franklin. Though he couldn't explain it, something was happening to the old man's face. It seemed to move and shift under his gaze. Maybe Jack was tired, maybe he was stressed out, or maybe it was just that his vision was temporarily out of whack. In any case it seemed to him that Ben Franklin was laughing, and he was pretty sure the joke was on him.

CHAPTER 2

ELECTRICLAND

With the cash secured firmly inside his jacket, Jack followed Mickey out the back door. Through a minefield of potholes and broken glass, they hurried toward Mickey's battered Buick. Used condoms and syringes were strewn about everywhere and Jack was glad he remembered to wear his old shoes. Not that he often bought new ones.

Once at his junk heap, Mickey dug for his skull and crossbones keychain. Jack watched impatiently as Mickey checked all four pants pockets and all four in his jacket, only to find it in the last one. While he pulled the keys out, he glanced nervously back at the bar and clumsily dropped them to the ground. He was trembling visibly. "Shit," he mumbled to himself and began groping for them in the dark.

Just then, three large men stumbled out the back door. They were thick, drunk, and mean looking. One wore a red bandana, another was wearing sunglasses, and the third had on a Harley Davidson jacket. He was also carrying a night stick.

The Bikers. Wonderful.

Jack thought he heard one of them say, "Where'd they go?" and his blood pressure began to rise. "Mick, you better hurry," he urged.

After what felt like an eternity, he heard a jingle and Mickey reappeared above the roof, twirling the key ring on his finger.

Jack leaned forward and clenched his teeth together. "Come on, let's go!" he implored and motioned back toward the malevolent-looking bikers in the dreary, yellow light.

Mickey glanced behind him and realized he better pick up the pace. They both got in and Mickey quickly pulled out of the parking lot. When they were finally on their way, Jack sat back and relaxed. He closed his eyes and breathed in deeply. And then he crinkled up his nose. The ashtray was crammed with half smoked cigarettes, the grey soot spilling over its sides. And greasy Taco Bell bags lay crumpled on the floor.

"You ever clean up this bucket of bolts?" Jack said.

Mickey glanced at the mess and then glared at Jack. "This ain't no limo service, you know. You don't like it, take a cab."

"Alright, take it easy. Jeez, that time of the month again, Michelle?"

Mickey ran his hand through his hair and swallowed. He looked at Jack and then back out the windshield. When his eyes returned they were glistening. "Sorry, man," he said through a throat full of gravel. "I'm just a little freaked out right now. I gotta go see that fuck Malone now and I'm not sure how it's gonna go. Didn't mean to be an asshole." He fell silent for a moment and drove on. Finally he said, "Look, man. I know I'm a fuck-up and I'm sorry for a lotta things. Coke's got me all screwed up. I know you don't believe me but I'm really gonna quit this time. Swear to God, hope to die." He wiped his brow with the palm of his hand so hard, Jack thought he was going to rub off some skin. Then in a low voice, almost to himself, Mickey said, "Can't keep taking everyone down with me.

Jack reached over and squeezed Mickey's arm. "Don't worry about it, man. It's cool."

Mickey wasn't convinced. "No, this time it's gone too far. I was outta control the other night. All I wanted to do was to party. Nothing else mattered." He then paused, swallowed, and spoke in a low, ominous voice, his eyes never leaving the road. "I don't know what it is, Jack, but I got a bad feeling this time."

He fell silent and reached for the knobless radio dial. He twisted it with the tips of his fingers until Led Zeppelin's live version of "No Quarter" filled the car. Jimmy Page set twangy guitar notes adrift in an enraptured Madison Square Garden. They rose and fell hypnotically, like a demon in flight, until everyone in the crowd fell under the rock master's spell. For a while, they both sat listening.

"Page is a fucking genius," Jack said.

Mickey nodded as if in a trance. "No doubt."

A red light stopped them at the intersection of Main and Line Boulevard, the area of Soundview which was quickly becoming the seediest part of town. Though the residents had long been enraged about the deteriorating conditions, no one in power seemed to care. The once bustling business center had sadly transformed into a diseased heart, which was now pumping poison.

"Look at this place," Mickey said, a disgusted look on his face. "No matter what you do, they keep coming back." Hookers and dope dealers were everywhere, prowling the street corners like scavengers, preying on the desperate and naive. And the sidewalks were packed with eager customers.

Jack sat up with curiosity. "Looks like business is good."

Mickey frowned. "You think it's Salazar again?"

"Wouldn't be surprised."

"Fucker never goes away."

Jack watched as a teenage boy with dirt on his face quickly approached a small time drug dealer he recognized. The two touched hands briefly, both scanning around nervously. They parted just as fast as they met, both disappearing into the throng. "Wilson's back," Jack said.

"Where?" Mickey said and searched the corners.

"Just missed him. Made a good sale too."

"Thought I got rid of that scumbag. Was he selling to a kid?"

"Looked kinda young to me."

"Fucker." Mickey blinked a couple of times, deep in thought. "Well if he's around, it means one of two things."

"What?"

"Either Shane and the guys are slacking off, or…"

"Or?"

"Or Salazar *is* back and he's serious this time."

Jack didn't want to think about that. "Maybe. But maybe Wilson's just trying to make it on his own."

"Doubt it. He doesn't have the guts."

At that moment, Mickey saw a young man approach an elderly couple. The old man began to point as if giving directions, when two other young men came out of nowhere and stripped his wife of her handbag and necklace. The old man tried to intervene, but before he knew it, he too lost his wallet and watch. Both were then unceremoniously flung to the ground and the three men disappeared into the crowd.

It was all Mickey could do not to give chase. "Did you just see that?!" he said.

Jack shook his head. "Unbelievable."

Mickey was about to pull over when some good Samaritans came to the couple's aid. Mickey watched with concern as they were consoled and helped to their feet.

Mickey ground his teeth. "Someone's trying to cash in again…Everything down here is organized."

"I don't know, Mick. We get a lot of amateurs, you know."

"Not *this* many. Look at all the hookers. All dressed up and classy. And that scam we just saw? *Someone's* behind this. I wouldn't be surprised if it *was* Salazar. *Fuck.*"

It was true. Even if there were freelancers, they didn't last long. Someone with muscle always came along and took over the action. And if the small timers didn't pay up, they soon ended up in a morgue.

The light turned green and Mickey drove on. "I don't

know when it happened, but this place is back to being a cesspool. Cockroaches all over the place." He took out a cigarette, lit it and looked at his watch. "Listen," he said, "I need the money. I better get going if I'm gonna get it to Frankie tonight."

"Then let's go."

"No Jack, I'm gonna drop you off. It's better if I go alone."

"What are you talking about? I'm going with you."

"No you're not, Jack. I'm doing this alone. I was the idiot who got myself into this and *I'm* gonna get myself out of it."

"But…."

"No buts, Jack. This is how it's gonna happen. Don't worry about me. I'll drop by later."

"I don't know Mick. You're in pretty bad shape. I can see you're achin' for some blow right now and this guy's obviously got plenty of it. You need someone to—"

"Forget it! You're not comin'. I mean it. This guy seems dangerous and I'm not puttin' you in the middle of it!"

Jack was about to say more, but realized his friend might be right.

Mickey sniffed and rubbed his nose with his palm. "Look, thanks, but I'm okay. Seriously. I'm just gonna go straight there, give him the money, and come home. No bullshit. I'll be back before you know it."

Jack just sighed. Even if he insisted on going, Mickey would just drive him home and sit in the car until Jack got out. Or until Mickey physically threw him out. Besides, he was really in no hurry to meet someone like Frankie Malone. He had met enough sleazebags in his life.

"Okay, fine. You win. But you better watch yourself. I don't want to find out you did any more blow. Especially with him. Leave the money and get the fuck outta there. Like you said. Don't screw around."

He gazed out the window and slowly rubbed his chin between thumb and forefinger. They hit another light and immediately to their right, Jack recognized a tall, sexy woman with long auburn hair leaning into the window of a black Trans Am. She wore a white tube-top over an unusually wide torso, and an orange leather mini-skirt hugged her narrow hips. Fishnet stockings clung to her legs and white stilettoes were on her feet.

The car was packed with exuberant college boys, and Jack was pretty sure none of them would be familiar with the true baritone of their new transvestite friend. No doubt they would be shelling out quite a bit of cash before they actually heard it, because Luscious Louie could keep up a sufficient falsetto for a quite a while. Perhaps all night. The only problem was once someone realized Louie was still anatomically intact, things would get a little ugly. Most likely then, Louie would pull out his gun and take whatever cash the boys had left.

Jack smirked as the tranny opened the car door and got in. The boys hooted in excitement, and when the light turned green, the Trans Am screeched away from the curb, leaving Mickey's Buick in a cloud of exhaust.

You'll get a real education tonight, college boys, Jack thought.

A car commercial came on the radio, and an obnoxiously loud idiot with a blow-horn voice began ranting and raving about rebates and cash back incentives. It was all so insulting

to your intelligence. Car sales. The call them "events'
and even "celebrations." What a joke. People go down to
experience these "celebrations" at car dealerships but never
see the games, the food, the dancing nor the confetti. All
they get are disillusioned old men desperately trying to make
their quotasin order to make their child support payments.
Jack reached over to change the station and Bon Jovi came
on, wailing through a fierce yet weary performance of
"Dead or Alive."

They passed by rows of dark alleys choked with garbage.
Jack frowned at the sight of his home town falling into such
disrepair. But he decided not to think about it. Way too
depressing. So he sought to distract himself with thoughts
of something more pleasant. Thoughts about the girl from
The Live Wire. He had seen her around, this cute young
brunette, but didn't even know her name. She had made a
pretty big impression on him at the bar, with her toughness
and classat the moment of her injury. Even though she could
have passed for a teenager, she exuded a confident maturity,
an unswerving grace which had left Jack wanting to know
her more.

"Listen, Mick," Jack said, "if I'm not going with you,
take me to The Shop. I want to see what happened to that
girl."

Mickey was lost in his own thoughts. "What girl?"

"The one who Favors hit. The little one with the dark
hair."

Mickey knitted his brow for a moment and then a
pensive smile dawned on his face. "Hmmmm," he mocked,
beginning with a high tone and dropping down to a low
moan. "So you got your eyes on little Tess, huh?" He then

stuck out his lower lip and nodded in approval. "I can't say I blame you. She's a little cutie." Suddenly a revelation hit him. "You like her!" he exclaimed and he reached over and poked Jack with each of those last three words.

Jack's cheeks turned the color of Campbell's tomato soup, and his efforts to block Mickey's pokes kept him off guard. As he tried to deny Mickey's suspicions, he couldn't help his voice from rising each time Mickey jabbed him.

"Get REAL! I just wanted to SEE! If she was o-KAY! Cut it OUT!"

Mickey was laughing loudly now, tears forming at the corners of his eyes.

Finally, through a sheepish grin, Jack admitted, "Alright, alright, yeah, she is kinda cute. But I do feel like it was all my fault. I coulda blocked the stick instead of ducking, you know? So I just want to see if she's at the hospital. You know, just to see if she's okay."

Mickey turned his head askance and frowned. "Man, are *you* a bad liar! Remind me never to ask you to cover for me. You are *so* full of shit, Bro. Don't bullshit a bullshitter. I've seen you like this before, and believe me when I tell you. You're hooked."

Jack knew Mickey was right. Already he was falling into his typical trap: creating a fantasy relationship with a girl he didn't know, nor had even interacted with in anything remotely resembling a normal situation.

When he realized he was doing it again, he chastised himself inwardly. More often than not, he was left disappointed, and he was getting tired of setting himself up for a fall. He told himself to calm down, to not get carried away hoping for what could be.

But it never lasted for long. He liked to dream. Especially when he thought, *really thought*, there was a chance this time. He had always been a romantic. Always looking toward the day he would find that special girl with whom he would share the rest of his life. He had never been lucky with love, running into more problems than anyone could imagine, but nevertheless, his heart was so full that he could only hope to one day find a woman whom he could give it to, so she could keep it in her care.

He had to know more about Tessa.

"Alright, stop giving me shit," he said. "So, uh, tell me what you know about her."

"Well, let's see. Not much, actually. Hmmm…I know her name's Tessa Dori. And I think I've seen her working down at Ma's."

"That grease pit?"

"Yeah, well, we all gotta make a living, don't we?"

"Yeah, I know. I ain't judging. So how old is she? She looks kinda young."

"I think she's about 23, 24, something like that."

"Huh, I thought for sure she was a teenager. I mean, she looks like she's around sixteen." Jack's face had frozen into a beaming, happy countenance.

Mickey glanced at him. "Jesus, man, nice perma-grin!" He started to laugh. "Holy shit, you're in love and she don't even know you!"

"Shut up."

Mickey smiled at him and shook his head. "Loverboy," he said. But after a moment his cheeks lowered and a look of concern came over his face. "You know what? I just remembered something. Her older sister is Maria. You remember her? We went to school with her."

Jack gazed out the window, frowning in thought. "Yeah, Maria. Year behind us. She was beautiful. A little stuck up, but she was okay. Didn't know she had a younger sister." He paused a moment, and scratched his head. "Mick, didn't she run away or something?"

"Yeah, that's right. Left a note, remember? Telling everyone not to look for her?"

"Right. She was friends with that girl Stacey from The Crazy Jester. She was the one who had the note. Anyone ever see Maria again?"

"No idea. Don't think so. From what I heard, she got hooked on drugs, got caught up with the wrong people and disappeared. Some say she's now one of those high class hookers with an expensive apartment in the city."

Jack was astonished. "Really?!"

"Yep."

Mickey drove on pensively toward the hospital. He then looked at Jack with sympathy. "Hey Jack."

"Yeah?"

"If Maria really is a prostitute, you know what that means, don't ya?"

Jack's eyebrows rose and his mouth formed a circle. When he replied, his voice came out hollow "I don't think I wanna know."

"Well, it is something to think about."

"You think she's turning tricks for Salazar?"

"Distinct possibility."

Jacks tightened his fists. "That son of a bitch. I'm so fucking sick of him…Jesus!" He shook his head anxiously.

He'd had enough dealings with Victor Salazar to last a lifetime and wanted nothing to do with him ever again. But his heart ached for Maria, and now Tessa and her family. He suddenly felt very cold. He swallowed hard and looked at Mickey. "You think Tessa's with Salazar too?"

Mickey considered this. "Not as far as I know. From what I heard, Maria ran off on her own and has had nothing to do with her family. Besides, if Tessa worked for Salazar, I doubt she'd be serving breakfast at a diner every morning."

Jack nodded, somewhat comforted. "You could be right." He then sat up and turned eagerly toward Mickey. "What else do you know about her?"

"That's it, Romeo. Find out the rest from her."

CHAPTER 3

THE SHOP

As Mickey drove away, Jack felt a gnawing sense of dread. Despite Mickey's insistence on facing Frankie alone, Jack knew there was bound to be trouble. By now, Jack was sure Mickey was craving coke again and he was afraid the temptation was going to be too strong. Mickey was entering the lair of a dragon and he had no shield.

Jack watched Mickey's Buick turn the corner and took a deep breath. There was nothing he could do about it now. He just had to trust Mickey's instincts and hope for the best. That and a little payer would have to do.

Without realizing he was being watched, Jack headed toward the emergency room under a bath of floodlights. Our Lady of Our Lord Hospital had been nicknamed "The Shop" on the streets because over the years, the people of Soundview had needed repairs about as often as a car needed maintenance. But instead of an oil changes, they got blood transfusions. Instead of tune-ups, they got stitches. And instead of new brakes they got new teeth.

Often finding themselves overwhelmed by the deluge of patients, the doctors practiced in a zombie-like trance, hurrying through each case before moving onto the next. They functioned on barely any sleep, were consumed with stress, and reaped little reward for their efforts. For every person they patched up, four new injuries arrived. And the faster they worked, the faster they came in. It was easy to become disillusioned, feeling their hard work at times was pointless, and they found themselves forgetting the reasons why they went into medicine in the first place. It certainly wasn't for the money. They were working for civil servant pay, for Christ's sake. And many of them burnt out only after a few months into their residencies.

When Jack entered the waiting area of the emergency room, he noticed a collection of bruised and slashed victims moaning and sitting on hard fiberglass chairs. Many of them seemed weary, as if they had been at the hospital for all eternity. And it looked as if they were going to have to have to suffer a little while longer, maybe *a lot* longer, before someone came along to make the pain go away.

An agitated, middle-aged Hispanic woman held siege to a jaded receptionist who had barricaded herself behind a glass pane. With the window between them, the hospital worker continued to ignore her until the Spanish woman lapsed into a rant in her own native tongue. When she was good and ready, the receptionist rolled her eyes, slid open the window, and said mechanically, "Have a seat and someone will be with you as soon as possible." She then shut the window and went back to whatever she was doing before.

The agitated woman slinked angrily back to her seat, ranting in rapid, staccato Spanish and flailing her arms as if swatting mosquitoes that weren't there. She took a seat next to a boy of around 15, probably her grandson, who was sitting on a broken chair, with his head down. Along with a goatee, long sideburns, and an aqua-colored muscle shirt, the boy now wore a split upper lip, cracked teeth, and a cheek full of shattered glass. Jack noticed his arm and felt a sudden slight pang in his stomach. He immediately recognized the tattoo. It was a curled up fist with the words THE POWER written above it.

So they were back, Jack thought, Mickey would love to know that.

The boy looked bewildered as he sat, wincing and flinching at sporadic intervals. Jack contemplated the life of violence the boy had presumably chosen. The Power, once a force to be reckoned with, was a collection of pushers and sadistic thugs who, under the direction of one Victor Salazar, had been terrorizing the residents of Soundview for some time. They stole for him, sold drugs for him, and extorted money from just about every small business in town. It was a booming business for Salazar, and there was little his victims could do. The police were unable to investigate, or chose not to, and anyone who went to the authorities faced retaliation.

The Power never kidded around. Their threats were kept promises.

Jack thought they were gutless punks.

A nurse opened the door to the emergency room, called a name, and another trauma case was ushered in. Jack waited quietly by the intake window, giving the nurse some time to realize he was there and she finally slid aside the glass. She must have appreciated his patience, for he was able to learn from her that Tessa was in fact being treated there. The only problem was, he wasn't a blood relative. They couldn't let him in.

It was an oversight on his part. He totally forgot about the rules of hospitals. But something inside urged him to see her. He checked out the security guard sitting near the entrance to the emergency room. He was a thin, elderly black man with a peppery beard and dandruff-caked bifocals. Jack could see his eyes were closed. His arms were crossed firmly across his chest, and his head bobbed up and down in unison with his deep and labored breath. Jack quickly glanced around, saw no one was looking, and slipped past him inside.

All at once, Jack was met with a frenzy of activity. Hospital staff raced around with gurneys, the patients upon them hanging on for dear life, like some grotesque version of a backyard wheel barrow race. The faces of the physicians were pale and haggard.

Jack scanned the room and noticed at least ten spaces divided by curtains for privacy. He peaked in the first one and saw an old woman laying down on a bed, heaving and spitting up blood into a container. He gagged and stepped back. This was not going to be fun.

He hoped he wouldn't have to look behind too many curtains. He imagined himself in some twisted version of *Let's Make a Deal,* with an insane Monty Hall wearing a white lab coat and stethoscope, asking him if he wanted what was behind curtain number two. The game show host danced in delight, his eyes blazing wildly, when Jack peered behind the curtain to see a muscular, bitter-looking man in his thirties getting his forearm sewn up. The patient was visibly drunk with bloodshot eyes, his heavy frame swaying slightly as he sat deliriously on the bed. A frightened woman was desperately trying to explain to the doctor how her husband accidentally put his hand through the storm door. Jack pictured the woman cringing in horror as her husband threatened to beat her senseless unless she let him in the house.

Each additional curtain revealed a progressively more heart-wrenching situation. After looking behind curtain number seven, he was about to give up, when he heard some promising voices. Suddenly, his chest filled with a cool, buoyant sensation. He angled himself outside curtain number eight to get the best possible view, and there she was. Tessa Dori was sitting at the end of the bed, wearing a white cotton halter top, tattered blue jeans, and navy Puma running shoes. She was frowning while a female Asian doctor tended to her forehead. Her friend Ashley, the blonde who had attacked Sticks Favors, was looking on with concern. She clutched Tessa's jacket tightly between her arms.

While she was being treated, Tessa gripped the edge of the bed. Jack noticed the tone of her arms and figured she must get a good work-out carrying around piles of meals on heavy plates. She had short, black hair parted just to the right of center, the left side falling over her forehead and continuing back behind her left ear. She had a waifish look, kind of boyish even, but upon closer observation Jack could see her soft feminine curves. She giggled and cringed as the doctor stitched away like an experienced tailor.

Finally, the doctor said, "Okay, just one more and you'll be all patched up." She deftly tied off the last knot, snipped off the excess thread, and turned toward the counter. Jack admired her work even if the wound looked like the stitching of a baseball seam.

Tessa looked off to the side and said, "Thank God that's over. I feel like a rag doll."

The doctor returned and took Tessa's face in her hands. She then made sure the gauze was secure. "You need to find safer places to hang out, Tess. I don't want to see you ruining any more of that pretty face of yours."

Tessa nodded and spoke in an ashamed voice, "Yes, Dr. Cho. Next time I'll be more careful." But once Dr. Cho turned away to write in her chart, Tessa looked at Ashley and scrunched up her face.

When Ashley giggled, the doctor looked up to see what was so funny. Ashley immediately looked at the floor and started scratching her head. The Asian woman looked back and forth between the two girls, frowned, and decided not to waste any more of her time. She handed Tessa her business card and instructed her to make an appointment to be seen in one week to get the stitches removed. She then said goodbye with a handshake and a practiced smile and threw back the curtain to leave.

She almost walked straight into Jack. Fortunately, for

him, he had anticipated her approach and was able to step away just in the nick of time. His sudden presence startled her for a second and she was about to ask what he was doing there when she was urgently called away.

Having escaped a potential embarrassment, Jack felt he better make himself known as quickly as possible. He looked in Tessa's room as she frowned, jumped down off the table, and said, "Is it me or did she treat me like I was twelve years old?" When Ashley shrugged, she said, "I'm twenty-three and everyone talks to me like I'm a kid."

"Well, you do kinda dress like a boy."

"What?!"

Ashley grinned guiltily. "I'm just sayin'...if you let me take you shopping..."

"Whatever," Tessa said and snatched back her jacket.

They started to leave and Jack took his chance. As they stepped out of the room, Jack stepped toward them and cleared his throat. They looked at him, somewhat startled, and then both registered surprise. They eyed each other with a quizzical expression and for a moment it felt impossible for Jack to speak. An electric current cut sharply, numbingly through him, yet he managed a look of concern.

"Hey," he said.

"Hey," Tessa said, her tone a mixture of confusion and curiosity. Ashley just gave him an icy stare.

"How are you?" he asked, nodding at her forehead.

"I'm okay. Just a flesh wound. Thanks. But...what are you doing here? Shouldn't you be out celebrating?"

Jack relaxed a bit. "I guess so. We actually didn't want to hang around there too long. The Wire's not the safest place to hang out. Especially when you just won a few bucks."

"Makes sense."

"Seriously, though, you okay? Looks kinda painful."

She smiled warmly and shoved her hands into her jacket. "It wasn't *that* bad. Looks worse than it is." She breathed in deep, raised her shoulders, and let them drop quickly. "Anyway, I'm back in one piece, as they say." The confused frown then returned and she said, "Didn't expect to see *you* here, though."

Jack pointed at the patch. "Well I felt bad about that. I kinda feel responsible, you know? Can I make it up to you?"

She thought about it for a moment. "How about half the prize money?" she said. But before Jack could respond, she giggled. "Just kidding. It wasn't your fault. But, um, what did you have in mind?"

"I don't know, a drink or something?" He held his breath.

She looked at Ashley as if weighing the possiblilty. "I'm not sure that's a great idea. I mean, I don't even know you."

"Oh, sorry. My name's Jack." He offered her his hand.

She took it with mock apprehension. "So…now that I know your name, I know you?"

Her hand was soft and smooth and Jack fought the urge not to let it go. His eyes sparkled. "Well, it's a start, anyway. I mean, everyone's a stranger at *some* point."

Tessa seemed to be enjoying this. "You might have a point. My name's Tessa."

Jack studied her face for the first time. Her naturally red lips widened to reveal straight, white teeth and she had the palest blue eyes he had ever seen. Her eyelashes were long and thick and her eyebrows angled upward, giving her an inquisitive, yet inwardly amused expression. Her skin was a creamy porcelain with light freckles sprinkled softly across her nose which crinkled slightly when she smiled. The only awkward thing about her face was the fresh gauze patch which now sat high on the left side of her forehead.

Jack was precariously mesmerized by her appearance. If he wasn't careful, he would easily stammer into foolishness. So he forced himself to concentrate on the person behind the face, because if he became too enamored with her, he would offer little in return.

Tessa was about to introduce Ashley when she noticed the blonde girl's hostile posture. She admonished her companion with her eyes as she said, "This sour sort is my cousin Ashley." The blonde was a good four inches taller than her, with long, curly hair and intense green eyes. Her irises had flecks of gold that blazed with ferocity, a startling contrast to her soft, olive complexion. She had a long, straight nose with pursed, taut lips, and wore a burgundy silk blouse over hip-hugging black jeans that she had tucked into fringed, suede boots.

Ashley made a gasping sound and shoved Tessa with her shoulder. "I'm not sour!" she protested.

"Yes, you are!" Tessa confirmed.

"Well, we don't know this guy," she protested and eyed Jack suspiciously. "And for one, I don't like the people he hangs out with."

Jack saw that this girl was going to be a nuisance. When he spoke, it was measured, as if defending himself to a prosecutor. "Wait a minute," he said, "If you're thinking about that guy Favors, I can assure you he's not my friend. If anything, he hates me so much right now that he's thinking of a way to get even..." Jack knew it was a mistake the moment it came out of his mouth.

Ashley sneered. "All the more reason to stay away from you. It's too dangerous to be around you." She pointed at Tessa's forehead. "Look what happened already!"

Jack's throat began to close up. He looked at Tessa and swallowed. "Maybe she's right," he said in defeat. "Well, feel better anyway."

He started to leave when Tessa reached for his arm. "I'm not worried about that Sticks guy. I've lived around here long enough to know how to take care of myself." She pointed at the patch on her forehead. "This is nothing, believe me." She glowered at Ashley, who crossed her arms and rolled her eyes. Turning back to Jack, she said, "Listen, it was really sweet of you to come down here. I'll take you up on that drink." She grinned widely. "Hospitals make me thirsty."

Without looking away from Jack, she said, "Ash, why don't you go on ahead? I'll catch up with you later."

Her cousin's jaw literally dropped open. "Are you totally de*ranged,* Tess? Did that pool stick just knock all the sense out of your brain? Look around you. We're in an *E-MER-GEN-CY* room! Don't you think you ought to tell your mom what happened?" She then pointed at her watch. "It's 12:30, Tess. You got stitches in your head and you have work tomor—"

She was cut off by Tessa's hand over her mouth.

"Jack, could you give us minute?" Tessa said. "I just have to take care of something."

Jack suppressed a smile. "Sure I'll wait outside."

While Tessa waited for Jack to leave, Ashley angrily

shoved her cousin's hand away from her mouth. "You can't—" she started, but Tessa shushed her with a finger.

"Listen," Tessa said, "I'm not a kid anymore." She looked up at the ceiling and raised her arms to question the heavens. "When will everyone stop treating me like a child?" She looked back sternly at her cousin. "Ash, this guy seems nice and I like him. Sometimes people are who they appear to be. How many guys would come down like that to check up on me?"

Ashley's arms remained crossed as if she were in some eternal hug with herself. But now she began tapping her foot. "Fine," she said, "then you deal with your mom when you stroll in at three AM with a gash on your head. Then you'll be sorry."

Tessa considered this for a moment.

"Just go another night. It's late, you gotta talk to your mom and you have work tomorrow, remember?" She looked past Tessa's shoulder. "I'm not sure I trust this guy yet, but if he really *is* a good guy, he'll understand."

"Okay, I'll tell him."

They started out from behind the curtain and were almost immediately flattened by a rolling bed wheeled in by a frantic medical. They were desperately trying to subdue a patient, a bald, obese man who was convulsing wildly. One of the doctors gestured toward Tessa and Ashley and yelled, "Someone get them outta here!" They didn't need to be asked twice. They started off and the curtain was rudely swung shut as the team began frantically working inside.

Jack watched anxiously as the two girls approached, not quite sure what he was about to hear. Both appeared on edge, nervously on the lookout for another gurney torpedo.

When they got to him, he said, "You guys want to get outta here? This place is getting dangerous."

Tessa nodded. "Yeah, let's. It's like a war zone in here."

"I know," Jack said. "We better leave before we end up in the hospital."

The girls both gave him an odd look and Jack could have sworn he heard crickets chirping. He swallowed and tried to loosen his collar. Ashley frowned at him while Tessa tried to figure out what the hell he had just said. When it dawned on her that it was joke, she smiled and said, "Stick to pool, Jack."

"Sorry," he said, "Just wanted to ease the tension." He cleared his throat and thought, *Just not at my expense.*

Tessa looked sympathetic. "Listen, Jack. It is kinda late. I really should be getting home. My mom's probably wondering where the heck I am and I'm gonna have to explain this to her." She pointed at the patch. "So...can I get a rain check?"

At first, Jack thought Ashley had won and convinced her cousin to blow him off. But Tessa seemed genuinely interested in him. He had no choice but to hope she meant it. "Sure, Tess," he said. "I understand. It doesn't have to be tonight. When's good for you?"

"Let's just see how things go the next couple of days, okay? Let me give you my number." She began checking her pockets, a look of uncertainty on her face. "I *think* I have a pen," she said, finally digging one out.

She chuckled and took Jack's hand. She flipped it over so his palm was facing up, and rotated her body into his. There, standing side by side, she leaned into him and wrote her number in his palm, close enough for him to catch a delicate hint of strawberries in her hair.

"Give me a call and we'll set something up." she said, then let go to face him again, her cheeks slightly flushed. She hesitated a moment as if caught momentarily off guard, then suddenly pointed her thumb back toward the reception area. "Gotta go take care of some paperwork now. Insurance stuff."

She started walking backwards and seemed to stifle a grin. "Well, nice to meet you, Jack. And thanks for coming by." Ashley took her by the arm and began pulling her along. Tessa continued to look at Jack as they moved further away.

"Sure, no problem," Jack called after her, "Talk to you soon."

Tessa said, "Oh, and congrats on the tournament. That was-"

And the last thing Jack heard her say was "HEY!" as Ashley jerked her around the corner and out of sight.

CHAPTER 4

AN UNEXPECTED ENCOUNTER

Jack left the hospital in a haze, his mind lost in memory. His heart had become unbound, released from its cynical leash. And once untethered, it now rose recklessly above clouds of despair. He started to walk home and could think of nothing but her bemused smile, her quirky gestures, and the appreciation she showed for his concern. He recalled again and again the feel of her hands, the scent of strawberries in her hair, and the warm way she leaned into him as she wrote down her number.

He wandered aimlessly in the streets, staring at his palm

and admiring her script. It was large and loopy, displaying a confident and feminine optimism. He smiled and ran his finger under her name.

Could she be the one? Is there really a chance this could happen? The possibilities made him dizzy. She was like an oasis of hope in the emotionless desert of his life. And her existence now somehow made sense of his own. Blinded by sentiment, he moved along, her image now guiding his every step.

Lost in thought, he inadvertently kicked a beer can, jarring himself out of his reverie. He looked up with a start and realized he hadn't a clue where he was. He squinted to make out the street sign halfway up the block, but it was too far away to see. All around, the stores lining the streets were closed, shielded by corrugated steel. The fronts were all covered with large swirls of spray paint. At first, the graffiti seemed indecipherable, a random splash of colors. But after Jack took a closer look, it all became clear. The unmistakable insignia of The Power.

He stared at the hostile, menacing fist, bright and proud against the dull, drab metal.

And the paint wasn't yet dry.

His eyes widened and he took a few steps back. He slowly turned once around, searching the shadows. Then all at once he began to run. The darkness closed in as he ran, the air thinning, making it difficult to breathe. It was as if he were on a treadmill going nowhere, suspended in time in some urban black hole. He headed toward the only light he could see, a lamppost up ahead, its eerie, conical glow flickering weakly on the pavement. It stood ancient and alone, a weary sentinel guarding the world from the ghastly horrors of hell.

Jack fled toward it, eager to get out of the blackness, when an ungodly shriek rose from an alley nearby. A loud crash ensued, along with a series of profanities, the curses echoing between the walls of the street.

He stopped in his tracks and held his breath. Peering into the alley, he saw nothing, but decided to give it wide berth.

He was about to break into another run when suddenly, out of the darkness, something shot out of the alley and onto the street. It was formless blur at first, all flailing arms and limbs, and it spun itself out in a whirlwind until once under the lamppost, it planted itself firmly, its head and torso quivering to a halt.

Sticks Favors then stood there, leering with contempt. He had another cue stick in his hands this time, and he held it out in front of him in a hostile, aggressive stance. No longer wearing the jacket of green felt, he was now all in black, save for the glowing green feather of a derby hanging askew on his shiny, white head. His right eye had been swollen shut from having been used as a battering ram earlier in the night, and there were fresh cat claw marks on his upper left cheek. His pallid lips quivered as he pulled them back in a hideous snarl.

Jack stepped back defensively, anticipating the worst. But Favors didn't attack just yet. Instead, his face melted into an odd, serene expression and he began to circle, as if he were having a pleasant evening stroll. He used his stick as one would a cane and moved with peculiar grace, like an Englishman strolling through Hyde Park. He began whistling a tune that somehow reminded Jack of the month of May, causing him to frown in bewilderment. Then Sticks' demeanor changed once more. He tensed up and he began jabbing the stick in the air, grunting and stabbing like a huge, one-armed praying mantis. He hopped in and out of the shadows, the cone of light an obscene spotlight for his malevolent performance.

"Look, man," Jack said, "I don't want any trouble. It was just a game. Somebody had to win. If you—"

There was a WHOOOSH! as Favors swung his stick perilously close to Jack's head. "Shut up, just you shut up, SHUT UP!" he warned. "You had your chance, smart guy. Now you're going to pay." He moved back into the darkness and let out another chilling, chalky cackle. Jack peered desperately into the darkness but it was impossible to see. He had to make a run for it.

He took off and was about to pass the lamppost on his right when the cue stick sliced through the air in an arc over his head, striking the lamppost neck high. Then, with all his might, Sticks Favors held the cue stick in place as Jack crashed into the shaft with his throat. His feet went out from under him, and he slammed to the pavement on his back. The air was forced from his lungs and he lay on the ground, struggling to breathe, paralyzed with fear.

Favors' head appeared out of the darkness. It hovered over Jack's prone body. "Oh, I'm awfully sorry," he said, "Did the poor wittle Banks fall down? You must always watch where you're going, you know. If you don't, you could get a boo-boo. You don't want a boo-boo, now do you?" His voice then deepened, "That's right, BANKS! You gotta watch your FLANKS! Or there'll be PRANKS!" He yelled these things in Jack's face, spraying spittle while Jack could do nothing but lay there, stunned and gasping for air.

Jack cursed himself for letting down his guard. Sticks, now confident with his advantage, grinned and backed away. He then began to dance an awkward jig, once again in an out of the conical glow. With both hands, he held the pool cue straight up behind his back as he hopped around, high stepping back and forth, his head jiggling around with glee. He bounced around, humming a discordant version of "Tea for Two," seemingly ignoring Jack as he lay writhing on the ground. Favors frolicked in the shadows, darting here and there, humming and giggling to himself as if celebrating some successful devious plan. He parried and thrust his weapon, repeatedly reciting strange poems of torment, emphasizing the words "flanks" and "pranks" as he savagely stabbed the air.

Jack fought to gain his breath. He mustered all his energy to turn on his side and was about to get to his knees when the cue tip recoiled off the pavement next to his head with a sudden WHACK! Jack peered up to see his assailant hovering above him, straddling over his prone body. Favors then lowered his head, stretching his neck with impossible elasticity until his face was inches away from Jack's. "I warned you not to fuck with me," he said. "Now I'm gonna have to hurt ya." He then rose up. Gripping the butt end of the pool stick with both hands, he lifted it over his head and paused in a momentary trance, as if about to perform some sacrificial rite.

The hesitation was all Jack needed. Adrenaline pooled from somewhere deep inside him and coursed through his veins, through every fiber of his muscles. Before Sticks could react, Jack clasped his hands together in a double fist and slammed them into his gut, causing him to mutter "Oof!" and stumble back beyond the conical glow.

Jack readied for his return. He grabbed two metal covers from the first garbage cans he could find and once again searched the darkness for his foe. He stood there in a defensive stance, the only sound being his heavy breath and his heart that now threatened to burst out of his chest. He backed up a few steps to adjust his eyesight, when all of a sudden Sticks came out of nowhere, twirling his rod like a propeller. He moved it side to side and above his head, like samurai preparing for attack. Jack just waited, somehow hoping he would lift off like a helicopter and fly away. Instead, Sticks let out a furious wail and lunged forward, swinging the stick with rage. Jack stepped aside, and with measured force, smashed the cue with a garbage can cover, shattering it to pieces.

All at once, Favors stopped and blinked. He gaped at the shards of his broken pool stick and seemed lost in questioning thought. He then dropped to his knees in anguish and began to sob, his strength now in fragments on the ground.

At first, Jack just stared in disbelief. *What a bizarre character!* He hoped this latest encounter would be the end of it, but somehow had his doubts. He was about to make a run for it, when he quickly changed his mind. Instead, a bitter resentment took him over, and in an uncontrollable rage he wound up his arm, stepped forward, and smashed the metal cover into his enemy's face. There was a loud, thunderous crash as he connected, and it felt as if he'd just struck a boulder. He stepped back defensively, ready for anything, but Favors just stayed there, rocking back and forth on his knees, a vacuous, comical expression on his face. For a few moments Favors swayed there, like a rocking pendulum, until he finally froze and crumbled to the ground. Jack looked at the lid, half expecting to see a mold of Sticks Favors' face, then took off for home, away from the sound of approaching sirens.

CHAPTER 5

ASHLEY AND TESSA

A shley's candy apple Mitsubishi Eclipse darted through the slums of downtown like a dinghy lost at sea, heedless of an oncoming storm. Ramshackle tenements hulked over the dreary streets, while sleepless scavengers peered out of alleys at the tiny sports car passing by.

Tessa gazed out her window, deep in thought. She was reclining back in her seat, her arms crossed over her chest and her head tilting to the right. Her brows were high, and in the dimness her pale, blue eyes glowed in reverie. A barely perceptible smile crept upon her lips as she hummed along with one of her favorite songs on the stereo. It was "Vienna" by Billy Joel, a hidden jewel off The Stranger, a largely underrated but flawlessly composed album. The song's wonderfully winding melody flowed smoothly into different musical passages, both seamless and complete, evoking images of European sunsets and couples in love, sharing ice cream at a sidewalk café. Tessa, being both young and full of desire, savored the image, and as the song played on she found herself yearning for romance. She hummed along sweetly and in tune, and when it reached a familiar verse sang quietly to herself:

> You got your passion
> You got your pride
> But don't you know that only fools are satisfied?
> Dream on, but don't imagine they'll all come true
> When will you realize
> Vienna waits for you?

At a red light, Ashley adjusted her rear view mirror. "I look like shit," she said, and attempted to fluff up her forelocks. She then frowned, pulled her blonde curls back into a pony tail, and secured it into place with an elastic terrycloth band. She gingerly touched a red blemish on her chin and winced.

"So what time is it anyway?" Silence suspended over the music as she continued to check herself out in the mirror. "Huh?" she said, asking a second time without a word. When she still got no response, she shot a glare at her cousin. "Hullo, anyone home?!"

That jolted Tessa back to the present. "Yeah, chill out,"

she said, and sat up. She cleared her throat and stretched out her arms. Yawning, she asked, "What time is it anyway?"

"That's what I just asked you."

"You did?" Her face began to flush.

Ashley was about to complain about being ignored when suddenly she fell into a fit of laughter. Tessa joined in and they cracked up together for some time. When the light finally turned green, the car behind honked impatiently. Ashely cleared her throat, wiped away a tear and said, "Okay, okay, don't have a canary!"

When they were moving again, Tessa looked at her watch. It was nearly 12:30 AM. Her stomach rumbled, reminding her she hadn't eaten all night. "I'm hungry," she said. "Let's go to McDonald's."

Ashley raised her right eyebrow. "Are you nuts? I'm not eating that crap!"

"Oh, come on. Please, please, please! I gotta have a burger now. Come on, I'm starvin', Marvin."

Ashley shook her head. "Nope, forget it. And stop calling me Marvin."

"I'll buy you a Shamrock Shay-ake," Tessa said, her tone suggesting a bald-faced attempt at bribery.

"A what?"

Tessa started to giggle. "You know, those green pistachio shakes made by the Evil Grimace's Irish uncle?"

"What the hell are you talking about?'

"You know, the McDonald's character?" she giggled. "They make those shakes around St. Patrick's Day."

"It's October, moron. They're probably doing something like pumpkin shakes now."

"Okay, so I'll buy you one of those."

"No thanks, I'll pass."

That got them laughing again until Ashley finally said, "You know, sometimes I wonder about you. I think you got novocain on the brain."

Tessa turned in her seat to face Ashley, clasped her hands together, and shut her eyes tight. "Please let's get something to eat! Please, please, please, with sugar and whip cream and a cherry on top!"

"Okay, okay, wacko!"

Tessa leaned over, took her face in both her hands, and kissed her hard on the cheek. "You're the coolest cousin I ever had!"

Ashley had to fend her off while keeping control of the car. "Get *off* of me!" she protested. "And Newsflash: I'm the *only* cousin you ever had."

"That too."

"*That too*," Ashley mocked, and then despite her efforts smiled again. "But I'm not eating any of those greasy fries. Look at this!" She pointed to the pimple on her chin and Tessa moaned with sarcastic concern.

"Yeah, that's right," Ashley said, "and once I have one, I can't stop. I'll end up stuffing my face with an extra large." She paused for a moment and looked at Tessa with suspicion. "You okay? You were kinda spacing out there for a while."

"Was I? No, I'm fine. Just thinking." She lightly touched the patch on her forehead.

"So what's the story? You really going out with that guy?"

Tessa turned to her, thought seriously for a moment, and then nodded. "Yeah, I think I will. Seems like a nice guy, Ash. A gentleman, I think. I mean, to come all the way to the hospital just to check on me? That says a lot. And there's something about his face I like. I mean, he's good-looking and all, but it's more than that. He seems honest, you know?" She looked out the windshield and nodded to herself. "Sometimes you can just tell by looking in someone's eyes. I think I'd feel safe with him." She paused and then smiled whimsically. "And I like the way he plays pool. It's kinda sexy."

Ashley glanced at her dubiously. "Just be careful, Tess. Guys are hard to read. A lot of times they seem nice and then turn out to be assholes."

Tessa looked at her with empathy. "Like Rick?"

Ashley's eyes moistened and she swallowed hard. "Yeah, like Rick."

"Do you want to talk about it?"

"Not really." The blonde looked in the side view mirror and made a decision. "Fuck it, I don't care anymore. You should probably know, anyway." She took a deep breath and continued. "He abused me, Tess. Made me feel like a loser. And when I couldn't give him what he wanted, he hurt me. Not like punches or anything, but he threw me around and called me names. Terrible names." Tears began to roll down her cheeks, but she composed herself almost immediately and wiped them away. She then took another deep breath. "Well anyway, it's done. I moved out a month ago. Now, I don't miss him at all."

Tessa took Ashley's hand and said, "Well at least you found the strength to get out. Good for you." She then sat back and looked at the floor. In a quiet voice, she said, "Must have been a nightmare." She shook her head in disgust. Then, more angrily, she added, "Sounds like a real jerk. No one needs that shit."

Ashley grinned suddenly, sniffed, and finished wiping her eyes. "You're a good kid, Tess. Understand why I don't trust guys now, right?"

"Of course, Ash. But I need to live my life too. And I need to learn from my *own* mistakes, you know, just like everybody else." She thought about Ashley's situation and really felt for her. "Sounds like you had it rough for a while, but some day you are gonna have to trust someone again. What's the alternative? To go through life alone? That's no way to live. I really do believe there are some good people out there. We just have to sense who they are... and I think this guy Jack may be one of them."

"Wow," said Ashely, almost stunned. "You are wise beyond your years, Miss Dori. Ever think about becoming a shrink?"

"Hmmm, not a bad idea. Maybe then I could help you with your anger management."

"What? What's that supposed to mean?!"

Tessa started to chuckle. "What's that supposed to mean? You nearly kicked the crap out of that guy at the bar."

"Oh, that. Well he deserved it! What an idiot, swinging that stick around with everybody there. And he coulda killed you!"

"Well you would have killed *him* if those bouncers didn't pull you away."

"Nobody hurts my baby and gets away with—" Ashley knew it was a mistake as soon as it came out. Tessa's smile froze, then transformed into an expression of resentment.

"Um, what I meant was..."

Tessa said, "You did *not* just say that. Baby? *Really?* Like Baby from "Dirty Dancing?" You gotta be kidding me."

Ashley was blushing now and was about to offer a flustered apology when Tessa suddenly held up a finger and grinned. "Got ya!" she laughed.

"Jerk!" Ashley exclaimed, as her face turned a shade of crimson. She dismissed Tessa's charade with an emphatic wave of her hand and smiled in embarrassment.

After a few moments of further ridiculing her cousin, Tessa felt a twinge of pain from her forehead. She winced and gingerly touched the patch. "What a weirdo that guy was," she said.

"Who?" Ashley asked.

"The bald guy from the bar."

Ashley nodded. "You mean freak."

"And what was with that jacket? It looked like it was made from that green stuff, you know, the stuff on the surface of pool tables? What do you call that, felt? I mean, who wears stuff like that?"

"Freaks do."

Tessa was still laughing when the next tune came on: "Scenes from an Italian Restaurant." "Oh, I love this song," she said and turned up the volume.

Billy Joel was playing the romantic intro when Ashley chimed in, clearly unimpressed. "Why do people love this song? It's all about divorce!"

Tessa ignored her and played air piano on her thighs. She then closed her eyes, swayed back and forth, and sang loudly over Ashley's complaints:

> A bottle of red, a bottle of white
> It all depends upon your appetite
> Get a table near the street in our old familiar place,
> You and I, face to face

When Ashley realized Tessa wasn't listening, she gave in and began to enjoy the song as well. They sang the next verse together, smiling at one another, enjoying their close bond:

> A bottle of white, a bottle of red
> Have a bottle of rosé instead
> I'll meet you anytime you want
> At our Italian restaurant

And as the song picked up and Billy began to roll, the girls laughed and sang, reveling in the good times which the loved are so apt to do.

CHAPTER 6

HIGH VOLTAGE

As Mickey drove on into the night, an unsettling, prickling feeling radiated from the deepest part of his chest to the very edges of his shoulders. His left leg fidgeted, bouncing up and down in front of the brake, and when he tried to swallow, it felt as if several balls of cotton had been crammed inside his mouth. He gazed unseeing at the white stripes of the road passing by as he contemplated his upcoming meeting with Frankie Malone.

Where had it all gone wrong? He thought back to the evening when the two of them had met and still couldn't begin to forgive himself. About a week before, after a particularly difficult day, Mickey had been having a drink at The Live Wire when a man in a pin-striped suit pulled up a stool next to him. He was a large, stocky man with thick, brown eyebrows and angry-looking eyes. Mickey measured the man without him noticing, and wondered what someone so well dressed was doing there.

The man ordered a double whiskey on the rocks, took a swig, and breathed out, refreshed. He then glanced around, taking in the sights until finally, as if by accident, his eyes fell upon Mickey.

"How's it goin'?" he said.

Mickey eyed him suspiciously. "Not bad. Yourself?"

"Been better. Had some shit go down today, don't even want to think about. Just looking to blow off some steam." He shrugged. "You know how it is."

Yeah, Mickey knew how it was. He'd been having a shitty day himself. The night before he'd gone on the worst cocaine binge he could remember, tearing relentlessly through his entire stash, completely out of control. Of course, it had been a blast while it had lasted, but now there was nothing left and no prospects of getting any more. He'd felt both physically and mentally drained. If he could only get one tiny little boost, he'd somehow manage to get through the night.

But the chances of that happening looked grim.

The man studied Mickey's face. "If you don't mind me sayin', pal, you don't look so hot."

Though Mickey was both pale and haggard, a slight flush appeared on his cheeks.

"Yeah, I know. Last night was pretty rough." He then

smiled, somewhat abashed, and said, "Actually, no. Last night was pretty awesome. Waking up, though, now *that* was a different story."

"Gotcha." The man took another swig of his drink and savored the burn as it ran down his throat. He then held the glass up to the light, admiring the dancing colors as they scattered through the ice. "You know what I do when that happens?"

Mickey turned toward him and leaned his elbow on the bar. "What?"

"Ever hear the saying 'hair of the dog that bit ya'?"

Mickey chuckled, "Yeah, I heard that one. The only problem is I don't have any more of that dog's hair and I'm broke. So I don't see myself gettin' any more."

A glint of eagerness flashed in the man's eyes. He looked warily around the bar and then back at Mickey. In a low voice, he said, "Are we talking about..." Then he sniffed and simultaneously rubbed his nose with the back of his hand.

They were, in fact, talking about the same thing. Mickey's body began to tremble, anticipating the chemical pleasure he knew all too well. Then his craving came on strong. Though it was cool in the bar, his armpits began to sweat.

"Yeah, we're talking about the same thing alright," Mickey said. He leaned in close, his eyes wide. "Why, you got any?"

The man broke out in a satisfied grin. "As a matter of fact, I do. Just got in some of the best stuff I ever had. Expensive as shit, but well worth it. Believe me." He craned his head and searched the bar. "Listen, two broads are on their way here and we're gonna have a little party back at the motel. You wanna come?"

Mickey's heart jumped at the idea. His usual suspicions were clouded by his overwhelming desire to get high. There was only one problem.

"Thanks, man. But like I said before, I'm broke. I gotta take it easy till I get paid at the end of the week."

"I gotcha," the man said and put an arm around Mickey's shoulder. "Been there myself. But if anyone offered me what I'm offering you, I'd jump at it. These girls are smoking hot." He grinned and rustled up Mickey's hair. "Forget about the money, pal. Let's go party." While Mickey considered this, the man raised his eyebrows and patted the pocket of his jacket. "I got a whole lot of fun right here."

That did it. The fact that coke was so near and available made him yearn for it all the more. He was beyond

making any rational decisions. He was going to party. He broke out in a wide smile and giggled nervously. "Okay man, you talked me into it." He shook the man's large, meaty hand and said, "By the way, my name's Mick."

The man winked. "Frankie Malone." He looked past Mickey's shoulder and said, "Looks like our dates are here. This is your lucky night, Mick."

It was anything but.

* * *

The girls were gorgeous. They were young and sexy and vivacious. They walked over to Frankie and he took one on each arm. They beamed alluringly at Mickey.

With a naughty sense of excitement, Frankie said, "Let's go, Mick!" and started to lead the girls outside. Mickey downed his drink as fast as he could. He left the bartender a couple of dollars and moved quickly after his new friends. When he got outside, he saw the girls getting into a navy blue Mercedes Benz. He was about to get into the passenger side when a voice inside him told him to beware. He hesitated, trying to figure out why it all felt wrong.

Frankie stood by the open door of the driver's side and motioned for Mickey to get in. "Come on, Mick, let's go. The girls want to party." When he didn't move, Frankie said, "Like the car? She's a beaut, ain't she? Too bad it's a company car. Would love to have it myself."

Mickey relaxed a bit but didn't move.

"You getting in, Mick? The girls are getting antsy."

As if on cue, they implored, "Come on, let's go!"

Something like this had never happened to Mickey before. It was all very strange. He could handle himself on the street, but when it came to unsolicited hospitality, he wasn't sure what to do. He was wavering between skepticism and exhilaration. The girls were smiling and giggling, blowing kisses to him. One of them was dangling a tiny plastic bag with white powder in it. She flashed him an inviting expression and he finally gave in. He got in the car and they drove off.

It was a night of pure, wild indulgence. The cocaine piled high and the liquor flowed forth. Music played loudly as the four of them did line after line and made goofy champagne toasts. The girls danced to the sexy beat of the music, stripping off their clothes while gazing at Mickey seductively. An erotic game of charades ensued, with the girls playing topless and wearing only panties. They climbed onto the beds and formed letters with their bodies, imploring Mickey to guess the dirty words that they spelled. Then they swarmed him, undressing him and pressing their warm, smooth bodies into his. They were tan and firm, and they rubbed their lips, hands, and legs all over him, offering up more and more cocaine as the night wore on. He even sniffed some coke out of their belly buttons, causing them to giggle and squeal out of control.

Mickey was in a state of euphoria. The coke and the alcohol intoxicated him, blurring his senses and distorting reality. His heart pounded with excitement as he reveled in the pleasures of both the chemicals and the flesh. All night long, the feel of the soft, young, bodies writhing under and all around him, electrified him beyond measure. And thus, it went on and on through the early hours of the morning, until he was utterly spent, passed out naked on one of the beds.

* * *

A sudden slap of shock bore a sharp pain through Mickey's head. He was cold, wet, and naked, with a pounding agony between his eyes. The blinds were wide open and the sun was shining as bright as day. "What the fuh?" he mumbled and tried to focus on his surroundings. He had no idea where he was, but then a vaguely familiar giggle helped bring him back to reality. When he finally came back to his senses, he rubbed his eyes and looked up. He saw the two girls and Frankie standing fully dressed and smirking at him. Frankie was holding the ice bucket which had just been dumped on his head.

"Wake up, lover boy!" Frankie said. "Rise and shine!" He tossed the bucket on the floor and rubbed his hands together to dry them. "We tried to wake you, but you wouldn't budge." He winked at the girls and they giggled again. "Listen buddy," he said, "the party's over. We gotta get outta here. There's just one last piece of business we gotta take care of. You had a good time last night, right?"

Frowning, Mickey found a towel to dry off and began to get dressed. "Yeah," he said, not amused.

"Well, my friend, that type of fun is expensive."

Mickey stopped and looked at Frankie, confused. "Yeah, but I told you I was broke. You said not to worry about the money."

"That's right, I did say that. I said not to worry about the money. I never said it was free."

Mickey said nothing.

Frankie looked at the girls, who just sneered at Mickey. He then turned his gaze back to Mickey, a mocking look of incredulity upon his face. He held out his arms. "You mean you thought this was all free?" He began walking and looking at the floor while shaking his head. "Nah, nah, nah, nah. No, pal. Parties like these are never free." He reached into his jacket pocket and pulled out a Colt .45, its dull steel shining menacingly in the dusty morning sunlight. He then walked over to Mickey, put his left hand on his shoulder, and pointed the muzzle up under his chin. "But don't worry, I'll give you a few days to dig up the dough."

Mickey's heart sank as it dawned on him what had just happened. He had been screwed beyond measure. In more ways than one. His voice came out, defeated. "What do I owe you?"

Frankie stepped back, a smug look on his face. "Oh, that can be worked out."

"What do you mean, worked out?"

"Depends on when you get it. You see, every day you don't pay me..."

"The amount goes up. There's a vig."

"Ding ding ding!" Frankie exclaimed. "Give the man a microwave for the booby prize!" The girls delighted in his sadistic sense of humor. His face changed and then Mickey saw for the first time how sinister his features could be. "That's right, junkie." He began to count on his fingers. "Now let's see: we had the coke, the booze, the girls, and... well, we'll even throw in the pot for free. You know, as a courtesy. That brings us to a grand total of..." He looked up and squinted as if he were calculating in his head, "about two grand."

"What!?"

"That's right, pal, and if I were you I'd get it quick. It's an extra $500 per day after today."

Mickey slumped back onto the wet bed in nothing but his jeans and hung his head. The joy from the previous night had dissolved into a desolate abyss of despair. He ran his right hand over his face and breathed, "Fuck me."

"Not today," Frankie said. "You had enough of that last night." He sat down next to Mickey and put an arm around his shoulder. "Listen, pal, I'm not such a bad guy once you get to know me. Hell, I might even find some use for you. Then you could have some more nights like this for free. Here's my card. My number and address are on the back. Get the money and bring it by." He stood up and walked over to the mirror to fix his tie. "My work is done here. Say goodbye, girls."

"Bye!" they sang, and slammed the door on their way out.

* * *

Mickey roused himself from his thoughts only to realize the traffic was moving at a snail's clip. He was tired, anxious, and angered from the memory of being suckered by some sleazy con artist and his two-bit sluts. He couldn't wait for the night to end, but the drive to Frankie's was taking forever. He furrowed his brow and realized the cause of the tie-up. The car in front of him was driving painfully slow. In the left lane, no less. *What is wrong with people? Don't they know the left lane is the passing lane?* He jammed his palm into the horn and blasted it for at least ten seconds. When the car in front of him finally sped up, he pulled out next to it and glared at the driver. There, hunched over and peering beneath the steering wheel was a shriveled old man. While appearing to concentrate on the road ahead, he extended his arm to the right and stuck up his middle finger.

Mickey rolled his eyes and shook his head. It was amazing that people like that were permitted to drive. It was obvious the old man couldn't see two feet in front of his face, so why was he on the road? Sooner or later there was going to be an accident and people were going to get hurt.

Mickey took a deep breath and tried to relax. He knew he shouldn't be taking out his troubles on the elderly. It was his fault and his fault alone that he was in this predicament in the first place. He realized he'd better pull himself together soon, or he was going to end up in deep shit.

He thought about guys like Frankie and it pissed him off. They came from a despicable breed of humans with no morals, no sense of conscience nor even a hint of humanity. They plotted and schemed, lying in wait for the right victim, then mercilessly moved in for the kill. It was a concept Mickey had never been able to stomach. And now, even *he* had become one of those victims.

It was tremendously frustrating. It seemed impossible to make Soundview a respectable place to live. With the condition of his home town deteriorating once again, it seemed apparent they had been fighting an uphill battle all along.

Clearly Victor Salazar was back.

Mickey knew about him all too well. For years, the mobster had been a blight on Soundview, relentlessly harassing and exploiting its hard-working residents. He'd emerged as a kind of jack of all trades in crime. Vice. Drug trafficking. Extortion. Blackmail. You name it, Salazar had a hand in it.

And it wasn't just all about business for him, either. He was known for his sadistic tendencies, gleefully dishing out punishment to anyone who got in his way. Like many criminals in Soundview, his reputation for cruelty had been built up on a bevy of rumors and it wasn't easy separating truth from reality. Mickey recalled a particularly disturbing one that seemed every bit as bizarre and unlikely as the one Jack had told him about Sticks Favors. Apparently, some years back, Salazar's accountant had fled with a considerable amount of his money. This infuriated him to no end, and for months, he made it his personal mission to track the traitor down. Eventually, he found him on a golf course in the Cayman Islands and proceeded to bash his head in with a five iron.

The story has it, that while Salazar was chasing the accountant around the course, a huge storm blew in, releasing a tremendous downpour. As Salazar was closing in, the accountant slipped on the wet grass and fell to the ground. While his former employee desperately begged for mercy, Salazar wound up and buried the five-iron in his head. Not yet satisfied, Salazar continued to bludgeon the accountant with the club, hacking away in some sort of savage, primeval trance, until he was finally struck down by a bolt of lightning. Only hours later after the storm had let up did a grounds keeper find the corpse of the accountant on a par three, his face down in a puddle of blood.

Salazar was nowhere to be found.

A series of small tremors shook Mickey out of this uncomfortable reverie. He had been off cocaine since the night with Frankie and the strain was making him crave it all the more. He yearned for that sharp, burning sensation in his nose and the smooth feeling it left as it slid down his throat. He wanted that alertness, that calming sense of well-being that made him feel everything was going to be wonderful, regardless of the situation. He breathed in deep, sniffed at empty air, and swallowed something that wasn't there. Then he wondered how he was ever going to get through the night.

He checked his directions and saw that he was getting close. He got off at the next exit and left the highway's flood lights behind. He sensed a sharp contrast between this place and his home town. The streets were no longer coated with grime, and even though the vents of his dashboard were caked with dust, he could tell the air outside was fresh and clean. The blocks were lined with thick, green hedges, dividing huge expanses of property, while gigantic trees loomed high, completely obscuring the October night sky. Mickey could see the limbs intertwine above, like a meshwork of giant arms closing in on him. He felt strangely claustrophobic under the canopy of branches, so he rolled down his window to let in the breeze. It was rich with the unfamiliar, almost alien fragrances of earth and vegetation. He reached for a cigarette and quickly lit it up.

The smoke felt smooth and comforting, the only thing at the moment able to calm him down. He looked at his watch and realizing he was late, began to notice the profuse perspiration under his arms. He increased his speed but had to be careful, as the directions took him up and down undulating hills and around treacherous blind turns. The street lamps tapered off, then finally disappeared, causing him to creep along in the gloom, with only the flickering of his headlights as a guide. At intervals, street lamps reappeared allowing Mickey to increase speed, but too often his car came perilously close to the edge of a cliff and Mickey found himself feeling tossed about on an endless sea of asphalt. He was beginning to get dizzy when, with a huge swell of relief, he finally stumbled upon his destination.

He pulled up to a wrought iron gate, sharpened spearheads topping its vertical bars like sentries in the night. A sign on it read "CAUTION: HIGH VOLTAGE!" It was flanked by two surveillance cameras on either side. Mickey began to wonder where Frankie had sent him. Did he really live in such a huge estate? With all this security? It didn't seem to make sense.

He rolled down his window. "Hello?"

A young man emerged from the gate house. He had a

blonde crew cut and a pock-marked face. His brown leather jacket bulged out on the upper left side and he was chewing a thick wad of gum. With an air of arrogance, he put his left hand on Mickey's roof and leaned down to scan the interior of the car. Chomping on the gum he said, "Who the fuck are you?"

Mickey eyed the bulge in the man's jacket. "Name's O'Leary. I got something for Frankie, um, Mr. Malone."

"He expecting you?" More chomping.

"Yeah."

The guard pulled a radio off his belt and switched it on. There was some static at first, then he pressed a button and spoke into it. "Frankie?"

Another crackle of static and then a metallic voice from the void responded. "Yeah?"

"I got some jerk-off here says he got something for ya."

"Who's got something for me?"

The guard frowned and looked back at Mickey. "Name again?"

Mickey clenched his jaws and spoke slowly. "O'Leary. Mickey O'Leary."

The guard stared at him for another moment and said into the radio, "Says his name's O'Leary."

The muffled voice said, "What's he got?"

"He didn't say."

"Well why don't you find out, idiot?"

The guard flinched as if he had been slapped. He took his finger off the speak button and looked at the radio. "Jeez," he said. He turned back to Mickey, a slight shade of rose beginning to appear on his neck. He cleared his throat. "What d'ya got?"

"He'll know. He told me to bring it."

The guard's neck was now turning crimson. He cleared his throat. "Listen, dipshit, you gotta tell me what you got or—"

The voice crackled back on the radio. "Clarence!"

"Yeah, Frankie?"

"Forget it. Just let him in."

"But you said—"

"Just let him in, moron!"

"Yeah, okay, sorry Frankie. I was just—"

The radio clicked off. Clarence stared at the radio again as if under a spell. He then cleared his throat and said to Mickey, as if he were in complete control of the situation, "Okay, no problem. You're lucky I was able to get you in." He scratched his head, winced a bit, and started toward the gatehouse. Without looking back, he said, "I'll just buzz you in."

When the gates were open wide enough, Clarence leaned out his window and grinned. "Enjoy your stay!" he said.

Mickey jammed on the accelerator and sped ahead. "Imbecile," he muttered.

Like everything near the highway, the property was blasted with flood lights, a security measure designed to obliterate all shadows and hiding places from any unwelcome guest. Even the spaces below the trees and shrubs were illuminated, visible from every possible direction. In awe, Mickey continued up a long, winding driveway which led to a sprawling mansion fronted by a large, flowing fountain. The water streamed from multiple jets in the well, and as the droplets hung in the air and fell, they were crisscrossed by a variety of colored lasers, creating a rainbow of cascading jewels.

Mickey got out of the car, and a man from the front of the house quickly approached. He was stocky, wore a three-piece suit, and his thick hair seemed molded to his head. His eyes were crazed with rage.

Mickey said, "Hey Frankie. I got—"

Frankie grabbed him by the jacket and slammed him up against the car. He jammed his forearm into Mickey's throat and said, "Don't 'Hey Frankie' me, punk. Where the fuck you been? I've been catching shit for you for days. What do you think this is, a charity? I ought to break your face right here for making me so look bad." He started to add pressure to Mickey's throat.

Mickey's instincts took over. He had been in this position many times before and the adrenaline only improved his performance. His heartbeat slowed. His breathing eased. And with a quick, fluid movement, he took the advantage. There was a swishing and a clicking sound as Mickey jerked his right arm around in familiar, instinctive motions. Suddenly Frankie felt something very cold and very sharp up under his chin. He froze, and his piercing glare faded into an unexpected panic. He eased up on his forearm.

Mickey said, "Back off, you fuck, or I'll jam this knife up through your skull."

Frankie hesitated and then began backing away, beads of perspiration appearing on his upper lip. He looked down toward where the switchblade was and a conciliatory expression took over his face. "Come on, Mick. I was just jokin'. You know, just having some fun. Like the other night—aaahhh!"

Mickey began to push the knife slowly upward. His brows lowered and his chin jutted forward. "Yeah, the other night. I remember. When you and those two whores fucked me over. I remember it like it was yesterday."

A ribbon of red began to trickle down the knife when three large men appeared, pointing machine guns at Mickey's head. They swore and cursed at him, demanding he drop the knife. One held the leash of a rabid-looking Doberman, snapping its vicious jaws.

Mickey slumped. He knew when he was beat. He lowered the knife and Frankie swatted it out of his hand. As it skittered away on the pavement, Frankie grabbed him by the shirt and drew back his fist. "You son of a bitch!" he yelled.

"ENOUGH!" a voice said from an intercom. Frankie froze and looked back toward the house. The voice said, "Bring him in. I don't want him touched...I mean it, Frankie."

The stocky man turned back to Mickey. His eyes burned with frustration and hate. He let go of the shirt with a shove and said, "This ain't over by a long shot, junkie. You mark my words."

Mickey straightened out his shirt and said, "Yeah, you and your army got it all over me."

Frankie took out a handkerchief and began to blot the blood from his throat. He stepped aside and said, "Let's go, douchebag. I wouldn't keep him waiting." He then bent over mockingly and gestured with an arm toward the house. Mickey looked back and forth between the armed guards and found no comfort there. They just stared back at him with hostility and motioned him to the door with their weapons.

It was then that Mickey began to piece it all together.

* * *

They took a few steps toward the house, but then Frankie paused and put a hand on Mickey's chest. "Hold it. Arms up." He came very close to his face and Mickey could feel the warmth of his breath. "I wouldn't do anything stupid," he said. "These guys love their toys." He then began patting him down.

Mickey just looked in the air. "Make sure you get a good feel, homo."

"Keep talkin', jackass," Frankie said, and with an air of smugness pulled open Mickey's jacket. He found an envelope there and was nothing short of bewildered when he saw all the cash inside. "What'd you do, rob a gas station?" A look of anger registered on his face, and to Mickey's confusion, he shoved the envelope back inside Mickey's pocket.

He then frisked his way down Mickey's legs and paused near his right ankle. While squatting there, Frankie looked up with a smirk. "Well, what have we here?" He pulled up Mickey's pant leg to reveal an ankle holster and a small pistol. He removed it and stood up. "What are you, some kind of half-assed secret agent?" He pulled out his own gun and jammed it in Mickey's back. "Come on, let's go." He shoved Mickey toward the doors and two of the armed guards followed.

They entered the house and led him down a wide, lavishly decorated hallway to an elevator. They descended a few floors and stepped out into an empty chamber. Then they walked to a large door, where Frankie punched in a code on the glowing keypad, which produced a happy chime and then a loud click. The door opened to a winding staircase that spiraled ever downward. Upon reaching the bottom, they stepped into what appeared to be a large living room, anchored by an L-shaped, shiny black leather couch against the far right corner. In front of the couch was a rectangular glass table. On the left wall was a vast entertainment center with a huge flat-screen TV. A state of the art stereo was playing Frank Sinatra, whose soft, throaty voice was singing about strangers exchanging glances in the night. Mickey immediately recognized the girl sitting in the corner of the couch with her bare feet folded underneath her. She had deep brown eyes, the color of dark chocolate, a small flat nose, and full lips. Her hair was cut short, dyed a platinum blonde, and she was wearing a bright pink tube top with cut-off jean shorts. She was filing her nails when she looked up to see who'd just arrived. When she recognized Mickey, she flashed a bright smile and held up her hand, fluttering her fingers around the emery board. "Hey, baby!" she called.

On the right, just before the couch was an extensive wet bar with rows of top shelf liquor sitting below a large, rectangular mirror. Behind the counter was a man of about fifty, well-toned for his age and standing just over six feet tall. While transferring some ice cubes into a glass with a pair of tongs, he studied Mickey with eyes the color of obsidian. His brows angled downward in an inadvertent, natural scowl that gave off the impression of a man accustomed to crushing the will of his enemies. He was wearing a brown tweed jacket with a white collared shirt left unbuttoned down below his chest. A silver cross on a chain lay around his neck, resting on a cushion of graying, curly hair.

Without taking his eyes off Mickey, he picked up a crystal decanter and poured some amber liquid into the glass. He swirled the ice cubes around, emitting a delicate, clinking sound, and took a slow, deep swallow. He then moved on to his next ritual, producing a soft pack of cigarettes, shaking one out and firing it up with a gold-plated lighter. He clicked it shut as the smoke spread toward his eyes, causing him to squint. He continued to look at Mickey through the haze and then moved out from behind the bar, planting himself in front of Mickey with his legs spread apart. He held the cigarette in his right hand, and rested his right elbow in his left. He took a deep drag and let out a huge plume of acrid smoke. His eyes were as black as coal. He studied Mickey for a moment longer, until a self-satisfied smile spread upon his face. He began to chuckle, then slapped his thigh, and broke out into a tar-coated cackle.

Mickey closed his eyes and felt dizzy. His stomach felt as if it were dissolving into hot syrup. *How could I have not seen this coming?* He began to think of all the things he had left undone and all the people in his life who were going to miss him. And it made him very sad.

The man began to pace in front of him, still laughing to himself, while looking at the floor and shaking his head. Every now and then he scratched his scalp with the hand holding the cigarette. He looked back up and Mickey thought he saw tears of amusement in the man's eyes. He pointed at him with the cigarette. "Now that was some performance you put on out there. You know, the way you flicked around that little knife of yours? Pretty impressive. What do you think, Frankie? Make an impression on you?"

Frankie said nothing.

He held out his hand. "I bet it did. Come on, let's see the knife."

Frankie handed it over and the man toyed with it for a few moments, appearing both fascinated and perplexed. He looked back at Mickey and said, "You gotta show me how to do that." He then paused, his face glowing in admiration. "So you're *the* Mickey O'Leary." He held his fingers up like quotation marks and said in an enthusiastic whisper, "The Man." Then he chuckled again. "So we finally get to meet. Well, I'm Victor Salazar." He searched Mickey's face for any glimmer of recognition or fear but was disappointed. His smile faded a bit, and then he offered his hand. With no other sane choice, Mickey took it. His palm was soft and firm, the nails perfectly manicured.

"So you're the one who's been messin' with my business in Soundview. I have to say, kid, I like your style. Fearless. Determined. And very...how should I say...*righteous*." He proceeded around the room again, this time nodding to himself, deep in thought. He continued to scratch his head with the hand holding his cigarette. Then he made his way around to the front of Mickey again. "You know, believe it or not, we're not very different, you and I." He lowered his gaze and teetered his head, as if acknowledging something, then said, "Of course, it seems we're on different sides now but, in the end, we all want the same things, don't we? Money. Women. Pleasure. Excitement. It's all there for the taking if we want it. We just gotta have the balls to just go out and grab it." He emphasized the point by reaching out quickly and snatching a fistful of air.

Mickey was looking down, but Salazar bent his head to look in his eyes. "That's what it's all about, isn't it, Mick? Balls. The greatest men in history took what they wanted because they all had huge ones. Napoleon. The pharaohs of Egypt. Julius fucking Caesar. They all had what it took and it brought them greatness. That's what life is all about in my book. And soon you'll see it the same way. It's all about survival of the fittest, my friend. Survival of the fittest."

Mickey remained quiet and wondered when he would get to the point. Actually, he didn't give a rat's ass about the point. He just wanted to get out of there alive.

Frankie's gun dug into his back and he arched forward.

"Frankie, put the gun away," Salazar said and tossed the knife on the bar. He gestured to the two gunmen, who moved away back toward the stairs. Frankie took a stool by the bar and put the knife in his shirt pocket.

"So Mickey, I hear you have a little something for me?" Salazar said.

Mickey took a quick glance at Frankie. "Uh, yeah."

Salazar raised his drink and spoke while he watched the ice cubes swirl. "How much?"

"Five grand, like Frankie said."

The glass froze at Salazar's lips. He swallowed and lowered the drink. "All of it?"

"Yeah, got it right here." Mickey reached into his pocket.

Salazar looked away and waved his hand. "That's okay, we'll get to that later." He glared at Frankie when he spoke next. "I was told that you might have some trouble in that matter." He walked over to the bar and leaned back against it. "How'd you get it? Relieve some people of their…shall we say, excesses?" He pantomimed quotation marks again to emphasize the word "excesses."

With the gun no longer in his back, Mickey relaxed a bit. He absently massaged his throat, which was red and roughened from Frankie's forearm. "No, some friends helped me out."

"Huh," Salazar said, now moving toward the couch. He stuck out his lower lip and rubbed his chin between his thumb and forefinger. "That's good." He was nodding in thought. "It's good to have friends. You do them favors, they do you favors. Everybody needs friends." He sidled in toward the corner of the couch and sat down as the girl instinctively shifted over to his right. He gestured toward the couch. "Mick, please, have a seat. Let's talk."

Mickey looked at Frankie and hesitated. He didn't want to sit and he didn't want to talk. But he moved slowly to the couch as if he were made of rusty metal. He tried not to look at what was on the table.

"Can I get you a drink?" Salazar asked.

Mickey sat down uncomfortably and again reached for his right pocket. "Listen, Mr. Salazar—"

Salazar held up a finger. "Shhhh," he said. "Relax. You're not refusing my hospitality, are you?"

"No it's just that…"

"Then have a drink. What'll it be?"

Mickey relented. "Just a Coke."

Salazar snickered. "Yeah, I'll bet." The whole room erupted with laughter.

Mickey's face turned crimson. In front of him on the table was a huge mound of white powder, along with several plastic packages full of it. There were two small mirrors on which sat some cocaine arranged in lines and a couple razor blades lying off to the side.

"You're a funny guy," Salazar said, trying to compose himself. "But I figured this was what you wanted anyway." He offered Mickey one of the mirrors and a small silver tube.

"Sorry," Mickey said. "I meant the drink. Coca-Cola? I'm laying off the blow for a while."

The smile faded from Salazar's face. He lowered his gaze and leaned back into the sofa. "Sounds commendable, Mick. I respect that. But why don't we make an exception, huh? Just for tonight, you know, in honor of our new acquaintance? Come on, I know how much you like it."

Mickey's eyes were wide and sober. He shook his head warily. "Thanks, but it's been getting me into too much trouble lately." He turned to look at Frankie. "And debt."

Salazar pondered this for a moment and said, "Yeah… well…I can understand that." He placed the paraphernalia back on the table, his eyes never leaving Mickey. He seemed to be losing his composure. With a perplexed look, he sat back, crossed his legs widely, and spread his arms over the top of the couch. "So you haven't had any since the night with Frankie?"

"No."

"One week, huh? Not bad. I guess it's a start but…I'll tell you a little secret. C'mere." He leaned forward and beckoned Mickey with his index finger. When his lips were next to Mickey's ear, he whispered, "I don't think you can do it." He then slapped him on the back and let out a loud guffaw that filled the entire room. He continued like this for a few moments, and when he finally settled down, he said, "Okay, seriously, Mick, I want us to be friends. There's something important I need from you, and in return, I'll get you anything your heart desires. You say you're quitting? Well, I've heard that before from many people, and if that's what you really want, that's your decision. But let me ask you something. Why would want you *want* to? I mean, let's be honest. It feels incredible, doesn't it? Makes you feel like you can take on the world!"

He looked at Mickey hopefully but saw nothing in his eyes. "Huh," he said. "You seem resolute. Be that as it may, there are other things I can offer you." He raised his arms and looked around the room. As you can see I have expensive tastes. And I can easily afford most of life's luxuries. You want to live a life of luxury, Mick?"

Mickey said, "Please, Mr. Salazar, I really need to get going."

"If you will do what I ask, I'll give you anything you want. Anything." He pointed his thumb at the girl sitting next to him. She had her hands between her thighs and was smiling timidly at Mickey. "From what I hear, you like Vanessa here a whole lot. You do me this favor? Any time you want her? She's all yours."

Salazar looked at the girl and nodded toward Mickey. She pointed at one of the mirrors with a questioning look and Salazar gave her the okay. She then picked up the reflecting glass along with one of the tubes and sniffed up some of the powdery drug. With her index finger she swiped up some more and tasted it, as if it were icing from a cake, and rubbed the residue between her upper teeth and gums. Now breathing deeply, as if consumed by some glorious rapture, she wiped her nose with the palm of her hand

and cleared her throat. She then rose and strutted toward Mickey, showing off her smooth, taut legs. Her stomach was firm, and in her belly button was a glittering diamond stud.

"Hey, baby," she said with a pouty face. "Miss me?" She straddled Mickey's waist and sat down in his lap. Mickey could see her eyes were a glowing white and her pupils were hugely dilated. Before he could decide what to do, she took his face in her hands and began to kiss him passionately. He could taste the numbing bitterness that remained in her mouth, and for a moment, gave in to his desire. Reflexively, almost in a trance, he kissed her back. Her hips began to undulate, arousing him to great heights, but it didn't produce the desired effect. Instead of drawing Mickey in, it suddenly jerked him back to reality, and all at once, he lifted her off him, stood up, and put her aside. He then moved away from the couch.

"Listen, man," he said in a shaky voice, "I really appreciate everything. Really. B-but there's some place I gotta be." His hands were shaking as he took out the envelope and held it out. "Here's the money, okay? Can we call it even?"

Salazar's scowl was no longer inadvertent. "Put...the fucking... money...back in your pocket." Frankie got up and the other two guards moved in. Salazar then chuckled and shook his head. "Why are you making things so difficult? Don't you even want hear what I have to say? I'm trying to be nice here and somehow I'm starting to feel like I'm being insulted." He got up and stood directly in front of Mickey again.

Mickey said nothing.

Salazar looked at him astonished. "Resolute," he said.

"Not smart, but resolute. Well here's the deal, Mick. You know about The Power, right?"

Mickey felt the men looming behind him and he began to sweat again.

"I'M TALKING TO YOU!" Salazar bellowed.

Mickey jerked himself upright. "Y-yeah. I know about them."

"Well they're not just a bunch of out-of-control punks. They work for me. They run various operations for me and earn me lots of cash. That cash is what allows me and my friends to enjoy the lifestyle to which we are accustomed. Four of these friends are right here in this room with us." He gestured to Frankie, Vanessa, and the two goons. "We've done well with our little enterprise, and we'd like to expand. The only problem is we keep running into a roadblock in one particular town where there's a boatload of business to be made. You know what town I'm talking about?"

Mickey shrugged his shoulders.

"Again with the muteness. Well I'll tell you what town I'm talking about, as if you didn't know. It's Soundview. And the roadblock is you."

A confused look came over Mickey's face. "Me? What are you talking about?"

Salazar continued. "You see, over the years we've tried to set up some framework for our operations, sent a few scouts in there, you know, to test the waters? But seems every time we try, our guys are being taken out by some pain-in-the-ass Irish boys. They're getting beat up, robbed, and outright demoralized. Do you know anything about this? Anything ring a bell for you? I mean, with a name like O'Leary, you gotta know something about these Soundview micks. So, do ya?" And the quotation fingers came out again. "Mick?"

Mickey was numb and exhausted and terrified, but he had to hold it together for just a little bit longer. "I don't know what you're talking about."

Salazar's eyes blazed. "I'll give you one more chance. What do you know about The Shamrocks?"

He swallowed hard and said, "Nothing."

With a smug expression, Salazar stepped back and nodded toward the men. The two henchmen grabbed Mickey's arms while Frankie stepped forward with a cold grin. He took Mickey's collar with both hands and jerked it down over his left shoulder. A loud RRIIPPP! was heard, and there, revealed on his upper arm was a large, green four-leaf clover.

* * *

"How do you explain that, tough guy?" Salazar asked.

Mickey tried to pull his collar back into place and glowered at Frankie. "It's just a tattoo, man. I'm Irish. Practically every Irish kid's got one of these on his arm. It don't mean nothing. And I don't know anything about no Shamrocks." He frowned as he massaged yet another new abrasion on his neck.

Salazar just stood there in disbelief.

Mickey said, "So can I get going now?" He reached into his pocket one more time to get the envelope.

Salazar grabbed his arm and held it there. "You go for the money one more time and I'll break your arm." He gave Mickey a threatening look, as if to dare him to doubt his words. He then thrust down Mickey's arm and began pacing the room again, looking at the floor and shaking his head as he had done before. The chuckling also came again. "You're something, kid. You are one funny guy. But sooner or later I'm going to stop thinking you're funny and it's gonna get ugly. Okay, time to stop playing games. Bring him in, Frankie."

Mickey watched Frankie walk over to a door that appeared to be connected to an adjacent room. He knocked on the door and a vaguely familiar voice answered. It had a deep, rich quality, both jovial and nonchalant. "Yeah, okay! Be right there, just give me a second!" Indecipherable mumbling was then heard along with the unmistakable sound of feminine laughter. After a moment, the door flew open and a portly, middle aged man appeared in a purple silk robe, with the letters GM in flowing script stitched on the upper left side. His hair was short brown, parted on the side, and a mutton chop mustache dominated the lower half of his face. He moved into the room with two young girls in negligees on each arm. When he saw Mickey, he let out a whistling, wheezing guffaw, which caused him to fall into a coughing fit. When he finally composed himself, he said, "Hey Mick! Long time no see! How ya been? Gonna join in the festivities?" He ambled over to the couch and sat down, somewhat distracted by the mound of cocaine.

Mickey felt that cold, prickling sensation again. This time it shot like a lightning bolt all the way out to the edges of his wrists. The air felt like it was leaking out of his lungs. Somehow he managed to whisper, "Fuck me."

He closed his eyes for a moment, a cinema show of memories flooding through his mind. When he opened them again, he was angry and glared venomously at the man. "I knew it. I knew you were a piece of shit. How long you been on the take, *Officer*?"

Frankie stuck his face within an inch of Mickey's. "Shut your fuckin' mouth or I will shut it for you."

Mickey just stared back in disdain.

Salazar pulled Frankie away and said, "So, I see you and Captain McGavin are old friends."

Mickey glanced over at the cop. "*Captain?* Oh, that's a good one. That's rich. Captain. Must be as good at giving bribes as taking them." He looked back at Salazar and said, "I wouldn't say friends. My pet snake is better company than this piece of shit."

The room burst out in laughter and McGavin's face dropped. "You better shut your mouth and listen if you know what's good for you. These guys mean business."

"Yeah, I know what kind of business they mean. By the way, lookin' real good, fat ass. Ever hear of a salad?"

Again the room erupted and McGavin's face took on a rosy shade of pink. He stood up and bolted toward Mickey but was blocked by the wall of the two guards' chests. After proclaiming in indignation that he didn't have to take that kind crap from anyone, he sat back down in shame.

Finally Salazar held up his hand. "Okay, enough!" He lit another cigarette and moved back toward Mickey. He took a drag and blew the smoke into Mickey's face. "McGavin's told me all about you, Mickey, so you can stop the bullshit right now. I know you're in tight with The Shamrocks. And I think you are their leader." He paused for a moment, clenching his jaws and grinding his teeth. When he spoke, it was with even, controlled malevolence. "From now on, you and The Shamrocks are going to work for me."

Mickey felt like a knife had impaled his chest. He knew in his heart this could never happen. The Shamrocks had been protecting Soundview from this very man for the better part of ten years, and whether or not they knew it, his family and friends had been relying on the club for their peace, their safety, their very livelihoods. And even if he tried to persuade The Shamrocks into joining a life of crime, a notion that was unfathomable to his own sensibilities, he knew it was absolutely impossible.

However, at the moment he had no choice but to simply play along. "Okay," Mickey said, "you got me. You win. I'll give it a shot. But you have to know I stopped being a Shamrock a long time ago. I don't even know how many of my guys are left. I might be able to do something, but I can't promise you I can convince them."

Salazar crossed his arms. "Oh, you'll convince them alright." He started pacing again. "You'll convince them. You see, Mick, a man like me only gets to be where he is through persistence. And brutality, if necessary. If I am unable to enforce my will, then no one takes me seriously. I lose respect. And a man in my position can't afford to lose respect. You know why? Because in order to run a business like mine, you need loyal people around you. People who both fear and trust you. Without respect, Mickey?" At this he started shaking his head. "Everything falls apart. Simple as that. Get what I'm saying?"

Mickey nodded.

"Good. Now my parents must have had a premonition when they gave me my Christian name. They must have had a feeling that I would win under any circumstance. You know what my name means, right? Victor?" His voice became vicious. "It means winner. And I will always win until the day I die. You understand me?" Mickey nodded again. "Now you will go talk to Shane Gallagher, or whoever the fuck is in charge of those little Irish pricks and you're gonna convert them within a week, or God as my witness, you will regret the day you were ever born."

He went over behind the bar to fix himself another drink. His demeanor softened. "Like I said, I don't want to get ugly in this. But if you force my hand I will not hesitate. You wouldn't want anything to happen to Tommie, now would you?"

Something snapped inside Mickey and before he even knew it, he was rushing toward the bar.

He didn't get very far. Before he moved more than a half a step, he was held back by the three big men.

Salazar just smirked.

Mickey's eyes blazed with fury. "I want you to understand something, you fucking…asshole. If you ever go near my brother, I swear by all that is holy, I will murder you myself. You can bet on it."

A flicker of fear appeared on Salazar's face before dissolving into a nervous smile. "Foolish pride," he said, "foolish pride." He nodded to Frankie, who now appeared smugly satisfied. The henchman reached inside his jacket pocket and produced a black, hand-held device with two opposing electrodes. As Mickey continued to glare at Salazar, Frankie jammed the device against Mickey's neck and pressed a button. A short buzzing sound filled his ears, and Mickey felt a high frequency vibration, then an excruciating pain in his neck. Before he knew what was happening, he fell into blackness. As he collapsed into the arms of one of the guards, Salazar said, "Get him out of here."

* * *

They started to drag him out when Salazar motioned Frankie over. "Soundview has been off limits for way too long," he said. "Like you said, it's a treasure chest just waiting to be dug up. If I don't take it, someone else will. And I will not let someone come in and take what is rightfully mine."

He gave Frankie a long look and then began straightening his hitman's tie. "I need him to get this done, you understand me? And I want some immediate results." He pulled a piece of lint off of Frankie's sleeve like a proud tailor. "I want ten grand by the end of the week. You know how that happens? Your little band of punks are going to go full force into Soundview and start shaking things up. I want to see some action by tomorrow."

Frankie's eyes opened wide. "Shouldn't we give the kid time to spread the—"

Salazar stopped him by putting his finger on his lips. "Uh ah ah!" he said. "We don't need any time because you are gonna make it happen. You see, Frankie, this was all your idea." He nodded over to McGavin, who was now looking very sober. "Yours and this fat freeloader sitting on my couch, doing my blow. The wheels are in motion now, Frankie. If we don't mean business, then we are nothing. And the only way we are going to prove it is if that kid out there brings The Shamrocks to us. See that he does it."

"Okay, Vic. You're the boss."

"Good. We understand each other. And one more thing."

"What's that?"

"Leave him with the money, Frankie. *All of it.* I mean it. I want it to remind him that he still owes me something. Maybe he'll even score some blow and realize that he'll always be a junkie. Then he'll figure out that we could be the solution to all his problems, not the source. Make sure those fat heads out there don't take any of it, either. And don't hurt him anymore. If he's in the hospital, he's no good to me. He may be tough, but he'll learn. The only way to protect his family is to do what I ask. Make sure he understands that."

Salazar paused. He grabbed Frankie by his lapels and pulled him close. "You got all that?"

Frankie swallowed, and a clicking sound came from inside his throat. "Yeah, sure, Vic. Like always."

Salazar stared back suspiciously. "I can't tell you how important this is to my reputation."

"Of course, boss."

Salazar relaxed. "Good," he said, "then go."

Frankie left and Salazar went over to the couch and sat next to McGavin. He picked up one of the silver-plated tubes and said, "You don't mind, do you?"

McGavin's forehead showed beads of sweat. His eyebrows were very high and his breathing was becoming labored. He shook his head.

"I mean," Salazar said, "I wouldn't presume to impose on your good time here, would I? You sure you've had enough?"

McGavin looked at the large pile of cocaine on the table. "Yeah, sure, Vic. I had plenty."

"Okay then. I guess I'll just have a little myself." He leaned over, snorted a fat line up his left nostril, and then another up his right. He drew it back deeply, wiped his nose, and sat back on the couch with his eyes closed. "You and Frankie told me this kid was gonna be a piece a cake. That all he cared about was getting high and—how did you put it?—he'd drown his grandma if it meant getting blow and getting laid. That doesn't appear to be the case, now does it?"

McGavin shifted in his seat. "I don't know. He seems a little different now. We used to bust him for possession all the time. And when he didn't have any, we'd catch him shaking down dealers. All he did care about was getting high. I don't know, maybe he is trying to get clean."

Salazar suddenly turned on McGavin and grabbed his robe with two fists. He shook the retired police captain so violently that his hairpiece flew off his head.

Spittle flew from Salazar's lips. "Listen to me, you fat-assed bald fuck! For your sake, O'Leary better come through. If he doesn't and word gets out that he defies me, I'll put your balls in a meat grinder! You hear me?"

"Okay, okay, Vic! Calm down! Jesus! What's wrong with you?"

Salazar's eyes cleared and he let go of McGavin. He shoved him away and sat back down. He smoothed his own hair back and breathed deeply again. McGavin hurriedly put his hair back in place with an uncomfortable glance at the girls. They were sitting at the bar now, barely suppressing their laughter.

Salazar now spoke more calmly. "Listen, George," he said, "the fact that you and Frankie miscalculated is of no consequence to me now. O'Leary will come through. He'd better, or we'll just have to pay his kid brother a visit."

McGavin looked down and began rubbing his face fiercely. He cleared his throat and finally dared to say something. "Vic, you sure you want to hurt the kid? I mean, he's got nothing to do with this. He's just a civilian."

Salazar looked at him like he was a revolting vagrant. "Who the fuck are you? Don't tell me what to do with my affairs. When I'm interested in your opinion, I'll ask you. Just keep your mouth shut, take my money, fuck my girls, and do my blow, okay? Now get out of my sight."

McGavin just sat there befuddled.

Salazar said, "Am I not speaking English? Go!" He gave Vanessa a signal and she got up and took McGavin by the hand.

"Give him a sloppy blow job or something," Salazar said. "Maybe that will clear his head."

As they were leaving, he added, "Straighten up, George. You're beginning to become a liability around here."

* * *

Frankie and the guards dragged Mickey's limp body up the winding staircase, to the elevator, and back through the house. Once outside in the cool air, Mickey began to rouse. When he woke, he realized his body was suspended between the two guards, one of whom held his wrists and the other his ankles. They began swinging him in a low arc, over the ground, back and forth with a steady cadence. In unison, they counted aloud, "One, two, THREE!" before launching him over the concrete edge of the fountain. He thrashed wildly in the air and landed with a *SPLASH!* into the icy cold water. He sat there humiliated, coughing and sputtering, while the guards went into hysterics.

Frankie came forward and tossed Mickey's knife and empty gun into the water. He said, "You have one week, you hear me? One week. In the meantime, we're gonna send some of our guys into your neighborhood to do some business. You see to it that they're left alone. I hear about any Shamrock bullshit, it's your ass." He paused as if to analyze the drenched and broken form sitting dazed in the fountain. All he could do was shake his head in disgust. "Have a nice night, junkie." He started walking back toward the house and nodded to the guards. They then proceeded to bash in his windshield with a couple of bats.

"Fuck!" Mickey moaned. But there was nothing he could do. He had to just sit there and watch his car get demolished. When it was finally over and he was alone, he rose from the fountain shaking violently. He made his way slowly back to his car, and opened the door. He pulled off his drenched jacket and rolled it into a ball. With his chest heaving, he used it to clear out as much of the broken glass off the seat as he could. He then got in the car and put his head on the wheel.

Quietly, the tears began to flow.

CHAPTER 7

A GROUNDED SOURCE

J ack lay on his back, his hands clasped between his head and a pillow. It was nearly 3 AM, but he remained wide awake, anxiously staring at the ceiling. He had heard nothing yet from Mickey and was struggling with the urge to succumb to grim speculation. If his mind could only let go, somehow slip off into the world of dreams, he would find out more in the morning.

In the dim light which flowed in from the street lamps outside, Jack listened to the light pattering of a newly falling rain. His amber eyes glinted with analytical consideration as he watched the shadows of water rolling down his walls in streaks. He felt helpless lying there, his ignorance of Mickey's condition prompting the mental bombardment of one bleak scenario after another, thus rendering the prospect of sleep impossible.

He rolled over on his bed and gazed upon a poster on his wall, the album cover of Meat Is Murder by The Smiths. Colored in drab green and gray, the poster depicted a young boy wearing combat gear, his face streaked with grime, his countenance a sobering look of fear. As in the past, Jack wondered how the illustration related to the theme of the album, but could formulate nothing. He guessed it really didn't matter. But the music itself had always reverberated through his blood, and for that, he would be eternally grateful. The wistful, melancholy sounds of Johnny Marr's guitar had so often soothed Jack's repressed yearnings. And Morrissey's haunting, lyrical delivery somehow helped him mourn the loss of love and future memories.

It had been several years since he had split up with Gretta, and only recently had his thinly veiled depression begun to fade. Spiritually and physically, no one had ever been closer to him. She was the only love he had ever known, and losing her had been the most difficult experience in his life. Even after all this time, he still felt the bond they had shared, and though it was distant in time and space, he found it hard to let go.

But that was until last night. Just the image of Tessa's bemused smile quickened his heart and gave rise to a new, growing anticipation of joy. He wanted to run with that feeling, the idea he actually could be happy again, but years of disappointment, along with a pervasive, persistent pessimism, tempered the idea with a healthy dose of reason. The fact was, he had only had a conversation with the girl. It was stupid to get carried away, even if the remote possibility alone brightened his impression of the world and somehow gave him hope.

It was nice to know someone like Tessa was out there, innocent and pure, charismatic and kind. But if he were to pursue her, there were other issues he needed to consider. Even if by some miracle he found his way into her heart, danger now loomed all around. With little provocation, for reasons unbeknownst to him, he had incurred the wrath of a violently unstable man, a person so filled with hatred and hostility that he was willing to go to great lengths to exact his revenge. How could Jack expose Tessa to this?

He groaned and turned over on his stomach, then pulled the pillow out from under his face and jammed it over the back of his head. How the hell was he going to deal with Sticks Favors? He racked his mind to come up with a solution.

Suddenly, a loud BANG! BANG! BANG! came from the direction of his front door.

He flipped over and sat up with a start, his heart slamming into the back of his ribs. BANG! BANG! BANG! he heard again and bolted to his closet to grab his old baseball bat. Wielding it so tightly that his nails left tiny crescents in his palms, he warily descended the stairs, stopping only a few feet from the bottom. Controlling his breath, he readied the club to swing. BANG! BANG! BANG! Had Favors really found out where he lived? How often was he going to have to fight off this lunatic? He steadied himself for another battle.

Unable to withstand another round of banging, Jack yelled, "Favors, get the fuck outta here before I bash your fuckin' head in!"

From outside the door came a hoarse and tired voice. "Open the door, Jack. It's Mick."

* * *

Although the voice sounded somehow unfamiliar, Jack knew it at once. He approached the door and twisted the deadbolt. When Mickey stepped inside, Jack could barely recognize him. He was soaking wet, his clothes clinging to his body, revealing just how frail he had become. His hands were jammed deep into the pockets of his water-logged jeans and his shoulders slumped forward, bearing the weight of his head which hung heavily toward the floor. For a moment he peered up, as if to read Jack's reaction, then self-consciously turned away.

Jack's concern turned into fear. Mickey's cheeks, now ashen and drawn, had taken on the color of a graying cadaver. His eyes had the dullness of fading embers.

He stood there shivering in a daze, his hair wet and matted to his head, not knowing what to say or what to do. Instead, he just looked blankly around, leaning on one foot, then the other, his sodden sneakers sloshing as he transferred his weight between the two.

Overcome by the sight of him, Jack took a few moments before he was able to say anything. When he spoke, all he could muster was, "Mick, what the fuck?"

Mickey just bent down and began to take off his Converses. With his eyes focused on the wet laces, he said in a barely audible voice, "I need a towel."

In angry exasperation, Jack looked off and muttered, "Jesus Christ." He started off towards his bedroom and glanced back with concern. "I'll get you some sweats. And some coffee. Black, right?"

From his position on the floor, as he worked on a knot, Mickey accepted Jack's hospitality with a feeble whisper.

They sat across from each other at the kitchen table, a hot bowl of chicken soup sitting untouched in front of Mickey. As he gazed at it, the steam flowed up and dissipated. He had showered and changed into dry clothes, but the deep chill that had seized his body still persisted.

Jack searched for anything in Mickey's expression that would reveal even a hint about what had happened. His eyes were bloodshot, his complexion pallid, and his hair was a disheveled mess, like the wig of some tattered scarecrow. And as he stared at his full bowl of soup, his nose began to run.

Jack turned to the counter and grabbed a roll of paper towels. He ripped off one and handed it to Mickey, who wearily blew his nose and said thanks. This sign of lucidity, however subtle, encouraged Jack, as it seemed Mickey was finally waking from his languid state. Jack had asked him at least a dozen questions, but so far, they had only been answered by the monotonous ticking of the clock on the wall.

"Freakin' nose is runnin' like crazy," he said as he grimly took a sip of his coffee.

Jack decided to try again. "Dude," he said, "why were you soaked?"

Mickey put the coffee mug on the table, pulled the blanket tighter around himself, and sat back in the chair.

Anger registered in his eyes. "Fuckers tossed me in a fountain."

Jack sat in silence, stunned.

"Then they smashed in my windshield."

Jack raised his eyebrows. After a moment, he got up to look out the kitchen window. The weak light that reached his back patio revealed heavy droplets splashing into growing puddles. "Jesus," he said. "The ride home must have sucked."

"Yeah, well that's nothing," Mickey said. "I was lucky to get out of there alive."

Jack's curiosity was gnawing at him. "Come on, man, you gotta tell me what happened." He held his arms out wide. "I'm in the dark here."

Mickey, his eyes now glistening, finally met his gaze. "I was set up."

"Yeah, Mick, I know that. Malone suckered you in for the five grand."

Mickey shook his head. "Malone works for Salazar, Jack. Frankie's just his errand boy. This whole thing came from Salazar. He got Malone to lure me in with women and coke, got me to deliver the money in person, then ambushed me."

Jack's eyes nearly popped out of his skull. All he could do was blink. "And he let you go? Holy shit. I mean, Jesus fucking Christ, Mick, you *are* lucky to be alive."

"I know. I was freaking out. I thought for sure he was gonna kill me."

"So all he wanted was the money? He didn't know who you were?"

Mickey reached over to his denim jacket, which was on the back of the chair next to him, and pulled out the envelope full of hundred dollar bills. He held it up for Jack to see and tossed it on the table. The package was so soaked through, it made a splat as it landed. "Keep it. You earned it," he said.

Jack opened the envelope and eyed all the wet bills inside. "This makes absolutely no sense to me."

"He never even wanted the money, Jack." Mickey said, his eyes thoughtful and distant. "He wanted me."

Jack sat back and looked at his friend with empathy. "So he knows about The Shamrocks."

"Yeah, he knows. Thanks to that fat fuck McGavin. I knew that son of a bitch was crooked. Now my whole family's in danger." He looked down and shook his head in misery.

"But I don't get it. He had you. Why didn't he just kill you then and there?"

"Don't you see, Jack? If Salazar killed me, The Shamrocks would go after him full force. He can't beat us. Not with his stupid band of goons. The Power never had a *chance* against us. The only way for him to win is to somehow get us to back off. He wants to use me for that. He wants me to somehow convince The Shamrocks to work for him."

Jack took a deep breath. His voice took on a pleading tone. "Mick, what are you gonna do? Those guys will never back down. Not from The Power or Salazar."

Mickey closed his eyes and shook his head. "I can't believe this shit." He shrugged off the blanket and went over to the wall, leaning against it dejectedly as he hung his head in despair. When he looked up at the ceiling, his eyes were brimming with tears. "What a life," his voice choked.

"Booze, gangs, whores, drugs. Look where it's gotten me. Jesus!" He went back to the table and buried his head in his arms.

Jack came around the table and placed his hand on his friend's shoulder. He didn't really believe in everything he was about to say, but he had to do something. "Come on, Mick," he consoled, "you never hurt anyone. At least not anybody who didn't have it coming. We both know Soundview needed The Shamrocks. You made that happen. And lots of people owe you their lives for that. The women and the coke? Who cares about that? What you do with your life is your business and no one else's. As long as no one else gets hurt, what difference does it make?"

Mickey didn't answer.

"Mick, you listening? It doesn't make you a bad person."

A muffled voice came out from beneath Mickey's arms. "Yeah, right."

"Seriously, why should it? Sure, sometimes you need to cut down, you know, for your own good. But other than that, you're not hurting anyone else, are you?"

Mickey stiffened and sat up. When he turned to Jack, his face was bloated and bleary-eyed. "Jack," he said, "if I don't get The Shamrocks to work for Salazar, he's going after Tommie."

"What?!"

"You heard me. So that thing you were saying about not hurting anyone else? That's all bullshit. I just put my little brother in some serious danger."

Jack started to say something, but his voice caught and he had to clear his throat. Finally, he said, "Tommie? Why would he go after him? He's just a kid!"

105

Mickey glanced at the ceiling and shook his head at an odd, askew angle. "Because he's a ruthless fuck, that's why. You know that. You've dealt with him yourself. He'll do anything to get what he wants, when he wants it." He sighed and pictured Salazar in all his arrogance. "No one's safe here anymore, Jack. Not even kids." He stood up, walked a few steps, and then bent to put his hands on his thighs. He breathed in deeply and blew out hard so his cheeks puffed out. "What a fucking nightmare."

"Mick, listen to me," Jack said. "All this that's happening now? Yeah, it sucks and we have to deal with it. We'll do whatever it takes to keep your family safe. But you have to stop blaming yourself for everything. Tommie's not in danger because of your so-called bad habits or because you're weak. Salazar's coming after you because you're the only one with guts enough to go against him." He looked hard into Mickey's eyes. "Dude, as much as you'd like to think, you're not a bad guy. A lot of folks around here actually think you're a hero."

Mickey stood upright, and it appeared as if a huge load had been lifted off his back. Just as quickly, he sat back down, somewhat abashed. He even managed a quiet chuckle. "Thanks, man," he said. "You always seem to know what to say." He thought for a moment. "You know, you're right. About The Shamrocks, I mean. It really was the best thing I ever did. It still doesn't change the fact that Tommie's in trouble. I just gotta figure some way out of this."

"Think we can stall Salazar for a while?" Jack asked. "Till we figure something out?"

"He said I had one week."

"A week, huh? Well that gives us a little time. Got any ideas?"

"Haven't thought about it much. My mind's all twisted up. And I'm fucking exhausted. Maybe I'll give Shane a call tomorrow. Maybe we can come up with some sorta plan."

"You mean like old times?"

"Yeah, like old times." Mickey considered something for a moment, then said, "I think Tommie'll be okay for now. We got seven days." He let out a deep yawn. "Right now I need to crash."

Jack was relieved to see Mickey in better spirits. "Okay, man," he said. "We'll call Shane in the morning." He nodded toward the living room. "You can use the couch."

Mickey got up and looked at his friend, a look of profound appreciation on his face. "Thanks, Man."

Jack smiled and said, "What do you want, a kiss goodnight? Get some fucking sleep."

CHAPTER 8

CHARGED, REBOOTED
AND RENAMED

Saturday Morning, October 14

Sticks Favors huddled in the back corner of his holding cell. Scrunched up into a ball, with his head tucked into his chest and his hands clasped firmly over it, he appeared like some giant water bug curled upon itself for protection. All through the night, he had sustained such a furious onslaught of physical and mental abuse that he now lay still, withdrawn into a loathsome state of catatonia. There, in the gloom, he remained motionless, in a vain attempt to block out everything that now assaulted his senses. But even with his eyes clenched tight, and his thoughts probing for some imaginary relief, the stench of urine still permeated the air, the rattling of the steel cages still rang in his ears, and the ridicule of his cellmates still tormented his mind.

The hazy borders at which reality ended and fantasy began were beginning to blur. He was getting close to the edge. Curiously close. Now near enough to the touch, he crawled out further, reaching toward the haze, where no one could hurt him and nothing left mattered anymore.

But just as his new world started to take took form, beginning to set his weary mind free, a cold voice jarred him out of his reverie, reining him back in. He turned on the voice, growling and defiant, not wanting to return. But it wasn't yet time. It wasn't meant to be. And it made him sad beyond measure. He longed one last moment for the cloudy, swirling colors of his wonderful, eternal dream, then reluctantly spiraled back down to his agony.

"MacCracken!" a harsh voice called out. "Stephan MacCracken! Where the hell are you?"

Sticks' white, glossy head emerged from his folded body, like some prehistoric albino tortoise, its shell caked with filth. He extended his limbs and stood up warily, his eyes darting about wildly, ready to flinch at any sudden movement. He stumbled toward the guard standing just outside his cell with his eyes half-shut and dried-up tear tracks visible on his grimy cheeks. "The name's Sticks," he croaked.

The guard scribbled some notes on a clipboard. "I don't

give a shit what you call yourself, scumbag. If you ain't MacCracken, you ain't getting out." He looked up and his expression registered surprise. "What the hell happened to your face?"

Sticks tried to smirk but the pain caused him to wince. He touched his swollen left jaw and said, "Electrolysis went bad."

"Oh, a comedian. Well your act could use some work, Groucho. You MacCracken or what? And don't bullshit me, 'less you want the other side of your face to look the same."

Desperately needing to get out the cell, he mumbled that he was indeed this Stephan MacCracken.

"Congratulations, dipshit, your grandma's here." The guard then yelled out of the side of his mouth, "Open seven!" His request was echoed from down the hall and a buzzing sound followed. The bars of the cage disengaged and swung open. After a quick glance behind him, Sticks sprung out of the cell and into the guard's arms, as if he were fleeing the clutches of some murderous fiend.

"Get off me, moron!" the guard said, shoving him back.

Sticks shakily offered an apology, and the guard just glared at him. "One more stunt like that and I'll throw your ass back in there. C'mon, move it!"

He shoved Sticks forward and escorted him toward the front of the police station. When they arrived, an old woman of about 70 years of age was berating a helpless man sitting on one of the benches. She was short and stout, and wearing a gray, floppy wig, thick horn-rimmed glasses, and a mean, shriveled face. Wildly gesticulating about some outrageous transgression, she wagged a threatening finger at the man, who, while leaning away and grimacing from her foul breath, desperately searched for someone, something, *anything* to save him from this berserk old hag.

The guard moved in quickly, practically dragging Sticks by the arm. "What the hell's going on? Hey, lady, take it easy!"

Mamsie turned on him in an instant. "Who the hell are you?" she screeched. "Oh, another crook with a badge, I see! Well, you don't fool me, copper. None of yer do!" She stared him up and down with a contemptuous sneer, her mouth silently working itself into a frenzy.

The guard just stood there dumbfounded, staring in disgust at the long white hairs that extended from the mole on her chin.

When her eyes fell on Sticks, she said, "So there you are, you little booger! I see you finally found a place that suits yer! I should let you rot in here for all that's good. Nothing but a low-life piece of shite is all you is!"

Sticks cringed at the sight her. She was wearing her stained, light blue house dress, loose brown stockings up to her knees, and dirty, moldering slippers. Over her shoulder hung an oversized white handbag. The odor of Ben-Gay surrounded her like a toxic cloud.

He considered fleeing back to the cell and begging them to let him back in.

The sneer remained frozen on her face as she adjusted her wig. "Alright, the paperwork's done, y'idiot. Bail's gonna cost ya twice as much as me by the time I get through with ye. Now git to the car afore I come to my senses and abandon ye!"

In one quick movement, she swung her bag in the direction of his head. But he was ready for it. Over the years, he had learned to anticipate her movements and was able to skillfully duck out of the way. The guard, however, never saw it coming. The heavy purse slammed into his neck like a sledgehammer, knocking him back several feet. Dazed by the blow, he was reaching for his gun when the entire room broke out in hysterics. Even the other officers couldn't hold back their laughter. He glanced around in humiliation, not knowing what to do, and finally decided it would be best just to get rid of them. "All right, all right, real funny." He reached for his neck, where a huge red welt was beginning to form. "Pain in the asses. I should do society a big favor and lock you both up. Now get out of my sight before I change my mind!"

"Bah!" Mamsie waved a hand in disgust. "Change your mind, my arse! Ye already got my 500 bucks for bailing out stupid here! And for what? Disturbin' the peace and resisting arrest? Nothing but a set-up to get my money. Yer all corrupt, I say!" She then proceeded to flog and kick Sticks out the door to the delight of everyone around.

The onslaught continued outside, all the way back to her monstrous, corroded Cadillac. Before Sticks could put on his seat belt, she tore out of the parking lot, throwing him back against the seat. The car raced past the sidewalk, nearly running down a young woman with a stroller, and as the mother looked on with astonishment, the Cadillac sped away with the blast of its horn. So awful was the sound that people on the street had to plug their ears. And when they looked toward its source, there for everyone to see was Mamsie's middle finger thrust defiantly at them all, out though her open car window.

* * *

After racing through the neighborhood streets, Mamsie skidded to a halt in front of a dilapidated home. Enclosed by a rusty, chain-linked fence, the yard was choked with weeds and the walkway, cracked in many places, led to a weathered split level house with peeling paint and rotted wood. The shingles on the roof were so loose, several had already fallen into the sickly shrubs that surrounded the house, and the clapboards hung at odd angles, fastened only in one or two spots by corroded nails. A dusty film covered the windows.

They got out of the car and walked toward the house. Sticks was bombarded the entire way by the throbbing in his head and by Mamsie's incessant nagging. They entered the house, which opened up to a musty room cluttered with worn, tattered furniture. Sticks took off his coat and walked toward the kitchen. Just before it was a door which led down to a den which had been converted into his bedroom. He opened the door and was about to go down when Mamsie decided it was time to conclude her diatribe. "Now you git down there in yer hole," she said, "and don't come out until you figgered out a way not to be shite!"

He started down the steps, but suddenly felt a sturdy foot in the small of his back shoving him forward, sending him tumbling down the stairs. There, in a crumbled heap, he vaguely heard Mamsie mutter, "Putz" before she left the house to do whatever she did during the day.

He lay splayed out on the floor, stunned by the fall and in complete, utter exhaustion. He wished there were some way to make it all stop, to end all his suffering and simply fly away. But it would have to wait. For now, he could barely move. First, he would rest. When he regained his strength, he would figure out a way to deal with his enemies. Then and only then would he be truly free.

He collected himself and rose slowly, groaning from the multitude of bumps and bruises he had sustained over the previous day. As he attempted to stand upright, the room began to spin and he found himself almost tumbling back to the floor. He wavered where he stood, then staggered toward his dresser and took hold of it until the dizzy spell finally began to subside. Then, once steadied, he took a deep breath and eased over toward his bed, falling upon it with a loud, metallic squeak.

Once the springs settled, silence enveloped the room, broken only by the intermittent sound of a passing car or the occasional songbird happening by. Perhaps the flat screech of an indignant blue jay, or the variable banter of a mockingbird; in any case, the birds came, offered their opinions, and went on their way. Sticks, however, continued to languish in the gloom of his bedroom, the darkness of which was disrupted only by the thin rays of sun that snuck in behind the blinds and crawled slowly across the floor.

So it was alone, in the solitude of his bedroom and with no one around as witness, that he finally let down his guard. He wailed there for some time, indulging his raw emotions, allowing his frustrations to all pour out until he could cry no more tears, until his energy was utterly spent. Then, as if some higher power granted him mercy, his breath deepened, his muscles began to relax, and he slowly descended into a state of twilight, leaving his squalid bedroom behind. His consciousness and sub-consciousness then blended into one, and he found himself reliving his past so vividly, it was as if he were there all over again.

CHAPTER 9

THE TURNING OF STICKS FAVORS

The odds had been stacked against him from the beginning. Stephan Oliver Favors had been born with a rare form of albinism called "acilia," a condition that not only deprived the body of all natural pigment but left it without any hair whatsoever. The lack of hair and almost translucent complexion gave the patient a very odd appearance indeed. When the pediatrician informed Stephan's young parents about their infant's condition, they panicked, unable to come to grips with the idea of raising such a freakish-looking child. So, after painful deliberation and a passing sense of guilt, they left him at an orphanage and were never heard from again.

From the onset, young Stephan was a quiet, inquisitive boy. He loved to look at picture books and learned to read children's stories at a very early age. He had an extremely active imagination, and by the age of four, had all the other children flocking to him to create some wondrous world of pretend. The kids loved this kind of play, for not only was it fascinating to them to play make-believe, it distracted them all from the hardship of a childhood without parents, without a place they could truly call home.

This worked well for Stephan for some time, but it was inevitable that problems would eventually arise. As the kids got older, they began to notice he was different. His appearance began to unnerve and even frighten some of the children, and he started to have trouble fitting in. Stephan's baldness could sometimes be masked by wearing a hat, but there was little he could do for the unsightly lack of eyebrows and eyelashes, and as he matured, his eyes began to glitter like emeralds, giving them a bizarre and unnatural shine.

By the age of seven, they began to whisper about him. They laughed at him, calling him names like "Baldy" and "Ghost Boy." Soon, he became a pariah among the others. Even the children he had thought to be close soon abandoned him, opting to run with the rest of the crowd rather than be known as the Ghost Boy's only friend.

During recess, he often frowned at the sight of the other children playing and laughing, smiling and touching, bringing into painful clarity what he was missing, and that he would be forever relegated to the life of an outcast. He spent hours by himself, wandering around the playground, silently crying, wondering if he could ever be happy.

This forced him into the one place where he could find sanctuary: the world of imagination. In particular, the imaginary world of books. There, he began to immerse himself in all the stories that were taught in school. By the age of nine, his literary abilities had become so advanced that he easily tore through children's classics like Tom Sawyer and The Wizard of Oz. His hunger for adventure became insatiable, and he greedily devoured tales like Peter Pan and Treasure Island, stories that swept him away to exotic lands, thrilling him with excitement and romance. He savored the adventures as best he could and even imagined himself as some brave and handsome hero. Sadly, however, at the end of each story he was coldly reminded of who he truly was, and how his life was meant to be.

Over time, he developed a deep resentment toward the other kids, especially those who subjected him to constant abuse. He sometimes lashed back, getting into fights and often making bad situations worse. By the time he was twelve, the administration had been forced to transfer him to other orphanages several times. He was fighting too much and making too many enemies. Finally, after one particularly nasty incident where Stephan broke another child's nose, it was decided the boy needed a change. It was time to explore a foster home.

Pappy and Mamsie MacCracken were essentially scavengers who took advantage of parentless children. The orphanage administration knew this all too well, but didn't seem to care. The elderly Scottish couple served a critical purpose. Over the years they had many times relieved the overcrowded orphanages of their burdens. They solved the problems no one else wanted to solve: they took in the children no one wanted. So whenever there was an opportunity to rid themselves of a problem child, the state jumped at the chance.

It was a perfect fit.

The MacCrackens were experts at exploiting the foster care system for financial gain. The custodial payments and tax exemptions offered by the state helped to line their pockets. They took the funds, keeping most of it for themselves, while offering the most meager of accommodations. The value of state money, however, paled in comparison to the cheap labor Pappy extracted from the children. For years the old man had only taken in orphan boys fit enough to labor long hours in his construction business. The boundless energy of teenage boys was ideal for the rigors of physical labor. And he worked them like slaves. Under his stern supervision, the boys would toil like beasts of burden, loading heavy beams, laying brick, and hammering nail after nail until their arms and legs were so sore with fatigue that by the end of the day, all they could do was nurse their aching muscles and fall into a deep and heavy sleep.

Pappy was a traditional craftsman, one who still valued the institution of apprenticeship. He worked the boys hard, but he also trained them in a trade: carpentry, electrical work, masonry. Of course, though, his motives were mostly self-serving; by promising the boys eventual certification, it gave them reason to stick around and work toward a goal rather than running away. Thus, he was able to hold onto the cheap labor only the foster children could provide.

With the last of their wards having grown up and

departed, the MacCrackens decided to take on one last boy. Pappy was getting on in years and was beginning to consider retirement. He realized he couldn't run his business forever. So, after thoughtful deliberation, he offered to "mentor" one last apprentice, with the idea of selling off his business within a few short years. Once the boy had learned the essentials of the trade, Pappy would try sell it to him for an exorbitant price and then live off the payments . They just needed to find the right boy. One who was quick to learn but easily duped.

They went through the familiar bureaucratic logistics until Stephan Favors was officially in their care. In their first meeting, the sight of the old couple made Stephan ill. He knew by now how to recognize cruelty, and he instantly saw through their façade. But he had no choice.

At first he wasn't sure which was worse, his new situation or his old. The MacCrackens were loud, belligerent, and verbally abusive. In her unique caustic manner, Mamsie would boss him around, inundating him with an endless amount of housework. And only after he finished was he allowed to go with Pappy to his workshop, where the craftsman gave him a crash course in the mysteries of brick, metal, and wood. There, under the old man's tutelage, Stephan learned how to build and became proficient in the use of all sorts of strange-looking machines: lathes, drills, electric saws. He was given a starter set of tools, which he maintained and practiced with for hours upon hours.

Finally, after several months of training, Pappy determined Stephan was ready to go to work. He joined Pappy's crew, which built houses. Most of his coworkers were illegal aliens who could barely speak English, and to Stephan's relief, seemed indifferent to his unusual appearance. There, men were judged only by their capacity for work, which put the boy at ease. It seemed as if he had finally found a place where he could apply himself with little distraction. Even when Pappy barked orders or was critical of his work, he didn't really mind. It only served to reinforce the standards of perfection and cultivate a work ethic that would eventually make him the best craftsman he could be.

He still went to school during the week, but it was at a public one now, with none of his former enemies ever around. He took a different approach to the other kids this time, laying low, blending into the crowds, and drawing as little attention to himself as possible. He no longer resisted or resented his outcast status, having convinced himself he was better off alone. A few kids tried to heckle him and to provoke him into reacting, but he merely slipped away before anything ever happened.

As time marched on, Stephan grew into a teenager under the roof of Pappy and Mamsie MacCracken. He lived very much in solitude, for outside of barking their orders, the cantankerous old couple barely acknowledged his existence. They didn't even eat their meals together. In the emptiness of his quarters, Stephan ate his dinner, did his homework, and finished off his day watching old movies on a staticky, black and white TV. There, in the shadows of that darkened room, as the wan light from his television flashed across his pallid face, he indulged in the same fascination with the tales he was introduced to as a young boy.

With the little money he had saved working with Pappy, he purchased a refurbished VCR and rented as many videos as he could. Every Sunday, he secluded himself in his room, opened a bag of popcorn, and allowed himself to become swept away by epic sagas of romance and danger; swashbuckling on the high seas or navigating perilous rivers in the depths of The Congo. He was entranced by movies like The Three Musketeers, The Count of Monte Cristo and Mighty Joe Young. He became enraptured by the heroes of the silver screen: Errol Flynn as Robin Hood, Clark Gable as Fletcher Christian and Johnny Weissmuller as Tarzan, King of the Jungle.. He was charmed by entertainers such as Gene Kelly and Fred Astaire, who danced elegantly in tuxedos with the most beautiful women he had ever seen. They were vibrant, handsome young men who exuded charisma and dazzled with their physical grace.

Stephan decided that he would try to learn as many of these dashing skills as he could. He studied the films closely and pantomimed the characters' actions in his bedroom mirror. He went to the library and took out books on fencing, tap dancing, and even make-up and magic. He dedicated himself to becoming an unforgettable all-around entertainer: a sort of one-man variety show combining magic, dance, and even bits of clownery. After endless hours of practice and rehearsal, he decided to enter several talent contests and variety shows. He never told Mamsie and Pappy because he knew they would laugh at him with scorn. So on the nights of the shows, he told them he was going to the movies and went out to face the audiences alone.

Finally he would show the world what he was capable of. He would dazzle them all with his talents in dance and song. He would dart around the stage, fencing and juggling, telling jokes and performing acrobatic feats. He would be admired, adulated, adored.

But as in life, his knowledge and hard work were for naught. His act was disjointed and poorly organized. He manically jumped from one performance to another without finishing the first, as the audience sat in uncomfortable silence, unsure of what he was doing or who he was trying to be. Soon, hecklers began their taunts. Sticks began to panic and moved at an even more feverish pace, in hopes of getting into a successful rhythm. But as he stumbled around the stage, dropping props and making a spectacle of himself, the crowd turned on him. They chased him from the stage amidst a chorus of boos.

With all his dreams shattered, and nothing left to do, he withdrew deeper into the only sanctuary he had left: the captivating world of cinema. He moved on to explore new, undiscovered genres: comedies, mysteries, classic detective films. One Halloween, he decided to go through some of the old horror movies made by Universal Studios. He was familiar with the stories of Dracula, the Wolfman, and the Mummy, but he was particularly intrigued by the tale of Frankenstein by Mary Shelley. That night, watching the 1931 version of Frankenstein starring Boris Karloff, he became fascinated by the so-called "monster" brought to life by a young mad scientist. Yet the feared creature wasn't really evil, Stephan thought. It had been brought into the world, an innocent being, both docile and tender. It was obedient and had the capacity to love, even appreciating the beauty of flowers and music. But a world unwilling to give him love turned on him, judging him solely by his appearance and causing the monster to lash out. To Stephan, it wasn't the creature who was the monster. It was the villagers. In the end, Stephan decided the creature was better off dead. What was the point of existence without acceptance and love?

With little hope of leading a normal life, Stephan agreed to take over Pappy's business when he turned 18. The MacCrackens allowed him to stay in the house, as long as he made his monthly payments toward the purchase price. He was familiar with all aspects of the business, he was able to use his hands, and it gave him a sense of purpose.

When Stephan was old enough, he began blowing off steam at the local bars. There, while acquiring a taste for beer and whiskey, he became intrigued with the game of pool. He was mesmerized by the swagger of the players and the colorful balls that careened around the table at different angles and speeds. He studied the players and their strategies, watching their every move, and when he felt ready, decided to take a crack at the game. It was a revelation. The first time he ever picked up a cue stick, it felt strangely familiar. It sat comfortably in his hands, almost as if it were part of him.

His abilities as a player developed rapidly. For the first time in his life, he was able to succeed in something while others looked on. And for the first time, he experienced something alien to him: the admiration of others. Soon, he developed a swagger of his own, theatrical and unique unto himself. With his knowledge of fencing and dance, he turned his pool game into a kind of performance art. He darted, spun, and parried, as if fencing with some invisible foe, evoking stares of incredulity. He approached the table like a stalking fiend and he attacked the game with a fervor that no one had ever seen. And he began to win. A lot.

One day he decided to craft his own collection of pool

cues. Each night, after the MacCrackens went to sleep, Stephan toiled in Pappy's workshop until morning. Using Pappy's lathe, he tapered specially treated wood into the shape of cue sticks, then finished them with sandpaper and varnish. He polished them until they shined and handled them with pride, caressing them like the lovers he never had. He developed a special bond with each and every one, for they were to be used to command respect from his peers, the respect he'd sought after his entire life.

To burnish his newfound identity, he recast himself as Sticks. Sticks Favors. The pool parlor virtuoso. The man who would win millions…and become a legend in his own right.

But his prowess soon gave rise to hubris, and he often showed off, taking his cockiness to distasteful levels and riddling competitors with insults. Alcohol only exacerbated his aggression. He thought the more he drew attention, the more he would be revered. He wanted to seem impressive, to somehow pique the interest of all the pretty girls, the ones with whom he never had a chance before. But as usual his actions backfired and the women only looked on with disgust.

And yet, he continued to win. His reputation grew. Rumors started to spread about his violent unpredictability, and, wary of his every move, his opponents invariably faltered, too intimidated to perform to the best of their abilities. Sticks, meanwhile, relished his dominance, and reveled in the feelings of intimidation he inspired in his opponents.

More experienced and talented players began to seek him out, if only to see if his outsized, outlandish reputation matched the man himself. These were players who were unfazed by pressure and didn't succumb so easily to Sticks' tactics, viewing him more as a clown than a formidable opponent. People started laughing at him again, and he started to lose his aura of invincibility. This infuriated him. With no other way to protect his image, he turned to violence, assaulting anyone who dared to beat him. He got into fights all over town and became banned from practically all the bars and pool halls. Then, just like everything else in his life, his once promising passion crumbled into bitter disappointment.

One night, he played horribly and lost at least a week's worth of wages. On his way home, he acknowledged the fact he was broke and had no idea how he'd pay Pappy for that month.

Now in his waning years, Pappy MacCracken had become tired and frail. A mini-stroke had softened him, and the once robust construction worker had become a caricature of himself, reduced to watching daytime talk shows and muttering to himself. Although Mamsie still remained a formidable presence herself, when the opportunity presented itself, Sticks enjoyed the sadistic pleasure of antagonizing the old man.

Upon returning home late that night and in a bitter state, Sticks decided to play Pappy a little melody. He browsed through his collection of rock and roll CDs until he came upon something that suited the occasion just fine: AC/DC's Highway to Hell. He turned the volume on his stereo all the way up, placed the CD in the carrier, and waited for the music to begin. Before long, Angus Young was heard jamming heavily on his guitar, his unmistakable sound sending deafening twangs throughout the house, shaking it to its very foundation. Sticks did the Angus strut, holding out an air guitar and lifting his leg up and down like a lever as he shuffled across the floor with puckered lips.

It didn't take long for Pappy to appear at the top of the stairs. He stood there livid, in his Fruit of the Loom T-shirt, stained boxer shorts, worn leather slippers, and threadbare robe, which stood open, its ties hanging loosely toward the floor. "Shut that goddamn crap off!" he demanded, waving his cane in the air. Sticks heard him, but he cranked the music up even louder and began dancing more spasmodically across the carpet. This caused Pappy to scream at an even more fevered pitch, his face turning purple and the veins popping out of his neck. Spittle flew from his lips as he strained to be heard, but his protests were drowned out by the irreverent wails of the singer, Bon Scott. He began slamming his cane against the wall, volleying forth a litany of imprecations, when he suddenly froze, clutched at his chest, and made an inaudible gurgling sound. He then slumped forward, teetered for a moment, and tumbled haphazardly down the full length of the steps.

Pappy MacCracken never got up again.

* * *

When Pappy hit the bottom of the stairs, Sticks stood flabbergasted, not knowing what to do. The old man wasn't moving, which was bad enough, but the idea Pappy might be dead terrified him to the core. He turned the music down and moved anxiously over to check on him. He wasn't breathing. Something was terribly wrong. A cold sweat broke out all over his body and he racked his brain about the situation. Was he really dead? And if so, could it be his fault? Could he be charged with his murder? He certainly had antagonized the old man, but it wasn't like he *tried* to kill him. Was that enough to be taken away? The thought of going to prison caused an unbearably cold feeling deep inside his chest. He knew he could never survive in maximum security.

Finally, he made a decision. He listened intently for any signs of Mamsie upstairs. He heard nothing, but he had to investigate to be sure. Sticks sidestepped Pappy's body and crept silently up to her bedroom. He cracked open the door and found her snoring away like a buzzsaw under a thick mound of blankets. Apparently, she hadn't heard a thing. It was a tremendous relief. Mamsie was always a deep sleeper, like a slumbering beast unafraid of what might be lurking about, but he still couldn't understand how she didn't hear the music. It was so loud that it had drowned out Pappy's entire conniption. Was she faking it? Was she just pretending to be asleep, planning on sneaking up on him with all sorts of accusations later? He had to find out. He tiptoed quietly into the room and stood precariously close to the bed. He was looking for any signs of her being conscious, when he found the answer to all his questions. For there, sitting on the night table, were Mamsie's prescription hearing aids, without which she was practically deaf. She hadn't heard a thing. Much like her husband in the room downstairs, she was at that particular moment dead to the world.

Sticks then went into action. Moving quickly, he returned to his bedroom and formulated a plan. As in some macabre scene from an old Alfred Hitchcock movie, he dragged the body up the stairs into the kitchen and laid it out on the cold linoleum floor. He placed the cadaver in an unnatural position, giving it the appearance of an unexpected collapse. Then, once satisfied with his work, he went back downstairs to anxiously await in bed.

The plan was to have Mamsie discover the body in the morning. Hopefully then, with little else to go on, the morticians would determine the death to be the result of a typical heart attack. No one need ever know the cause.

The night was an eternity. Sticks lay there in the darkness, his eyes wide open, painfully aware of the dead body that lay stiffening on the floor above. He jumped at every creak, started at every sound, and on rare occasion, when he could stay awake no longer, fell into a fitful state of slumber. In his restlessness, he was riddled with all sorts of nightmares, horrifying images of the corpse in the kitchen sitting up, turning its attention towards him, and slowly making its way toward his bedroom. It would trudge down the stairs with a clumsy THUMP! THUMP! THUMP! and drag its moldering body to the front of his bed. There, it would loom in front of him, wavering like a zombie, until an expression of hateful recognition appeared upon its face. Sticks would look on aghast, too paralyzed to move, until the corpse finally fell on him and throttled him where he lay.

When the dawning light awoke and the early birds began to sing, Sticks finally heard Mamsie stirring in the upper portion of the house. With his heart in his mouth, he anxiously listened as she made her way down the steps. A moment later, when she let out a shrieking wail, he came running up the stairs to see what was wrong. He did his best to act dismayed and even went to some lengths to comfort the old woman, and when the authorities were called and the police arrived on the scene, he acted as if he were in a complete state of shock. He answered every question in a feigned condition of numbness, and even, when he felt the time was right, broke down into tears.

The detectives and the forensic coroners took all the information they needed and eventually, to Sticks' ultimate relief, the authorities concluded the cause of death was a stroke, an unfortunate passing of natural causes. The case was then closed.

In the ensuing months, Mamsie mourned as much as her cold disposition would allow. She never wept, claiming that "crying is for pussies," instead moving about in an emotionless, trance-like daze. She would wander through the house staring vacantly, sometimes standing for long periods in different rooms, perhaps reliving some fragmented memories of the life she had with Pappy. Only on occasion would she revert back to her normal self, when she would begin to chastise Sticks and order him around the house again. But those moments were short-lived. Mostly her mind was elsewhere.

Sticks was fine with this. He welcomed this lack of lucidity because he was utterly petrified she would begin to suspect him. And he wasn't far wrong. Before long, he began to feel her eyes upon him. In between her vacuous spells, she would glance at him with curiosity, as if piecing together the solution to some mystery. Every once in a while, he would catch her in her suspicious stare, only to have her suddenly look away and appear busy with some random occupation. This unsettled Sticks to no end. It was as if she were trying to read his mind, and it started to unnerve him.

As the months rolled on and the shroud of grief slowly lifted, Mamsie began to see things more clearly.

One night, without warning, she confronted him about the night Pappy died. She demanded immediate answers and he simply panicked. He began stammering and looking away, scratching his head and wrapping his arms around his body. A high-pitched whining sound rose from his stomach and all he could do was slink away in fear. It was enough to convince her something was up, but what? The coroner said it was a stroke, which was enough to kill anyone. So why did the moron act so guilty? It was enough to make anyone suspicious, so she just decided to watch him more closely. And also put a lock on her bedroom door.

Time passed on and the two of them avoided each other as best they could. The unspoken truth hung between them, but they still needed each other in a precarious, symbiotic way. She needed what little income he provided from the fading contracting business and he needed a place to stay. They came to merely tolerate each other's existence, however uneasily.

After his arrest on the night of the pool tournament, Sticks had no one else to turn to. So he had called Mamsie to come bail him out. It was the last of a series of humiliating events, finishing off one of the worst days of his entire, pathetic life. It was as if some higher power was telling him something, making him aware that nothing, from that day forward, would ever be the same.

He had nothing left.

In a packed house full of spectators, he had lost the biggest pool tournament of the year in humiliating fashion, thus rendering his strategy of intimidation useless, once and for all—the fatal blow to his already withering reputation. Thanks to Jack Banks, no one would ever back down from him again. He had been beaten up by a girl, banned from The Live Wire, bested by an enemy he had ambushed on the street and, last but not least, sexually molested in jail. And if all that wasn't enough, he had to swallow what little pride he had left and ask a hateful old witch to come bail him out.

* * *

Surfacing from the fitful reverie of his past, Sticks' awareness slowly emerged. He began to feel the pillow on his face and the clothes on his body. He clenched his eyes shut and fought his rising consciousness, not wanting to return.

"HEY!" a loud and shrill voice cried out, startling him out of the last vestiges of sleep. He cringed and instinctively put up his hands to protect his face.

Mamsie stood there pointing at him, her jaw thrust forward and her voice rising to a fevered pitch. "Get up you good-for-nothin' and do something with yeself! I'm so sick-a your laziness. That bail is gonna cost you! Not me! Jest see if I don't mean it! Yer gonna clean up this entire house, startin' with this pigsty right here, ya hear me? And none a yer bullshite! I'm gone out for bingo. When I get back, you better be bustin' your arse!"

Sticks sat up slowly and swung his legs over the side of the bed. He had been in a deep sleep and was still in a stupor. He wasn't ready for Mamsie's voice, and her tirade began to painfully echo inside his head. His eyelids were puffy, especially the bruised one, and he slowly raised them to look at the clock. It read 6:30 pm . He had slept away the entire day.

"Don't ye hear me?!" the hag cried again.

Sticks finally looked at her. The familiar odor of Ben-Gay permeated the room. She stood there, fists on stocky hips, her crooked, matted wig perched above a pinched face of granite. She was working her mouth again, moving it around furiously, as if trying to come up with some other sort of insult to fling in his direction.

He didn't see it coming. He suddenly saw a light, heard a sudden SMACK! and felt a sharp burning sensation on the side of his face. His eyes began to tear.

"Don't ye look at me like that," Mamsie warned. "You ain't nothing special. We took care-a you way too long and this is how you are? Yeah, that's right. I know what you did." Her breaths got deeper and more hurried, more desperate-sounding. "You did something to Pappy. I just know it. And I'm gonna find out zactly what you did. Sooner or later, I will. So you better watch your step, mister, and mind what I tell ye! Now get to work!"

She sneered, climbed the stairs, and slammed the door as she left the house once again.

He sat there stunned, trying to digest what had just happened. So she finally came out and said it. She had suspected him all along. It was just a matter of time before she went to the police, made her accusations, and convinced them to come take him away.

He began to panic.

For a moment he remained there, frozen, not knowing what to do. Suddenly, he bolted off the bed and darted up the steps. He crashed through the storm door and tumbled out onto the lawn, just as Mamsie was backing out of the driveway. He ran towards the car, waving his arms, begging for her to stop so he could somehow plead his case. But once in the street, she floored the gas pedal and peeled out, shooting dirt and pebbles backwards and leaving him in a cloud of dust.

* * *

In a complete state of turmoil, he watched the car disappear. For a while he just stood there, clenching and unclenching his fists. Slowly, he began to tilt his battered face forward, jutting out his lower jaw and making deep, wheezing sounds. An old man walking a Chihuahua happened by unaware, but once he saw the monstrosity Sticks had become, quickly scooped up his pet and hurried away. The lap dog whined and its bell collar jingled as they faded away into the distance.

He gazed around the neighborhood, seeing it differently. All the houses were decorated for Halloween. The people across the street had covered their hedges with white silken webs and tiny black plastic spiders . A green-faced witch hung from the eaves of the roof, sitting on her broomstick along with a mischievous black cat. Fluttering bats had been hung throughout all the trees and freshly carved jack-o-lanterns sat glowering on porches.

At the house to the left, fake tombstones were scattered across the lawn, embellished with hideous, decaying zombie-like figures digging their way out of the ground. A sudden movement amongst the headstones caught Sticks' attention, and for a moment, he believed he saw the form of a hovering white head. It floated eerily across the lawn with some undisclosed purpose, and when Sticks strained to look closer, he noticed two glowing white hands clutching some strange, unidentifiable object. The head turned toward him with an ugly, mutilated face and grinned menacingly, as if to communicate some preordained, sinister secret. It lifted its hands to reveal a long tapered shaft topped at the end with a glinting, sharpened blade. The apparition made eye contact, nodded in acknowledgement, and then drifted spookily away. Through the gloom, Sticks lost sight of the strange phantom, but as it disappeared, he heard a blood-curdling howl that sent him fleeing with his arms raised in terror, toward the sanctuary of his own backyard.

He ended up near Pappy's workshop, an oversized shed so large it practically took up the entire yard. He backed up against its doors, his eyes bulging and his heart beating dangerously out of control. His mouth was dry and he tried to swallow, but it only made a metallic, clicking sound. He pressed his hands firmly against the doors, as if for no other reason than to know something solid was there. He looked toward the sky. Through the skeletal branches of a withered, dying oak, he saw the thin crescent moon lean forward behind a floating wisp of cloud. The gnarled fingers of the tree seemed to caress it, like a sickly old miser pawing at a precious jewel . Darkening clouds seemed to converge from all around, forming ugly, accusing faces, both merciless and cruel. They pointed at him and sneered, labeling him a murderer, demanding his death.

He groaned and held his head in his hands. What was he going to do now? She was going to tell! She was going to tell and he was going to hell! They were going to take him away and place him with all those horrible maniacs who would torture and beat him. He was going to be raped and violated worse than he had ever imagined. And when they were done with him, he would be executed. Executed and sent to hell!

His desperation began to erode his mind. His thoughts fragmented and went asunder. He knew where he was, but everything began to change. The world seemed to rotate upon itself, turning everything inside out until he began to see things from a new but vaguely familiar perspective. It was as if he had been there before, but he knew not when, nor what he did there. The edges of everything began to blur. They softened into a state of grayness, where his actions became automatic and without reason. Like a character in one of his books, he began to move toward his predetermined fate. His one ultimate purpose: to avenge the hate he had suffered his entire life. He would kill them all. Yes, that's what he would do. He'd kill them all and that would be the perfect ending of his own tragic tale. And oh, what a glorious ending it would be!

BASTARDS! Every last one of them! Everyone he had ever met had tormented and abused him. His entire life he had been alone and besieged in a cold and loveless world, and now they wanted to torture him forever. Well, he had a surprise in store for all of them. A wicked surprise indeed. If he was going to hell, then he would be damned if he was going alone. He was going to take some of them with him. That was for sure.

He lifted away his hands to reveal a face contorted by menace. Then he opened the shed and went inside. It was dark and dusty, smelling of oil and varnish . In the darkness he reached up and pulled the string on the bare, hanging light bulb. He squinted from the sudden brightness and covered his eyes until they adjusted. He then proceeded to scan the contents of the shed. There were stacks of wooden beams and boards, along with crates of iron rods and castings. Sturdy, well-worn benches held a bevy of electric tools used for cutting and finishing.

He went over to the wood. Here, his selection would be critical. He had to choose well. He took his time browsing through the piles, and when he happened upon one particularly hefty beam of ash, it spoke to him. Deep in his bones he understood that this piece of wood was to someday help fulfill his destiny. He was ecstatic. He lifted it out carefully and carried it over to one of the benches. There, he took his time to make precise measurements with a practiced eye. He prepared to bring it to life. He put on his safety helmet, giving him the appearance of some strange alien warrior, and brought the beam over to the saw. He flicked on the machine and it loudly came to life. Then he proceeded to cut the beam down, the whirring blade ejecting fountains of sawdust that rained down lazily on his head. Once it was cut to its proper size, he spun it on the lathe, tapering it down just the right amount until it took the shape of a sturdy pool stick. He sanded it down until it was smooth, then brought it back to the saw, where he cut it in half.

Then he moved on to the next step. He took the thicker half and placed the newly cut end toward the saw. He turned on the machine again, and when it began to whine, he carefully pushed the end back into the blade, cutting a three-inch slot into the wood. He then drilled two precisely measured holes into either side of the two remaining extensions.

When that was done, he went over to the metal and chose a long and heavy piece of steel. He took it to the vise, cut off a chunk with a blow torch, and cooled it off in a bucket of water. After filing it down to his exact specifications, he brought it over to the old-fashioned whetting stone. There, he sat and began to pump wildly away at the pedal, bringing the grinding wheel into motion. As the stone began to rotate into an ever-increasing speed, Sticks' expression shifted from one of manic determination to giddy anticipation. When the spin was finally fast enough, he held the metal firmly to the stone, sending flickering sparks flying around the confines of the workshop, like the embers of fireworks falling down from the sky. The RIIIINNNNGGGG of the grinding droned in his ears. He cackled.

Once the metal was sharpened to a razor-thin double edge, he drilled two holes into its base and screwed it into the thicker end of the tapered rod. The thinner half of the pool stick was then slotted to fit perfectly over the blade so that unless dislodged by the proper amount of force, it held firmly into place.

A little paint, a little lacquer, and it was complete.

He stood and marveled at what he had just crafted.

Oh, what a masterpiece! His most treasured piece of art! To the death! He was going to live by the game and they were going to die by the game. And now, more than ever, he was ready to play.

* * *

Mamsie stayed late at bingo that night. Her mind was distracted and on more than one occasion, she missed hearing the host call one of her squares, at one point even costing her an opportunity to win a toaster. She was getting fed up with the boy. He had become useless and lazy, and lately even defiant. Pappy's construction business was becoming neglected, work was being left unfinished, and the clients were becoming enraged. He was losing their accounts and the income was drying up. Now he had gone and gotten himself arrested.

There was no way in blazes she was gonna tolerate the behavior of a hooligan. He'd better turn himself around or he'd be out on his arse in no time. She didn't really think the boy had killed Pappy. Her husband had died of a stroke. The coroner said so. But she sadistically relished the horror it inflicted upon the boy when she threatened to turn him to the police. He damn near wet his pants every time . Well, she'd be damned if he was gonna be a parasite. He had better done some work around the house or she just might put the finger on him for spite. Enough was enough.

While at the church, Mamsie always drank her tea with a special ingredient smuggled in past Preacher MacGregor. Often, while no one was looking, usually when one of the ladies yelled "Bingo!", she poured "a little pick-me-up" in her cup underneath the table. She had prescribed herself a little more "pick-me-up" than usual that night and, driving home, she decided to forego the tea altogether, opting instead to swig directly from her flask.

As the brandy ran down her throat and burned her insides, she thought bitterly about the money wasted to bail out the boy. "Disturbin' the peace! BAH!" she muttered to herself. "Resistin' arrest! I'll give you resistin' arrest. Let's see him resist arrest for murder!"

She floored the accelerator and sped down her street, screeching to a halt just inches in front of the garage. A thin film of moonlight glowed from behind the sickly grey clouds . She opened her door and staggered out of the car, her ratty gray wig sitting crooked on her head. She regained her balance, peered up at the house, and saw a strange flickering purple light, flashing like a strobe from inside the boy's bedroom window. She frowned and muttered to herself, wondering in disgust what the hooligan was up to now.

When she approached the front of the house, she saw that the storm door was now broken, hanging loosely on one hinge, with the wooden one left curiously ajar. When the light switch didn't work, she became frustrated, then gradually incensed. "STEPHAN!" she screeched. "What kind a game is ye playin? Fix the goddam lights!!" AC/DC blasted from his room again, and just as before, Angus Young's defiant electric guitar came to life, only to exasperate a McCracken once more. As she approached his door, the purple light continued to flicker out from his stairway below. Mamsie crept warily forward. "Don't ye hear me, boy?" she meekly inquired. "You better mind me or I'll toss you out! You see if I don't!" She listened carefully by the basement door but was answered only by the music. "Where the hell are ye, goddamn yer hide!"

She started deliberately down the steps, which groaned and creaked loudly even above the sound of the music. The purple light got brighter as she slowly descended and then the music suddenly stopped. All she could hear was an electrical buzzing that accompanied the cadence of the flickering light. A sudden ringing buzzed in her ears and she felt dizzy, clutching the banister with her bony hand for support. An emotion that had been foreign to her all her life began to stir inside her. She was afraid. Perspiration beaded on her upper lip and her hands started to tremble. A dry, coppery taste filled her mouth. When she spoke, an unfamiliar voice, both meek and uncertain, came out. "Boy? Is you here?"

Eventually she reached the bottom of the stairs and turned stiffly to her right, freezing in place. A dark, inanimate figure was hunched over, sitting on the bed. Its head was down and tilted forward, its features obscured. All that was visible was a round and shiny ball that seemed to hover and glow upon the lifeless sitting form. It sat motionless, bathed in the flickering illumination that radiated fitfully from an ultra-violet light.

Mamsie remained frozen. "Boy? Has ye lost yer head?" she said, as he began to stir. He craned his neck forward and Mamsie suddenly gasped. Stick's wounded eye was a swollen mass of mangled tissue. But that wasn't as bad as the one that looked at her. It seemed to look *through* her. In the dim illumination of the hesitant purple light, the eye was dark and vacant, an empty black hole, devoid of any sign of life. The rest of his features were also blank, deadened, yet somehow in motion.

But then his eyebrows lowered, and his expression twisted into a loathsome grimace. Once again, his jaw jutted out, revealing his lower teeth, and he began to wheeze. His hands gripped tightly on what appeared to be a sturdy staff and he began to bang it on the floor in a steady rhythm.

Mamsie blanched. She no longer recognized Stephan, who had somehow transformed into this abomination that now tormented her. The terror robbed her of the control over her weak and rigid body. A light pattering sound came from the rug beneath her and the stench of urine filled the room.

The dark form on the bed rose and slowly drew near, carrying the pool cue. "How was bingo, Mamsie?" it demanded. "Did you win anything?"

"I...I...uh...n-no," Mamsie stammered.

"What's the matter?" it taunted. "Cat got your tongue? Was it a black cat, you witch? Did it rip out your tongue? Or are you just so happy to see me, you just can't find the words?"

"N-no...I mean, y-yeah I'm glad to see ye..."

He was extremely close now, almost to within inches of her face. "Well, you didn't answer my question. DID YOU WIN ANYTHING!?"

"Um, n-no, not tonight."

"Well, then. I got a prize for you right HERE!"

The creature jerked off the top half of the pool cue, revealing a long, sharp double-edged blade. In one swift motion, it pulled the spear back and thrust it violently up under Mamsie's rib cage and deep into her heart. She let out an UUUUHHHH! and began convulsing wildly on the stick. The creature grinned insanely, holding fast to the spear as blood spurted out in every direction. She continued to rattle there, dancing some grotesque jig of death, until she ultimately fell limp upon the stick. When she finally went still, the creature's leer slowly faded, and with blank curiosity, he began to examine her lifeless form. After being satisfied that she was once and for all gone, he pulled out the blade and unceremoniously dumped her corpse to the floor. He glanced around the room, which was now splattered with blood, and the psychotic expression returned to his face. He began to wheeze again and quietly chuckled to himself. After all the years of torment, he had finally figured out his ultimate purpose.

Sticks Favors then brought his arms in close, doubled his body over, and let out a bone chilling howl of rage.

Chapter 10

The Shamrocks Get Amped Up

Saturday Afternoon, October 14

Liam Cullum was having a bad day. Not only had he woken up with a splitting headache, but he hadn't won a poker hand all afternoon. His temperament was volatile to begin with, so it was a wonder that his bad luck hadn't resulted in somebody's head getting bashed in. He had precious little patience for even his closest of friends, and if his luck didn't change soon, someone else's was going to run out.

A burly, rugged sort of ruffian, Liam had lank, rust-colored hair and a perpetual, shadowy beard. Born and raised in the toughest part of Belfast, Liam had fled to the States a few years back, after inadvertently beating a man to death in a barroom brawl. He spent his first weeks in New York surviving as a renegade of sorts, shaking down small-time dealers and pimps to survive. It was during this time that he first met Chris Doherty, who now sat across from him at the table. Doherty had a slim build, a pointy nose and brown beady eyes. On his head he wore a small fedora that always seemed to be slipping off his head. It had been Doherty who first met Liam on the streets, and being impressed by his toughness and strength, decided to introduce him to Shane Gallagher, the sole leader of the Shamrocks after Mickey had moved on.

Liam's steel blue eyes now seethed with anger as another pile of his money was scooped away. He had been getting lousy cards all day long, and his dirty fingernails were starting to make deep imprints on the inside of his hands.

As they anted up for the next game, he lit up his stubby cigar. Between his meaty fingers, it looked like a misshapen extra thumb, the end of which blazed with smoky, smoldering embers. He glowered across the table at Doherty, whose luck that day had been simply ridiculous. The bastard had just won the last two hands and was now smirking and shuffling the cards.

Liam puffed on his stogie. The only thing keeping his temper in check was the music on the stereo. U2's "War" was playing loudly in the room, with Bono's proud indignation crying out against oppression and injustice everywhere. All of the Shamrocks were huge U2 fans. Not only did they love the adrenaline-surging rock, they were drawn to the band's passionate, vivid evocation of Ireland, the beloved home from whence they all came.

Doherty was mixing the cards over and over again, bantering with some of the other guys, when Liam shot up from his chair, knocking it over and onto the floor. "STOP YER FOOKIN' YAMMERIN AND DEAL THE FOOKIN' CARDS ALREADY!" he bellowed.

The talking stopped and the satisfied smile on Doherty's face faded. He hesitated for a moment, a brief look of surprise in his eyes, and then a glimmer of humor returned to his gaze. He had known Liam for a while now and knew how to handle him, so he chose to be careful. "Easy, big guy," he said calmly. "I gotta mix em' now, don't I?"

A younger, lean and muscular boy was sitting next to Doherty. He was leaning back in a comfortable recline, his legs crossed at the knee and a beer mug in his hand. An ample mop of jet-black hair sat upon his head, combed back into a well-tended mullet. His ivory-colored teeth gleamed through the smoky haze as he grinned at Liam with impish arrogance. "Yeah," he said, "you don't wanna keep getting the same shitty cards, now do ya?"

"You'd best shut it, Logan, if you know what's good for ya," Liam warned.

Logan just waved his hand and said, "Stop you're whinin' and just start winnin'"

With that, Liam suddenly lunged forward and would have had his hands wrapped firmly around Logan's throat if it wasn't for the timely reaction of several Shamrocks. Being familiar with Liam's frequent outbursts, The Shamrocks were always ready for him. They restrained him with many arms, but his rage was boiling over. With the strength of an ox he was about to overcome their grip when a familiar voice of reason brought him back to his senses. "Take it easy, Nitro," the voice said,

Liam slumped. He recognized the voice instantly. Shane Gallagher, now wearing a Notre Dame sweatshirt and a green bandana stepped out of the struggle to face him. He had curly, black hair and bemused, blue eyes. He put a reassuring hand behind Liam's head. "Save it for the bad guys, huh!" he laughed.

Fully aware that he'd better listen, Liam reluctantly settled back into his chair and relit his cigar. He scowled at Logan once again and blew a cloud of smoke in his direction. "Yer lucky Shane's here, you piece of shite," he said, "Next time I'll shove the whole fookin' deck down yer throat."

That elicited a nervous chuckle from the group, signifying a temporary truce. It was safe to resume the game. With a suppressed grin, Doherty began to deal again. Liam glanced at his cards and was encouraged: he'd been dealt a pair of pocket aces. His heart quickened as he strained against revealing his good fortune. He now had a chance to win back some of his money, but he had to be careful not to push anyone out of the hand so as to build up the pot.

A few more cards were dealt and the players continued to bet. Liam was now sitting pretty. The pot was much larger now, and after another ace had been dealt on the table, a couple more players folded The only ones left in the game now were Liam and Doherty. Finally it was time to call. Liam flipped over his two aces and taunted, "You got fooked up the arse, Doherty. Trip aces."

He started to reach for the pot when Doherty said,

"Not so fast, big boy." He coolly flipped over a king and a jack, revealing a straight. Liam's face froze. In his drunken haze, he had forgotten that a straight would have him beat. The space above his head seemed to shimmer, like the air above baking asphalt in the summertime. His eyes bore into Doherty, as he let out a ferocious roar and flipped the table over, sending a cascade of cards and bills flying everywhere. And once again, Liam needed to be restrained.

After one long guzzle from a bottle of Jack Daniels, Liam sat muttering over his losses with his hand firmly around the neck of the bottle. Just then, an unfamiliar voice nearby said, "Man, inside straight on the river? That must suck."

Liam couldn't believe what he was hearing. Was someone actually trying to mock him again? Sitting at the table, he had run his hand through his hair and was now holding his head and looking down. He peered up to see who had just spoken and didn't recognize him. The stranger had, pale blonde hair, amber-colored eyes, and an even, straight nose. Liam was about to unstraighten it. "What the fook did you just say?"

The man realized he had just upset the wrong guy. He held up his hands. "Nothing, man. I just know how it sucks to lose in this game."

Before the stranger could react, Liam shot up and grabbed him by the throat with two massive hands. "I'm gonna throttle ya, piss-boy!" he yelled and slowly began to close on his victim's windpipe.

The stranger was about to crush Liam's testicles with his knee when Liam heard a metallic click from behind. Before he knew it, an arm jerked back his head, exposing his throat, which suddenly had something cold and sharp against it. A tremulous and angry voice whispered in his ear, "Calm down, buddy. Just let him go and you won't be choking on your own blood."

Liam slowly let go of his victim and was subsequently released. He spun around to see a pale, lanky young man with sunken brown eyes pointing a switchblade at him. He was wearing a denim jacket and Converse high tops. Stunned, Liam looked around the room at his brothers in disbelief and said, "You guys gonna let these idiot bahsteds come in here and do this? We gonna let some lame-ass fookers pull knives in our own place? Look at em'. This one looks like a fookin' junkie." He reached for a chair and said, "Come on, let's show em' what for!"

But instead of a rally, all Liam got was an uneasy silence. Shane just stood casually next to the man with the knife. He beamed at Liam with amusement.

Liam was exasperated. "Come on, Shane!" he pleaded. "Let's show these guys a lesson!"

Shane just warmly put his arm around the shoulders of the man in the jeans jacket. He shook his head and laughed. "Nitro," he said, "I'd like you to meet a couple of my old friends. This 'junkie', as you called him, is Mickey O'Leary. And the guy you almost strangled here is Jack Banks."

* * *

Liam just blinked, frozen, at a complete loss for words. And the room erupted in hysterics.

"Don't worry Nitro," Shane said, "you didn't know."

Mickey stepped forward and put a hand on Liam's

shoulder. It felt like a boulder. "No worries, Brotha," he said, "you can make it up to me on the streets."

Liam just stood there with a furrowed brow as he attempted to sort out his colossal blunder.

Shane then reached out and gave Mickey a strong embrace, slapping him firmly on the back. Stepping away, he held onto Mickey's shoulders and grinned. "God," he said, "It's so fooking good to see you. It's been way too long, Brotha!"

"You got that right," Mickey agreed.

Jack watched the exchange with a warm heart. He had always been awed by the bond Mickey and Shane had shared, for the pair had been through so much together as the founding members of the Shamrocks. It was amazing after all these years, the two were still in one piece. They had bravely risked their lives for what they believed in, and Jack had admired that to no end. He just hoped in this case, everyone would come out alive.

Mickey asked for the three of them to speak privately, so Shane led them back through a dimly lit hallway to a room guarded by two very muscular boys. Shane produced a key chain, unlocked the door and told the two guards they were not to be disturbed. Once inside, Mickey brought Shane up to date, explaining how his cocaine habit had caused him to lose focus, allowing a two bit hood like Frankie Malone to sucker him into a trap set up by their old adversary, Victor Salazar.

Shane was outraged.

Since time was of the essence, the three of them immediately began to formulate a strategy. What they came up with was a desperate plan with obvious flaws, but it would the best they could do given the circumstances. Jack was dubious to say the least.

Upon reaching their conclusion, Shane opened the door and whispered to one of the guards. A few moments later a tentative knock was heard. Shane said, "Yeah, it's open!" and two teenage Shamrocks came in.

Jack knew them at once. Despite their adolescent changes, Jack still recognized them from the bratty little punks they once were. He found himself amused by their seemingly instantaneous transformation and silently marveled how quickly time flew by. Dan Logan had become a very handsome lad, with thick, wavy hair and sparkling white teeth. Despite being in the gang, he had somehow managed to win the starting quarterback position on the high school football team. This good fortune, in combination with his favorable looks, made him very successful with the ladies as well. With everything going so well for him, Logan had grown quite a bit of an ego, and a smugness to boot.

Patrick Meaghan slunk in behind him, his eyes wide with apprehension. He wasn't the brightest bulb in the box, and over the years his uncertainties had prevented him from developing any sense of his own individuality. In high school, he rarely strayed very far from Dan Logan, and rather than expose his own insecurities, felt content to follow the quarterback around as a dog does his master. It had its benefits, being associated with the most popular guy in school, for Patrick never really had to apply himself, leaving most of the thinking to his childhood friend. It also didn't hurt that wherever Dan Logan went, the hottest girls in school followed. And that got Patrick laid as well.

Patrick was a squat and stocky boy, but lean and quick;

physical attributes that served him well on the football field. He was the starting middle linebacker on the team and was considered one of the better defensive players in the division. His position was based on instincts and quickness, so his lack of creative thought didn't hinder him too much in games. He had a pug, porcine nose, beady eyes, and a bit of an acne problem. And he knew all too well if it weren't for Dan's magnetism, he would have had a rough time with the girls, indeed.

"Guys, you remember Mickey and Jack, right?" Shane said.

Dan grinned and went over to shake Mickey's hand. "Course!" he said. "Me and Pat have been buds with Tommie forever! How've you been, Mick? Haven't seen you in a while!"

Patrick followed suit, gripping Mickey's hand with exaggerated deference, but barely making eye contact. Both of the teens then nodded in acknowledgement toward Jack.

Shane offered them both a seat on a beer-stained sofa. They looked at him with anticipation and curiosity. "So what's up, chief?" Danny asked.

Shane hesitated at first, irked by the familiarity with which he was addressed. After a brief icy stare, he said, "We have a problem, guys, and we need your help. Mickey here has run into some trouble with The Power and now his family is starting to get dragged into it. Mickey, as we all know, can handle himself, but Tommie is now a target."

Danny and Patrick exchanged glances and said almost simultaneously, "Fuck me…" Danny then bolted up out of his seat and said, "Just tell us who they are and we'll fuck 'em up! We'll knock their teeth out! We'll bash their brains in!" He began gesticulating, swiftly jabbing the air with his right hand, then his left, aggressively pointing his fingers for emphasis. Patrick, as if on cue, jumped up and joined in the charade of bravado.

Jack glanced anxiously at Mickey, who stood leaning against the wall. His right arm was set firmly across his waist, and he was holding his left elbow as he stroked his chin.

Logan continued with his frenzy. "We'll kick their faces in! We'll slap them silly! We'll…"

Mickey stepped forward and smacked Danny on the side of the head so hard, it left the quarterback's perfectly groomed hairdo a mess. Patrick ducked and retreated back toward the couch.

Danny said, "Hey Mick! What the—? What's your problem? Jesus! Now my hair's all fucked up!" He went over to the Guinness mirror and began to re-comb it. Mickey followed him over, grabbed a huge clump of his hair, and jerked him over toward the couch. He shoved him onto it.

"YOU THINK THIS IS A FUCKING JOKE!?" Mickey roared. "Tommie's life is at stake here, and you two clowns are acting like idiots! This is serious shit, assholes!" His eyes blazed with fury as he glared at the two teens. After a moment he just shook his head and forced himself to calm down. "Are you guys up for this? This ain't just about bangin' heads at a brawl. I need you guys to watch Tommie's back!!" He took a deep breath and continued. "But I need you to do this in secret, you understand? This is a huge year is for him. This is his big chance to make something out of his life. He can't succeed if he's constantly worried there's a bullet with his name on it. So we need to protect him without him knowing what's going on. That's why I need you guys. You're his best friends, you're always together, and you guys know how to fight. We'll give you guns, knives, whatever you need, but you have to keep it quiet and never let him know the deal."

He paused, watching Danny and Patrick nodding, wide-eyed.

Danny stood up, rubbed his throbbing scalp, and said, "Absolutely, Mick. Tommie's our boy. We'll do whatever it takes."

Patrick hesitated, swallowed, and glanced up at Danny. He wasn't sure he was up for it, but if he was with Danny, he knew everything would be alright. Danny always knew what to do. He stood up as well and said, "Yeah, we can do it. Shamrocks forever, right?"

Mickey looked over to Shane and Jack and shrugged. For the moment, it was all they could do. They simply didn't have the time to conceive a more viable plan. He sighed and said, "Okay, Shane vouches for you guys. To be sure, you'll both need a piece and a blade outside all secured areas. And remember, whatever it takes, keep Tommie close at all times."

"Course, Mick," Logan said, rubbing his scalp. Patrick nodded warily.

"Come on," Shane said and motioned the boys over to a large trunk in the corner of the room. He unlocked the combination padlock and pulled it open with a shink! He then lifted the lid, revealing a cache of guns and knives. Danny and Patrick came over, eyeing the weaponry with reverence and anticipation. Danny absently rubbed his hands together like a little boy getting ice cream; Patrick simply licked his lips. Shane moved aside a pair of Ak-47's. For this kind of job, the boys just needed a couple of nine-millimeter pistols and switch blades.

The teenagers felt the weights of the weapons in their hands.

"I'm counting on you both," Mickey said, as cold as ice. "Do not fuck this up."

* * *

After the two teens left the office, Mickey plopped down on the couch and let out a heavy sigh. Jack sat down next to him and Shane hopped up on his desk.

Jack didn't want to set Mickey off again, but he needed to be heard. "You sure this is the right thing to do, Mick?" he said. "I mean, I know we've thought about it, but those two guys ain't Rhodes scholars, you know. Shouldn't we think about this a little more? I can keep an eye on Tommie too, you know. I can move my schedule around a bit and…"

Mickey abruptly stood up. "NO! I'm not getting you mixed up in this! I'm not taking you down with me too!" He began pacing around the room and running his hand through his hair again. "I'm gonna keep a close watch on Tommie myself. And when I can't be there, Dan and Pat will. Those guys have been friends since they were little snot noses and they've always looked out for each other. They go to school together and they hang out together. They'll be there for Tommie when I can't. Simple as that."

Jack looked deflated. "Well at least keep me in the loop, Mick. I don't want to see you or Tommie hurt." He swallowed. "Let me help somehow."

Mickey considered this with a furrowed brow. He

suddenly became acutely aware of a throbbing near his throat. The taser wounds Frankie gave him the previous night were swelling into blisters and it felt like two hot pokers were boring into his neck. He imagined Jack tied up in Salazar's den, his face bloody and bruised. He quickly changed the subject.

"So what ever happened with that girl last night?" Mickey said with a smirk. "I totally forgot about the hospital. Was she there?"

Jack's cheeks turned a subtle shade of pink. "Yeah," he said, "she was there. She was getting stitched up in the ER."

"Really? So...did you talk to her?"

"Yeah, she's pretty cool. She took it all in stride. Tougher than she looks. And kinda funny too."

Mickey raised he eyebrows. "You just like her ass."

"Didn't really notice," Jack lied, "but she does have nice eyes."

Mickey looked at Shane and nodded toward Jack. "Nice eyes. Right. Whatever." He plopped back onto the couch. "So what's next? Did you get her number?"

Jack's face lit up. He held up the palm of his hand and showed what was left of Tessa's phone number. He remembered how she leaned into him as she wrote in his palm. As if in a trance he said, "She smells good too."

Mickey slapped his thigh and exclaimed, "HA!" He sat forward, eager to hear more. "So did you call her yet?"

Jack quickly sat on his hands. "Are you kidding me?" he said. "She just gave me her number last night and you want me to call her today. WAY too soon. That's like a cross between stalking and desperation!"

Mickey looked at Shane, who raised his eyebrows and

nodded askance. "That's right, Mick," he said. "You can't call the next day. It's a rule."

Mickey frowned and said, "That's bullshit, man. You gotta go for it while you can. Life is short, my friends. When opportunity knocks..."

Jack said, "You're nuts. I'm waiting at least 'til tomorrow. I'm not gonna screw this up, no matter what you say. Girls can smell desperation." He paused for a moment and looked at the floor. "She can wait anyway. I'm more concerned about Tommie. I'm just not sold on the plan. Mick, what if...."

"Jack, stop worrying about it. It's my problem. I can take care of my little brother. You should worry more about your own life. Just call her, man. I haven't seen you this excited about anyone since Gretta." He noticed Jack wince and knew it was a sore subject, but he pressed on. "It's been a long time, dude. Too fucking long if you ask me. You need some better company than me. Let's face it, she's a lot cuter than me and probably a lot safer to hang out with."

"Come on, Mick. That's bullshit," Jack said. "You're good people, man. Don't say that."

Mickey's eyes moistened and he looked away. "Whatever," he said.

"Okay, I'll call her, but don't shut me out now when you need me the most."

Mickey suddenly beamed. "Okay, but today. Not tomorrow. Not Monday. Not next week. If you can get a date out of it, I'll know at least I'm doing something right."

* * *

As in years past, Mickey led the way and approached the dais that stretched out in front of the clubhouse. A resounding round of applause rose up from the youths, punctuated by boisterous whistles and cheers. Jack passed behind Mickey and sat to his left, while Shane sat down to his right. Mickey, now heartened by this once familiar atmosphere of admiration, felt his strength and his sense of importance roar back.

In front of a large picture of James Cagney playing the gangster in Public Enemy, Mickey remained standing and leaned forward with his hands on the table. He surveyed the room of smiling and encouraging faces, youths in awe of what they perceived as greatness.

Mickey stood up tall and raised his arms to quell the cheers. His face then became serious. "Thanks, guys," he said, and when the noise died down he began his speech. "It's great to see so many of my old friends again. And I'm also proud to see that our efforts of the past have continued. Since I've been gone, our streets have remained safe, thanks to all of you."

An enthusiastic roar erupted, followed by a chant of "SHAMROCKS! SHAMROCKS! SHAMROCKS!" accompanied by the rhythmic unison of pumping fists. Mickey again quieted the group. "I'm also encouraged that so many new faces are eager to join us in our cause." He glanced at Liam and added, "And I'm happy to see that we've continued to recruit well."

Somewhat abased, Liam raised his fist and the crowd erupted once again.

"But now we are needed more than ever. Some of you may remember the name of Victor Salazar." A ripple of hisses and guttural curses sounded from the crowd. "Well, his strength has grown again and he now has The Power working the areas downtown."

He paused for a moment, not sure how the next part would be received. Yet he had to press on.

"As bad as that sounds, it's not the whole story. I come here today not as the former leader of The Shamrocks but as an old friend who needs your help." He paused, looked over at Jack, and then said, "My family has been threatened."

"Let's kill the fooker!" someone yelled.

"Fook him, let's kill *his* fookin' family!" another cried.

Mickey held up his hands again. "A little while ago, in a moment of weakness I admit, I was tricked by Salazar and I became indebted to him. How this happened is not important, but what I will tell you is this: We are now living in very dangerous times and we all need to be extremely cautious. Watch your backs."

Mickey took a drink of water that had been brought to him. He cleared his throat and paused, unsure of how to proceed. Finally, he came out with it. "To repay my debt to Salazar, he wants me to convince you guys to work for him."

The room became silent; the men grimaced in anger and resentment. Then a surge of protest began. "So this is why you're here?" a voice shouted above the curses. "You want us to join that old fook? Go fook yerself!"

People stood up and started jeering. Suddenly Shane bolted out of his seat. "SIT THE FOOK BACK DOWN AND SHOW SOME RESPECT! Let the man finish, for fook's sake!"

Like beaten curs, the crowd settled down and took their seats again.

Mickey continued, "Of course I'm not gonna ask you to

turn your backs on your families. I started The Shamrocks so we could live our lives without worrying about our parents getting mugged, our sisters being raped or our children getting hooked on drugs. It worked out well for a while, but at this very moment Salazar is planning on taking over Soundview. *All* of Soundview. And if he succeeds, no one will be safe." He stood upright and folded his arms across his chest. "I think we can still protect ourselves and somehow stop this mother fucker once and for all."

A loud, enthusiastic cheer rose up from the crowd.

Mickey scanned the room with pride. He made eye contact with as many faces as possible. "I want you to know I will fight this with everything I have. I will never give up. But right now I need all of your help. Salazar's plan is starting with me. He has threatened my brother and if I don't give him what he wants, I'm not sure what he'll do." He leaned forward with a threatening expression and said, "I say fuck him. I'm not delivering shit."

Mickey absently rubbed the area on his neck where he was tasered. "I'm gonna kill the motherfucker," he proclaimed, "I don't know when and I don't know how, but I promise you it will happen!"

The crowd erupted again and Mickey raised his arms to quiet them down.

"In the meantime," he said, "we need to stay strong. Within the week, Salazar is planning to release The Power all over town. And we need to be ready for them."

"FOOK THEM!!" someone yelled.

"Are we gonna kick some serious Shamrock ass?" Mickey shouted.

"YEAH!" came from the crowd.

"Are we gonna fuck up some Power?"

"YEAH!" echoed the crowd.

"NOBODY'S GONNA FUCK WITH US!"

"YEAH!" volleyed forth in a deafening roar.

Now their fists were pumping eagerly in the air.

Mickey's voice swelled with a forgotten righteousness and pride. "SHAMROCKS!" he yelled with a pumping fist. "SHAMROCKS!" he chanted and all the men stood up and joined him. "SHAMROCKS!" they all yelled together. "SHAMROCKS! SHAMROCKS! SHAMROCKS!"

And as they mustered, their chants blasted through the walls of the rundown warehouse, the sound of a collective spirit, preparing to battle whatever lay ahead.

CHAPTER 11

LIVE CONNECTIONS

After the rally died down, Mickey, Shane, and Jack called some key members into the office to give them their orders. They were to be stationed in certain areas throughout the town and were warned to be prepared for any aggression by The Power. Jack had wanted to discuss more options with Mickey, but he would have none of it. He was going to spend some "quality time" with his little brother, who at that moment was at the house studying for midterms. He told Jack to go home and relax. He'd call him later.

So Jack left the clubhouse, his mind spinning from everything that had arisen in the past couple of days. The afternoon was overcast with a thick blanket of clouds; the drabness accentuated by a fine sprinkling of mist. Jack shivered, put up his sweatshirt hood and picked up his pace until he arrived home. After entering his house, he checked his mail, took off his sweatshirt, and realized he was hungry. He mixed some Bumble Bee tuna with Hellman's mayonnaise, put it on some whole wheat toast and added some wise potato chips to his plate. A tall glass of coke with ice was his beverage of choice and he brought his lunch into the den.

He threw on the TV and was instantly disheartened. It was a playoff game between the Red Sox and the Royals, a harsh reminder that Boston had just knocked out the Yankees in the first round, and he couldn't care less about the remainder of the baseball season. He flipped around the channels until he came across "Jaws", probably his favorite movie of all time. It was the scene where Chief Brody was chumming for the shark, complaining of the stink from the bucket. "I can drive slow ahead," he says, "Come down here and scoop out some of this shit." With that, the gigantic shark suddenly emerges within five feet of Brody and scares the shit out of him. With wide eyes, Brody backs into the cabin and tells Quint with a cigarette dangling from his lower lip, "You're gonna need a bigger boat."

Jack smiled at the line, one of the most famous quotes in movie history.

He looked at the clock and thought about what Mickey had said. 'Life is short my friends. When opportunity knocks…' Jack rolled his eyes. It was now four o'clock, the day was passing by, and he had no valid reason, according to his prodding friend, not to call Tessa. He picked up the phone and dialed her number. After several excruciating rings, her voice mail picked up. A warm, friendly voice said, "Hey, this is Tess. You know what to do at the beep!"

Jack cleared his throat and gave his best rendition of a confident, relaxed guy.

"Hey Tess, this is Jack," he said, "Just calling to say hi. Hope you're feeling okay. Give me a call when you get a chance."

He left his number, hung up, and tossed the phone onto the coffee table with a clank. "Mickey, you're an asshole," he muttered. Surely she had a life. Probably out with some friends or even some guy. *I'm an idiot*, he thought, and lay back down to stare at the ceiling.

He was ambivalent about being single. There were times when he was content to be left alone, coming and going as he pleased, with no one telling him where to go, or what to do. But then there were other times, like now, when he missed the romance and intimacy of being in a relationship. He began to reminisce about Gretta and the experiences they shared all those years ago. He thought about their vacation in Jamaica, when he had made love to her while she was only half wearing her sun dress. Then the time they went hiking and spontaneously made love in the middle of a secluded field, only to have a group of bird watchers with binoculars emerge from the woods nearby. The lazy summer afternoons by the Sound, floating together on rafts and falling asleep as the water lapped lazily upon the shore. He could still almost feel her warm, soft body and smell the sweet perfume on her neck. All these memories danced in his mind in an endless loop as he lay staring at the ceiling. And it was in this reverie that he dozed off, with a faint smile on his lips and a tear rolling down his cheek.

* * *

R I I I N N N N N G G G G ! ! ! ! ! … … … . RIINNNNNNGGGGG!!!.........Jack was instantly jolted out of a deep state of blackness, his left arm flailing out and knocking over the watered-down Coke on the table.

"Shit!" he exclaimed and grabbed some paper towels to wipe up the spill. After a couple more rings, he cleared his throat and answered it.

"Hello?" Jack croaked.

A sweet-sounding voice answered. "Hi, um, is this Jack?"

"Yeah?" he croaked again.

"Oh, sorry. It didn't sound like you. It's Tessa."

Jack's chest turned cool and prickly. "Hey, how's it going?" He flinched at the sound of his voice. "I'm sorry, could you hold on a sec?"

"Sure," Tessa said, still a little confused. "No problem."

Jack threw the phone on the couch and ran to the bathroom. Although he was twenty feet away from the phone, Tessa could clearly hear him gargling. When he picked up the phone again, she was giggling hysterically.

"Hey, sorry about that. My throat's a little dry," he said

"Apparently!" she said brightly. "Is everything okay? I can call back later if…"

"No, no, I'm fine," he said, "I was just dozing when you called."

"Well, I wasn't sure it was you." More giggles. "You sounded like some old chain smoker."

Jack chuckled. "Nah, I don't smoke. But my voice does sound a little deep when I wake up."

"Were you actually *gargling*?"

"Yeah, busted."

She burst out laughing again and Jack couldn't help but join in.

"Too funny," she said, "So what's up? How's it going?"

"Pretty good," he said, trying to sound as relaxed as possible. "How about you? How's your forehead?"

"Oh that. It feels a little sore, but not a big deal. My mom freaked when I came in late with stitches on my head. I guess I can't blame her. But I still think she overreacted a bit."

"Well, that's what parents do. But at least we give them something to stress about. Keeps 'em busy."

"I know! What would they do if they had nothing to worry about?" She laughed and said, "Sorry I couldn't answer when you called before. I was at the library, studying for a mid-term. Had to turn my phone off."

"Really? What are you taking?"

"Gross anatomy."

"Oh, that's cool. I took my share of those classes. I'm a biology teacher over at McArthur Middle School. Do you have to dissect a corpse?"

"No, which was actually disappointing. I was kinda looking forward to getting my hands in the middle of some guts."

"Seriously?"

"Yeah, I've always wanted to be a nurse since I was little girl. The human body fascinates me."

Jack thought that *her* human body fascinated *him*. "That's pretty awesome, Tessa. You seem like someone who would be good at taking care of people. You have a very positive attitude. That goes a long way towards helping others, you know. I think only certain types of people can handle being around the sick, let alone help them. People like you are badly needed." He suddenly thought he was laying on the accolades too thick and he cringed.

"Thanks, Jack. That's sweet," she said. "I realized I wanted to be a nurse after years of taking care of my dad."

"Really? He was sick?"

"Yeah, he had a bad case of diabetes. It was very hard to control, even with all the insulin shots I gave him. Probably because he was the worst kind of patient." She paused and her voice became a little choked. "I loved him beyond words, but he was the most stubborn person I ever knew. Even though he knew it would eventually kill him, he kept smoking and drinking much more than he should have." She swallowed. "It's hard to change some people, Jack. They live for their vices."

"Wow, you lost your Dad? So sorry to hear it."

"Thanks, appreciate it. I still think about him all the time. His passing inspires me to look for ways to *prevent* illnesses, not so much treat them. You know, helping people to be proactive about their behaviors and not fall into bad habits."

Jack thought of Mickey and *his* bad habits.". "Yeah, Tess. I know what you mean. Lots of people get into things that are bad for them. There's just something about that quick fix that can be really hard to resist. I mean, some people are lucky and they can do whatever they want. But for everyone else, too much of anything isn't good."

"Well I say anything in moderation is okay, as long as you're not sick and it doesn't hurt anyone else."

"Makes sense."

There was a pause in the conversation and Jack felt he better act quick, or an irreparable, uncomfortable silence would ensue.

"So," he said, "when can I buy you that drink I owe you?"

"Jack, you don't owe me anything. It wasn't your fault."

"I know, you're right. But I'd still like to take you out. I'd like to get to know you."

"Well, that's different. Of course! That would be nice."

Without thinking, he blurted out, "What are you doing tonight?"

There was another pause and Jack immediately thought he blew it. *I'm such a loser,* he thought to himself.

After an eternity, Tessa finally said, "I think I better study tonight. I'm way behind."

Jack was deflated but he tried to sound unfazed. "Oh, okay," he said, "we'll do it some other time."

Tessa could sense the disappointment. "No seriously, I'm not just blowing you off. I do have to study. Let me think... It would be nice to hang out, but I am ridiculously busy with work and school. Let's see...I'm working tomorrow morning...what do you think about coming down to Ma's tomorrow? I have a break around eleven. Buy me a cup of coffee?"

"Hmmm, interesting. Yeah, that sounds cool."

"Okay then, see you tomorrow at eleven?"

"Sure."

"Great, see you then."

"Okay, then have a nice night."

"You too, Jack. Bye!"

"Bye." And he hung up with a light tingling sensation running all over his scalp.

* * *

Mickey was exhausted. Not only had he been traumatized the night before, but he had barely slept and was now being forced into becoming a body guard. And on top of that, he had to figure out a way to take out the most dangerous man he had ever known.

All he wanted to do was sleep.

He was driving a rental now, while his even more battered Buick was being repaired, and was a few blocks away from his house when his cell phone rang. He didn't recognize the number, so he answered it curiously.

"Hello, Mick?"

"Yeah," Mickey answered. "Who is this?"

"It's George. George McGavin."

Mickey held the phone away from his face and looked at it with a frown. "What the fuck do you want? How'd you get this number?"

"Wait, Mickey, just hold on. Don't hang up. Salazar doesn't know I'm calling you. You need to know something."

"Why should I trust *you*? You fuckin' sold me out."

"Look, Mick, I didn't know what the deal was. I was just hanging out there one night and Frankie comes in with Salazar and starts asking a lotta questions. About The Shamrocks. I don't know what they want and I really don't give a shit. I'm partying. I'm wasted and some naked hottie is all over me. So they ask me who ran The Shamrocks and it just came out. They ask me if you like to party and I said shit yeah, you do. Let's be honest, Mick, you *do* like to party."

"Not anymore. And it's none of your fuckin' business. What do you want, anyway?"

"Look, I ain't no saint. I'll be the first one to admit it, but…Salazar's out of control this time."

Mickey's stomach dropped.

"He was serious about going after Tommie. I'm just warning you."

Now Mickey's heart skipped a beat. "What did he do? WHAT DID HE DO?!"

"Nothing, Mickey. Calm down. Nothing yet. But I just thought you should know."

"I gotta go. I gotta go. I gotta make sure Tommie's okay."

"He is, Mickey. And I'm sorry this all came down on you. I wish I could help but I'm in a tough spot myself. I'm caught between Salazar and Internal Affairs."

"Well, that's what living the good life gets you."

"I guess. But be careful, Mick.

There was silence. Then Mickey said, "Yeah, you too."

PART 2

CHAPTER 12
SHORT CIRCUITED AMBITIONS

Saturday Evening, October 14

Barney O'Leary was sitting at the dinner table enjoying a tall glass of Guinness. He was a stout man, once quite thin and agile, but since retiring as a firehouse captain four years prior, had put on considerable weight. This was in no small part due to his well-known predilection for beer. For as long as he could remember, each swallow of the cold, dark ale satisfied and refreshed him in a way that no other drink could. He was fond of declaring that his order of allegiance in life was God, family, his fire station, and beer. It was as if every bottle he opened up was some sort of high privilege that no one else seemed to understand.

He stared transfixed at the strings of tiny bubbles flowing up from the bottom of his glass and took another large gulp. He closed his eyes and swallowed, feeling it tingle his throat, then opened his eyes with a big smile. A big white mustache of foam covered his lips. He wiped the foam off with his sleeve and said, "Damn, that's good!"

Nearby, a woman of similar age wearing a starched white apron was stirring a pot on the stove. The savory aroma of beef stew hung in the air, causing Barney's mouth to water. "So when's dinner, Ma?" he said, "I could eat a horse!" He then let out a huge bellow of laughter and everyone at the table rolled their eyes.

Barney was a contented man. He had worked Firehouse #39 for twenty-five years, sustaining his fair share of burns and bruises, but nothing serious enough to send him to the hospital. Over the years, his seeming invincibility had earned the nickname "Achilles." It wasn't really luck that had kept him safe, but a sagacious ability to anticipate dangers and an uncanny agility to dodge them whenever they occurred. Fortunately for him, nothing had ever surfaced as his Achilles' heel, but people were beginning to think it would be his lust for beer that would eventually do him in.

Back in the late '70s, his firefighter's salary had enabled him and his young wife Mary to purchase a three-bedroom house on the edge of town. It was modestly sized, without much of a yard, but it did have an attic and a basement and at the time was just large enough to hold his growing family. His two older girls shared one bedroom, another was for the boys, and when needed, lower family room was used for sleeping quarters as well. The house could be tight at times for such a large family, but they adapted as best they could and rarely felt claustrophobic.

On this particular night, the house felt warm and alive with the activity of family. Barney's two married daughters had brought their families over to celebrate his sixty-fifth birthday. Katie had been married for five years and had provided him with two grandsons, Ryan and Sean, while Meg had a two-year old daughter named Shannon and another "in the oven," Barney had liked to say. His daughters had given him very little grief growing up and he had developed a deep affection for them since they were little girls. He still joked with them at every opportunity and they would often give him big hugs and kiss the top of his head as he sat proudly on whatever seat served as his throne for the day.

His younger sons were brimming with potential. Donnie, who was in the sixth grade, was excelling at McKenna Elementary School and was a top candidate for the athlete/scholar award at the end of the year. And Tommie, well, Tommie was an entire story unto himself. He was going to make the O'Leary name famous someday.

Barney listened to his daughters gossip while the little ones ran around giggling in the living room. It was 6:15 and he hadn't a bite to eat since lunch. He took another swig of his beer to quell his hunger, but after a lame attempt at stifling a belch, his stomach made a loud gurgling noise. At this, the girls suddenly stopped talking and looked wide-eyed over at their dad before bursting out in laughter. Meg said, "Ma, you better hurry or Dah's gonna eat one of the kids!"

Mary, still stirring, turned her head toward her husband with a knowing smile. "Nah, they wouldn't satisfy him," she said. "They're too sweet!" She then opened the oven and with a padded mitt took out a large loaf of freshly baked bread.

"That smells loovely, me darlin'," Barney said. "How much longer?"

"When Mickey gets home, we'll eat," Mary said, and everyone knew that was the end of the conversation.

* * *

Barney had always thought his oldest son would be destined for great things. When he was a boy, Mickey made friends easily. Some days it felt to Mary that the doorbell wouldn't stop ringing from kids looking to play with him. He exhibited a special kind of charisma; a unique balance of fairness and toughness, which he used to break up fights and settle playground disputes. After a while kids would come to him to air grievances, which he always seemed to handle with a keen sense of playground justice. He would retrieve a stolen ball or chase away a bully, leaving the rest of the kids in awe. He was like a glowing light to which the rest of the children were drawn.

In high school, after prodding from his parents, Mickey decided to join the basketball team. The combination of agility which he inherited from Barney and the lankiness from Mary (who was a track star in her own day) gave Mickey the rudimentary skills to excel at the game. He had tremendous hand-eye coordination and an innate sense of leadership, so before long he became captain of the team.

Unfortunately, however, life had its own set of plans for Mickey. And they didn't include basketball. During an ill-fated ski trip, a near lethal combination of pot, Southern Comfort, and a youthful sense of indestructibility had sent him precariously down the wrong ski slope. As he turned down a particularly steep part of the trail, he hit a patch of ice, picked up speed and flew out of control over the side of a hill. If it weren't for a strategically placed safety fence, it would have been all over for the young Mickey O'Leary. Taking into account what could have been, he considered himself lucky enough to walk away with merely a hairline fracture in one thumb and a bone chip fragmentation in the other. For years he wondered why he had sustained such strange injuries (having snapped a six inch beam in the fence in half), only to one day realize it was due to his grips on the ski poles. In any event, he never forgot how he survived the accident, for as he flew over the side of the hill, he thought for sure he was going to die. Perhaps some majestic spirit intervened, giving him another chance to fulfill some greater destiny. Or maybe it was simply fate. Either way, it just wasn't yet his time.

Mickey took his injury and the loss of basketball in stride. He maintained a close bond with his teammates, so he continued to attend practices and cheer the team on during games. After a while, though, he began to lose interest. He had lots of friends, many of whom weren't athletes, and as the season wore on he slowly distanced himself from the team, attending fewer practices and games.

The school years flew past and Mickey did just enough

to get by with B's and C's. He had no intention of going to college because his real desire was to follow in his father's footsteps and join the fire department. After graduation he eagerly went through the application process. He filled out the forms, got some references, and took a physical.

One day, about a month after his physical, he was called in to speak to the fire commissioner in his dad's district. Mickey was so excited that he skipped breakfast and arrived thirty minutes early for the meeting. He was numb with anticipation, waiting to hear the news that would make his father so proud. Finally the secretary told him the commissioner would see him and led Mickey inside his office.

Artie Connor was sitting at his desk wearing a white-collared shirt and thin black tie. His commissioner's badge was on the upper left side of his shirt. His half-eye reading glasses were pushed down toward the edge of his nose and he was studying a file on his desk. Connor didn't look up but waved Mickey in and continued reading. Mickey took a seat in front of the commissioner's desk, his mouth dry and sweat building under his arms.

Finally Connor took off his glasses, tossed them on the desk, and sat back. He put his hands behind his head and stared at Mickey for what seemed like an eternity. After an excruciating silence, Mickey said, "So, you wanted to see me?"

Connor stared for a moment longer and then got up and walked over to the wall, which was hung with awards, plaques and photos, many of Connor himself with various local dignitaries, shaking their hands and accepting recognition for one achievement or another. He stopped in front of one shot where Connor was standing with Mickey's father, holding fishing poles and an impossibly large sea bass in front of a boat named Lass of the Sea. Connor gazed at the picture wordlessly before finally speaking.

"Mickey," he said, "your father and I have been pals for a long time. We fought fires together for years. Before I got promoted to commissioner, he saved my ass on many occasions and for that I will be forever grateful. We've fished together, played golf together, and even my wife and your mother Mary have become close friends."

He turned around and glowered at Mickey, his eyes ablaze with fury. "So you can imagine how it feels for me to realize their son is on drugs."

Mickey's heart sank. "What are you talking about? I don't—"

"Save the bullshit, kid." He went over to the desk and tossed Mickey the file. "You tested positive for marijuana, cocaine, and other various narcotics. What do you have to say about that?"

Mickey was devastated. He had no idea they would be testing him for drugs. He thought the blood and urine tests were just to see if he was healthy. If he had known…Jesus Christ!

Connor said, "Needless to say we can't have a junkie running through blazing buildings trying to save people. Lives are at stake in this line of work and we can't afford to have guys with questionable character handling emergencies."

Mickey closed his eyes, leaned his elbow on the desk, and ran his hand over his face.

"Christ, kid. Your old man risked his life for years

raising you and this is how you turn out?" He spun Mickey around and grabbed him by the shirt. His voice quivered with anger. "Now this is how it's going to work. You are going to tell your dad that you're no longer interested in becoming a firefighter. Tell him you'd rather do something else, like join the Coast Guard or whatever the fuck. I don't give a shit. But under no circumstances is he to know you're disqualified from the fire department because of your little drug habit, you hear me?"

He paused then and his face softened. His eyes seemed to moisten, and when he spoke next it was more of a whisper. "It would break his heart."

Mickey got up and stood next to the commissioner, his head still hanging low. When he spoke his voice came out dry and low. Finally, he said, "He doesn't have to know anything. He doesn't even know I applied. It was gonna be a surprise."

CHAPTER 13

UNPLUGGED

Disappointment and despair hung around Mickey like a black cloud the week following his meeting with Artie Connor. Not only would he never see the pride in his father's eyes the first time he put on a firefighter's uniform, but he hadn't a clue about what to do with the rest of his life. When his parents asked about his plans after graduation, Mickey would just shrug his shoulders and say he needed some time to work things out. He would take a few courses at the community college, get a job, and pay rent for his room downstairs. He was young, he had time on his side, and soon something would come along to show him the way.

So he spent most of his time hanging out with kids in the neighborhood, those who had little interest in college or a career. Most of them had just gotten out of high school, had no expenses, and were still living at home. They got by on small jobs and had an overabundance of idle time.

They often spent their nights in the woods by the lake, lighting bonfires and drinking beer. Circled close to the flames, they stood around smoking joints and listening to classic rock on giant boom boxes. Night after night, the young rascals would goof around and play air guitar to Rush, The Who, or Led Zeppelin until someone would smash a bottle against a blazing log, causing swirls of sparks to float in the air. All the stoners would then gaze in awe at the twisting specks of orange light and, in turn, begin throwing all sorts of debris into the fire until Mickey finally regained order.

By this time, he was unquestionably the leader of the group and always had the final say. Because although he'd experienced his fair share of setbacks in his young life, he still maintained his good looks, still had his athletic physique, and still got all the girls. And if there was one thing that drew admiration from young men, it was success with good-looking girls. If you were tough on top of that, well then, you were simply royalty.

By the age of 19, Mickey had proven himself to be a fearless and tremendously skilled street fighter. After high school, with the little money he had made doing odd jobs, he joined a local kick-boxing gym where he lifted weights and trained for hours on end. The training would not only serve him well on the streets, but it eventually earned him a job as a bouncer at a local tavern. Most of the nights at the pub went without incident, but every once in a while, some of Mickey's friends would arrive all coked up just looking for a fight. They never started one; Mickey would never allow it. But if any fathead on steroids began acting up, Mickey would just make a signal and all hell would break loose. It was a blast. Some of the boys laughed as they let their fists fly, some even laughed while they were taking punches. "Is that all you got, bro?" they taunted. Or, "Come on, man, you can hit harder than that, can't you?!" And after every scrum they would meet up outside the bar in hysterics, running away before the cops ever came.

Soon there was a brawl in the bar almost every night, usually pitting Mickey and his friends against other groups from all over the town, guys who were also looking to let loose some pent-up teenage angst. The bar owner became frantic with all the violence and when he learned of Mickey's involvement, fired him at once.

Mickey laughed it off but soon wondered how he and his pals would fill the void. Not long after being cut off from the bar, the guys were getting restless and edgy. Fights began breaking out amongst themselves and Mickey knew they were going to need to find some other release.

* * *

Late one Friday night, they were milling around one of their hang-outs, a place in transition, and not necessarily in the right direction. The corner deli, with which they had all become so familiar throughout their youth, had recently changed hands. The old owner, Dennis Landsbury, was gone, and it gave everyone a vague notion of disorientation (a feeling they weren't ready to acknowledge) that their youth would soon be behind them and many of the things that had become a constant source of stability were now fading away. The past was growing more distant, their childhoods getting farther away, and every additional change in town heightened a gnawing sense of anxiety.

Dennis had been beloved by the community for years. The kids had so often been sent to the store by their mothers to pick up last-minute necessities for dinner, that it had become a weeknight dusk-hour ritual. Every evening Dennis would see parades of young familiar faces, most of them out of breath coming to his store. He would say, "Hey kid, what'd your mom forget tonight?" or "Ran out of ketchup again, sonny?" or "Can't have dinner without some Coke, sunshine!" His sandwiches were large and tasty and he made his salads (tuna, egg, potato, and such) fresh every morning. He would ask about your family, your grandmother's health, or your dog's new puppies.

But one day, without much of an explanation, he decided he'd had enough and sold his place. People speculated that his health was failing, that he had an expensive girlfriend, or that he had a bad gambling problem and needed to sell the store in order to pay off his debts. In any event, he was gone in the blink of an eye.

The new owner was a hardened Colombian named Jaime. He pronounced his name "High-may" and if anyone said his name incorrectly, he would instantly throw them out of the store. He had no desire for friendly banter and he seemed to care little for the cleanliness of his store or the quality of his food. The bagels that Dennis had brought in fresh every day were now kept around until they hardened into a flavorless bricks. He would microwave them to soften up the staleness and then slather them with heavy butter to mask the cardboard taste. Shane, who was good friends with Mickey even then, once hurled one of the bagels through Jaime's window after breaking a tooth on the petrified lump of dough. Jaime never even bothered to fix the broken glass.

Most people regarded Jaime as a bitter immigrant who appeared to get by selling smutty magazines, lottery tickets, and garbage food to the drunk kids who came around late at night. But Mickey had heard some rumors, and that night, he and Shane were going to find out the truth once and for all.

It was 12:30 AM and Mickey and his crowd had just left a bar down the block. Some of them were stoned and the munchies were coming on strong. They headed down to the deli, which the guys had jokingly nicknamed "The Grossery." Mickey and Shane, however, weren't interested in food. They entered the store and waited on line while Jaime and his associate Pedro irritably served their customers..

When Mickey got to the front of the line, Jaime said, "What do you want?"

Though he was a little nervous, Mickey tried to act casual. "Got any chewing tobacco?' he asked.

Jaime's eyes instantly narrowed and he glared at both boys with suspicion. He looked toward the door and then to Pedro. "No, we never carry it."

"Well maybe you have some in the back," Mickey said.

"Nope," Jaime said, staring at Mickey now with a dawning curiosity.

"Maybe in your car, then?" Mickey said.

Jaime's severe expression eased, but he appeared very alert now. "I might at that," he said,"

Why don't we go take a look." He nodded to Pedro, who scowled at Mickey and Shane and muttered under his breath in Spanish. Mickey thought he heard him say something like "stupido," but he didn't really care. The tingle of adrenaline was propelling him forward.

They followed Jaime out back, where he motioned them to walk with him. "My car's on the other block," he said and the two boys followed. They turned a corner into an area that was poorly lit. Suddenly, Jaime spun on them brandishing a barber's razor.

"You punks fuck with me, I'll cut you up!" he whispered harshly. "I'm not fucking around here. You want the shit, show me the money!" Mickey's heart pounded away in his chest. He reflexively put up his arms, but he also knew Jaime had nothing to gain by attacking them. Mickey was only showing interest in doing business and that was what drove Jaime. Business. The Colombian pusher was only laying down the rules.

Mickey held his breath and slowly proffered a roll of five twenties. Jaime looked back and forth between Mickey and Shane and then snatched up the bills. "Follow me," he grumbled and led them to a brown, dented, dirty sedan. He opened the passenger door, put a key in the glove compartment, unlatched it, and pulled out a tiny zip-locked bag. He slapped it in Mickey's palm but didn't let go of his hand. "You tell anyone about this, I kill your mother," he growled, and then stormed his way back to the store.

Mickey bent over his new prize and gazed at the little white packet with anticipation and delight. His eyes sparkled and his heart began to race. It was all he could do to keep himself from running as fast as he could in any direction. He was going to feel goooood within moments. He poked at the packet in the palm of his hand and then held it up to whatever dim light was left in the street. He was simply overjoyed.

Shane leaned in close to get a good look himself. "Do you think it's the real stuff?" he asked.

"It better be," Mickey said, "We just gave him a hundred bucks." He peered at the packet more closely and then shrugged his shoulders. "Well, there's only one way to find out. Come on."

He sat down in the shadow of the car and motioned Shane down next to him. Even though he hadn't yet sampled the coke, Mickey was already humming and feeling his body tense up. He looked past Shane and then back over his shoulders. Once he was satisfied they were alone, he took out a tiny coke spoon, opened up the packet delicately, and dipped the spoon into the powder. He scooped out a little mound and brought it to his right nostril. He snorted deep, and did the same with the other nostril. He then dipped the spoon in again, but this time he pinched the powder off the spoon and rubbed it between his lips and gums.

The chemicals went to work. There was no doubt it was good stuff. A surge of ecstasy raced through his body and he began to slowly pant. He handed the paraphernalia and the packet over to Shane and stood up. He closed his eyes and breathed in deeply. The physical pleasure was indescribable.

"This is amazing," he said and lay back down on the grass. He clasped his hands behind his head, and gazed up at the stars. "I wonder where the Big Dipper is."

Shane grabbed his crotch and said, "I got your Big Dipper right here."

"Ha!" Mickey said. "That's not what I heard. You're grabbing empty space there, my friend."

"Bite me," Shane said and sniffed up some of his own coke. He then rubbed his nose and blinked his eyes hard in disbelief. "Hey man, this shit's way better than last time."

"No doubt," Mickey said. "No doubt."

Mickey sat up and they looked at each other. When they saw the dilated pupils in each other's eyes they began to crack up. "Dude," Mickey said, "you better wipe your nose off. You don't want the chicks to think you're a cokehead."

Shane chuckled and said, "What, those guys? They're all drunks and potheads! Who cares what they think? They'll probably want some themselves. Oh, and by the way, you got some on your lips too."

Mickey wiped his lips and said, "Is it gone?"

"No, it's right here." It was on the right side of Mickey's lips, and Shane pointed to his own right side. Mickey looked at Shane and mirrored his movements, wiping the left side of his lips.

"Is it gone now?" Mickey asked.

"No, it's on this side!" Shane said, and pointed to Mickey's right side. Mickey wiped at it, smearing the powder.

"How about now?" Mickey asked.

"It's right there, you dope! Here, let me get it."

Shane reached over and Mickey turned his head, blocking Shane's efforts.

"What are you doing!?" Shane said and tried harder to get to Mickey's face. Mickey fell back on the grass in hysterics, covering his face and curling up in a ball to shield himself from Shane.

Shane began to laugh too and said in exasperation, "Let me see, you idiot!"

When Shane finally gave up, Mickey looked up with tears in his eyes. His face was even more smeared.

"It's still there, you moron!" Shane exclaimed and tried to get to Mickey's face with even greater fervor.

"Who you calling a moron, you dipshit!?" Mickey said, and before Shane knew it, he was lying on his back with Mickey sitting on his chest.

"Get the fuck off me, you asswipe!" Shane yelled.

"Make me," Mickey said, sat back, and feigned a yawn. While Shane struggled futilely, they both heard a window open.

A disembodied voice yelled, "You two hooligans better get off my lawn or I'll call the cops!"

The two boys got up and bolted away, laughing boisterously. As they ran, Mickey mimicked the man and said, "You two hooligans!" in a deep and garbled voice.

CHAPTER 14

THUNDERBOLT AND LIGHTNING RODS

They raced all the way back to Jaime's Gross-ery to find their friends hanging out in front of the store. Sean Murphy had his back up against the wall with Maggie Lonnigan pressing into him. She was kissing him fiercely and running her hands through his hair. Another couple was opposite them, making out against the hood of a dusty blue Nissan. Jimmy Casey had just finished drinking a can of soda and was demonstrating how low he could extend a string of spit from his mouth toward the ground. There he stood, bent over, the spit hanging about four feet down as the others looked on in disbelief and disgust.

Mickey snuck up behind and shoved him so the spit touched the ground. Startled, Jimmy reflexively sucked the spit back into his mouth. This was met with a combination of laughter and revulsion from the group. Jimmy just grimaced, spit, and shoved Mickey back with an embarrassed smile.

Mickey looked around in spirited disbelief. "So this is it for tonight?" he asked. "Damn, you guys are starved for entertainment!"

At that moment a shiny black Toyota sped by with a weathered brown van in hot pursuit. The van was blasting its horn and a man was yelling out its passenger window for the smaller coupe to pull over. The two vehicles then turned the corner and disappeared, followed by the sound of screeching tires and a crash. There were some guttural threats, a scuffling sound and then the shrieking of a woman. Mickey looked at Shane, his face stretched into an expression of disbelief. He yelled, "Let's go!" and made a move toward the cacophony. Several of the group began running down the block, but Shane said, "Guys! Wait!" and waved them back toward his car. There, he opened his trunk and began distributing all sorts of hand held weaponry: bats, clubs, tire irons. He handed Mickey a Louisville Slugger and said, "Go! I'll be right there!" Mickey gave him a quizzical look, but there was no time for questions. He took off, running as fast as he could to catch up with the others. Once assured he was alone, Shane reached deep into the trunk, lifted up the spare tire and pulled out something else.

The ruckus continued to ring out as Mickey approached

the corner. As he turned it, he finally saw what was happening. The Corolla was halfway up the curb, its hood covered in trash, with several garbage cans strewn about the sidewalk. The van was angled in front of the smaller car, clearly having cut it off and forcing it up onto the curb. The back doors of the van were wide open and it had no license plate. Skid marks from both vehicles stretched out behind them for several yards. A skinny man with bleached, spiked hair was attempting to drag a girl toward the back of the van. He had one arm around her waist and the other hand over her mouth. She kept biting down on his hand, causing him to howl in pain, and each time he pulled his hand away, she either cried out for help or cursed at her assailant.

Further down the sidewalk near a tall hedgerow, two young men were grappling fiercely. One of them, wearing a charcoal pull-over fleece, was frantically yelling toward the girl. "Gretta!" he yelled, "Leave her alone, you fuck!" but his words went ignored.

Another man, the size and shape of a body builder, stood facing the approaching boys with a massive set of arms folded across his chest. He had a purple Mohawk, a big, hooked nose with a ring in it, and studs running up and down his ears. He was wearing a turquoise blue tank top, and his arms were covered in tattoos. He grinned malevolently as Matthew Mullin launched himself at him. The giant simply caught him in midair, effortlessly lifted him up over his shoulders and threw him down squarely on the top of his head. The boy convulsed briefly, then lay listless on the ground.

Gretta squeaked in shock behind the hand that was covering her mouth, her face streaked with tears. The spiky-haired man holding onto her, stared in unbridled admiration. "Bloody hell, Bolt!" he said in an astonished Cockney, "Smashing!"

Bolt just kept on grinning, his face seeming to grow in size. "Come on!" he said to the rest of Mickey's gang, "Who's next?" He brought down his arms in a pectoral flex and let out a penetrating howl that seemed to reverberate all around.

Mickey licked the inside of his lips. They were still numb from the cocaine. He wiped the sweat off his brow and found himself almost involuntarily in motion. The combination of the coke and the adrenaline he was now feeling seemed to propel his body forward. Whether or not he had control of his body, one thing was clear: There was no way he was going to let these punks take this girl. He took a step toward the body builder and raised the bat.

Bolt held out his hands and beckoned Mickey toward him with a taunting, waggling of his fingers. His grin grew even wider now, and his head seemed to swell like an inflating carnival balloon.

Mickey blinked hard and violently shook his head to clear his senses.

"Let her go," he said in an even voice. "I don't know who the fuck you are, but this is our town. Take your bullshit and get the fuck outta here… NOW!"

Bolt slapped his thigh and pointed at Mickey as he let out another high pitched cackle. His face was turning amorphous now, with different parts of it swelling and contracting in all kinds of directions. "Okay, tough guy," he chuckled, "You wanna play ball? I'm gonna shove that

bat so far up your ass it'll be coming out of your mouth."
He then made a move toward Mickey.

Mickey readied to swing the bat when a sudden loud
CRACK! pierced the air. Startled, they all turned toward
the sound and saw Shane pointing a smoking handgun up
toward the sky. Everyone went silent.

"Listen, you FOOKS!" he said. "Leave the girl alone
and get the fook outta 'ere before someone gets hurt. I ain't
jokin'."

For the first time Bolt's eyes showed a glimmer of fear.
His cockiness faded and his face seemed to deflate. He
looked around, his arms at his sides and his fists clenching
and unclenching.

Shane could see he was stalling, trying to formulate a
new plan. "You hear what I said, fookface?" He came closer
and leveled the gun in the direction of Bolt's head. "Let
'er go!"

At that moment, the boy in the charcoal fleece freed
himself and ran over toward the girl. The man with the
spiked hair was still holding her, but was too fixated on the
gun to see him coming. Before he knew it, the boy pounded
him in the jaw, knocking him to the ground. The girl, now
freed, cried, "Jack! Oh my God! Jack!" and reached for him.
He led her away as she sobbed in his arms.

Shane was now a few feet away from Bolt, pointing the
gun at his face. The big man simply sneered in defiance.
"You have no idea who you're dealing with." he said.

"No," Shane said, "and I don't give a flying fook. So
what I suggest you do 'ere is take these rats of yers, get in
that piece of shite van, and get the fook out of here before
I use this thing."

Bolt weighed his options. He wasn't used to taking orders from anyone on the streets.

Shane thrust the nozzle of the gun up under Bolt's chin. "I'm not telling you again. MOVE IT!"

That seemed to shake Bolt out of his stance. He turned to the girl and said, "We'll see you soon, Kitty."

"Fuck off, asshole!" the girl shrieked.

He puckered a set of thick, wet lips and made a kissing gesture towards her. It made a long, drawn out sucking sound. Then as he moved toward the van he meowed and hissed like a cat, making himself laugh all over again. As this was happening, two of Mickey's group got a hold of the guy who was fighting with Jack and threw him into the side of the van. He seemed to freeze there, as if stuck to the side panel by Velcro, then slowly slid down to the ground in a daze. When he tried to get up, he stumbled, but then managed to get himself into the passenger side of the van. Spike then realized he'd had enough and awkwardly dove into the back of the van, slamming the doors shut. When Bolt was finally inside the brown vehicle, he rolled down the window and said, "Remember the name Salazar, punks." He started the engine and put it in gear. "Soon, he's gonna be in all of your nightmares."

Mickey said, "Yeah?" and began pounding the van with his bat. The rest of the gang joined in, smashing the windows, headlights and taillights before Bolt sped off, back to whatever hell from which they came.

CHAPTER 15

GRETTA, THE CROOKED COP
AND THE CRAZY JESTER

After the van disappeared, Mickey tried to digest what had just transpired. He had been looking for excitement, but this? His heart was pounding, his mouth was dry, and his chest was heaving. Yet he felt a sense of exhilaration that was intoxicating.

He sought out Shane, who was tucking the gun behind his back into his pants. Mickey cocked his head slightly to the side, frowned, and said, "What the fuck are you doing with a gun?"

Shane just shrugged and said, "Me uncle gave it to me. Knowing me he thought I might need it someday. He was right now, wasn't he?"

"Yeah, well, just make sure you don't shoot yourself another asshole."

They both chuckled nervously and glanced around. The rest of the gang was talking excitedly about the previous scene. The girls, who had witnessed everything at a distance, were gesticulating wildly with their hands and speaking in rapid outbursts. The guys took the recap to another level, bragging about their bravery with shadow boxing and kicks in the air.

They carried on like this for a short while, until Mickey realized Matt still lay motionless on the ground. He hurried over to the boy and flipped him onto his back. Once he ascertained his friend still had a pulse, he breathed a sigh of relief. He tapped him lightly on the cheek but got no response. He looked at Shane and shrugged his shoulders.

Shane reached over and slapped Matthew hard across the face. "MATT!" he yelled. "WAKE UP!"

The boy groaned and reached to feel the top of his head. "Ah, fuck," he breathed and looked up to see his hand covered with blood. "What happened?"

"You should see the other guy!" Mickey joked with relief. "Billy!" he called out. "Get your car and take him to the Shop. And fast. He needs a doctor."

Billy took off and was back with the car in an instant. With the help of the others, he loaded Matthew into the car and sped away. After they were gone, Mickey glanced toward the girl and her boyfriend, who were leaning on the Toyota, seemingly in an eternal embrace. He went over to see how they were doing. The girl, Gretta, was inconsolable. Her head was tucked into her boyfriend's neck and her sobbing could be heard from twenty feet away. She was a petite girl, with straight brown hair, wearing tight black jeans and a teal and purple windbreaker. Her hair was so long it extended all the way down her back.

As Mickey approached, the boyfriend offered to shake his hand. "Don't know how to thank you," he said, "Not sure what woulda happened if you guys didn't show up." His eyes were hazel, almost golden, revealing both intelligence and a certain vulnerability which Mickey recognized immediately.

"Banks?!" Mickey exclaimed, "What the fuck?!"

Clarity came to the boy's face. "Hey Mick!" he said, "What's up, Man?" A look of astonishment appeared on his face. They exchanged a quick, sturdy hug and Jack said to his girlfriend, "Gretta, this is an old friend of mine, Mickey O'Leary. God, we've known each other since...Jeez, since the first grade!"

"Actually since kindergarten," Mickey said with a grin.

"Yeah, that's right!" Jack said. "When we were kids I used to ride my bicycle to his house after school. We would do all sorts of things! Remember reading all those Mad magazines?"

"Yeah, that was awesome. Jack here was a huge Godzilla fan"

"Oh my God, that's right!" Jack said, "We used to watch monster movies in his kitchen all the time. Sometimes there would be one every day after school on the 4:30 movie. Remember Monster Week?"

"Of course!"

"Those hard pretzels your mom used to give us were the best! And all those Christmas sucking candies!"

The two boys stood there, shaking their heads and smiling at the nostalgia, remembering the times they both were being introduced to the world. They never knew back then that all would be ever changing, always leaving that precious part of their lives farther and farther behind.

Jack continued to gush. "We were on the high school basketball team together too. He was the captain. A great leader, this guy." He gazed at his old friend in appreciation. "Figures you came to help. Thanks, Bro. Don't know how to repay you."

"Forget about it. We heard screaming. Had no choice."

Gretta stood in silence, but still visibly agitated. Her deep brown eyes were smeared with mascara, and she seemed to be looking every which way at once. She glanced up briefly at Mickey and said, "Well, we still owe you anyway. Thanks so much."

With a subtle smile, Mickey nodded and finally accepted some appreciation. "So Jack, it's been like forever. What have you been up to?"

"I'm teaching over at McKenna now."

"No shit. Really?"

"Yeah. Biology. It's a living."

"Huh, that's awesome. I always knew you'd make something of yourself."

"It ain't rocket science."

"Yeah well, beats driving a cab all night long."

"That's what you do now?"

Mickey swallowed, still scarred from his failed drug test

and the rejection from the fire department. "Yeah, well I had other plans but they fell through. I'll come up with a better idea at some point."

"I'm sure you will. Listen, Mick," Jack said, "Give me your cell phone. We gotta get together to catch up."

"Sure, we should play some hoops sometime."

"Of course. I haven't played in years, but who cares? Pool's actually my game now."

"Really?" Mickey said, "You should come down to the Crazy Jester, then. We hang out there all the time and they got a pool table in the back."

"Oh yeah? Sounds great! I could…"

Gretta grabbed Jack by the arm and shot him a look of exasperation. "Sorry to interrupt 'the good old days'", she said, holding up her fingers in mock quotation marks, "but helloooo! I was just almost kidnapped and I'd really like to get the fuck out of here."

Jack reached out for her. "I know, hon. Sorry. I wasn't thinking. It's just a real coincidence that—"

Gretta suddenly recoiled. "You know what? Don't touch me," she said. "This is actually all your fault! If we had gotten outta here months ago like I asked, this never would have happened. I hate this fucking place! I told you a long time ago I didn't like what was going on around here, but you wouldn't listen." She then made her voice sound stupid and masculine. "'We'll move, Babe. Don't worry. Maybe next year,' Isn't that what you kept saying? 'Maybe next year?' Well 'maybe next year' almost got me kidnapped and raped and God knows what else! If it wasn't for your 'hero' here, I might have been…" She trailed off, then looked one more time at Jack with an expression of deep regret. Finally, in barely a whisper, she said, "I would have married you."

Jack was aghast. He reached out for her again. "Come on, Grets, don't do this."

She knocked his hands away. "No, I'm done talking. You two can catch up and go brawling for all I care. I'm outta here." She walked over to pick up her pocketbook, whose contents had spilled onto the ground. Then she got in her car and locked the doors with a firm, decisive click. With an open hand, Jack slapped the window and said, "Come on, Gret! Open up!"

But instead, her face fell into a deep expression of despair and she sped off into the night.

* * *

Jack stood motionless, staring after the receding tail-lights. His neck was red, his back was aching, and his left eyebrow was rubbed sore. But his physical state was of little concern. Gretta had essentially been his entire life for over a year. What was he going to do now?

Mickey walked over to him and put his hand on his shoulder. "She'll come around, dude," he said. "Don't worry. She's gonna realize this wasn't your fault and then come running back. This shit happens all the time. They blame you for everything just because they can."

Jack looked down and shook his head. "No, man," he said. "You don't understand. I've never seen her look at me like that before. I think she means it this time." His throat caught on his words and his eyes began to glisten. He breathed in deeply and let it out shakily. "I don't know, man. I got a bad feeling about this. She told me that if anything like this happened, she was gonna leave." He swallowed hard. "This is bad, dude. Really bad."

Mickey saw that his old friend was almost inconsolable. He felt deeply for the guy. He looked around and saw that everyone was staring. "Come on, guys. We better get out of here before the cops come." He looked over at Shane. "Especially you with that piece of yours. Get out of here!"

The gang began to disperse, but Jack just sat down on the curb bewildered, running his hands through his hair. His eyes were closed in remorse. Mickey walked over and sat down next to him. "Come on, pal," he said. "Let's get a drink and talk about it."

"Yeah, let's go to The Crazy Jester," Shane suggested, "We can shoot some pool."

Mickey looked back up at Shane. "Didn't I tell you to get outta here?" He stood up and moved close to his Irish friend. "Listen, Man," he whispered intensely, "my boy here's in deep shit. I need to talk to him for a bit. But you got a gun and the coke. Now get lost before the cops come. Seriously!"

Shane finally relented and moved away at a brisk pace before breaking into an all-out sprint. Mickey watched as he disappeared back around the corner.

He then went back and sat down again next to Jack. "So what do you think?" he said. "You want to shoot a couple-a games?"

"Yeah, I guess so." He looked up, wiped both of his cheeks on his sleeve, and said, "I don't have my stick, but fuck it. Let's go."

Mickey said, "Now you're talkin'. We just gotta go back to the Gross-ery and…"

But before Mickey could finish, a cop cruiser with its

lights ablaze tore around the corner and skidded to a halt. A uniformed officer of medium height, slightly overweight and with a mutton chop mustache stumbled as he hastily emerged from the car, causing his hat to fall off and his billy club to rattle on the ground. He scrambled to retrieve both, causing his sparse, brown hair to fly in all directions. Once again fully equipped, he placed the club in his belt and put his hair and hat back into place. When he spotted Jack and Mickey, he put his hand on his gun.

"You two!" he ordered. "Get up and put your hands where I can see them!"

The boys complied as they rose to their feet.

"Get over to the car and put your hands on it!"

They did as he said. He frisked them both, emptied their pockets, and examined their IDs. Mickey thanked God he made Shane leave.

"You're that O'Leary kid," the cop wheezed. "Weren't you the kid who led the high school team to the States?"

Mickey looked up and said, "Yeah, well, we both were on the team."

"Huh," the cop said. "Okay, you can take your hands off the car." He gave them back their wallets. "You're Barney's kid, aren't you?"

Mickey nodded.

"What're you kids doin' out here? I heard reports of brawls and gunshots."

Mickey looked over at Jack to see if he wanted to say anything. After careful consideration Jack said, "Actually, officer, everyone's gone now, but ten minutes ago a whole lot of shit was goin' on. I was driving with my girlfriend on the way home when outta nowhere this van cuts us off. I get out to see what the problem is and one guy jumps me. My girlfriend tries to help me and another guy grabs her and starts dragging her into the van!"

The cop's eyes narrowed. "Are you shittin' me, kid? You better not be screwin' around."

"No, I'm totally serious. If it weren't for Mickey here and his friends, I don't know what woulda happened."

The cop moved closer and took Jack's face by the chin. He could see the bruises beginning to swell up. He looked back over at Mickey. "So you're still a hero, huh, kid? How'd you stop it?"

"Me and my friends heard some screamin' so we came to see what was goin on. There were a bunch of us and we kicked their asses pretty bad, so they got scared and took off ."

The cop then said, "The call said there was a gunshot. Who's got a gun?"

Mickey said, "I don't know anything about no gun. All I know is there was a lot of fighting and crashing goin' on. Maybe that was the noise they heard."

"Hmm, okay." the cop said. "So where's the girl?"

Jack said, "She was really upset and I don't blame her. Actually she got pissed at me. She blames me for not taking her away from this place. She thinks it's been getting too dangerous around here and I'm starting to agree. Too little too late, I guess."

"Where is she now?"

"She took off in her car without me, so I'm not sure. Maybe home, maybe not. I tried her on her cell phone, but she's not picking up. Her name is Gretta Reece."

The cop looked back at Mickey. "So who were these guys? Can you describe them?"

"Well," Mickey said, "it's all kind of a blur. I don't remember much about the other two, but one guy was really big. He had a Mohawk, tattoos all over his neck and arms, and studs all up and down his ears. One of the guys called him Bolt."

"Did you get a look at the van?"

"It was just a beat-up brown van."

"Get the license plate?"

"That's what's so weird. There wasn't any."

"Huh," the cop said again. "Well, that complicates things."

"Sir," Jack said, "have things like this been happening around here lately? I mean, girls just getting kidnapped like it's nothing?"

"Well, let's put it this way. I'd stay off the streets if I were you. Any time you hear about unmarked vans driving around, it don't sound too good." He studied the two young men for a moment and then made a conclusion. "Okay, I'll look into all this. And check on your girl. Give me a call if she doesn't show up." He handed the boys his card. It was a blank white card that said Officer George McGavin and a cell number. No official department seal, no other markings.

Mickey and Jack exchanged a dubious glance.

Then Mickey suddenly sucked in some air and raised his finger. "Oh yeah," he said, "I just remembered. The big guy, Bolt? He said something about a guy named Salazar. Like he was some sort of badass that we would regret screwing with. You ever heard of him? A guy named Salazar?"

McGavin's eyes widened. "Salazar?" He looked a little unnerved. "Why? Whatdaya mean?"

Mickey said, "I don't know. I think I've heard that name before. Some kinda drug dealer or somethin'."

McGavin shot forward and grabbed Mickey by the shirt. His face was twisted into a furious expression. "Listen, you punk! Victor Salazar is a personal friend of mine. He's got a lot of friends. Many *powerful* friends. And he's a legitimate businessman. If I hear you slandering his name around town, I will personally make your life a living hell." He looked back and forth between Jack and Mickey and let go of Mickey's shirt. He shoved Mickey away and then walked back to his car. Before he got in, he said, "Now you two get the fuck outta here before I book you both for disturbing the peace." Then, to himself, he muttered, "Waste of fuckin' time."

He sped away with his lights on.

The boys watched the car disappear. They glanced at each other, shrugged, and started walking back toward Jaime's Gross-ery. As they moved through the scene of the scuffle, Mickey first looked at the drops of blood from Matt's head and spotted the empty bullet casing from Shane's gun. He stooped to pick it up and then glanced back to where McGavin's car disappeared.

"That's got to be the worst cop I've ever seen," he said.

* * *

A short while later, Mickey and Jack caught up with Shane, who was waiting for them outside the Crazy Jester. He was standing under a large wooden sign painted bright with the picture of a fool balancing on one hand and juggling three balls with the other. The fool was clad in multi-colored harlequin clothing, resplendent with bells at the ends of his three horned cap and curly tipped shoes. He had a disproportionately large head, a hooked nose and was grinning wildly.

As they started toward the door, Mickey hesitated and found himself transfixed by the sign. He frowned, shook his head and muttered, "Nah…" before following the other two into the pub.

Inside on the right was a long, wooden bar with a counter against the wall holding numerous bottles of various spirits. A cash register sat in the center, with a mirror above it spanning the length of the entire counter. Three TV's broadcasting different sporting events were hung high on the wall. Several men were sitting and drinking, watching the games with varying degrees of interest. A girl in her early 20s sitting behind the bar glanced up at them. She had green eyes and bobbed brown hair with a streak of magenta. She wore low-cut designer jeans and a powder blue T-shirt tied up at the waist to reveal a flat mid-riff and belly ring. A tiny diamond chip subtly glittered in her nose as she stood up. She sighed and reached over toward a stack of cardboard coasters and absently tossed three of them on to the bar.

"Hey Mick," she said flatly. "What can I get you guys?" Jack noticed her sad, vacant gaze.

"Hey, Stayce," Mickey said and then turned to Jack. "What're you havin'?"

Jack said, "You got Michelob?"

"We got Michelob Ice."

"Oh," Jack said, "how about Molson Golden?"

"Yeah," Stayce said. "Oh wait. No, we only have Molson Ice."

"Figures," Jack said. "Just gimme a Corona."

"Yeah, that sounds good," Mickey said, "Coronas for us too."

The girl left to get the drinks and Mickey said to Jack, "Man, you're pretty particular with your beers."

Jack said, "Yeah, well, I like Molsen and Mich. Both go down real smooth. We used to drink them all the time in high school. Don't you remember?"

Mickey had a faraway look in his eyes. "Yeah, we used to drink a lot of Molson, come to think of it."

"Yeah, all those times we used to play quarters?" Jack said. "That was all with Molson and Michelob."

"That's right! And remember St. Paulie Girl? That was a good beer too."

Jack said, "I wonder why they had to change all those beers?" He shook his head. "Seems like everything's always gotta change, no matter how good it is. You finally find something you like and something's gotta come along and ruin it. New and improved, my ass!"

Stayce came and delivered the Coronas with little wedges of lime stuck in the top. The boys twisted the wedges around the lips of the bottles and pushed them down into the suds. Jack took a sip and tasted the tartness of the lime, which made his face pucker. "Well, that ain't a bad substitute, anyway," he said.

Stayce lingered for a moment, watching the boys sample their beers. Mickey turned to her. "Hey, you okay? You seem kinda down in the dumps."

She looked between the three of them, hesitated, and

finally said, "Yeah, well, only my best friend in the world took off with her sleazebag boyfriend like three weeks ago, and I ain't heard shit from her since." Her jade-colored eyes glistened as she looked off in thought, and then appeared to wince. "Ah, fuck it. People suck." She turned to the booze rack, took a bottle of Jack Daniels and poured herself a shot. She downed it as if it were lemonade and wiped her mouth with her sleeve. She then began to towel off the counter.

"Wait a minute," Mickey said, "are you talking about Maria?"

Stayce swallowed hard. Her next word came out choked. "Yeah."

"So your best friend just took off without telling you? That's fucked."

"She left a note," she said. "Big fucking deal. All her friends and family, the ones who cared about her all her life? She just takes off and leaves them a note saying something like 'Goin off to see the world. Thanks for the memories. Don't look for me.' You believe that shit?"

"And no one's heard from her since?" Jack asked.

"Nope," Stayce said, "But I wouldn't be surprised if some bad shit happens to her. Her so-called boyfriend was a real sleaze bag. Never liked the guy."

"You're talking about Maria Dori?" Jack asked incredulously

Stayce glanced at him for a moment. "Yeah." Her eyes began to tear up. "I gotta run," she said and hurried toward the bathroom.

The three boys were left pondering the idea of a close friend disappearing without a trace.

"Fuck this," Shane said, breaking the silence. "Let's shoot some pool."

Jack and Mickey agreed and moved sullenly toward the back of the tavern. A skinny boy wearing tattered jeans and a battered brown leather jacket was putting quarters into the jukebox. He was wearing a skull cap and was very pale. Jack thought there was something very odd about him.

As Shane racked the balls, Jack checked his cell phone one more time. No messages. He put it in his pocket and looked for a decent pool cue. They were mostly warped and the tips were chipped, but he settled on one that was in reasonable shape. Shane rolled the cue ball to Jack and told him to break. The once-pristine white ball had cracks all over it, and the table felt was marred with beer stains and cigarette burns. The whole area around the table reeked of sour ale.

But Jack was in his element. His thoughts were focused on pool. The angles. The spins. The banks and the leaves. Nothing else mattered just then.

After he broke, he began sinking balls left and right with a precision that neither Mickey nor Shane had ever seen. Maybe on TV, but never in person. After the sixth ball fell effortlessly into the side pocket, Mickey said, "Dude, what the fuck? You gonna let us play too?"

Jack just smiled without looking up and sank the last ball of the game. "Maybe if I'm feelin' generous. Got any more quarters?"

Shane shook his head and said, "Yeah, I got some. But I ain't puttin' 'em in all night if you keep winnin'."

Mickey smiled proudly and handed Jack some coins. "You were always good at settin' up plays in basketball. I guess this is kinda the same. But man, that's pretty awesome. How'd you get so good?"

Jack answered as he racked the balls again. "We had a table in the frat house at school. I played a lot and I guess it just took. It's weird how some things just come natural. Well, sorta natural. You still gotta work on it to stay good." He broke the balls up again with a crack and once more began sinking them in an orderly fashion.

Mickey walked over to Shane and said under his breath, "He's gonna be a while. Let's hit the bathroom."

Shane smiled knowingly at Mickey. "Now you're talkin'." The two then disappeared into the men's room.

While Jack was busy emptying the table of the colored balls, the pale boy with the skull cap looked on with fascination. He took in every move, every turn, every nuance of Jack's performance. The boy edged closer to the table, quietly singing along to the songs he had chosen from the jukebox, but his gaze never wavered from the show Jack was putting on. Slowly, as if in reverence, he approached the table and gingerly placed some quarters on the edge, reserving the next game.

Jack barely noticed; he was so focused on the game that he was oblivious to all distractions. Just as he sank the last ball, Mickey and Shane nearly fell out of the bathroom, laughing hysterically. Jack looked up and had to smile at the fun his old friend was having.

Mickey saw that Jack once again had cleared the table. "What, we take too long for you? Jeez, you're unbelievable!" His eyes were a bright white now and his pupils were dilated. His breathing came out quick and hurried.

The pale boy started to say, "I got winners," but before

he was able to get it out, Mickey put his arm around Jack and said, "Fuck this. Let's get another drink. I ain't gonna stand here and watch you put on a clinic all night." And as the three of them went back to the bar, the boy was left standing awkward and alone, abandoned in the now empty pool recess.

At the bar the three boys ordered more beers. Shane got caught up in a hockey game and Jack once again futilely checked his phone.

"How you holdin' up, dude?" Mickey said. "I gotta admit, that was one fucked up situation earlier today. When do you want to go check on your girl?"

"Soon. I think I better let her cool off. I'm sure she didn't go back to my place, so there's no rush. But I've never seen her so pissed."

Just then, a loud slam came from the area of the pool table and the pale boy yelled, "MOTHERFUCKER!" Some of the patrons glanced curiously over, then went back to their own business.

"So what the hell happened back there with your girlfriend?" Mickey asked.

"It was really weird. I'm still trying to figure it out. One minute we're driving home, and outta nowhere this van pulls up behind us and starts honking its horn. That lunatic, Bolt? Was that his name? He rolls down the window and starts yelling at Gretta like he knows her. Starts cursing at her and demands that we pull over. She becomes terrified and speeds away. They chase us, cut us off, and we crash into a bunch of garbage cans. I get out, which was probably a bad idea, but what am I supposed to do? I'm like 'What the fuck is your problem, Man?' and all hell breaks loose.

Thank God you guys showed up. I don't know what would have happened if you didn't." He shrugged and shook his head. "I still don't get it."

Another loud flurry of profanities sprung out from the back of the pub. A burly man from the bar turned toward the pool table and yelled, "Hey pal, wanna keep it down!? We're watching a ballgame over here!"

The boys returned to their conversation. "Whatever," Jack said. "As long as she's okay. Hopefull we can all laugh about it someday."

"Amen to that," Mickey said, and they clinked their beers in a toast.

Suddenly the pale boy began singing at the top of his lungs to a song on the jukebox. He sang along to the tune, dramatically emphasizing each verse as if it were his own personal anthem. Jack recognized it as "The Punk Meets the Godfather" from The Who's Quadrophenia. The boy sang out loud and with escalating passion:

> I'm the guy in the sky
> Flashing high, flashing eyes
> No surprise I told lies
> I'm the punk in the gutter!

"Shut the fuck up!" the guys at the bar yelled, angrier now.

Jack asked, "So what have you been up to since high school? Didn't you want to be a fireman like your dad? Whatever happened with that?"

Now it was Mickey's turn to fall silent and stare into his drink. His voice became low and somber. "That's another story for another time, my friend."

Jack decided not to push the matter. "Well in any event,

it's real good to see you again, Mick. Let's not lose touch again, okay?"

With that, Mickey's face lit up and he said, "You got it, bro." And as they clinked their beer bottles together for the last time that night, they heard, "MOTHERFUCKER!" once again.

Almost in unison, three big guys from the bar said, "THAT'S IT!" and made a move toward the back. But by the time they got there, the back door stood open and no one was left in sight.

"Fuckin' whack job," one of the guys muttered, and they all returned to the bar.

CHAPTER 16

SHOCKING DISCOVERIES
IN SHANGRI-LA

Jack was lying on his couch studying an empty matchbox. It was all black, save for the strip of flint on the side and the words *Shangri-La* printed in purple script on its face. He idly pushed the tiny drawer in and out, in and out, over and over again. He felt as depleted and bereft, as devoid of purpose, as the tiny cardboard box he now held in his hands.

He tossed it on his coffee table and again picked up the hastily scrawled letter Gretta had written just moments before she left. He still couldn't believe she was gone. When he had arrived home the night after everything went wrong, it was as if she had vanished into thin air. Everything of value to her was gone. Her clothes, shoes, and jewelry were completely cleaned out. The only signs of her ever having been there were her toothbrush, a half-smoked pack of cigarettes, and the empty box of matches. Like himself, Jack thought, anything that could be replaced had been left behind.

Through the haze of watery eyes he read the letter once again:

Dearest Jack,

I wish I could explain to you the real reasons why I am leaving. It's not your fault. You're the sweetest guy I've ever known. You've always been good to me. You've treated me like a lady, unlike most of the men in my life, and I'll always love you for that.

But things have become very complicated for me lately and I can't keep looking over my shoulder. I can't keep being afraid all the time. Something had to give and after tonight I realized it was time for me to go.

I'm sorry I said those mean things to you before, but I was scared and pissed off. You know me; when I get worked up, I have trouble controlling myself. I'm sorry I took it out on you.

Anyway, I guess there's not much more to say, but thank you for everything. I've had a great time with you, but now for both our sakes, I have to go. I'm so sorry. You're the last person on earth I ever wanted to hurt.

Please don't look for me.

G

After the first time he'd read the letter, he called her cell phone over and over. He drove by her place several times and even parked on the block to see if she would show up. Not once did her car appear. He spoke to her landlord, a nice old woman named Lucy Gibbons, but she had no more information than he. Upon hearing his concerns, Lucy did her own inspection of the apartment but again found little of significance left behind. Gretta had paid up till the end of the month, but it was still upsetting for her to disappear without a trace. Unnerved, Mrs. Gibbons asked Jack to contact her if he learned anything

He had nothing to tell her just yet, but he was determined to find out.

It all seemed very strange. They had been together for just about a year, and the more he thought about it, the more he realized how very little about her he knew. She was always very vague about her family, and rarely did she reveal anything significant about her prior life.

The night after he had spoken with Gretta's landlord, Jack took a drive over to the Shop to see if he could find her. She was a nurse in the emergency room and had worked odd hours, mostly in overnight shifts. He'd never had any reason to visit her there, preferring to sleep through the night, so he hadn't ever seen her at work. Yet to his dismay, after questioning several of the emergency staff, no one at the hospital knew who she was.

So there he lay on his sofa, searching his memory for any clues of his girlfriend's whereabouts.

Don't look for me.

Those words seemed so eerie.

Wasn't that what Maria Dori had written in her note when she ran away? It seemed oddly coincidental that two young girls would both disappear from the same town, around the same time, and ask their loved ones to leave them alone.

He put down the letter and picked up the empty matchbox again.

Shangri-La.

An ill-reputed strip joint on the dark side of town. He turned the box over and saw the phone number. After a brief call, he got up and grabbed his coat.

* * *

It was close to ten o'clock when Jack left the house. The street was dark and eerily quiet, the only sound from a dank breeze drifting lazily through the trees. Even the crickets were silent, as if they were watching him, waiting breathlessly for his next move. Despite the feeling of unease he was compelled to find out who Gretta really was and why she had ultimately left. His mind was a hurricane of emotions, and as he pulled out of his driveway he knew deep down his half-assed investigation was already a mistake. Nothing good could ever come of it.

He drove for about fifteen minutes and pulled into a parking lot facing a long, wide cement building. There were no windows on the side of the structure and its entire length was painted jet black. A huge neon sign was mounted upon it: a flashing purple replica of the logo on the matchbox, bearing the words SHAN-GRI-LA in thick, flowing script. The syllables would light up in order, with a distinct pause between each, until the entire name of the club was in sight.

Then it would flash three times before going dark, starting the whole sequence once again. Below the pulsating name was a depiction of a scantily clad woman sitting back in a suggestive pose. She had on high heels and her long legs were crossed and kicking slowly. Her full-breasted body was propped up by her left arm with her right hand running seductively through her hair.

As Jack contemplated the sign, the parking lot began to fill up. Young men were spilling out of cars, drinking beer and laughing, their excitement obvious as they moved toward the club. Ready as he ever was, Jack followed the crowd through the doors. There were two massive bouncers at the entrance, the first checking IDs and the second one frisking everyone for weapons. Once inside the door, Jack found himself in a vestibule with a girl sitting behind a glass window. The cover charge was $20, but he grudgingly handed it over. Without making eye contact, the girl took his money in exchange for what looked like a raffle ticket. She pointed to her right, looked past Jack, and yelled "Next!" He followed her directions toward another bouncer, who took his ticket, stamped the back of his hand, and then pulled back a thick, black velvet curtain.

The first thing Jack noticed was a long extension that jutted out from a curtained stage into the center of the room. Chairs and tables were arranged around its perimeter. In the seats were all kinds of men, young and old, drinking, smoking cigars, and leering at the pair of half-naked women who were dancing around the platform. Several of them barked loud, lewd remarks at the girls, and the crowd voiced their approval of the catcalls with laughter and cheers. Jack took note of the piles of folded up bills in front of each patron and instantly knew their purpose. They were ready for use when the girls came around.

On the catwalk were two shiny, silver poles that extended from the floor to the ceiling a good fifteen feet above. The two young girls were in lingerie and moved seductively around the poles. One was dressed in a teal-colored satin teddy, had a milky white complexion, blonde hair, and sparkling green eyes. The other was more exotic-looking. She was very tall with cinnamon skin, almond-shaped eyes, and wore a dark, see through black dress with slits running all the way up her thighs. The show had just begun and the girls were already working the men into a frenzy with their slow and sensual striptease. They strutted around the poles, swaying from them, leaning against them, and even caressing them. By the time the girls had their clothes off, they had the men exactly where they wanted them.

All along the stage the girls worked the room, visiting any man who showed interest and especially the ones who had cash laid out in front of them. They would slowly move closer, making eye contact and launching into their coy charade: convincing each guy that he was the only one for her. She would thrust her firm, full breasts in his face and run her long, perfumed hair over his head until he offered some cash. Then she would allow him to place the bills under the thin strap of her panties, tolerating the extra caress she would usually receive in the exchange.

Jack wanted as little to do with the scene as possible. While the girls were certainly beautiful, he saw through the entire façade. The idea of getting physical with a girl as a business transaction had no appeal to him whatsoever. It was empty, crass manipulation. So he ignored the women and searched around to find a way to get the information he wanted.

He went to the bar and ordered a beer. The bartenders were beautiful girls as well, but they weren't dancers. They simply served the drinks. And they seemed to carry an air of disgust toward the whole atmosphere, especially the guests. The barmaid served him curtly and looked at him with disdain. He wondered why she worked there if she was so repulsed by the place. He guessed she had her reasons.

An adorable Asian girl sat down on the stool next to him. With a flirtatious smile she asked, "You want any company, baby?"

"No, actually…" he said and reached for his wallet to pull out a picture of Gretta. He was about to ask her if she had ever seen his girlfriend, but as soon as she realized he wasn't interested in a lap dance, she simply scowled and slinked away.

He decided to try another method. He glanced around and before long found what he was looking for. A middle aged man wearing glasses and drinking a martini was sitting alone at a small table for two. Luckily enough, there was an empty one beside him. Most of the customers were crowding the stage anyway, so the outer tables were left vacant. He took a seat and waited for the right moment, not wanting the man to be startled by an aggressive approach.

After the opening act ended, Jack decided it was as good a time as any.

"Wow, those girls were hot!" he said to the man with the martini.

"What was that?"

"The girls. The ones dancing? How hot were they?!"

"Oh, those two? Not bad. But I'm just waiting for my favorite to come out."

"You have a favorite? Huh. You must come here a lot."

"Yeah, once in a while. It's a little pricey but, hey you gotta pay for it one way or another."

"What do you mean?"

The man studied him for a moment and then frowned. He leaned over and said, "You know, by the time you get laid in the real world, it's already cost you. You gotta pay for dinners, shows, flowers, gifts, all kindsa stuff. And then the sex isn't even that great half the time, you know? So you might as well cut to the chase, find the type of girl you dream about, and get on with it."

Jack was stunned. "So you're telling me…you're saying you can be with any one of these girls in here?"

The man's eyebrows rose up to his forehead. He suddenly sat up straight and began darting his eyes all over the place. "Wait a minute, you ain't a cop, are you?"

Jack chuckled, "Who, me? You kiddin? Nah, I'm just a regular guy. School teacher, actually."

The guy looked at him suspiciously. "If you're a cop, this is entrapment, you know."

Jack laughed at the man's paranoia. "Don't be ridiculous. I'm here because I'm looking for a girl myself. She told me she was working here. Look, I have a picture." He pulled out his wallet and showed it to him.

The man looked at the photo and then suspiciously back at Jack. "You're kidding me, right?"

"No, I met her at another club last week and she said she worked here. She told me to stop in. I thought maybe she was a dancer, but from what you said, I guess I can expect a little more."

The man looked again at her picture. "Huh," he said, "Looks just like 'the girl next door' here. Strange seeing her this way. She looks like she could be my daughter."

Jack was starting to get agitated. "So you've seen her here before?"

The man looked at Jack with a combination of humor and incredulity. "Son," he said, "that picture you got there? That's Ecstasy. She's the one I come here for. She's coming out next."

Jack's stomach dropped. His face turned pale and he thought he was going to be sick. "Are you sure?" he said.

The man said, "I don't know, I guess so."

Jack shot forward and grabbed the guy's shirt. He knocked into the table and spilled the martini on him. "ARE YOU SURE!?" he yelled.

"Yeah!" the man yelped. "Now get off-a me!"

Jack stood up and looked around. He didn't mean to make a scene and didn't want to get thrown out. Not before he saw her. "Sorry," he said and threw the man a twenty. "That should cover your cleaning bill." As he walked away, the guy yelled after him, "This won't even cover the drink!"

Jack didn't hear it. He scanned around for a hidden vantage point. He wanted to get a good view of the stage without being seen. As he settled into a dark corner, the music ended and the dancers quickly collected their tips and disappeared behind the curtain. He checked his watch and swallowed. He shrugged inside his shirt and let out a tiny, high pitched, whining noise.

A stunning-looking blonde, topless, appeared out of

nowhere. "Hey, handsome," she said, "haven't seen you around here before."

Without removing his eyes from the stage, Jack said, "Get lost." His voice sounded gravelly.

The girl frowned, called him an asshole and moved on.

The spotlights dimmed and a palpable sense of anticipation filled the air. "Crazy" by Seal began to play, the sultry, futuristic song with which Jack had become all too familiar. It was one of Gretta's favorite songs. As the crowd got more excited, a slow, sinking feeling gripped his stomach. They were all about to be entertained by his girlfriend.

Suddenly, a loud percussive note struck, and blinding light flashed up behind a girlish form, framing her silhouette in swirls of mists. The men roared. She emerged from the glare, strutting to the music and playing to the crowd in front of the stage. Jack could see that she was dressed in a sexy cat outfit: a sleek black teddy, with thigh-high stirrup-fastened stockings, long black furry gloves, a cat-eared tiara and a long, bushy tail. Even the makeup on her face looked feline.

He knew all too well the shape of her body, the way she danced. She slinked forward on her hands and knees, making stalking, predatory movements, perfectly choreographed to the music. At first she was somewhat limited by her platform boots, but as soon as they came off, she was free to explore the stage. She glided from one side to the other, seducing any man who made eye contact and silently signaled she would later return, for a more intimate encounter.

Moving back toward the center of the stage, she began working the dance pole. Jack couldn't believe his eyes. Never in his wildest dreams did he imagine his very own girlfriend in lingerie, pole dancing in front of a hundred delirious men.

And yet, her performance was incredible. Her tiny physique enabled her to shimmy up and down the pole like a small, feral animal. She climbed and twisted and spun upside down from her legs, like a nubile gymnast competing at some theatrical, erotic version of the Olympics.

When she finished her performance on the pole, she began to strip off her clothes. She was seductively shy, slowly removing one article at a time until she revealed her smooth, firm body. The stockings came off, the teddy came off, and everything else until she was left with nothing but her G-string. She then crawled to the edges of the stage, where she toyed with the men, posing her body in different sexual positions as she collected her money.

Jack was revolted. Had she been doing this the whole time they were together? All those nights she was supposedly working at the hospital? What the hell was wrong with her? He wanted to grab her and shake some sense into her.

He felt so completely humiliated, so he decided to return the favor.

He moved back toward the stage to where she was teasing a group of men. She was on all fours now, showing her ass to a customer, who was placing dollar bills in her thong. Jack stepped forward, took something out of his pocket, and slipped it under her G-string.

The men started laughing. Gretta froze, then turned and sat down. Against her skin she felt a long, thin plastic object. She grabbed it and looked at it.

It was her toothbrush.

She squinted at Jack, seemingly unaware it was even him.

He sneered at her in disgust and said, "You forgot it. I figured you might need it working in a place like this."

She blanched, stumbled to her feet, and ran toward the curtains. She was met there by three large men, who appeared out of nowhere from the side of the stage. She pleaded her case and gesticulated wildly, while showing them the toothbrush and pointing at Jack. One of the men took it from her and they let her go. He said something to the other men and motioned toward Jack. The bouncers sighted him and quickly approached. A voice over the loudspeaker ordered someone named Fantasia to report to the stage.

Jack thought about taking off, but before he had a chance, was surrounded by the three men with whom Gretta had just spoken. They ushered him over to a private area that had its own bar and was cordoned off by thick, velvet ropes. A man was sitting on a black, velvet couch built out of the wall. He wore a tailored, white-collared shirt unbuttoned low enough to reveal a bed of curly chest hair, and what appeared to be a thick, golden lightning bolt hung around his neck. His black eyes blazed with cool, measured curiosity as Jack approached. Next to him was a girl with smooth, tanned skin, short, straight platinum hair, and deep brown eyes.

He gestured for Jack to sit down. He was drinking bourbon on the rocks, lifting the glass to drink with the same hand in which he held a cigarette. Each time he took a sip, the smoke got in his eyes, causing his face to twist into an ugly grimace.

Jack sat down as one of the bouncers handed the toothbrush over to the man with the gold chain. The man studied the bristles for a moment, turning it around in his hands several times and then said, "Not bad, but I prefer Oral-B myself. They get to the hard to reach places."

The bouncer began to chuckle but was stopped instantly by a glare from the white-shirted man, who sat back on the couch and studied Jack. His stare was as icy as a glacier. "My top earner is crying backstage," he said. "Says she's done for the night. Won't tell me why." He looked at the toothbrush and said, "So what the fuck is this? Some kinda half-assed joke? I can tell you one thing. I ain't laughing. Want to explain yourself?"

Jack loathed the man instantly—loathed his smug, superior manner. This was the guy responsible for turning a girl like Gretta into a whore. Probably forced her into it and wouldn't let her go. But he had to be careful. If he wanted to get out of there in one piece, he had to play it cool. "That girl, Ecstasy?" he said. "She's my girlfriend. She took off on me a few days ago without a word. I put two and two together, found her here, and came to say goodbye."

The man leaned forward. His raised his eyebrows and spoke with a fair amount of incredulity. "Your….your girlfriend? You mean from here, right? You're a regular?"

"No," Jack said, "I mean like a real girlfriend. We'd practically been living together for the last six months."

The man looked at the bouncer, who shrugged. His eyes moved back to Jack. "Son," he said, "you understand the type of place we run here? I mean, these girls, they don't just dance. Our customers can have just about anything they want for the right price, if you get my meaning."

"Yeah, well, I'm starting to figure that out. I just wish I knew that a year ago."

"So you didn't know she worked here?"

Jack shook his head. "I thought she was a nurse."

"A nurse?"

"Yeah, it was a good cover for her, I guess. That way she could be here all night, pretending to be working the night shift at the hospital."

The man nodded and then picked up the toothbrush.

"So what's the deal with this?"

"Well like I said, she took off on me the other night. Cleaned out all her stuff. This was all she left behind. Figured I'd return it to her."

"In her G-string?"

Jack looked at the bouncers and then back at the man. "Guess I was kinda pissed. No offense to you."

The man stared at him for a moment, but then his expression lightened up and he fell into a fit of laughter. When he composed himself, he motioned to a waitress. "What's your name, kid?" he asked.

"Jack."

He offered his hand and Jack wisely took it. "Jack, the name's Salazar. Victor Salazar. What're you having?"

Jack froze. Instantly, he began to feel the sweat under his armpits. He blinked as if in a daze.

This is Salazar? You've got to be fucking kidding me.

"Kid?" Salazar asked, a little impatiently.

Jack swallowed, then managed "A beer."

"You sure? You might want something a little stronger because of what I'm about to tell you."

"No thanks. A beer is fine."

"Suit yourself."

The waitress left and Salazar continued. "Jack, my friend, you're a lucky man. Now, I know you may not see it this way, losing your girlfriend and all, but you soon will. You see, Ecstasy, your girlfriend, is very important to me. You saw her on the stage, so you now know what she can do. Men come back here week after week just to see her. Some come to see her perform and others with different needs come to get…well, let's just say…a little more intimate. She's a talented and beautiful girl and she's extremely valuable. I can't afford to have her upset in any way because when she's upset, it affects her performance and that affects business. You follow?"

"Yeah."

"Okay, good. Now a moment ago I said you were a lucky man. Do you know why I said that?"

"Not really."

"It's because on rare occasions, when you catch me in the right mood, I can be extremely generous." He paused and chuckled. "There's something I like about you, Jack. You haven't said much, which is good. Guys who can't shut up always say the wrong things and piss me off. Then there are guys who want to show how tough they are. That pisses me off too. But not you. You seem like a straight up, respectable guy who just got involved with the wrong girl. My girl."

Salazar took a drink, lit up another cigarette, and sat back, letting it all sink in for Jack. "Now if another guy came in here looking for retribution, he might say or do the wrong thing and get himself in a lot of trouble. A guy like that, if he was fucking one of my top earners for a year, I would say that guy owes me a lot of money, you catch my drift?"

Jack nodded, just waiting for the moment when he could get the hell out of there.

"But I'm gonna let you go under one condition."

"What's that?"

Salazar leaned forward, his eyes communicating the deepest threat Jack had ever seen. "Don't try to save her. I can't tell you how many guys have come in here, 'fallen in love', and tried to take one of my girls away to give them a better life. I can't blame them. These girls are young, sexy and very, very convincing. Of course guys are gonna want to save them. But Jack, make no mistake. Every one of those guys eventually went away, and mostly in a very bad way. So my advice to you, and I want to be very clear about this, is to leave her alone. Don't talk to her. Don't write to her. Don't even send telepathic messages to her. As of tonight, your relationship with Gretta is over. Got it? You agree to this and I'll forget about everything you owe me. Deal?"

Jack breathed in deeply and reached out his hand. "Deal."

"Great," Salazar said and stood as if to dismiss him.

"Thanks," Jack said. "But can I ask you one more question?"

"What is it?"

"How much does she charge, you know, for everything?"

Salazar looked at the bouncer and they both smirked at each other. Holding his smirk, he looked back at Jack and said, "Thousand bucks a night."

"You're kidding," he said, his voice barely audible.

"Dead serious, kid."

* * *

The following afternoon was awash with rain. All day long, thick clouds the color of slate held vigil over the school grounds, releasing a downpour of biblical proportions. By the time Jack left his classroom to go home, the parking lot was flooded everywhere. He had to navigate huge puddles on the way to his car, with nothing but his battered briefcase to keep him from getting drenched. And it wasn't working too well.

His day had been a disaster from the start. Not only had he woken up exhausted from a night of fitful sleep, but in his early morning haze, he had forgotten his lesson plans at home. After that, it had gone from bad to worse, having to break up a fistfight in one of his classes and spilling coffee on a stack full of essays he had yet to grade. He was hating life, to say the least.

As he approached his car, a small figure holding an umbrella materialized out of the gloom. It was a girl, wearing boots and a raincoat, but Jack couldn't make out who it was. The rain was being driven sideways by the wind and no matter how he tried, he couldn't prevent it from getting into his eyes. After getting close, he blinked hard and his vision came into focus. To his astonishment, it was Gretta.

His eyes widened and his chest tightened. He glanced frantically in all directions, over her shoulder, to his left and right, and back behind him. He could barely see anything, so he relaxed a bit, thinking if he couldn't see anyone, no one could see them.

When he finally looked back at her, he saw a familiar expression which had a completely different meaning to him in the past. Her soft, brown eyes were like those of a fawn, timid and wary, exuding the need for protection and yet somehow alluring. Jack had always found that gaze to be intoxicating, stirring his desire to cuddle with her. But now he saw more. She was afraid.

"Hey," she said. She was shivering.

Jack said, "Get in."

She hurried around to the passenger side while he opened his own door. While inside the car, he unlocked her door and started the engine to bring in some heat. She opened her door, deftly closed her umbrella, shook it off, and got in. She pulled back her hood.

"What are you doing here?" Jack said.

"I needed to talk to you."

"You know, you're gonna get me killed," he said.

She flinched at those words, but she pressed on. "Well that's one of the reasons I came here. You—"

"Are you sure you weren't followed? Does anyone know you're here?"

"Jack, please. I wouldn't have come if I thought you'd be in danger. As long as I show up for work tonight we're okay."

Jack shot her a look of disgust. "Work. Nice occupation. Pay's good though, right?"

She forced a painful smile. "I deserve that, I guess. I lied to you and I'm sorry."

"You're sorry! Do have any idea how I feel? Our whole relationship has been a lie! All those times I thought you were going to work you were…you were doing that?! I'm…I'm…" He trailed off. "I'm just completely blown away."

Gretta sat back against the door and tucked her left foot under her. She pleadingly gazed at Jack, who could see she was struggling to keep her emotions in check. No matter how hard it was for her, she was determined to talk to him.

He just sat there and looked at her. She had become a stranger to him. She was only a few feet away, yet it felt like they were a continent apart. Not long before, he could have reached out and touched her, squeezed her thigh or caressed the back of her neck, and it would have given them both a sense of warm ease. Now, the rift was immense. He felt hollow.

Barely able to speak, he managed, "I met your boss, you know."

She nodded. "Charming guy, isn't he?"

"He warned me to stay away from you."

She reached through the barrier and took his hand. "That's what I needed to talk to you about," she said. "You'd better listen to him, Jack. He's a dangerous man. He likes it when people try to fight him. He thinks it's a game. And he always wins. He's powerful. He's got lots of money and he knows how to buy people. Don't even think about going to the police. No one will help you, trust me. And if he finds out you're causing trouble, and he will find out, it will only come back to haunt us both."

Her hands were icy cold, but he had no desire to warm them. The thought of her dancing around naked was bad enough, but the idea of her having sex with strange men was beyond revolting. He was having trouble getting past the betrayal. He let her hand go.

"Don't worry," he said, "I'm not gonna get into a fight with a guy like that. I may be naïve, but I'm not stupid."

Gretta forced a painful smile. "Jack, you're not naïve," she said, "Believe it or not, what we had was real. I fell for you. Pure and simple. I wasn't pretending. I may have a fucked up life, but I still know what it's like to be in love. Jack, you're amazing."

Jack swallowed hard. He turned away to gaze ahead and all he saw was a fogged up windshield with rainwater streaming down the glass. His throat felt like it was closing in on him. He knew no matter what was said, he would probably never see her again. "Whatever," he croaked. "It doesn't matter. It's still over." He shut his eyes and shook his head.

She reached over again and touched his shoulder. In a choked voice, she said, "I know. I wish things were different. I was stupid to think it would somehow work out. I guess I was in denial."

Jack turned back to her. "So what happened the other night? Those goons who attacked us? They work for him?"

She nodded, wide-eyed and sober. "Yeah. When I didn't show up at work for a few days, he had those jerks track me down. I had a feeling that was gonna happen. It's one of the reasons I was pushing for us to move. I thought somehow we could get away from all this." She looked down and ran her hand through her long brown hair. When he saw her face again, a tear was streaking down her right cheek. She sniffed and said, "I guess I was the naïve one."

"But why did you make such a scene? You said everything was my fault. Why'd you do that? It made me feel like shit."

"I know. I'm sorry about that too. My head wasn't right. I was scared and upset and I was finally realizing we could never stay together. My hopes of slipping away with you had just been ruined and I didn't know what to do. I had to figure how to leave you in a way that somehow made sense. I couldn't bear it if you knew the truth." She paused and searched his eyes for a moment. It only confirmed what she already believed. "So now you know. And from now on you'll always think of me as a whore."

Her face crumbled and the real tears came now. It

melted Jack. Even though he had been betrayed, he still felt sorry for the girl. He bent over toward her and took her in his arms. She sobbed there for a long while—a time that was somehow suspended between their crumbled relationship and their certain future apart.

Jack handed her some tissues. He felt like he was dying inside. "So what happens now?" he said. "I mean, it sucks that we're done but, what's gonna happen to you, Gret? You're telling me you're stuck there till he just decides to let you go? That's slavery. How the hell is that possible?"

As she wiped her eyes she said. "All it takes is ego and money. The world never changes, Jack. The powerful will always prey on people like us."

Jack gritted his teeth. "It kills me that I can't help you."

Gretta sat up soberly. "Jack, please don't get any ideas," she implored, "it will only hurt us both. I've seen what he can do. It's better if you stay out of it." She sighed and wiped her eyes again. "Look, I got into this business for a number of reasons. I had nowhere to go. No home, no family, and to be honest with you, I actually enjoyed making money from sex. It gave me a charge. And I made a hell of a lot more money doing it than I could have doing anything else. But somewhere along the line, I began to want more. I wanted to connect with someone. And then I met you. It made me reevaluate my life and I realized I wanted a change. Unfortunately that change is just gonna have to wait a while. I don't know, maybe if I save up enough money, I can buy myself out. But until then, I guess I'll just have to keep plugging along." She forced a bittersweet smile and sighed. "I'll survive."

It was silent for a moment but for the pattering of the raindrops of the roof of the car.

"So that's all I guess," she said, "Just add it to the list of crazy experiences you've had in your life." And for the last time, in a gesture that had become so familiar to Jack, she held up her fingers in mock quotation marks and said, "It could be that 'time back when you were with a stripper and didn't even know it.' Should always make for a great story at parties."

Jack shook his head. "It'll never be just a story, Gret. It will always be much more than that."

Her fragile smile faded. She shot forward and kissed him passionately. He put his hands on the back of her head and pulled her face to his, wanting with his kiss to somehow leave her with a part of himself.

When she finally pulled away, she held his face in her hands and tried to take a mental picture, one she would remember forever. Then her eyebrows furrowed poignantly. "I'll miss you so much." she sobbed, then quickly opened the door, slipped out, and disappeared into the rain.

CHAPTER 17

MICKEY TAKES CHARGE

The next day, Mickey pulled his cab up in front of Gino's for a couple of slices before his afternoon shift. He'd never imagined he would be driving a taxi, but since he got fired from the bar, he needed to find *some* way to make some money. For the time being, it was the best job he could find. It would only be temporary of course, and the tips were good enough for him to sock away some cash, possibly to use for community college. Jack had clearly made something of himself. So why couldn't he?

His stomach rumbled as he put the cab into park. He

hadn't eaten anything but a half of an English muffin for breakfast and he was starved. He was already looking forward to some of Gino's famous "square pizza." He liked it just out of the oven, when it was thick and moist with the cheese melted and dripping. If he had to wait for a fresh pie, that was fine. The reheated cardboard slices just didn't do it for him.

He ate in silence, washing the pizza down with a Coke and thinking about the events of the past weekend. He was happy to be back in touch with Jack, a real straight-up guy who was cool and sane all at once. Many times in Mickey's life, when he needed advice (and was willing to accept it), Jack was there to offer the so-called voice of reason. It was going to be good having him back in his life and in return, he was going to try to help his old friend piece his life back together, no matter what it took.

Mickey's thoughts were interrupted by the sight of Gino himself entering the parlor door. It was odd seeing him this time of day since he always worked nights and weekends, leaving the day shift to his employees. He caught Gino's eye and waved, but the proprietor looked away and hurriedly ducked back into his office. Mickey frowned.

There was only one worker behind the counter, and as more people began to file in for lunch, the line began to grow. The tables that weren't occupied were cluttered with trays, soggy paper plates, spilled parmesan cheese and half-finished cups of soda. The sole employee was running around in a harried state, taking orders and removing pizzas from the oven. Gino reappeared, tying on his apron, and began to prep the ingredients for new pizzas. He started by sprinkling flour onto a big rectangular tray and then dumping onto it a glistening mound of dough from a shiny, silver bowl. He kneaded it and flattened it until it filled out the entire tray. He then ladled some tomato sauce into the center and spread it out. Deftly, he tossed shredded mozzarella around the platter as evenly as possible and once he was satisfied, the whole thing went in the oven. Between making pies, he would wipe his hands on his apron, take orders, fill cups with soda, and accept the customers' pay.

Mickey hadn't seen Gino work the counter in years. He watched for a while, and when the traffic finally died down he went over to say hi. As he approached, Gino finally acknowledged him, reluctantly. There was a dark bluish crescent below his left eye and his lower lip was swollen, with a vertical scab running through it.

"Hey, Gino." Mickey said warily. "How's it goin'?" He nodded toward the counter. "Never thought I'd see you makin' pizzas again. What's going on?"

"Hey Mick," Gino mumbled. He winced in pain and touched the scab in the middle of his lip.

"Shouldn't you be out playin' golf?" Mickey asked, "Where's Johnny?"

Gino swallowed. "I had to let him go."

Mickey's brow furrowed. Johnny had been a part of Gino's for over fifteen years. "Really? What happened?"

Gino looked over to his only remaining employee and decided the kid could handle the dwindling traffic for the moment. He motioned for Mickey to follow him back toward his office. As they entered the room, Mickey detected a distinct, musty odor, typical of a space with poor ventilation. On the walls hung a multitude of black and white framed photos of various Italian celebrities. Frank

Sinatra, Joe DiMaggio, Robert De Niro, Tony Bennett, Al Pacino, John Travolta, Frankie Valli, Joe Pesci, James Gandolfini. All frozen in time and grinning widely, as if nothing could be better than to hang out with Gino in his secluded, dingy lair.

The pizza proprietor offered Mickey a chair and sat down behind his desk. From one of his drawers, he took out a bottle of anisette and two small glasses. He poured the drinks and they both lifted their glasses to say "Salute," then drank. Mickey tasted the essence of the licorice, then felt the liqueur bathe his stomach and chest with warmth. He sat back in anticipation to hear Gino's story.

The aging Italian man looked around his office forlornly, swallowed hard, and finally said, "Mick, I've had this place for over twenty years." He sighed and shook his head. "I just don't think I can keep it up."

Mickey was shocked. "What do you mean? This place is jumpin'! You barely got enough seats for everyone."

"That's not it. Business is good, it's just…"

"What, is everything okay? Someone sick in your family?"

"No, Mick it's not that, thank God." He rolled his eyes up and crossed his chest. "God forbid."

He gazed at Mickey as if debating with himself whether or not to reveal anything further, then finally said, "Listen, Mick, you're a nice kid. I always liked seein' you in my place. You're a good customer. But everything's changin' around here. It ain't *safe* no more." He touched his lip and winced again. "You see this?" He pointed to his eye. "Three punks come around here a few weeks ago and tell me I'm gonna need 'protection' from some 'bad dudes.' They tell me I gotta pay them two grand a month or they ain't gonna be responsible for what's gonna happen. I was like 'two grand a month? I barely clear that after expenses!' They just shrug and act like they don't give a shit. And they say, 'Don't get stupid and call the cops because if the wrong people find out I been squealin', things'll get worse.'"

Gino poured himself another drink and offered one to Mickey, who declined. He continued, "So now I gotta cut corners, let people go who've been loyal to me their whole lives, and start making pizza again myself. Forget about retirement. That's outta the question now." He sat back and looked at the ceiling. "It's crazy. I don't know what the heck is going on around here no more." He looked hard at Mickey now, a sad, desperate man looking for answers. "*You* spend a lotta time in the streets, Mick. You notice anything different?"

For the moment, Mickey ignored the question. He was too stunned and mesmerized by the businessman's dilemma. "Jeez, Geen. That sucks." He nodded toward the Gino's bruises. "So….is that what happened to your face? You miss a payment?"

"I guess you can say that. I wasn't ready to hand over two grand just like that. I mean, that's a lotta dough and I don't know if I should take these kids seriously. Plus I still gotta pay Johnny and the others. I just don't have it handy. So they come by a few days ago and jump me as I'm leavin' the store. All I got is about eight hundred bucks on me. They take it and then slap me around. They say next time if I don't have the whole two grand, they'll crack my skull."

Mickey rubbed his eyebrows, deep in thought. He considered Jaime, the coke dealer at the Gross-ery, then

Dennis, who had up and left so abruptly. And Bolt and the crew who had just attacked Jack and Gretta the night before. "There definitely are some new scumbags in town. Maybe it's all connected somehow."

Mickey groaned and leaned over, putting his elbows on the desk. He began to rub his face with his hands. He stopped but kept his eyes closed and thought carefully. Pointing blindly in the air he asked, "Was there a guy they said they worked for? Salazar? Does the name Salazar ring a bell?"

Gino's eyes opened wide and he pointed at Mickey's chest with gusto. "That's it!" he half-yelled and half-whispered. "Yeah! Salazar! That's what they said!"

Mickey gritted his teeth and nodded in affirmation.

* * *

The following Thursday Mickey was off, so with little to do, he idled away the early part of the day sitting on the floor between his couch and coffee table, watching mind-numbing TV. By the time he got antsy, it was already two in the afternoon and he was alone in the house. His dad was at the firehouse, the kids were at school, and his mom was out to lunch with one of her friends. They had converted the lower den into an apartment for him and he was happy to pay his parents a reasonable rent. And unbeknownst to him, it was all for his benefit. They were saving his money to give back to him later in life, if and when he decided to buy his own house. It was a kind of forced savings system the O'Learys had adopted and it was working quite well.

The apartment was a comfortable one, equipped with a bathroom, a large bedroom, and a spacious combination kitchen/living room. The kitchen was open onto the living space, so in the rare event he attempted to put a meal together, he could still see a ballgame on TV. Usually he either ordered in food or, when he wanted a nice home-cooked meal, just went upstairs and ate with the family.

Mickey was, in fact, paying his own way. That meant he could come and go as he pleased. As long as he handed over the cash to his dad the first of every month, he lived by his own rules. No one would bother him about coming in late. No one cared if he slept until noon. And he could bring in girls in the middle of the night without anyone knowing. He had his own private entrance! It was perfect.

So there he sat, on a lazy weekday afternoon, with no one around and all the freedom in the world. The window shades were drawn, the door was locked, and the television was on. And there on his glass coffee table was a small packet of white powder.

Mickey picked it up and examined it closely. His hands were trembling slightly in anticipation of the euphoria. It was a strange phenomenon, almost feeling high before taking the drug, but it happened almost every time. Mickey didn't take much note of it. He couldn't get to the coke fast enough.

He carefully pulled open the tiny zip-locked baggy and tapped out some powder onto the table, then with a razor blade cut up the coke into two parallel lines, one for each nostril. He rolled up a dollar bill and snorted up both lines. His nose burned, and almost instantly, a sense of pleasure exploded through his chest. The drug dripped from his nasal cavities down to his throat, leaving a bitter taste, but he liked it. It gave him energy. It gave him optimism. And it gave him the feeling that he could do anything in the world.

He looked over toward the window, where rays of light were peeking in from behind the shade. It was a gorgeous day. He had to get out, go for a walk, go into town, see some of the coolest people in the world whom he loved and who loved him right back. He got up, put the dollar and the baggy in his pocket, put away the razor in his bathroom cabinet, and wiped away any stray white crystals. Giving the room a once over to make sure absolutely nothing incriminating was left lying around, he grabbed his sweatshirt and denim jacket and left.

Outside, a cold front had shoved the dreary weather away and the air was now cool and breezy. The sky was a metallic blue with the brightest sun Mickey had ever seen. His eyes had yet to adjust from the dimness of his apartment and he held his hand up to block the blinding rays before putting on his sunglasses. Wisps of renegade clouds in various feathery forms raced across the sky, shepherded along the way by the strong gusty winds.

Yellow leaves freshly stripped from the trees floated around as Mickey walked down the block. He headed toward Ma's diner where he could have a cup of coffee and read the paper. Maybe he'd get the coffee and paper to go and read it on a bench at the park. Yeah, that would be nice.

He turned the corner and walked up Delaney Street toward Main. School had just ended for the day and the buses were leaving the grounds brimming with little kids, who were practically hanging out the windows. The school field was surrounded by a chain link fence, partially to keep the kids safe from the traffic, but mainly to keep them from straying. Some kids were still lingering on the playground while others unlocked their bikes for a leisurely ride home.

Mickey crossed the street and headed for the sidewalk which ran along the soccer field. He liked watching the kids since he knew a lot of them from the neighborhood and thought maybe he'd recognize a few. In the near distance, a teenager with long, blond frizzy hair leaned up against the fence. He wore baggy jeans and a dark down vest over a hooded sweatshirt. A New York Yankees cap sat on his head, twisted at an odd angle, and a clump of hair grew out of his chin, bound together by a tiny rubber band. He was a couple of inches shorter than Mickey and skinnier by about thirty pounds. A schoolboy of about 10 years old was timidly holding out some money toward him.

It was Timmy Lonnigan. Maggie's little brother!

The teenager had a smug expression as he reached out to take Timmy's money, but as soon as he noticed Mickey, his smirk vanished and he immediately turned away from the boy. He then put his hands in the pockets of his vest, lowered his head, and began walking away at a brisk pace.

"Hey! YOU!" Mickey yelled. "YO! GET BACK HERE!"

The teenager picked up his pace, but Mickey ran after him and grabbed him from behind.

"Hey! Get the fuck off-a me!" the teenager protested.

Mickey threw him up against the fence and thrust his face a mere inch from the young man's. "What the fuck were you doing back there? That's my friend's little brother."

The teenager struggled in Mickey's grip and tried to push him away. "Nothing!" he grunted. "Get off of me!"

Mickey clenched his teeth. "Not till you tell me what you were doing."

"I don't know! The kid came up to me and started asking me stupid questions. I told him to get lost." He started to reach down toward his pants pocket, but Mickey sensed it and flipped the teenager around like a rag doll so his chest was up against the fence. He then shoved the kid's face into the mesh, the metal wires pressing hard into his flesh. "OOOOWWWWW! STOP IT!" he managed through mashed lips.

With one arm behind the kid's neck, Mickey began to pat him down. He struggled to break free, but Mickey shoved him harder against the fence and spoke closely behind his ear. "Move again and I'll bash your face in."

When he was finished emptying out the kid's pockets, Mickey had found four packets of marijuana and a switchblade. "What the fuck is this, asshole? You selling this to kids?"

The teenager gasped for breath.

Mickey flipped him around and jammed his forearm up against his throat, forcing him back against the fence. "ANSWER ME!" he demanded.

"Okay, okay!" the kid gasped. "You're choking me!"

Timmy was standing there watching, completely dumbfounded. Mickey turned to him and yelled, "Get out of here! Go home! And if I catch you buying this shit again, I'm telling your folks!"

With that, the little boy bolted away as fast as his little legs could carry him.

Mickey glared back at the teenager. "What the fuck is wrong with you? The kid's ten fucking years old. You don't have enough scumbags to sell to?"

"Sorry, man. But I got no choice."

"What do you mean you got no choice?"

"My boss. He wants more sales. He says business gotta go up and he don't care how. Says to sell to kids if I got to. And I gotta come up with the money or I'm dead meat."

Mickey paused for a moment to absorb what he was hearing. "Who you talkin' about? Who's makin' you do this? Sellin' to kids?"

"This guy I know. Fronts me a buncha weed and I gotta sell it all. I get some stash for myself and make a little money, but most of it goes to him."

"What's his name?"

"I don't know his name. Wouldn't tell me."

Mickey pressed harder on his throat, and the kid made a sound like NNGUNNK!! Mickey eased up and the kid began to cough. Once he caught his breath, he cried, "Okay! Okay! Stop! Please! He'll kill me if I tell you!"

"Okay then, punk," Mickey said. "I'll make it easy for you. I'll give you a name and you just nod if I'm right. Got it?"

The teenager looked resigned. "Whatever."

Mickey examined him closely so he wouldn't miss any reaction. "Salazar."

The kid's eyes widened and Mickey knew immediately who he was dealing with. He eased off the teenager's throat and stood back, absorbing the enormity of the situation while the kid rubbed his throat in despair. Mickey frowned, rubbed his forehead, and thought for a long moment. The cocaine was still circulating through his brain and his mind was running wild. Finally, an ill-advised idea materialized in his mind, an idea that would change everything for him and those around him forever.

"You tell your motherfuckin' boss that he can forget

about doin' business around here from now on," he growled at the teenager. "Tell him...tell him The Shamrocks are running things now." Mickey nodded to himself and said, "Yeah, The Shamrocks..."

The kid continued to gasp until Mickey had had enough. "You heard what I said, right? And if I see you around here again, I'm gonna shove your head into a wood chipper. Now get the fuck out of here."

While the kid stumbled off, Mickey sat down on the curb and lit a cigarette. He took a drag and gazed ahead, deep in thought. In a voice that exhibited both wonder and disbelief, he said, "Fuck me." He then felt in his pockets for the bags of weed, and smiled.

.

CHAPTER 18

AN ILL-ADVISED IDEA

Across the street from Cunningham Park stood a large factory that had been built by the Gallagher family after the end of Prohibition. Shane Gallagher was in fact the descendent of a long line of successful ale brewers, some of whom had emigrated from Ireland back in 1937. For decades, the Gallaghers had dominated the industry, both back in Ireland and the U.S., concocting one variety of beer after another: ales, lagers, stouts, pilsners, blondes, reds, everything. People travelled for miles around just to tour the facility and sample the multitude of novel and tantalizing flavors that it produced.

The business thrived, with the majority of the profits being sent back to Ireland for proper use.

When tragedy struck in the 1950s, everything changed. Without warning, an aggressive strain of influenza ravaged the family running the American factory and the business never recovered. Anyone familiar with the nuances of the business in America died and none of the Gallaghers back in Ireland had the ability to take over. The interests of the family back home had veered toward other ventures, namely gun-running for the IRA, and they no longer had the desire to invest in brewing. The once-thriving factory was then shut down and eventually leased to various operations, all of which defaulted for one reason or another. Without tenants, the property fell into disrepair and was left vacant for long periods of time.

As a teenager, Shane was visited by his favorite Uncle Seamus, with whom he had developed a close and mischievous relationship. Seamus had taught Shane the ways of the streets in Belfast, giving him an education on how to survive amongst the toughest of scoundrels. Seamus had some ambitions of his own for America and he had a proposition for Shane, wherever it might go. He offered to pay for Shane to establish himself in America, with the idea of scouting around to find any connection with which to trade in munitions. There were no serous obligations with such an arrangement. Seamus knew his nephew had wanted to move to America for some time and wanted to help the boy reach his dream. Any connection would be a bonus.

So with a substantial subsidy from his Uncle Seamus,

Shane left for the U.S. to "be on the lookout" for anyone interested in dealing for guns. Seamus wasn't expecting much, but he kept in touch with is nephew in case something came up. So, with the family's blessings, Shane moved into the old brewery. He converted some connecting offices into a large apartment and then redesigned the south east wing into a clubhouse of sorts. It had several rooms, the largest of which had space for two pool tables, two dart boards, four poker tables, and a wet bar. This was where he and his friends spent most of their time: goofing around, drinking beer, and competing at various games of leisure.

There were two other rooms of note: a music studio that had been set up for friends belonging to a rock band, and a more private "office" that Shane used mostly to entertain young women. In this private room there were a large sofa bed, couch, recliner, coffee table, desk, and large TV. That day, Shane, Mickey, and Jack were sitting on the couch drinking glasses of beer that had been tapped from the wet bar. The stereo system was blaring the usual propaganda about how purchasing some product, which would no doubt change their lives and make all their dreams come true.

Shane got up and walked purposefully toward the tuner on the radio. "More fookin' commercials than music on this piece of shite!" he said and began turning the dial. When he came upon a song he recognized, he let go of the tuner and turned up the volume. "Oasis! That's what I'm fookin' talkin about!" It was no coincidence that his favorite band was led by two Irish brothers. He was also proud that he shared the same last name as Liam and Noel Gallagher. But more than that, he was completely taken in by the power, the passion, and the adrenaline surge the music sparked. Especially the song they were all listening to just then:

> All your dreams are made
> When you're chained to the mirror and the
> razor blade
> Today's the day that all the world will see
>
> Need a little time to wake up wake up
> Need a little time to wake up
>
> Need a little time to rest your mind
> You know you should so I guess you might as well
> What's the story morning glory...

All pumped up, Shane went over to his desk, took out a small zippered case and brought it over to the table. Mickey took his feet off the table and sat forward eagerly. Jack just remained reclined on the couch looking on with confused curiosity.

"Just like the song, eh?" Shane said, unzipping the case and pulling out a small mirror, a razor blade, and a tiny vial of coke.

Mickey said, "Yeah, I could use a little something to wake *me* up!"

Jack looked back and forth between the two of them and frowned. "Are you serious? You guys called me down here for this? I thought we were gonna talk about some important stuff. I don't got time for this shit."

Shane looked at him and chuckled, his bright blue eyes maintaining their ever-present sparkle. "Try some," he said.

"It might make you feel better. God knows, you've had a lousy week."

"Sorry, man," Jack said, "Not into it."

"Really?" Mickey said, "How come? Just a little toot and you feel like you can do anything! Makes me feel great."

"Yeah, well, not me." Jack said, "I tried it a couple of times, just to see what it was like, you know? And I get it. It feels good at first. But when it starts to wear off I don't like it at all. You can't fall asleep and your heart races non stop. Feels like a heart attack waiting to happen if you ask me. Who needs it?"

Shane and Mickey just looked at each other and shrugged. "Okay, more for us!" Shane said and began to tap out some of the white powder onto the mirror.

"Mick," Jack said, "can we just get on with it? You guys can do this later. I got tests to grade."

Mickey said, "Okay just one line. I think better this way."

"Whatever," Jack relented.

Mickey bent over, snorted up the line, stood up, then closed his eyes and breathed in deeply. He then opened his eyes and began pacing around. "Okay," he said, "So let's talk. Jack, you know a lot of weird shit is going on around here. Your girlfriend almost got kidnapped the other day and then she just disappears. Just like Stayce's friend Maria. Then I find out gangs are taking protection money from all over town. Gino the pizza guy just told me yesterday how he was being shaken down by a bunch of punks. And for all we know, Dennis from the deli was run out of town by the same people. I even caught some sleazebag selling weed to a ten-year-old kid. Right by the school!"

Jack sat forward and placed his beer on the table. "You think all this stuff is related?"

Mickey glanced at Shane, who was looking at Jack and nodding. Then Mickey looked back at Jack. "Yeah, we do," he said. "Bolt said he worked for some guy named Salazar, Gino said the gang mentioned his name, and the guy selling the weed said he was working for him too!"

Jack was at a loss for words. He stared at the rim of his beer bottle, replaying the scene from Shangri-La. In a serious and somber voice, he said, "Guys, you're not gonna believe this, but I met him two nights ago."

Mickey was about to light a cigarette, but his lighter never reach the tip. "What? Salazar?!" he exclaimed, "Get the fuck outta here! Are you sure? How? Why?"

"You're shitting us!" said Shane.

"No I'm not. He owns that strip club Shangri-La over near Portsmouth. I thought Gretta might be working down there, maybe as a waitress or something, but boy was I wrong. I went down there looking for her and one thing led to another and before I knew it I was being held captive by a bunch of muscle heads. I was lucky to get out of there alive."

"Wait a minute," Mickey said, "Start over. You actually *met* this guy? We gotta know everything, Jack. Don't leave out any details."

Jack relayed the story of how Gretta had cleaned out both his and her apartment, leaving barely a trace, and how he was able to track her down. Although he was embarrassed to admit he had no idea he was sleeping with a stripper, it made him feel better to get it off his chest. He also could sense that Mickey and Shane had some plan to retaliate against Salazar and he thought they should know everything.

"That sucks about Gretta, man." Mickey said, "I feel your pain. But tell us more about this guy Salazar. What kinda sleazeball is he?"

"The biggest," Jack said. "He was a cocky son of a bitch. He essentially told me if I ever tried to see Gretta again, he'd kill me."

"That fooker!" Shane said. "I'll fookin' kill him meself!"

Mickey looked tense. He leaned over the coke, cut up another two lines and snorted them up before Jack had a chance to protest. Apparently he was too caught up in the scenario to care.

Mickey sniffed deeply, and then wiped his nostrils with the back of his hand. He then handed the mirror to Shane. "Jack," he said, "this guy must be paying the cops to look the other way. That's the only way he could be getting away with it."

"Fookin' A," Shane said breathlessly as he sniffed some coke himself.

Mickey began pacing again, inhaling deeply and moaning with pleasure each time he breathed out. When he spoke, he gesticulated wildly with his arms. "This guy is bad news," he said, "The cops sure as hell ain't doing anything and if we don't do something ourselves, who the hell is gonna stop this creep? Hell, Jack, he's forcing your girlfriend to be a hooker! She wants out and he won't let her! Sounds like sex slavery to me. Don't you want to do something about it?"

"Fookin' A!" Shane said.

Jack looked back and forth between the two, Mickey

pacing and pleading with him and Shane bent over the mirror. These were not the types of people who should be planning a war against a man as powerful as Salazar. His chest felt cold. He held his hands out with the palms up and turned his head to the side. "Listen, guys, this dude has a lot of money and a lot of dangerous people working for him. I know Gretta's in trouble, but she made some bad choices to get there. She even told me to stay away because if Salazar ever found out I was trying to help her, she would suffer the brunt of it. And to be honest with you, I don't want to end up in the trunk of some car with a bullet in my head."

This gave Mickey some pause. He finally stopped pacing, crossed his arms and leaned his back against the wall to absorb Jack's words. His face was sympathetic, trying to understand his friend's quandary, but he wanted to address the bigger picture. "Look, Jack," he said, "I know this all sounds crazy, but I've thought about this a lot and I really think something has to be done. If the cops won't help, I want to be the one to stop this guy."

"You mean we," Shane said.

Mickey looked at Shane and smiled. He went over to him and put his hand on his shoulder. "Yeah, of course we. Couldn't do it without you, bud. I'm just sayin' what it means to me." He looked back at Jack, who seemed to be disappearing into the couch. "Jack, right now I'm nothing. I was a high school basketball star for a while and then that ended. Then I wanted to be the fireman my dad could always be proud of and that didn't happen either. Now I'm driving a cab and still living with my parents. Jack, I was meant to be much more than this."

His eyes began to well up, and he went back over to

Shane, who handed him the mirror. Two fresh lines were waiting for him on its cool silver surface. He did the lines, breathed in deep, and was happy again. "You see, buddy, I can save our town and do something worthwhile at the same time. I'll be making something of myself. I'll have a purpose again, Jack. Don't you see? It's my calling!"

"Fookin' A!" Shane said.

Jack stood up and went over to Mickey. "Dude," he said, "you can do anything you want if you just put your mind to it. Is it worth putting your life at risk just to feel like you're making a difference?"

Moved by Jack's concern, Mickey cocked his head and reached out his hand. Jack took it in a handshake and Mickey leaned into him slapping his back with his left hand. "You're such a dude," he said. "Thanks for the concern, but I've made up my mind. If you don't want to do this thing with us, I'm totally cool with it. We'll keep you out of it."

"But how are you guys gonna do this?" Jack said. "Like I said, he's got goons all over the place, not to mention some cops."

Mickey looked at Shane and said, "Your turn."

Shane's crystal blue eyes beamed. They contrasted starkly with his pale skin and black mustache and beard. He stood up, clapped his hands, and rubbed them together. "Okay, Jack, my friend. If you want to know the details, you're gonna be involved in some ways. If you don't want to be involved at all, we can't tell you anything."

Jack was torn. He certainly did not want to be in a war with a crime lord, but he was very curious to know how they would go about it and he did want to contribute in some way. "Well, what if I helped give you some advice, you know, strategies or stuff like that? It might help to have some input from outside the battle, so to speak."

Shane looked over at Mickey, who was standing with his right arm across his stomach; his right hand was holding his left elbow and his left hand was rubbing his chin. "Yeah," he said, "I like the idea. He was always a good strategy guy in basketball. Always knew the best way to attack the other team. I like the idea."

Shane shrugged and said, "Okay. Well this is the deal. Mickey and I know lots of lads who love to fight. These guys have lots of energy and they're just waiting for something to do. Some of them we all know from school and others we know from the streets. Like I said, they love to fight and if they heard some bastard was trying to kidnap their girlfriends, put their families out of business, or sell drugs to little kids, they would do anything to stop it. *Anything.* Trust us Jack, we got the people." His face shined with pride.

"But Salazar's got money, experience, probably guns," Jack said.

"I can get guns," Shane said, "I have connections back in Ireland. Me Uncle. He's been runnin' guns through Canada for years. If we can get the money, he'll send us the guns. All I gotta do is give 'im a call.

"Huh," Jack said. He stuck out his lower lip and nodded. "You sure your guys are gonna know how to use them?"

"Once we get the artillery, me uncle will send over some IRA men to give us a little trainin'. We'll take some hunting trips into the mountains, you know? Set up some war camps and have at it. Not only learn how to use the guns, but strategies, hand-to-hand combat, guerilla warfare, all that kinda shite."

Jack looked over to Mickey, who was nodding with the widest grin he had ever seen on his face.

PART 3

BACK TO PRESENT DAY

CHAPTER 19

UNLIMITED CAPACITY

Saturday Evening, October 14

Mickey practically burst through the front door when he arrived home. He had sprinted from his rental on the street and was panting in a cold sweat as he entered, anticipating the worst. His hair was in disarray and his eyes were wild with fear. But even in this extreme state of agitation, he couldn't help but be pacified by the atmosphere of his home.

The first thing he noticed was that the air was so warm.

It seemed to caress his skin and melt away all the tension he was feeling. James Taylor was playing on the stereo, his velvety soft voice telling a soothing story of friendship and comfort. And the delicious aroma of his mother's famous beef stew permeated the air, a scent both appetizing and familiar.

Mickey smiled when he noticed his little nephews playing on the floor. At first they were startled by his frantic entrance, but once they recognized their beloved Uncle Mickey, their little faces lit up with great excitement. They launched themselves at him like little torpedoes.

He had to be ready. He knew what was coming. In a survival reflex he had learned through experience, he turned his body so his hip would absorb their impact. It was a good thing he did, because they hit him with a full head of steam. It seemed to him they would purposely run headfirst like a series of battering rams into his balls, causing him to double over, so they could take him down with ease. Not this time. Protecting his family jewels, he was able to thwart their attack, battling back with tickles and noogies until the little ones were giggling out of control. The laughter had always been contagious to Mickey, and he followed suit, reveling in the joy.

"About time you showed up!" Mickey heard, and he looked up to see his older sister Katie grinning and leaning in the kitchen doorway, her arms crossed against her chest. His younger sister Meg appeared behind her, rocking little two-year-old Shannon in her arms. "Ah, the fair prince has arrived. Now we can all rejoice!"

While staving off his little assailants, Mickey grinned

and said, "And there are my two favorite ladies. Can't tell you how much I've missed the nagging."

The sisters exchanged glances and laughed. Katie said, "Nagging he calls it. Can't wait till he gets married. Then he'll know from nagging!" They both giggled and returned to the kitchen.

While Mickey was still in his nephews' grasp, he realized he desperately needed to know something. "Tommie! Is Tommie here?"

Meg called back from the kitchen. "In his room, Mouseketeer!"

Mouseketeer. As a boy he hated that nickname. It had always irritated him when his sisters called him that, but on that night, it felt just fine.

Mickey's mom appeared, drying her hands on a kitchen towel. "Come on, kids. Soopper's ready," she said. The children ran into the kitchen and she came forward to give Mickey a kiss on the cheek. "What happened? You forget it's your father's birthday?"

Mickey's surprised expression said it all. Mary O'Leary just smiled and shook her head. "Head's always in the clouds, isn't it? Don't worry," she whispered, "we have a cake and a card. We all signed it. It's in my night table in the drawer. Sign it and we'll give it to him with the cake."

"I'm sorry, Ma. You have no idea what's been goin' on and—"

She held up a finger to her lips and he immediately fell silent. She had that effect on him. "Don't worry about it, Luv. Just go get your brothers." She paused and looked at him for a moment, a little frown on her face. She took him by the chin and examined him. "You okay, child? You look a little pale."

His face turned pink and he took her wrist gently. "Yeah, Ma. Everything's fine. Don't worry about me. It's Pop's birthday. I'll go get the troops."

Still a little suspicious, Mary said, "Well, alright. Guess you'll be okay once you get a decent meal in ya."

Mickey smiled. "If that's your stew, I'm gonna be just fine."

"Of course it is. You know it's your Pa's favorite. Now go, we're all starved."

As Mickey ran up the stairs, she yelled, "And don't forget to wash your hands! That means all of ya!"

Mickey took the steps two at a time. When he reached the second floor, he took a left toward Tommie's room. Donnie, the eleven-year-old, had a bedroom down the other direction. "Donnie, dinner's ready!" he yelled as he approached Tommie's room.

"'Kay!" Donnie yelled and bolted out of his room toward the stairs. Mickey caught his eye and they both saluted each other before the little boy disappeared down the stairs.

Mickey knew exactly what Tommie was doing in his room and didn't even bother to knock. It wouldn't do any good, for the high schooler was almost never found in his room without his earphones on. It drove his parents crazy because they had to physically come get him every time they needed him. He simply never heard their calls. So he had to live with everyone just entering his room without knocking. He didn't care. The only things he ever did there were study and sleep.

Mickey turned the doorknob and slowly pushed the

door open. There his brother was, sitting at his desk with a textbook and a notebook open upon it. A desk lamp shined a bright, yellow light on his studying material, which he pounded fiercely with two pencils he was using as drumsticks. His head was bobbing back and forth, no doubt to his favorite grunge band from the '90s, but his eyes were focused on the lesson he was absorbing.

Mickey leaned in the doorway, smiling and shaking his head, much in the way Katie had done with him earlier. He took in the moment, both relieved and thrilled that everything was fine. At least for now. He went over to Tommie and pulled out one of his earphones.

Tommie looked up to complain, but when he realized it was Mickey, smiled broadly. He swiveled his chair around and leaned back. "Hey Mick, what's up?"

Mickey said, "Whatcha doin', Tommie Boy?"

Tommie pointed to his notes with his pencil. "This trig shit is killin' me. Got a midterm this week." A worried expression suddenly appeared on his face. "I think I'm gonna fail."

"Oh please," Mickey said, "you say that before every test and you ace 'em all!"

"No, seriously, they really loaded up on me this time. I freakin' hate midterms!"

"Well I ain't worried about you," Mickey said. "All you do is practice and study. So don't go telling your friends you're gonna fail because they're gonna start hatin' you when you get all A's again." He leaned over to look at Tommie's notebook and all he could see were swirling letters, numbers, and symbols. "Jeez, that stuff looks like hieroglyphics to me."

"Hieroglyphics! Nice word." Tommie said. "You learning to read books now?"

Mickey grabbed him in a headlock and started messing up his hair. "Don't be a wise-ass, pipsqueak! I can still kick your ass. I don't care how big you get!"

Tommie laughed. Then Mickey took Tommie's headphones and said, "What're you listening to now, Pearl Jam again?"

"No. Green Day this time."

"Can't go wrong with them either." Mickey put the headphones in his ears. He could picture Billy Joe Armstrong with his jet black hair, jamming out some post-punk guitar and belting out lyrics about stupid, corrupt American politicians. He listened for a moment, letting the power punk pound on his eardrums before giving the earphones back. "Good stuff," he said, "but how you can study with all that rattling in your ears, I have no idea."

"Comes with practice," Tommie said.

Just then, Donnie appeared at the door and whined, "Come on! They're gonna kill you guys if you don't get down there!"

Mickey grabbed Donnie by the waist and started carrying him over his shoulder down the hall. "Let's go, Tommie," he called over his shoulder. "We gave them enough of a head start. I'm sure they'll still complain when we eat most of the food!"

Tommie followed them down to the kitchen. When they got there, Donnie squirmed out of Mickey's arms and hopped up onto his seat at the dinner table. Everyone else was seated, the table was set and Mary was putting the finishing touches on her husband's birthday meal. Steaming, savory beef stew, warm baked bread, corn on the cob and a colorful, crispy salad.

"Look what the cat dragged in." Mickey heard and looked in the direction of his father, who was glowering back at him, one of his arms resting over the back of his seat. "Kept us long enough. Your cab get another flat tire or something?"

"Barney!" Mickey's mother exclaimed.

"It's okay, Ma," Barney said, keeping his eyes on Mickey, "I was just wondering where our prodigal son has been all day long. Were you working or just wasting more time with those hoodlum friends of yours?"

Mickey dropped his shoulders and put his hands in the pockets of his jeans. He gazed back sadly at his Dad. Rather than attempting to defend himself, he said, "Happy Birthday, Pop."

Before Barney could respond Mary moved in behind her husband and put her arms around his neck. "Let's not spoil the evening before it starts, Luv. Everyone's here now. Let's have a nice dinner." She pecked him on the cheek and he glanced up at her, the woman who had always made him smile. His tense expression melted and he patted her arm. "Your right, Hon. You're right."

"Good," she said and went back to the stove to retrieve the rest of the food.

But after Mary moved away, Barney couldn't help himself. He looked back toward Mickey as he found his seat. Mr. O'Leary then addressed Tommie without breaking eye contact with his oldest son. He reached for his napkin and snapped out the folds in the air, as if expressing some remnants of disgust. "How's the studying going, Tom?" he said, "Kicking butt on the field *and* in the classroom?"

"Yeah, Dad," Tommie said, "Trig's kinda tough, but I think I can handle it."

"'Course you can," Barney said, "You'll make a great role model someday. Unlike other people I know."

The last sentence hung in the air, until Barney finally said, "Okay, Tom, why don't you say grace."

Mary placed the salad on the table and sat down for the prayer. Tommie glanced uneasily at Mickey, but then closed his eyes, folded his hands and proceeded to thank the Lord for the meal they were about to receive. When he finished, they all said "Amen" and began to pass around the dishes in a frenzied state, their mouths watering in anticipation of a hearty, delectable meal. Being back in such a familiar, comfortable place, Mickey's charisma took over and he began to crack jokes, tossing familiar taunts at his siblings. It had been a while since they had all been together, so they welcomed his ribbing. Even Barney gave in to a few chuckles.

Relieved that his father had begun to relax, Mickey was finally able to take in the whole scene. Everyone was in a great mood. The food was delicious, better than usual, and as they ate the siblings continued to banter all evening long. There was sarcasm, laughter, and a deep, enveloping sense of contentment.

Mickey watched Tommie almost the entire time. It was unusual to admire one's younger brother. Generally it was the older one who was the idol. Maybe Mickey saw in Tommie everything he could have been himself. There was no question Tommie had it all. Good looks, intelligence, talent, charm, and most of all ambition. He was going to be a great success story someday. That was for sure. And everyone knew it. Mickey just had to see that it stayed that way, no matter what. He just wasn't sure how it all would play out. If only he had just a little more time...

CHAPTER 20

COFFEE AND SPARKS FLY
AT MA'S DINER

Sunday, October 15

Robert and Gladys Tannenbaum went out for breakfast every Sunday morning. They had several favorite eateries, and each week after careful deliberation, they set out for a warm morning meal to begin their day. If they wanted bagels and cream cheese, they chose Itzie's over on Delancy. If they preferred pancakes, and had the time to wait, they drove to IHOP. And if they were in the mood for good old-fashioned egg specials, they walked to Ma's classic kitchen style diner.

The Tannenbaums had lived in Soundview for just over thirty years, long enough to observe with sadness its moral and physical decline. They had put their children through college and seen their professional careers blossom. They were all now married and living elsewhere. Their kids had pleaded with them to move away to a nicer neighborhood, but this was their home and the only way of life they knew. They were familiar with the stores, the restaurants, the shops, and all the business proprietors. If the town had become a little rough, they could endure it as long as they remained careful. The only annoyance was that their friends no longer wanted to visit them. They were all afraid to come. This bothered Gladys more than Robert, who didn't mind one bit not having those "pain in the asses" over to the house. So they simply had to do the traveling themselves in order to socialize and decided to live with the minor inconvenience.

Gladys was a sweet little woman with a warm disposition and finicky preferences. She kept her wardrobe simple and neat. She shunned glamorous excesses and was content to age naturally, unlike the many women who fought physical maturation through facelifts and liposuction. Her mother and grandmother had ripened without interference and she preferred to do things their way. People would just have to love her for who she was and not for what some plastic surgeon could sculpt.

Robert, who shared his wife's indifference to fashion, often found himself in a world of anachronism. The style of clothing that suited him best reflected times past. He preferred polyester pants and shirts of solid bright colors, which embarrassed his grown children to no end. At family gatherings, his ensembles of lemon yellow cardigans often clashed with turquoise blue bellbottoms. And when he questioned the apparel of his sons, he never understood why he was met with such incredulity. He wondered how his kids would ever learn to present themselves without his guidance.

That particular morning, the Tannenbaums entered Ma's and were instantly greeted with the aromas of warm, buttery eggs, salted, meaty bacon, and the bitter heartiness of freshly brewed coffee. After moving their seat several times due to being too near to the door, the kitchen, the bathroom, or "loud screaming kids," the Tannenbaums finally settled into a booth, where Gladys could view the rest of the world which happened to be dining at Ma's that morning. She got a particular kick out of an obese man sitting alone and feasting on a banquet of scrambled eggs with heaping sides of ham, bacon, and sausage. He wore a tee-shirt depicting a grinning boar in a chef's hat. Under the face was the phrase "I Dig Pig." Gladys chuckled and told Robert to turn around and look. Robert briefly glanced behind him, only to return to his original position with a shrug.

Tessa came over and asked if she could get them anything to drink. She had been edgy all morning, having had little sleep the night before. Between worrying about her midterms and anticipating seeing Jack again, she had tossed and turned all night, waking up cranky and dreading the mob scene that was Sunday mornings at Ma's. She had more than her usual cup of coffee and was now jittery and wide awake, the compounding effects of the caffeine surge.

Despite her inner chaos, Tessa appeared calm and offered the warm, welcoming waitress smile that had come to be expected at Ma's. She was wearing a powder blue cotton dress that came down to her thighs and a white pocket apron to hold her order pad, extra straws, napkins, and, most importantly, her tips. She wore white Keds sneakers and her hair was held back behind her ears by a plastic blue headband. Her bangs fell forward above her stunning eyes, which were accentuated by the color of her outfit.

The Tannenbaums said they didn't need any menus, for they knew what they wanted and were kind of in a rush. They were trying to make a movie. Tessa looked at her watch, which read 10:45 AM.

"Really?" she said, "Where are you going to a movie? I'd love to find a place that shows movies so early."

Unnerved, Mrs. Tannenbaum said, "We're meeting friends out of town and seeing the movie by their neighborhood."

"Oh, how nice," Tessa said. "What are you going to see?"

"Um, we don't know yet, but it's an early show," she replied.

Tessa just nodded and smiled, knowing they were full of it and simply wanted to be given preferential treatment. "Okay," she said. "I'll do my best to put your orders through."

Gladys smiled back and said, "Okay, I'd like two eggs over medium with the yellow loose and the white all cooked. Wheat toast dark, with the butter on the side. Bacon done medium. And a Diet Coke with a separate glass of ice." She said all this somewhat self-consciously, in a sort of kind and pleading way, with her right hand face down and the fingers spread, as if hovering above an imaginary plate of food that would soon be there.

Tessa nodded and scribbled down eggs over easy, wheat toast, bacon and a Diet Coke. She poked the pen on the pad, leaving a dot, and looked over to Robert. "And you, sir?"

Robert smiled at Tessa as well. "I'll have lox, eggs, and onions," he said, "with a toasted bagel and cream cheese on the side." He paused as if for emphasis before adding, "And I like it hot." His nostrils flared and he jiggled his head as he smiled, smitten by Tessa's natural charm. His hand also illustrated the plate of food that was to come out exactly as he wanted it. He handed her back his menu and said, "I'll also take a hot cup of tea with that. Thanks, dear." It came out "thanks, dee-ah," as he flared his nostrils once again.

Tessa made no note of the man's temperature preferences, but she nodded amicably and took their menus. "I'll be right back with your drinks," she said and went to put in their orders.

After she left, Gladys raised her eyebrows and nodded at her husband. "Isn't she adorable? And sweet too. I wonder if she's single. She would be perfect for Josh, don't you think?"

Robert looked back over his shoulder at Tessa, who was getting Gladys' Diet Coke at the soda fountain. "Yeah," he said, "but don't you think she might be too young for him?"

"I don't care. I'm gonna ask her anyway." She opened her pocket book and took out her set of family pictures. "Nothing ventured, nothing gained."

At that moment, bells jingled as the front door flew open. A handsome young man with tousled blond hair, alert amber eyes, and an athletic build walked in. He scanned the room, apparently looking for someone. He was wearing a weather-worn, brown leather jacket over a dark, hooded sweatshirt, blue jeans, and casual brown shoes. The Sunday newspaper was folded under his arm. The hostess, a young girl named Veronica whose curly brown hair was tied into a thick, scruffy pony tail, came over and brought him to a booth near the door. Jack threw the paper on the table and sat down, facing the length of the diner. Almost immediately his eyes fell on Tessa and his heart skipped a beat. He saw she was busy and decided to wait until she was free. He opened up the paper and pretended to read. His mouth was dry and he began to feel warm, so he took off his jacket and hoodie. The moment the bus boy brought him a glass of water he took a deep, long drink.

Tessa had noticed him immediately. As soon as bells rang, she glanced toward the door. But though she recognized him right away, she quickly spun around and became completely absorbed with the soda fountain. After filling up a glass with Mrs. Tannenbaum's diet coke, she filled another one with ice and then went to prepare Mr. Tannenbaum's tea. She then put the beverages on a tray and set off to deliver them. She had to pass Jack on the way, and when their eyes met, she acted as if she were surprised to see him. Smiling abashedly she said, "Oh, hey! How are you?" She nodded at the drinks as she moved by and said, "Give me a sec, I'll be right back." She then hurried toward the rear of the diner.

"Sure," Jack said, admiring her as she moved away. *Is this really happening? Is this girl really interested in me?* He smiled to himself and a cool sensation briefly filled his chest. To calm himself down, he flipped to the sports section and began reading an article about the upcoming World Series. He found it hard to concentrate. He realized his hair must be a mess from the wind, so he fixed it as best he could without a mirror.

At the Tannenbaums' table, Gladys immediately asked Tessa if she would like to meet a nice Jewish boy. Before Tessa could answer, Gladys thrust a picture in her face. "He's a very nice boy…and a doctor." Gladys beamed with pride. "Just take a quick look. Handsome, don't you think?"

Tessa didn't know what to say. Anyone knowing her could easily see how flummoxed she was, and all she could do was take hold of the photo. "Um, yeah," she said, looking at the picture of a clean-cut, dapper young man with inviting grey eyes. If she were to meet him under normal circumstances, she may have been interested. But the idea of the guy's mother trying to fix him up with a stranger was a little weird. "He is cute," she said, "but um…" She looked over toward Jack. "I'm kinda involved with someone. Sorry, but thanks."

Gladys cleared her throat and put the picture away. "Will it be much longer?" she said, "We really need to be on our way."

"Should be just a few more minutes," Tessa said and moved quickly back to the front of the diner. *Okay, stay cool, Tessa. We'll have a cup of coffee and see how it goes. RELAX!* She slid into the booth opposite Jack, took a deep breath and failed to suppress her huge grin. "Hey," she said, and let out a shaky exhale.

Jack, sensing her excitement, felt an irrepressible elation. He leaned back and crossed his legs under the table, trying to appear at ease. "So how's your shift going?"

A barely perceptible thread of electricity passed between their eyes.

"Not bad," she said.

"Busy morning?"

"Yeah, this place gets mobbed on Sundays. Overwhelming sometimes. And I'm so tired. I wish I were back in bed." She said all this with her eyes both bright and wide.

Jack was a little dubious. "Rough night?"

"Yeah. Didn't get much sleep between studying and…"

"And?"

Tessa paused. Her cheeks slightly flushed and she looked out the window. "Just things. I have a lot on my mind."

"Stressin' about school?"

She returned her gaze to him. A knowing smile appeared this time, like she had a secret to share with him, but it was a secret he already knew. "Yeah, among other things."

It was Jack's turn to be pleasantly unnerved. To change the subject, he nodded at her forehead. "I see you graduated to a Band-Aid."

Tessa's touched her wound with her left hand. "Yeah," she said, "didn't want to walk around with that ridiculous patch on my head. It stings a little, but no big deal. My mom had a cow the other night when I got back from the hospital. And my idiot cousin had to tell her the whole story. I just wanted to get some sleep and all hell breaks loose." She sighed and pulled at a paper napkin on the table. "My mom can be such a pain. Everyone is so protective of me. It's so annoying."

"Well I can understand why they'd be so protective. I'm sure there are lots of people who really care about you"

"Thanks!" Tessa said, "that's nice of you to say.

Just then a DING! pealed out from the kitchen window.

Tessa began to get up. "I gotta get that. Um, can I get you anything? Coffee or something?"

"Yeah, sure. You guys have any oat bran muffins?"

"I'll check. And coffee?"

"Not a coffee drinker. I'll take a cup of tea with half and half."

"Oh, like the English have it."

"I guess so."

"Honey?"

"What?"

"Very funny. Honey?"

"No, Sugar."

Tessa grinned again. "You sure, sweetie?"

Jack laughed. "Just bring the sugar."

"Sure, be right back," Tessa said, and glided away.

At that moment, the front door swung open and a thickset, burly young man entered amidst swirling brown leaves that followed him in. He had lank, reddish hair and a stubbly beard. His eyebrows were furrowed and his lips were twisted into an intimidating snarl. After glancing around suspiciously, his gaze fell on Jack and his expression softened into muted surprise. He raised his eyebrows and lifted his chin in a silent question, but Jack just shrugged, looked around briefly, and shook his head.

Liam Cullen also shrugged, though a little disappointed, and motioned to someone outside to come in. Chris Doherty entered, shuddering from the cold and trailing in his own mini-cyclone of leaves. "What's up?" he said, rubbing his hands together for warmth. He scanned around the diner himself and said, "Any scumbags here?"

"No, just you." He elbowed Chris and nodded toward Jack. "He says nothing's goin' on." He sighed and took a menu from the counter. "We gotta hang around here anyway, so might as well get some'in' to eat." They sat down at the counter, to the right of the entrance to the kitchen.

Meanwhile, Jack got up and went to the bathroom. As he opened the door he was overwhelmed by the odors of urine and the disinfecting discs from the latrines. The acrid smell irritated his senses, reminding him of the mothballs that his grandmother used to put in her closets. He went over to the mirror and confirmed his concern about his appearance. His hair was a disheveled mess. He splashed some water on his hands and fixed his hair. As he thought about Tessa, he smiled incredulously and shook his head. A strange, yet pleasant tingling sensation began to run along his scalp. That was when he heard a crash, followed by a distressed female voice he instantly recognized as Tessa's.

* * *

As Jack was in the bathroom contemplating all the possibilities with Tessa, two more men entered the restaurant. The first one was big and muscular, with a large, hooked nose that had a ring running through it. He had a Mohawk haircut, dyed a garish aqua and about ten stud earrings in each ear. His neck and arms were covered in a tangle of tattoos. The second youth was skinny, with spiked, bleached blonde hair and a goatee. "No, wait, Bolt," he laughed in a Cockney accent, "You can't, bloke! You're daft!" His teeth were rows of rotten stumps.

Bolt immediately noticed Liam and Doherty and flashed them his new seven-inch switchblade. "You two pussies fuck with me and I'll butcher you up. Stay the fuck out of my way." While watching them closely, he grabbed his friend by the shirt and said, "Keep an eye on them, Spike." The skinny one took out a barber's razor, pointed it at Cullem and Doherty, and continued his high-pitched nervous giggle.

Bolt turned toward the rest of the people in the diner and yelled out, "Where's Ma?" As he looked from one shocked patron to another, he was met with horrified silence. He went over to a small family in a booth and grabbed the father by his shirt. He pulled him over and screamed in his ear. "Helloo-oooo! Where the fuck is Maa-aaa!?"

"I...I...I...d...d...don't know!" the poor man managed to stammer.

"Hey!" a man said from behind the counter. "What do you want? Ma's not here anymore."

Bolt shoved the family man back in the booth and turned toward the proprietor. "Who the fuck are you?" he demanded.

The man who had spoken up was middle aged and slight of build, with a balding hairline and tired, liquid eyes, one of which was beginning to twitch. His voice became choked, as he spoke quietly and apprehensively. "I'm Peter. I run the place now. What...um...what can I do for you?"

"What you can do for me is open up the register and give me what you owe me."

"Owe you? What do you mean owe you? I've never seen you before in my life."

"Well get used to seeing me now. One thousand bucks a week." Bolt smiled ominously. "Protection money."

"Protection money? What are you talking about? I don't need your protection."

Bolt came close, grabbed him by the shirt and spoke quietly into his ear. "Um, yes, you do. You're gonna need a lot of protection." His breath was foul.

"F-f-f-rom w-w-what?" Peter asked.

Bolt stepped back and grinned, revealing a chipped front tooth. "Why, from this!" He picked up a pastry stand that was sitting on the counter and threw it through one of the glass refrigerators. It made an earth-shattering crash, and several of the patrons screamed and moaned. A number of them made a move toward the door.

Tessa, who had been watching indignantly, had had enough. She was in the aisle between the counter and the tables, having just served some customers, and she moved forward. "Leave him alone!"

Bolt swung around and grinned like a letch. "Oh, what have we here? A brave little lass! Aren't you a tasty breakfast?"

Tessa stood as bravely as she could and said, "You jerks better get out of here before we call the cops!"

Bolt bent over in hysterics. "The cops?! Oh that's a good one. The cops! Fine! Go ahead, call 'em! We'll have a party! You can be my date!" He grabbed Tessa by the arm and spun her around so he was behind her. As she struggled, he put his mouth against her ear and rubbed his groin on her behind. She felt the moisture of his breath as well as its stench as he said, "You like that, bitch? You're not so tough now, are you?"

Spike was laughing at this, and Doherty was about to

make a move, but Liam held him back. Doherty frowned, but Liam just silently nodded toward Jack, who was now moving rapidly down the aisle toward them.

* * *

When Jack heard the ruckus from the bathroom, his heart leapt to his throat. He threw open the door to see what was going on. What he saw was utter chaos. Tessa was being molested while Liam and Chris were being held back with what appeared to be straight edged razor.

What the fuck??!!

Jack half-walked, half-ran at them, his emotions a boiling cauldron of unbridled fury. He picked up speed as he approached them, and before Bolt could react, he slammed his fist into his skull so hard that the whole diner could hear the smack. Bolt's eyes rolled up in their sockets and he made a choking sound. He finally released Tessa and crumpled to the ground.

She stepped back, staring with disbelief at the brute, who had only a moment ago held her in his grasp. She shuddered and made a quick spasmodic movement of her shoulders, as if to unburden herself of something revolting. Her face then contorted with rage as she stepped forward and kicked the unconscious Bolt in the side. "Asshole!" she said.

Spike was in a desperate spot. Though he was outnumbered, he couldn't let Jack get away with knocking out Bolt. He had to cut him, if for no other reason but to teach him a lesson. He yelled, "HEY YOU WANKER!" and began slicing the air with his razor toward him. Jack fell away, instinctively pulling Tessa down with him, and kicked his foot up into Spike's stomach. The British punk let out an OOOOFFF! and doubled over in a moan. Liam yelled HEY! and when Spike spun toward him, an entire boiling pot of coffee splashed into his face. It burned into his flesh with such excruciating agony that he dropped the blade, threw his hands to his face and shrieked like a little girl. He then proceeded to flail about blindly, stumbling and bumping into things until Chris grabbed him by the jacket and threw him outside.

Jack slowly stood up and helped Tessa to her feet. She then rolled into his arms and he held her there until her shivering and panting died down. During their embrace, Jack did his best to take off his brass knuckles inconspicuously. As he put them in his pocket, the other waitresses came to comfort Tessa. Liam, with a wary eye still on Bolt, put the coffee pot back and went over to talk to Peter.

"You gonna call the cops?" he asked.

Peter considered this and said, "I'm not sure. They've haven't been much help around here lately. Probably wouldn't even show up."

"Well, don't worry. Me and my mate here, we'll keep an eye on the place for ya. We'll make sure this won't happen again."

"Thanks, appreciate it. But, if you don't mind me askin, why do you care so much?"

Liam shrugged and said "Someone's gotta do something. Like you said, the cops around here suck."

Peter nodded, his mouth slightly ajar.

Meanwhile, Jack, Veronica, and another waitress led Tessa into the kitchen. "Oh my God, are you okay?! What an animal!" Veronica exclaimed. Tessa reassured them that she was fine and decided it would be best that she take the rest of the day off. She asked Jack to take her home since she didn't want to ride the bus back alone. She got her jacket and told Jack she was ready to leave.

On their way out, Jack looked over toward Liam and Doherty. "You guys okay to finish this?"

Liam said, "No problem. We're good at waste management. You know how it is."

Jack saluted them and took Tessa outside.

The rest of the diners were murmuring about the spectacle when Peter announced he was closing for the rest of the day. He apologized for the inconvenience and conceded that no one would be asked to pay their bill. Everyone then began filing out, warily side-stepping the fallen Thunderbolt.

When it was their turn to pass by, The Tannenbaums regarded him with snobby indignation. And as they hurried out the door Gladys muttered, "The service here is terrible."

CHAPTER 21

A WALK IN THE WOODS

As Jack was driving Tessa home, it occurred to him that the chaos surrounding them both was what had actually brought them together. These strange set of circumstances had not only served to introduce the two, but it was now becoming evident that a developing bond was beginning to form.

He glanced over to see Tessa staring ahead, deep in thought and quietly wringing her hands together. "You okay?" he asked her.

She breathed in deep and said, "I'll live." She looked at

him with her light blue eyes. Her face was pale in the dreary light that filtered in from the overcast sky.

She furrowed her eyebrows. "What is it with all the weird things happening around here? I mean, it just seems like every time I look up insane shit is going on. Nut jobs coming out of the woodwork, people getting robbed, fights all over the place. And the cops aren't doing a thing about it." She took a deep sigh and searched Jack's face for an answer. "I mean, don't get me wrong, Soundview has always had an edge to it, but lately it seems like everything is spinning out of control. Am I crazy or have you noticed it too?"

Jack looked ahead at the debris-cluttered streets. The wind was still blowing, and he followed he the paths of a few plastic bags that swirled ever higher into the brisk, autumn air. "Well, yeah, Tess," he said with a nervous chuckle, "Let's see, two days ago a psychopath goes ballistic at The Live Wire and today I have to cold cock some guy just to keep him from molesting you."

Tessa gasped and her hands flew to her mouth. Her pallid cheeks suddenly turned a subtle shade of rose. "That's right! You were there both times!" She gave him a playful, suspicious look. "I hope this doesn't happen every time I see you."

"Me, too. Trust me."

This got an endearing giggle out of Tessa, but even as he said it, Jack shifted in his seat. His thoughts briefly turned to Mickey's problems with Salazar, their amped up plans with the Shamrocks, and last but not least, his late night encounter with Sticks Favors. Just within the past few days he had become an uncanny lightning rod for trouble and it was beginning to unnerve him to no end. How could he make any promises to this girl? He decided he'd better tell her at least some of the truth, if for no other reason than for her own protection.

He took a deep breath and said, "To tell you the truth, though, I have heard a few rumors about the town that are pretty hard to believe."

That got Tessa's undivided attention. "Really? What have you heard?"

"Well I don't know if it's true or not, but apparently there's this drug lord who is trying to take over the town. Again, I don't have any real facts, but I wouldn't be surprised if those two guys back there worked for him. Supposedly he runs that gang of drug dealers, The Power? And now he's trying to make his presence known."

"Are you serious? You mean it could get worse? Who the hell is this drug lord? Do you know his name?"

Jack swallowed. "Not sure. I've heard many different names, but mostly just speculation. People talk, you know? And like I said, it's just a rumor. But it couldn't hurt to be more careful about where you go and what you do. I hate to say this but based on what's happened the past few days, we should be ready for anything."

"Wow," Tessa said, "I can't believe this! This is very upsetting." She shook her head and fell silent in thought. Suddenly, she gasped and sat up with a start, running her hair quickly behind her right ear. She spoke in a hurried and agitated state. "Jack, there was this drug dealer a few years back. I heard a lot of stories about him when I was in junior high. Kids were getting lots of drugs back then and my sister…" She trailed off, shut her eyes tight and hid her face with her hands.

Jack pulled over and shut off the engine. He sat with his back to the door and faced her. He wasn't sure what to do. He wanted so badly to comfort her, but all he could do was sit there and wait for her to stop crying. Finally, as her sobs dissipated, he softly said, "Tess," and gently reached over to take her left hand in both of his. "You don't have to talk about it if you don't want to."

She wiped away the remnants of her tears with her sleeve. Embarrassed, she continued to look down, but she was grateful for his sensitivity. She let out a self-conscious chuckle and said, "Look at me. I'm such a wimp. I shouldn't even care anymore. It's been such a long time." She sighed, faced him, and gave a self-conscious smile. Jack couldn't imagine the pain of losing a sibling. His heart ached for her. She shrugged. "Oh well, we all have baggage, I guess."

"Of course," Jack said with a reassuring smile. He paused for a moment and came up with an idea. "You want to go for a walk? I think we could both use a little fresh air."

Tessa considered this briefly then shrugged. "I don't see any reason why not. Sure. Where do you want to go?"

"How about the Croon's Lake? There's a bike path around it that people use for walking in the woods. What do you think?'

"Yeah, that sounds nice. It's always pretty this time of the year."

"Okay, let's do it."

Ten minute later, Jack pulled up on a side street that bordered the west side of the lake. To their left on the other side of the street was a residential neighborhood with some of the largest homes in Soundview. Many of them had been decorated for the autumn season, their front porches adorned with bales of hay, bright orange pumpkins, and all kinds of amorphous squash in various shapes and colors.

Jack got out of the car and was going to open Tessa's door for her, but she was out by the time he got to her side. There was a chill in the breezy October air, which caused her to shudder and tighten the belt of her coat. Jack reached behind her, closed the car door and placed his hand on her back. Just the idea of touching her gave him a secret thrill.

"Let's go this way," he said and guided her toward the bike trail heading north. As they approached the path, they could see the lake peeking out through the clumps of trees ahead. Off in the distance, some mallard ducks were cruising around the surface, lazily searching for food, while regal swans patrolled the area with an air of grave suspicion. In a small clearing near the lake, a man and a boy of about ten were fishing off a small pier. Jack noticed a sign post saying that it was illegal to take more than 8 "black crappies" in one day. Jack wondered how many people knew that a black crappie was a fish and was about to crack a joke, but decided to leave it for another time.

They moved deeper into the woods, and as the shadows of the canopy enveloped them, a rich vegetative aroma filled the air. The brown leaves which littered the trail crunched under their feet.

Jack wondered if Tessa was ready to talk. "Sorry I upset you in the car," he said.

Tessa raised her eyebrows. "What? No. You kidding? You don't have to apologize, Jack. I'm the one who should be apologizing, carrying on like that. That had nothing to do with you. I was just thinking about my sister and I guess with all that's happened lately, I kinda..." She stopped walking, smiled and shrugged her shoulders. "Don't worry. It won't happen again."

She searched his eyes, trying to evaluate his level of sincerity. In her experiences, she had learned that it was very difficult to read people. But she sensed a certain compassion in Jack, and though she wasn't sure why, she was beginning to feel she could tell him anything. So she decided to talk about it. She *needed* to talk about it. "Jack, about four years ago my sister Maria ran away. She left a note saying she was destined for greater things than being a caretaker for my father and that she wanted to see the world and be left alone. She told us not to look for her. We were all devastated at the time and my mom, of course, still hasn't gotten over it. Especially since my father died. I still in some ways resent her for abandoning us. But I've learned to deal with it. Life goes on, you know?"

Jack had his hands in his jacket pockets and was looking at the ground as they walked. He didn't want her to know he was already aware of Maria's story. He thought it would be best for Tessa to explain it herself, in her own personal way. Without raising his eyes he said, "No doubt about that. What other choice do we have?"

"Not much. I mean, sure we have to live with a lot of things we can't control, but it doesn't stop you from wondering what happened."

Jack kicked at a leaf which flew into the air and circled vertically before it settled back onto the ground. "So you're still not sure what happened?'

Tessa shook her head. "Not really. Sometimes my mom and I speculate about it. We called the police when she ran away but they couldn't find her. We even hired a couple of private investigators but both quit without any explanation. Personally I think it had something to do with her boyfriend."

"Really?"

"Yeah, I knew when I first met him there was something wrong about him. He was a bit older than her and he rarely smiled. I found out later on he was a drug dealer. I think his name was Frankie."

Just then, a loud rustling sound came from the trees just off the path. Suddenly a large raven emerged from the leaves and flew toward them. Jack grabbed Tessa and ducked, causing the black scavenger to veer away and land on a big wooden branch on the other side of the trail. It cawed at them in arrogance.

They looked at the bird in disbelief. "What was that?!?" Tessa exclaimed.

"Freakin winged rat," Jack said.

"Did that thing just try to attack us?"

"Probably has a nest nearby. Let's go."

Jack was flabbergasted. Could it be the same Frankie Malone who swindled Mickey? He had no idea what to say next. He was torn between the truth and the desire to protect this poor girl. After a few moments he decided that whatever was going on, he was going to be honest with her. She had obviously suffered from the consequences of Salazar's long reach, and he felt she should know as much as possible.

"I think I know who this Frankie guy is, Tess. And I think he's a big part of what's been going on lately."

"Really? You serious? Are you sure or is it just a rumor?"

Jack swallowed. His words came out slightly choked.

"I'm not a *hundred* percent sure. I sort of think it's this guy who's been causing a lot of problems around here, but I'm not positive."

"Maybe you could help me find out what happened to my sister!"

Jack's heart skipped a beat. "Tessa, listen. I shouldn't be telling you any of this. But if Maria got mixed up with the Frankie I know, I'm not sure it's a good idea to be asking a lot of questions. This guy is connected with some extremely dangerous people. The less you know, the better." He paused, looking back and forth between her eyes. "But having said that, I think you should know as much as possible because I…" He looked down and blinked a few times, as if in deep thought. "Because even though I just met you, I really care about you." He looked back at her lovely, attentive face. "More than I've cared about anyone in a long time. It may seem strange to say that, being that we just met, but…I just don't want any more bad things to happen to you." He took her hand. Then he lightly touched the band aid on her forehead. "Tessa, for what happened at the Live Wire and Ma's? I'm *so* sorry."

Her heart open, Tessa returned his gaze. She smiled subtly and squeezed his hand. "Jack, please. You can't take responsibility for the idiots in this neighborhood. It's a rough town. I grew up here. It's not the first time I've had run-ins with morons and it won't be the last. But I do know what you mean. So much has happened the past few days and… yeah, I've been in the middle of some weird stuff, but it's not your fault. If anything, you've been amazing. I mean, if you weren't there today…" She looked down. "I don't know what would have happened."

Jack said, "I don't know. I just seems like I've been some sort of lightning rod attracting these lunatics."

Tessa put a finger to his lips and shook her head. "No, Jack," she said. "It's not you. The truth is I can get a little reckless. Even though it can be dangerous, I kind of put myself in situations where I can get hurt, because I think I'm tougher than I am. I shouldn't have gotten in the middle of it at Ma's. I just thought I could handle that jerk. I just wasn't thinking. I'm the one who should be sorry for dragging you into it. I guess I thought nothing would happen to me with all those people around."

Jack nodded in understanding. "Well, let's just agree that it's nobody's fault and that we'll both be more careful. The fact of the matter is that right now this neighborhood is more dangerous than it's ever been and we can't afford to be reckless, okay?"

Tessa gave him a toothless smile. "Okay."

A strong gust of wind bent back the tree tops setting free a bunch of newly released leaves. The raven cawed again back down the trail behind them. Tessa suddenly felt tired. "Jack, could you take me home now? I think my bed is calling my name."

* * *

Shortly thereafter they pulled up in front of Tessa's house. They both got out of the car and Jack walked her up to her stoop.

Tessa searched for something to say. She looked down and moved around some pebbles with the toe of her shoe. She then glanced briefly at her front door.

"My mom's gonna wonder why I'm home so early," she said.

"Why don't you tell her that it was slow and Peter sent you home?"

Tessa chuckled. "Slow? At Ma's? On Sunday morning? No, that won't fly. That place is always packed."

"Yeah, I guess you're right. You could tell her you were worried about your midterms and decided studying was more important, right?"

She considered this for a moment and said, "I guess that could work. She might buy that." She smiled a wide grin for the first time since they were sitting together in the booth earlier that morning. So much had happened since then. "Thanks again, Jack," she said, "For everything."

Suddenly she stood up on her toes and brought his face close. He felt her soft, warm lips press passionately into his and before he could respond, she was releasing him. Through his daze he heard her say, "Call me, Jack. And let's have a *real date* next time." She waved to him from behind the storm door and then was gone.

CHAPTER 22

FRANKIE MEETS THE TASER

Friday, October 20

Bolt sat on the couch in a feeble daze. His expression was blank, and his eyes were fixed on a spot on the wall across the room. His mouth hung open and a string of drool trailed from the corner of his mouth. Although his skull was wrapped in a huge bandage, it was still evident that underneath lay a substantial indentation just above his prominent brow.

Next to him was an agitated figure whose entire head

and neck were also wrapped in gauze. He was gesticulating wildly as he attempted to speak through the bandages, in spite of his burnt, swollen tongue. In vain he tried to utter "The Shamrocks!", but all that emerged was "Thah Thrambrouth! Thah Thrambrouth!"

Victor Salazar swirled his glass of whiskey on the rocks and peered incredulously over the rim at the two sorry figures on his couch. He looked over at Frankie and said, "Is this some sort of a joke?"

Frankie was standing at attention in the middle of Salazar's den, in almost the very same spot Mickey had been a week ago. It was Friday afternoon, Salazar had just returned from the Caymans, and although he was sporting a nice Caribbean tan, he was anything but rested. His hostile takeover was struggling. And he wanted to know just what in the fuck was going on.

Salazar watched with intrigue the fidgeting mummy on his couch. Finally, he broke his own spell and said, "So Frankie, are you telling me these are two of your best guys?"

Frankie cleared his throat. "Uh, yeah. Thunderbolt there has been a terror on the streets for years. Nobody ever messes with, um, him."

"Well it sure looks like someone fucked him up now. What's with King Tut?"

"Um, well, we think someone sorta threw boiling coffee in his face."

"Uh-huh. And this happened while they were shaking down a diner?"

"We think so."

"And this was in O'Leary's neighborhood?"

"Yeah."

"Shamrocks?"

"We think so."

"Wasn't O'Leary going to shut down The Shamrocks? I mean, that's what you told me, right? That this kid was a pushover junkie and you would have him working for us in no time?"

"Uh yeah, it's just that he seems to be resisting a little…"

"RESISTING?! RESISTING, YOU SAY?! Take a look at these guys. These are two of your best guys and he's reduced them to gibbering idiots! Last time there was resistance like that, the Nazis were taking cyanide underground!"

Salazar walked over to Frankie and stood inches away from his face. His voice trembled as he spoke low and measured. "Do you have any idea how this makes me look?"

Frankie swallowed and said, "I know how it looks, but I can take care of it if—"

"Take care of it?! Are you fucking kidding me? I gave you a week to work on this punk and he's spitting in my face!" He began pacing and walking around in circles. "I should have known. I should have known when you guys brought him here that he was gonna be difficult. But I was relying on your judgment, Frankie, because you were so sure about it. 'Oh, he'll crack easy, Vic', you said. 'Yeah, he's a pushover junkie, we'll have those Shamrocks working for us before you know it.' Whatever gave you the idea that was gonna happen?!"

"*He* said it would." Frankie pointed over to George McGavin, who was sitting nervously on the couch near the two invalids. The same purple silk bathrobe hung around his portly figure, but the girls were gone and he certainly was no longer in a jovial mood.

McGavin shot up and said, "Now wait a minute, I never guaranteed anything!"

Frankie yelled, "Oh yes, you did! You told me he was a coke fiend who would do anything for it and…"

McGavin yelled back at the same time, "I'm sorry if you and your thugs can't control one punk who…"

A deafening bang rang out throughout the room, and the two frantic men flinched and froze. Victor Salazar stood holding a smoking Colt .45 pointing down at a corner of the room. The only sound left in the room was the ringing in their ears.

Salazar picked up his drink and began swirling the ice cubes around the glass. He gazed into it, peering at the tiny eddies made by his motions. He made his way over to McGavin, whose lips were quivering in fear. "I never liked you, George," he said. "I simply tolerated you because you have friends." Salazar smiled and McGavin felt a shiver down his spine. "Friends in high places. But now, you've put me in a difficult position. You've compromised my credibility. And now I have to work harder to gain back my respect, you FAT… FUCKING…WALRUS!"

McGavin said, "Now wait a minute!"

"SHUT THE FUCK UP AND DO NOT SAY ANOTHER WORD OR GOD AS MY WITNESS I WILL DISEMBOWEL YOU, YOU BLOW-HARDED BUFFALO!"

Salazar nodded to one of the guards, who shoved McGavin's bundle of clothes into his gut. Salazar smirked again, and he took another huge swig of his drink. He then breathed in deep and shot out an ice cube from his mouth, striking the police captain squarely in the forehead.

McGavin's head jerked back from the impact, which left an angry red welt above his eyes. The guards snickered sadistically, but Frankie remained silent, both rigid and aghast.

"No more freeloading for you," Salazar told the corrupt cop and moved to within inches of his face. "I never want to see you alive again. Now get your fat ass out of here!"

McGavin didn't need to be told twice. He ran out of there as fast as he could, dropping a dirty blue sock on the way out.

"Now you," Salazar said as he walked over to Frankie. He gazed at his right-hand man with sadness and regret. "What am I supposed to do now, Frankie? He looked deeply into his eyes and was almost pleading as he spoke. "You know how this makes me look, don't you? If I can't rely on you to enforce my will, you're no good to me. You understand that, don't you?"

He stopped and studied Frankie, who had been his partner in crime for so many years. Putting his hand on Frankie's shoulder, he said, "You've been a loyal and efficient soldier for a long time, Frankie. But you're slipping. And it's putting everything at risk."

He nodded the guards over to Frankie. When they grabbed his arms, Frankie began to struggle.

Salazar walked over to his desk and took out the square, black metallic object. When Frankie saw the Taser, he gasped. "Come on, Vic," he pleaded. "You don't have to do this. I'll get The Shamrocks, I swear! Just give me a coupla days and I'll have O'Leary begging for mercy. Please!"

Salazar pressed the button on the Taser and watched in fascination as the blue threads of current passed between the electrodes. He pressed the button again and again, transfixed by the small yet menacing device. "Amazing how these things work," he said.

His expression cleared and his eyes turned black again. He glowered at Frankie, who now wore a white mask of fear. Then Salazar stepped forward, and Frankie's agony could be heard echoing throughout halls of the entire mansion.

* * *

Early that Friday evening, Mickey opened the front door and peered outside. It was still light, the sun setting to the west, bathing the clouds with a pinkish hue that spilled out between the giant clumps of cotton suspended in the sky. The air was unseasonably warm for that time of year, so Mickey took off his sweatshirt. He stepped out onto the porch and searched around cautiously. Then he called back inside for his younger brother.

A few houses down the street, a desperate Frankie Malone sat in his car by the curbside. He watched Mickey silently through a pair of heavy black binoculars.

He was livid. Not only had Mickey made him look like a fool, but he was losing his credibility with Salazar. At this point, it was too risky to rely on anyone else, and he wasn't going to sit around and wait for another disaster. It was time to take matters into his own hands.

He felt oddly cool at the moment. This was a familiar routine to him. Over the years, he had stalked, kidnapped, and even killed many unsuspecting victims. Now it was exhilarating to be back out in the field, preparing to take down a target, especially someone who had disrespected him one too many times.

Tommie followed Mickey out onto the porch. They descended the concrete steps together and continued on to the curb, where they got into Mickey's Buick, fresh out of the repair shop. The windshield had been replaced, but they were still waiting for a few parts, and some dents from the night at Salazar's still remained. Frankie threw the binoculars onto the seat and winced from the pain in his neck. The angry red burns from Salazar's taser were now welting up into blisters, and throbbing discomfort gave him even more incentive to take down the O'Learys.

As Mickey's car began to roll down the block, Frankie put his own into gear and drove toward them. But before he could close in, two other cars, a blue Mustang and a silver Camaro, pulled up behind the Buick. The Camaro followed Mickey down the block, but the Mustang slowed to a crawl, preventing Frankie from keeping up with them. By the time Mickey reached the end of the street, Frankie was still stuck behind the Mustang. He tried to pass it, but every time he moved to the right or the left, the Mustang followed suit.

Frankie furiously blasted his horn, keeping his hand on it for one prolonged, irritating sound. The car in front of him then stopped altogether. Frankie rolled down his window and yelled, "Move it, motherfucker!" *I'm gonna tear this guy a new asshole*, he thought. Shane Gallagher suddenly emerged from the Mustang. His face was painted green and he was wearing a leather cap with side flaps. The hat was pulled down so low that most of his face was covered, and his dark windbreaker was unzipped halfway. He was reaching into it with his right hand as he quickly approached.

Frankie scrambled to get out, but Shane slammed his

door shut with his hip trapping the middle-aged mobster inside. "What the fuck?" said Frankie. "You son of a bitch, you don't know how sorry you are gonna be!" He reached inside his suit jacket and pulled out his gun.

Shane grinned through the door and pulled out his own gun. "Hey, you got a nice one!" he said. "Is that a Colt .45? Love those little bahsteds!" The whites of his teeth and eyes shone bright against the lime green paint on his face. On his cheek was painted a white four leaf clover.

Frankie was unnerved. In his haste to make something happen, he had forgotten about The Shamrocks. And he had lost his advantage. Before he had a chance to make a move, Shane waved his hand above Frankie's car, signaling ten other Shamrocks to swarm down upon it. They appeared out of nowhere, from out of parked cars, behind hedges and trees and shadows everywhere. There they were, all wearing ski masks and green jackets and adorned with four leaf clovers of all sizes and shapes. And they were all pointing guns at his car.

In a flash, Frankie put the car in reverse and floored it, shooting recklessly backwards. The men moved quickly away from the back of the car. Frankie put his right arm on top of the passenger seat and turned his head backward to see where he was going. As he flew in reverse, another car entered the street and they nearly collided. Frankie jammed the wheel to the right, backing over a mail box and onto someone's lawn. Then he put the car into drive, jerked the wheel to the left, sideswiped a parked car, and sped away.

One of the youths said, "Should we chase him?"

"Nah," Shane said, "we're good. Let's go tell Mickey."

With that, the youths scattered, shouting, "Shamrocks! Shamrocks! Shamrocks!" and disappeared as fast as they came.

Chapter 23

Snow White

Late Friday Night, October 20

The young woman sat at her vanity, carefully applying mascara. Not that she really needed any make-up. She had always been a natural beauty, and throughout her life she never had any problems attracting the opposite sex. Whether it was the naïve young boys in high school or, more lately, unsuspecting lustful men, she merely needed to flash a smile and they were instantly under her spell. Her jet black hair flowed in generous waves over her heart-shaped face, and her long eye lashes accentuated porcelain blue eyes that seemed to possess a hypnotic quality over men. She had milky white skin that contrasted her full, red lips, and her teeth sparkled with every mischievous grin. She was a slim 5'7", with a body that had stayed firm into her late twenties, and her proportions suited men just fine. When she shopped for clothes, she rarely needed anything tailored; even off the rack, the clothes fit the way they were supposed to when they were conceived by the designers.

Though she sometimes got a thrill from dazzling everyone with her elegance, usually she preferred to wear more comfortable clothes. And of course she couldn't help but look adorable in a sweatshirt and jeans. Sometimes it was a burden, being the object of men's desires, but she quickly learned to utilize it as an advantage to get what she wanted in life. And she wanted a lot. She had a taste for opulence.

As a teenager, she had flirted with the idea of becoming a model. On more than one occasion, an agent had noticed her natural beauty and attempted to convince her to make it a career. It seemed a distinct possibility. She began to get excited by the idea. But when her father became ill, all her ambitions came crashing down.

She had loved her father dearly. He was the heart and soul of their family, a jovial man with a tremendous amount of charisma. He would play piano and sing at parties, radiating life and joy. But he too often indulged in the pleasures of life, and his passions for drinking, smoking, and decadent cuisine led to his ultimate demise. Even after he began to deteriorate and needed living assistance, he would still smoke his cigarettes and eat his chocolate bars without heeding anyone's complaints.

His decline, and the idea of his mortality, hit his daughter hard. As he started to fade, she found it hard to be around him at all. The prognosis was grim and it was turning their once happy family life into a constant source of stress. Her home had somehow converted into some sort of amateur intensive care unit, with her mother and younger sister tending to him at all times. She soon refused to help in her father's care, unable to watch him deteriorate in front of her eyes and cope with the reality of death.

Though she may not have realized it, she had actually inherited her father's desire for indulgence. Since boys had always liked her, she found it easy to lose herself in the pleasures of sex. It helped distract her from the tensions she was feeling at home. She began sleeping around, having sex with many different partners, without any real urge for a long-term relationship. She had no interest in getting to know any particular boy, for she had seen all too well what tragedies could befall someone held dear. She simply had no inclination to give her heart to anyone. Some called it nymphomania, but she just saw it as an outlet. A hobby that provided a much-needed distraction for an emotionally strained girl.

Her behavior began to take its toll on her family, just about the time she graduated from high school. Her father was suffering from kidney failure and it was only a matter of time before he died. So her mom and her sister began to ask her to take a more active part in nursing her dad. But she just couldn't bring herself to do it. She rebelled, staying out even later, and sometimes never even coming home. She started doing more and more drugs, becoming addicted to cocaine and staying up all night on binges with people she barely knew. When her expensive habits led her to steal money from her family, she realized it was time to leave. So she ran away.

Not long after her eighteenth birthday, she met a man who had taken a keen interest in her. He said he knew lots of famous people, many of whom were photographers for high fashion magazines, and she was a rare beauty, who, once introduced to the right people, could become a top model in no time. She wasn't sure she believed him at first, but he had enough money and coke to keep her interested. He introduced her to a life of excitement and wonder. He treated her like a queen and took her out to glitzy restaurants in the richest parts of the city, always ordering the most exquisite dishes and expensive champagnes. He bought her clothes in the latest styles and took her to celebrity events where she socialized with some of the most famous people in the world. And he brought her to extravagant fashion shows and parties and introduced her to everyone as the next big star.

She was in awe. It didn't matter that no lead ever went anywhere. In the end, she never got called for a big photo shoot or for an acting audition. She just ended having sex with people posing as photographers and agents. That was fine for her. She never really had much in the way of ambition so she was content as things were. Frankie set her up in a beautiful apartment with the most spectacular view of the city, and all she had to do was have sex with him. Not a bad deal. He didn't seem to act like she owed him anything and he only came around once in a while. He paid her bills, gave her an expense account, and often left her alone. As far as she was concerned, it was the perfect set-up. She no longer had to face the cadaverous remnants of her father or the constant nagging of her mother and her holier-than-thou, self-righteous little sister. She had an exciting new life with new and interesting friends. She never looked back.

But then things started to change. Frankie began introducing her to important friends with whom she was expected to have sex. At first it was no big deal to her, since she was used to promiscuity. But some of the men began making bizarre requests. Some wanted to role-play, while others desired kinkier things. When one man asked for a hand job while wearing a baby outfit and drinking a bottle of milk, it was just too much. She called the guy a freak and threw him out of her apartment.

That night she realized she could no longer deny the fact she had become a prostitute. These men were paying Frankie to have sex with her, and the idea of being a whore hit her hard. When she confronted Frankie, he tried to calm her down. He said it was no big deal. The guy she threw out wasn't an important client. But he insisted she continue to "entertain" some of his wealthy friends. He told her not to take everything so seriously; just relax and have some fun. But when she resisted, Frankie turned a fierce, beet red and threatened her, warning that if she didn't do as he said, he would throw her out on the street. "You'll do what I tell you or you'll end up giving ten dollar blow jobs with the crack whores on Eleventh Avenue!" he snarled.

It frightened her beyond measure, the prospect of street life, but even more terrifying was the fact that she had nowhere else to go. She certainly couldn't go back home. She never even went to her father's funeral. She would never be able to overcome the disgraceful way in which she left. Given the alternative, she decided to suffer the few indignities that occasionally came her way.

One night, it changed forever. Frankie came in furious. He ordered her to strip and get on the bed. She obeyed warily, figuring something was wrong and he just wanted to have sex as an outlet. She did as she was told, but he took her violently, squeezing and hurting her, slapping her and shoving her face in the bed. When he couldn't come, he got dressed, called her a fucking whore, and marched out, slamming the door behind him.

Since then, the only time she ever heard from him was when he called on her to entertain another one of his guests. The clients began to turn on her, as if Frankie had told them it was okay, even recommended, to be violent with her. She accumulated bruises and scars all over her body. Soon, it became intolerable.

On several occasions, she had packed and then unpacked a small suitcase, wrestling with the idea of leaving completely and starting a life somewhere anew. She still had quite a bit of money left in her expense account, and lately, the tips from her clients had paid off pretty well. The problem was that Frankie would never let her leave. She made too much money for him. So she realized that at some point she was going to have to run away.

It was a dangerous prospect, the idea of trying to escape, for she knew that Frankie was the kind of man who would hunt her down, maybe even kill her if she tried to leave. The idea made her shudder. But what was she supposed to do? Her life of luxury and excitement had turned into a painful, humiliating nightmare. She felt trapped. The clients were coming more and more often now, and the brutality was getting worse. It was time to leave.

There was just one thing she needed to do before she left. In the event someone came after her, she had to be prepared. The idea of running away with no one for protection was terrifying, but at this point there was no other escape. Once she got far enough away she would feel safer, but there was no way she was doing it without a gun. So through her connections she procured a small pistol, one equipped with a silencer. The quieter the better. If something went down, she had no interest in attracting attention

She emptied out her expense account, packed her small suitcase, and was getting ready to leave when she got the call. Frankie was heading over and he was mad. She wasn't sure what he was so upset about, but it didn't matter. He was coming over and he would be there soon.

This was not good.

She couldn't just take off at that moment; she didn't have enough time. She needed a head start. As soon as Frankie found out she left, his people would be swarming the city looking for her. She would undoubtedly get caught and she didn't want to think what would happen to her then.

So she dressed up in his favorite outfit: a teddy, silk nylon stockings, and high heels, all in white, and hoped she could please him enough to assuage his foul mood. Then, when things had calmed down, she would finally leave.

She sat at the vanity and examined her face. She was paler than ever. Her stomach churned. She fought to hold her hands steady while she put on her lipstick and powdered her face. The hard life was beginning to take its toll on her beauty. Even if she wanted to stay, it was only a matter of time before she became used up. She sighed shakily and opened her drawer, from which she removed a small vile of coke and a mirror. She tapped out a small quantity onto the mirror and with a razor blade divided it into small lines. She looked one more time at herself in the vanity mirror and then bent down to do two lines, one in each nostril. She left a couple of lines for Frankie, in hopes that it would ease his mood.

She wondered what he had been so upset about. Lately she had been obedient to the clients and never mentioned that she was unhappy. She hadn't ever hinted about leaving, so what was it?

Then, a cold feeling struck in the pit of her stomach. The bank account! Was it possible he found out she took the money? He may be mean, but he wasn't stupid. He probably even checked the account once in a while to see how much money was withdrawn. His name was on the account, so of course it was possible.

She got up quickly and went over to the closet. The cash was in a bag on the floor. She had to hide it, but where? After a few moments of deliberation, she put it on the high closet shelf, pushed it into the corner, and covered it with a couple of cashmere sweaters.

She sat on the bed. What if he came in and accused her? Should she play dumb? Who knows what he would do to her to find out the truth. Torture? And what if he found the money? At the very least, she would lose the only security, the only chance for her to make a new life.

Everything was spinning out of control. Her mind kept

coming back to one grim scenario, the one and only solution that could save her. She hoped it would never come to that.

The elevator bell dinged and her heart leapt in her chest. She closed the closet door and went back over to her vanity. She heard the key push into the lock, and the door was open.

"Where are you?!" Frankie yelled.

"I'm in here," she called, singing a little to sound relaxed. She heard his heavy footfalls approach the bedroom. He entered and stared at her. It was an icy stare and it froze her to her seat. She forced herself to smile and got up. She walked over to him as seductively as she could and said, "Hey, baby, where you been? I missed you!" She put her hand on his chest and went to kiss him when he forcibly shoved her onto the bed.

"Where is it?" he growled.

He knew. The girl frowned and said, "Where's what?"

He took two quick strides and slapped her so hard, she saw a blinding flash of light. He then grabbed her by the shoulders and began shaking her violently. "Don't give me any of your bullshit! Where's the fucking money?!"

Her mind was spinning in a thousand directions, and all she could say was, "What money? Please, you're hurting me!"

He threw her down and said, "Okay, you wanna play games? Fine with me." He started to look around the apartment. Finally, he said, "I know it's here somewhere." He searched frantically through the drawers, emptying them and tossing her clothes all over the place. "So you decided to leave me, huh?" he said. "To take my money and disappear?" He came back over to her and grabbed her by the wrist. "Let me tell you something, sweetheart. Nobody steals from me and gets away with it. I mean *nobody*. Especially no two-bit tramp like you!"

He shoved her back down and went to the closet. She had to move fast. Her life hung in the balance. She reached under her pillow and pulled out the gun. As soon as she had her finger firmly on the trigger, she heard, "AHA! I knew it, you cunt! Boy, are you gonna pay for this."

He reappeared. When he saw the gun pointed at his face, his smugness dissipated. His malicious grin faltered and he just stood there stupidly, not knowing what to do next.

"Drop it," the girl said.

Frankie Malone had been in this situation before and it had always turned out in his favor. Many of his prostitutes had attempted to get the best of him, but they were always too stupid and weak. He just had to stall until the moment was right. He began to smirk. "What are you gonna do with that, shoot me? I bet you never even fired that thing before."

She didn't answer. She just continued to point the gun in his face, though her hands were trembling.

"You don't want to use that thing, Hon. You don't want to *kill* me, do you? It's okay now. I'm not mad. I just don't want you to lie to me, that's all. Just give me the gun and we'll forget the whole thing. Come on, we'll do a couple of lines and have fun like we used to."

As he moved toward her, she yelled, "DON'T MOVE! Just drop the bag and put your hands up!"

That was when he first took notice of the silencer. A thread of fear stirred deep inside of him. He dropped the bag and made a subtle move toward the inside of his jacket.

"PUT YOUR FUCKING HANDS UP!" the girl

shrieked and Frankie was shocked into obedience. He put his hands up, but not fully, his arms bent at the elbows.

She stood there, a stunningly gorgeous young woman with raven black hair and the face of a cherub, wearing a white teddy and pointing a fully loaded, silenced handgun at a notoriously dangerous criminal. She felt empowered. "Now slowly turn around, you son of a bitch!"

He did as she commanded.

"Get on your knees."

He started to sweat. "Come on, honey," he said. "You don't have to do this. Just take the money and I'll forget about the whole thing."

"I don't think so, Frankie. You never forget anything."

"You'll never get away with this!"

"I said get on your fucking knees!"

He slowly knelt and said, "You don't want to do this. You're fucking with the wrong people. You kill me and—"

The high-pitched sound of the silenced pistol went off and the back of Frankie Malone's skull exploded. His brains and blood splattered all over the room and he collapsed like a sack of potatoes onto the floor.

The girl gasped and brought her hand to her mouth. Her chest heaved and she whimpered wordlessly before she bolted into the bathroom and threw up into the toilet. After a few bouts of dry-heaving, she stood up and closed the lid of the toilet. There she sat, hugging herself and silently crying, images of her past appearing in her mind. Cooking dinner with her mom. Laughing and singing with her dad. And pushing her little sister on the swings. It was all over. She would never see any of them again.

Finally she stood up, took off the lingerie, and showered

quickly. There was no time to lose. She toweled off and put on fresh underwear, a sweatshirt, jeans, and sneakers. Then she put on her long woolen coat and grabbed both the bag of money and her suitcase.

But as her hand reached for the door handle, she stopped. She still had a chance. If she left her apartment this way, she most certainly would be sought for murder. Not only by the police, but by any one of Frankie's sleazy friends. What could she do? How could she mislead them? And then an idea came to her. Why didn't she think of it before?

She dropped her bags and ran to the kitchen, then opened one of the drawers and took out a thick roll of duct tape. She ran over to Frankie's corpse and, while holding her breath and scrunching up her face in disgust, took his two wrists and bound them behind his back. Then she cut off a small square of the tape and in the same manner placed the tape over his mouth. She ran to the bathroom, collected her white shoes and lingerie, and shoved them in a plastic bag. She put it along with the gun in her suitcase and then evaluated the scene. It would have to do.

She took her stuff, walked over to the window, and climbed out onto the fire escape. A cold wind whipped around the building, and she shuddered. Then, as quietly as possible, she descended under a veil of darkness.

And Maria Dori fled into the night.

CHAPTER 24

IN AN OUTLET OF RAGE
(A FATEFUL DECISION IS MADE)

Saturday Morning, October 21

Nikos Moustakas was worried. He felt an uncomfortable knot of fear in the pit of his stomach and he didn't like it. He *never* felt this way. In fact *he* was the type who instilled that feeling in others. Only a few times had he felt that way before, once when the orthopedic surgeon told him he would never compete in body building again.

At age twenty-four he had snapped his patellar tendon squatting four hundred pounds. After that, he was resigned to bouncing at bars and busting heads for the rest of his life. And though he enjoyed throwing beatings to drunken loudmouths, he knew he was destined for greater things.

His life had changed after one particular bar brawl. During this scrum, Nikos had lifted a juke box over his head and brought it down on top of a drunken patron. The victim ended up in a coma for a week and Nikos was soon arrested for attempted manslaughter. He thought he was doomed. He had no money and believed he was headed for a good long stint in prison.

That was, until he was visited in his cell by a man named Frankie Malone. He was sympathetic to Nikos' situation, said he had been in his position many times before and not to worry. He had new friends now. Nikos was the kind of man they needed. So Frankie posted bail for him, hired a good lawyer, and got him off with a sentence of six months probation and community service.

After his release, Frankie introduced him to his boss. Victor Salazar was a man who could get him anything he wanted. Money, beautiful women, a life of luxury, you name it. All Nicky had to do was collect some money owed to Mr. Salazar once in a while, and if the money wasn't available, throw some beatings until it was. It seemed like a dream. Like doing what he was born to do. He made lots of money, had his pick of some of the hottest women he had ever seen, and got to appease his sadistic side.

But now all that was in jeopardy. It was 10:00 AM on Saturday, and just like every morning he was bringing his boss the paper. With his heart in his mouth, he gave his familiar rap upon the door.

"Yeah, Nicky. C'mon in."

With sweat beginning to soak the shirt under his arms, Nicky opened up the door. Salazar was in his bathrobe and pajamas, sitting at his desk going over some figures. He was wearing half-eye glasses on the edge of his nose and his hair was messed up from a long night of sleep. A steaming cup of coffee sat next to his paperwork. He looked up, took off his glasses, and gave a big grin. But when he saw the look on Nikos' face, his grin immediately faded. "What's up, my man? You look like you just saw a ghost."

Nikos cleared his throat and said, "There's a problem with security."

"Why?" Salazar demanded, "What do you mean?"

Nikos swallowed. "The morning shift never showed up."

"What? *Nobody*? Are you pulling my chain?"

"No, Boss. I'd never do that. I went out to get the paper and only Carlos and Charlie were out there. I went over to Clarence at the gate and he said the night shift left, but none of the morning guys came in."

Salazar said, almost to himself, "Those were Frankie's guys." He looked up at Nikos. "You think Frankie's called them off? You think after the other night Frankie turned on me?"

"You'd better take a look at this." Nikos handed him the newspaper and left.

Salazar couldn't believe his eyes. There, on the cover, was a large picture of Frankie Malone, next to a headline that made his heart race:

Reputed Mobster Found Murdered in

Luxury Apartment

Frankie Malone, alleged underboss to the Salazar crime family, was found dead in his posh uptown Manhattan apartment earlier this morning. According to the police, he was murdered execution-style, with a bullet to the back of his head, his hands bound behind his back, and duct tape covering his mouth. Police are looking for witnesses but have come up with few leads. Most of the neighbors questioned stated they knew nothing of the incident, although one reported hearing some sounds of an argument.

For years, Frankie Malone had been suspected of racketeering, drug trafficking, and vice. Some even allege Mr. Malone had been the mastermind behind The Power, the violent gang that has been terrorizing and extorting local businesses for years.

Mr. Malone's murder poses many questions about the future of the Salazar crime syndicate, and investigators believe it may signal a challenge to the supremacy of the crime lord. Some residents of Soundview, the town under the most recent siege by The Power, hope this to be true. One local proprietor said, "I'm telling ya, I think it was The Shamrocks. Last week a coupla low-lifes from The Power came in to rob my store. Then outta nowhere come these Irish kids and beat the hell outta 'em. Not only do they give me back the cash, but they drag these punks outta my store and get rid of 'em. One of the kids had his shirt ripped in the fight and I saw a four leaf clover on his chest. The same thing happened a few days ago down by the Korean deli."

Another resident had a similar story. "My sister was walking home late with her boyfriend the other night and these three punks from The Power jump them. They knock out her boyfriend and God only knows what was gonna happen. My sister thinks they were gonna gang rape her or something. Then a car pulls up and a bunch of kids with clubs empty out. The Power see they're outnumbered and take off. I'll never forget what my sister said happened after that. One of the kids said, 'Don't you worry, love. The Shamrocks are here to protect ya.'"

Stories like these have encouraged and even empowered local proprietors. Tired of being bullied for years, one convenience store owner said, "Now it's time for these hooligans to get their comeuppance. I got me some mace, a bat, and I even got me a registered gun to protect my store. And if all this don't work, The Shamrocks will show up. Guaranteed."

The excitement The Shamrocks are stirring among the residents is evident, but investigators may need to consider the young band of Irish vigilantes in the murder of Frankie Malone, their sworn enemy. The question now is how Victor Salazar, a man feared for so many years, might deal with this group of Irish youths. Time will only tell.

Salazar sat motionless for a long time. He continued to stare at the photo of Frankie, his partner in crime for decades. The room was deathly silent but for the relentless ticking of the clock and the drumming of his fingers on the desk. One by one in sequence, he lifted his fingers then tapped them back down again. His thoughts were a whirlwind. Had O'Leary done this? Would that little prick actually kill Frankie, his most trusted accomplice and

J. M. Abrahams

biggest earner? Sure, Frankie fucked up and needed a good kick in the ass once in a while, but this?

This whole O'Leary thing had turned out to be one big cluster-fuck. Even if the snivelling punk had nothing to do with it, it didn't matter. Everyone *thought* The Shamrocks had something to do with it. The newspaper was practically fucking announcing it.

Something had to be done soon. He had to get his credibility back or he'd never be able to get capable security again. *Fucking cowards. Taking off at the littlest hint of a challenge.*

Well I'll show those Shamrocks. I didn't get here by backing down from any peach-fuzzed kid with a Swiss army knife. I've handled much bigger threats than gang leaders and I am not going to let any two-bit punk run me outta town.

He made up his mind. He pressed the button down on his intercom.

CHAPTER 25
CITY LIGHTS (THAT'S AMORE)

Saturday Night, October 21

Jack wiped the beads of sweat from his brow and looked eagerly at the clock. He was taking Tessa on a "real date" that night and he was praying it would all go well. He showered, shaved, put some gel in his hair, then threw on his best jeans, a pair of black casual shoes, and a navy and black button-down collared shirt. He sprayed on some Calvin Klein cologne, and was finally ready. He inspected his reflection in the mirror and hoped he was handsome enough for her. He thought he was decent-looking, but he never knew what was attractive to women. Over the years he had seen so many beautiful women with some very average looking guys. He guessed those guys just happened to be in the right place at the right time, lucking out beyond measure.

Or maybe looks weren't as important to women as he thought. He went into his living room and dialed Tessa. She picked up after two rings.

"Hello?"

"Hey Tessa. It's Jack."

"Hey Jack, how are you?"

"Good. So…are you almost ready?"

"Just about."

"Okay, I'm ready to leave. I should be there in about ten minutes."

"Okay, great. Just do me a favor. Call me on my cell when you're almost here. I'll come down and meet you outside. I just don't want you to have to answer a million questions from my mom. She gets really protective and she'd probably give you the third degree. Remember, my sister's boyfriend didn't work out so well."

"No problem."

"Thanks."

"So, see you in a few?"

"Yes. Looking forward to it."

"Me too," Jack said, and he smiled as he hung up the phone.

* * *

As Jack pulled up in front of her house, Tessa was

standing on the stoop, clad in a thin leather jacket which tied firmly around her waist and flared out stylishly around her hips. Her hands were in her pockets and she was leaning against the railing. She ran down the steps and got into his car. She smiled widely, leaned over to kiss him on the cheek, and put her seatbelt on. "So," she said, "where are we going?"

"It's a surprise," Jack said.

"Ooooh, I love surprises."

"Well I hope you like this one."

"I know I will."

They drove out of the neighborhood and Jack proceeded to the Long Island Expressway, headed west. Tessa began to speculate where they were going, but decided to wait before she made any guesses. She wanted to find out more about Jack. He was still something of an enigma to her.

"So, what do they have you teaching in biology these days?" she asked.

"Oh, same old stuff. I gave a class in evolution today."

"Oh, cool. I like that stuff. So what did you talk about? Darwin and the Galapagos?"

"No, to tell you the truth, that part to me isn't really that interesting. I mean, yeah, so there are all these different kinds of finches on these different islands, but so what? What I think is really cool is the 'survival of the fittest' idea. You know, how certain animals reproduce better because their traits help them survive?"

"Yeah, I always thought that was interesting too. How do you teach that?"

"Well, one example that's been taught for years has to do with these moths near London during the Industrial Revolution."

Tessa nodded, completely attentive. "Yeah, I vaguely remember that from Intro Bio. Didn't the moths change color or something?"

"Well, what happened was there were a lot of trees around there that had light-colored bark. When all that coal was burned in the mid-1800s, the trees started turning black from the soot. There were these moths, called peppered moths, that were white before all the pollution. The theory goes that when all the white moths rested on the now dark tree bark, birds saw them more easily and ate them all up. The few dark moths that existed were better camouflaged, so the birds couldn't see them, and they survived to reproduce more. Before, there had been many more white moths; after the factories sprang up, the dark moths kind of took over."

Tessa did her very best Sigmund Freud impression, which left a lot to be desired. "Hmm, veddy interestink."

Jack chuckled. "There is some controversy about how the data was collected, but the example works for me. I also give other examples of camouflage in natural selection to my students. Take for example the rattlesnake. Most of them live in the desert, where the rocks and dirt are usually brown and black, you know? That's the color of rattlers. They blend into the ground and ambush anything that comes along. Now take your typical rainforest vine snake. They live among the green vegetation and are the exact same color. They're also long and thin just like the vines, so it's almost impossible for any creature to see one unless it's moving. Unwary lizards have no chance crawling around vine snakes."

"That's so cool, Jack. I bet you're a great teacher."

"Thanks."

The expressway rose and suddenly the Manhattan skyline became visible, the skyscraper lights beginning to glitter in the early dusk. "So," she said, "going into the city? This is a surprise."

Jack just smiled and said nothing. They eased their way through the approaching tolls and descended into the Queens-Midtown Tunnel. When they re-emerged into the bustle of Manhattan, Jack headed downtown. "So," he said, "what do they have you learning in nursing school these days?"

Tessa said, "Cute. Well we did a lot of microbiology today. Basically all about viruses. Nasty little buggers."

"I know," Jack said, "those things can knock the hell outta ya."

Tessa nodded. "You got that right. I had mono a couple of years ago and I was out of commission for a month. Chills, night sweats, the worst sore throat in the world, and on top of all that, I broke out in hives all over my body."

"Yikes."

"Sorry. Too much information." She thought for a moment. "You know," she said, "if it weren't for our immune systems, we would all be eaten up by microbes in no time."

Jack agreed. "I don't get sick often, but when I do, I feel like I'll never be normal again. I lie in bed thinking I'll never be able to get up in the morning and deal with all the nonsense of everyday life."

"I know exactly what you mean," Tessa said. "So I guess when we're normal, we have to remember to appreciate it and get the most out of our days."

"Absolutely. You never know when you're gonna get sick again, and not just with viruses. You hear about tragedies every day." He looked over at Tessa. "It's really too bad what happened to your dad. It must have been very hard on you when he passed away."

Tessa looked out the window and swallowed. "It was hard. But even more frustrating because he could have avoided getting sick if he only took care of himself. I kind of blame him for all the pain he caused himself and my family."

Jack nodded. "Losing people you love is about the worst thing that can happen. And life can be very unfair. You never know when a tragedy is about to hit you. I had a couple of very close friends who I went to school with. Their names were Charlie and Rena. They were perfect for each other. I was living in a dorm with them when they met and even remember the night they went on their first date. They were both extremely health-conscious, almost to a fault. I used to mock them for never eating anything unhealthy. And of course they gave it back to me about eating so much meat and fried foods. Anyway, eventually they got married and had a little girl. At some point Rena began feeling weak and Charlie took her to get checked out." Jack shook his head. "She was diagnosed with a brain tumor."

Tessa gasped and her hand flew to her mouth. "Oh my God!"

"Yeah, she didn't last a year. It was horrible. I mean, I couldn't believe it. Here was this beautiful, sweet young girl who ran five miles a day, and she ends up with this rare incurable disease. Just unbelievable."

"Wow."

"Well, one thing Rena taught me was to savor every

good moment in your life because you never know when something can go wrong."

"Amen to that."

Jack nodded to himself and then looked over to Tessa. He took her hand and smiled. "So for Rena, let's have the best date ever tonight."

Tessa squeezed his hand and said, "It already is."

* * *

After they parked, Jack led Tessa on foot along the streets of lower Manhattan. The evening had warmed up since they left, and throngs of pedestrians moved in large masses along the avenues. Tessa noticed the crowd growing denser and moving along with them in the same direction. She hadn't been to the city in a while, and she wasn't quite sure where they were. Then she saw all the people turning around the corner of Mulberry Street. She gasped with excitement and took Jack by the arm. "Oh! Little Italy! I haven't been here in ages!" She looked at his satisfied expression and said, "Nice job! I guess with a last name like Dori, I had to like Italian food, right?"

Jack smiled knowingly. "Well, I figured the odds were with me."

"Hah!"

As they strolled amongst the crowd, Jack and Tessa took it all in. Above them, between the buildings on either side of the street, were strings of tiny white lights wrapped in streamers of red, green, and gold, They arched up in the centers to form large luminescent bells, and one after the other they hung, forming a festive cavalcade of color up and down the street. Bakeries lined the sidewalks offering a dizzying array of Italian pastries, and the sweet aromas of the cakes and cookies swirled around them as they walked down the block. Souvenir shops stood narrowly between the restaurants, offering tiny sculptures of the Roman Coliseum and colorful T-shirts with shapes of Italy in red, white, and green.

Everywhere small potted evergreens wrapped in bright red bows dotted the sidewalks, and beneath the awnings of the restaurants stood chalkboard stands on which were scrawled the specials of the day. Even the sounds conjured up images of old Italy. Mandolins and accordions played wistful romantic ballads, and both Jack and Tessa felt as if they had been whisked away to a simpler time, when serenity and romance were the ways of the world.

Finally they settled on a tiny little ristorante called Giuseppe's, where they were ushered past the maître d' stand by a little mustachioed man named Enzo. After promising them the most wonderful culinary experience they could imagine, he seated them at an outdoor table so they could enjoy the warm evening air and watch the strollers pass by. The tablecloth was checkered red and white, and the white candle in the middle emitted a warm, reddish glow. Jack suggested ordering a white zinfandel and Tessa smiled and nodded in assent.

While Enzo was getting their wine, a busboy brought some fresh bread and a tiny dish of olive oil. Jack asked for some butter and the boy returned with it in no time. The bread was soft and warm, but the butter pats were frozen solid, and Jack knew that trying to spread it on just left whole chunks of butter on a mutilated piece of bread. So he heated up the butter between his hands until it was soft enough to spread. Tessa was quite amused by this whole process and simply sopped up the olive oil with her own piece of bread and took a bite. It melted in her mouth.

The drinks came and Enzo proceeded to tell them about that night's specials. With a flourish, he described a mouthwatering array of exotic dishes that sounded so delicious, they were tempted to order everything, After naming each entrée, Enzo would ball up his fist and kiss his fingertips with an explosive opening of his hand, exclaiming, "Ah! Delizioso!" or "Mama mia! It's-a so good!" Tessa giggled, and when he was finished they thanked him and said they still needed a moment to decide.

After Enzo moved out of sight, Jack said with an ecstatic expression, "Sautéed-a-lightly with a-mushrooms and oon-ions, in a nice-a light-a cream sauce."

"Stop it," Tessa said with a laugh, "you're killing me." She looked over her shoulder for Enzo and added, "Aw, he's sweet."

"No, I like him," Jack said. "I just think it's hysterical the way they always hold up their fingers like that when describing food." He had to do it again. "Nice-a light-a cream sauce."

"Stop it!" she laughed again.

"Okay, so what're you gonna order?" Jack asked.

"I'm not sure."

"You want to order different things and share?"

"Hmm, that sounds interesting. What did you have in mind?"

"Well, how about splitting a shrimp parmigiana and a veal marsala? That way we can have something with a tomato sauce and something with a mushroom sauce."

"Sounds great, let's order. I'm starvin', Marvin!"

Jack looked at her curiously. "Surely, you didn't just call me Marvin, did you?"

"Nah, it's just an expression…and don't call me Shirley."

They both groaned at the corniness and took a much-needed drink.

Jack summoned over Enzo, and they ordered their meal. In addition to the entrees, they decided on baked clams and Caesar salads for appetizers. "Eccelente!" Enzo said as he took away their menus.

After he left, Jack said, "I always like to share different foods. I like a variety."

"Of course," Tessa said, "why not?"

"Well I've been on dates with women who had all these restrictions on what they will or won't eat."

"Like what?"

"Let's see, I've dated vegans, vegetarians, women who don't eat red meat, women who are allergic to shellfish, allergic to dairy, lactose intolerant…I even went out on a date with a girl who said food in general 'didn't appeal to her'. I think the only food she said she could eat was stuffed shells or something like that. I don't know, I think she had some sort of medical condition. She said she had been tested by a lot of doctors and they still couldn't figure out what was wrong with her."

"Sounds like a mental case to me."

"Probably. Well, anyway, I'm glad you're a normal eater."

"I don't know about that. I feel like I'm gonna pig out!"

"Don't worry, I'll be too busy stuffing my own face to notice." He picked up his glass of wine and held it out. "Let's toast," he said.

"Okay, what should we toast to?"

Jack looked deeply into her pale blue eyes and said, "To friendships with potential."

"I like that," Tessa said and clinked his glass.

They sipped the wine, relishing its blend of tartness and fruit.

"Mmmm," Tessa said, "that's good."

"Yeah, I usually have white zin with Italian food. It goes really well."

"Look at you, the connoisseur."

He shrugged his shoulders. "I dabble," he said.

Tessa looked at him for a moment, seeing him differently than she had before. Then, realizing she was staring, she suddenly put down the wine glass and reached for the bread, almost knocking it over. She caught it, avoiding disaster, and Jack said, "Nice save."

Her face turned a mild shade of rose and she said, "Sorry, I'm such a klutz. I guess I'm a little nervous. I'm not used to dating."

Jack said, "You don't date much?"

"Not really. With school and working at the diner, I really don't have much time. I mean, I go out with my friends once in a while, but dating? Let's just say it's been a while. How about you?"

The image of Gretta sobbing in his car suddenly flashed through Jack's mind. His smile faded and he winced a bit. He cleared his throat and looked away.

"Jack?" Tessa asked, "You okay?"

He reached for his drink and took a generous swallow.

"Was it something I said?" Tessa asked.

"No, uh, I just remembered something I forgot to do at work. Sorry I spaced out. What did you ask?"

"We were talking about dating." She tilted her head down to make eye contact. "You sure you're okay?"

He couldn't help but admire her genuine concern. "Yeah, I'm fine." He began to feel warm inside again. "You want to talk about dating? I could probably write a book."

"You have some good stories?"

"You know it. There are some real whack jobs out there."

"Okay tell me a good one."

"Alright, you asked for it. A couple of years ago, after a recent break-up, some friends convinced me to try one of these internet dating services—"

"Don't tell me," Tessa said. "An internet crazy."

"You have no idea. Well, this girl Lisa contacts me on the website telling me I seemed interesting and she'd like to get to know me. She had just moved back from Arizona to live with her parents and was looking to meet a nice guy. We spoke for a while and then she told me she had a confession to make."

"Here it comes," Tessa said

"Well to me, this wasn't a big deal. She said that she had had an accident when she was in Arizona. She said she lost about half of her index finger in some bizarre incident. That really didn't matter to me. She seemed nice, was cute, and lived close by. Missing part of a finger wasn't a deal breaker. So we made plans to get together. But on the night of the date, I called her to confirm and she answered all upset. Said her sister had just had a miscarriage and she felt she needed to be with her. She said her brother-in-law was a real jerk and wasn't gonna stick around to console her. He had told her sister something like, 'Why should I hang around, I'm not gonna get you pregnant tonight anyway.'"

"Oh my God!"

"I know! The guy went out to drink and play pool!"

Tessa shook her head. "Unbelievable. The guys some women choose."

"I know. Well, anyway, I said I was sorry to hear about it and she should be with her sister to support her. We agreed to go out another night later in the week. So I called her the night we were supposed to go out and she began to apologize again. She said her brother was in town for the holidays and he accidentally burned her forehead with a cigarette. She said it was bad and she was too embarrassed to see me. I wondered how bad could it be that she didn't want to see me, but she said it was really was pretty bad. I tried to convince her that it wasn't a big deal and she finally agreed to see me, though very reluctantly. So she insists on coming to my place and when I answer the door, I couldn't believe my eyes. She had this perfect circle of a burn right in the middle of her forehead and she had rubbed cover-up right into it."

"You're kidding!"

"Nope. And I gotta tell you. That burn didn't look like an accident. She tried to tell me this story that her brother was smoking a cigarette on the back porch, and she snuck up behind him to scare him. He somehow jumped, throwing his hand back and accidentally burning her forehead. But if you saw this burn, you would know it was no accident...I think some jealous ex-boyfriend must have found out that she was dating, pinned her down, and burned her squarely between the eyes."

"Oh my god!!"

"That's not even the half of it. So some time later, we go out to dinner, she drinks three vodkas during the course of the meal, and then after dinner we go back to my place. She asks me if I smoke pot and I'm like, 'Yeah, once in a while.' So she whips out this huge baggie of this bright green weed that looks really exotic. She rolls a joint and we get stoned on my terrace. This is all fine, but then she starts craving a cigarette and asks me if it's okay if she smokes. I tell her to go ahead and have one, even though I don't smoke cigarettes myself, and don't really like the smell. We talk for a while outside and then we come back in to watch some TV. While we're watching, like two or three different times she suddenly shudders violently, like she's having some memory of a really bad experience. I chose to ignore it because she was a nice girl and, I thought, I don't know, maybe I could somehow comfort her."

At that moment Enzo appeared with the baked clams and the salads. There were six clams on the dish, along with two slices of lemon and two tiny forks. They squeezed some lemon juice on them and dug in. The lemon complemented the chewy clams, which were blended with bread crumbs and flavored with butter and garlic.

As they ate, Jack continued. "So we went out a few times and I became curious about her finger. Understandably, she was reluctant to talk about it, but after a few drinks one night she told me the whole story. She said she was training to be a social worker in Arizona and was working with some drug rehab cases."

Tessa said, "I know where this is heading."

"I don't think you do. She gets a call one night which

happens to be the night of the Super Bowl. She was at a bar, having a couple of drinks, you know, her kind of drinks. Vodka on the rocks. She must have been on call or something so she had to answer the call. What she was doing drinking while on call, I have no idea. Well, now she has to go pick up a crack addict and drive her to some sort of rehab meeting. And not only is it stupid driving drunk to begin with, but what kind of message does it send to a crack addict if your sponsor or whatever she was is driving drunk?"

"I know!"

"It gets better. This girl Lisa tells me she picks up this drug addict and decides to smoke pot with her in the car! With her rehab case! So then of course she needs to go pick up some cigarettes. She drives to a gas station and leaves this girl in her car. Now here is the craziest part. When she gets back to the car, the girl is smoking crack!"

"Holy shit."

"I know. Lisa is like, 'What are you doing, put that away!' and they start struggling in the car for the pipe. The drug addict reaches into Lisa's glove compartment, pulls out Lisa's loaded gun, they struggle some more and the gun goes off."

"You've got to be kidding me."

"Nope."

"What the heck is she doing with a loaded gun in her glove compartment?"

"I have no idea, but the bullet took off half her finger and she had to have all these surgeries to repair it. It turns out there were all these complications and she ended up losing more of her finger than was expected. Poor girl. What a fiasco."

"That is some story."

"I know, I mean, even if she was making up the whole thing, that was one screwed up girl."

"So did you break up with her after hearing all that?"

"The funny thing is I didn't even get a chance to. She told me that night she wasn't really as ready for a relationship as she thought. She said she needed to be more comfortable in her own skin before she could be comfortable with anyone else."

"Huh!"

"Yeah, imagine that. Apparently, the first sane thing she ever did was break up with me. Welcome to my world."

* * *

They both started laughing and their dinners arrived. Cheered by their obvious enjoyment with each other, Enzo smiled as he laid down the food. "Be-a very careful," he warned them, "the plates, she's-a very hot." It was true. The mozzarella cheese was bubbling on top of the tomato sauce, which smothered the breaded shrimp, and the veal was still sizzling amidst the mushrooms in the marsala sauce. They wasted no time and began to eat. Enzo was right. It was one of the most wonderful culinary experiences they had ever had. Neither could remember a dinner tasting so good.

"So," Jack said, "tell me about some of your dating disasters."

"After that story? Too much pressure!" She thought for a moment and said, "I don't think I have any soap operas to tell, but I have been out with my fair share of morons. Like, there was this one guy who when I told him I wanted to be a nurse asked me why anyone would want to clean the shit off of old people."

"Are you kidding?" Jack exclaimed, "What an idiot!" He shook his head. "Hey, that reminds me of a friend of mine who's a special education teacher. She said she went out on a date with some guy once and he asked her over dinner what it was like working with retards."

"Sounds like the same guy," Tessa said.

"Yeah, that would be something, huh? What did he do for a living?"

"I don't remember. After he made that crack, I was like 'Check please!'"

"Huh," Jack said, "so all these guys were rude like that?"

"No, not all rude, but just kinda boring. I haven't really met anyone worthwhile until…" She stopped herself.

Just then, a group of men on the street began to sing. There were a couple of musicians, one playing the accordion and the other the mandolin. They sang "That's Amore," the Dean Martin classic from the '50s. Some of the diners joined in with enthusiasm:

When the stars make you drool just like a pasta fa-zool

That's amore

When you dance down the street with a cloud at your feet

You're in love

When you walk in a dream but you know you're not

Dreaming signore

Scuzza me, but you see, back in old Napoli

That's amore

Tessa took full advantage of the distraction and turned to watch the musicians.

"I love this song!" she said and began to sing. She turned back to Jack, who did his best to sing along as well. Normally, he wouldn't find much enthusiasm for such a song, but with Tessa there, it was easy to get caught up in the romance.

But he was dying to hear what she was about to say before. When the song ended and everyone finished applauding, she turned back to face him all aglow. "So," he said, "what were you about to say before the music started?"

"Oh," she said and cleared her throat. She looked around for Enzo and said, "Could we get more wine?"

"Sure," Jack said, and caught the waiter's eye. He ordered two more glasses and then decided not to push her. "You sing pretty well."

"No, I don't. You're just saying that."

"Should I tell them to come over here to serenade us?"

"No, that's okay. It would be kind of weird with them right on top of us."

"Yeah, I know. They would start to sing "Bella Notte" and it would feel like that scene out of Lady and the Tramp."

"Then you would have to roll a meatball over to me with your nose."

He laughed at that, and his eyes sparkled at her easy sense of humor. He couldn't remember meeting a girl so witty.

She smiled at him and said, "Jack, what I was about to say before was that you're so different from all the guys I've met. You're fun to be around...and thoughtful. Ever since I met you, you've been really considerate. That means a lot."

Jack shifted in his seat. "Thanks. Appreciate that."

The wines came and they both took another much-needed drink.

Tessa kept gazing at him analytically. "I mean it," she said. "But you're also an interesting guy...and funny."

"Well thanks again. And while we're at it, let me say that you're one of coolest girls I've ever met. You're brave and smart and considerate yourself. You're also not stuck up and selfish like most of the girls I've dated. And that's surprising to me because..."

"Because what?"

He gazed at her in astonishment, as if he were attempting to contemplate some of nature's wonders, like shooting stars or giant waterfalls. "Because you're just about the most beautiful thing I've ever seen."

Tessa's eyes widened and she looked away for a moment. When she spoke, her voice was quiet and raspy. "No one's ever said that to me before." She looked back at him. "My sister was always the beautiful one and I was the tom boy." She shook her head slowly and held his gaze. "Wow."

He slowly reached across the table and smiled easily. "Well it's what I think."

She squeezed his hand and said, "Then that's all that matters, isn't it?"

* * *

They finished their dinner and Jack left a big tip for Enzo. Tessa gave the waiter a big kiss on the cheek and thanked him for a wonderful experience. Enzo, somewhat abashed, waved to them as they left and said, "Grazie, signore, signorina! Buona sera!"

341

They both waved back and said, "Buona sera!" in utterly unconvincing Italian accents.

They strolled back down Mulberry Street arm in arm, leaning close to each other and taking in the sights. They stopped to get a batch of zeppolis doused with a thick coat of powdered sugar. With each bite, powder ended up on their faces and they had fun wiping it off each other as they moved along.

They found their way back to the parking garage and Jack drove them home. In the car, Tessa hummed "That's Amore" quietly to herself, which made Jack smile. They were home just before eleven. Jack walked her to her door and there they stood again, after another emotional interlude.

Tessa looked thoughtfully up toward her house and then back to Jack.

He started to say, "I had a nice time—"

She cut him off by firmly pressing her lips against his. This time she lingered there, and Jack had time to kiss her back. He pulled her body close to his and they smiled as they kissed, a profound and unfamiliar passion coursing through them. It was a feeling of surprise, a longing feeling that, now having a chance to express itself, seemed to want to persist forever.

The porch light turned on and Tessa suddenly broke free. She had a desirous expression on her face, not wanting to leave but knowing it was time. "I'd better go," she said.

Jack held her hand a moment longer and said, "Okay, I'll call you."

"You better."

"I will. Don't you worry."

She smiled and said, "Okay. And Jack?"

"Yeah?"

"As you're falling asleep tonight, do me a favor."

"What's that?"

"Thank your friend Rena for me."

CHAPTER 26

THE ELECTRIFYING CHARGER

Saturday October 28

It was a cool and bright Saturday in October, with a crisp breeze lazily rustling through the trees. The sun angled sharply toward the west, bathing the landscape with its warm autumn rays, creating a spectacular explosion of orange, crimson, and gold. And as the leaves danced in the autumn air, twisting and turning in a kaleidoscope of color, the sun waved a bittersweet goodbye to those who shared its days of summer warmth. It wasn't a sad departure, but a gesture of appreciation for time well spent. And as it waved farewell in the distant horizon, the sun shimmered in a grand finale of radiance, blaze and hue.

At this moment, however, few were distracted by this landscape of beauty. A high school football game was being played, much closer than anyone had anticipated; and an excitement, almost tangible, electrified the air. The first place Treemont Tigers had been expected to rout the visiting Soundview Chargers, but a tough fought, down-to-the-wire battle was unfolding between the divisional rivals.

The crowd watched with breathless anticipation as Soundview launched one last desperate drive. The Chargers were trailing 17-13 with thirty seconds left in the game, and forty yards stood between them and the winning score. Up until that point, the Chargers had battled remarkably, but the Tigers were a much bigger and more physical team. They had dominated the league the entire season and weren't about to let anyone beat them in the waning moments of a game. Not on their home field. And definitely not The Chargers.

The Tigers were confident and cocky, but the Chargers had a weapon; a force to be reckoned with. And the weapon was slowly taking over the game. A gladiator, standing six foot one with one hundred and ninety-five pounds of pure chiseled muscle, Number 88 was fast and strong and had the surest hands the league had ever seen. Even at the age of seventeen, the player knew he had been meant for the game, and dedicating himself completely, had pledged to become the best wide receiver the world would ever know.

The Tiger fans were on their feet howling and whistling, urging their defense to stifle the Chargers' last-ditch attempt.

The brass band played disjointed and out of key while the cheerleaders hopped and danced with youthful exuberance.

The Chargers huddled to call the next play. Number 88 leaned in, hoping for his number to be called. But there was some time left on the clock and the coach wanted them to move a little closer to the end zone to increase their chances of a score. The play was to be a hand-off to the running back, a sweep toward number 88's side to the right. 88 would be blocking, a task he enjoyed, though not as much as catching touchdowns. But he was ready.

The huddle broke and the quarterback walked up to the line of scrimmage, surveying the field. "Blue 23! Blue 23!" he called. "Hut! Hut! HUT!" The ball was snapped and there was an instant crashing of pads and helmets. The players grunted like primordial beasts as they battled each other and a deafening roar rose from the stands. The quarterback took the ball, rotated clockwise, and handed the ball off to the speedy running back, who headed toward the right. Number 88 faked as if he were running out to catch a pass near the sideline, and his defender followed. But after a few steps, 88 stopped dead in his tracks and the defender's eyes widened. Before he could react, 88 plowed so hard into his chest that it lifted his body off the ground and onto the turf.

With his own defender already knocked out of the play, 88 moved back into it. A speedy, bulky linebacker was hurriedly pursuing the ball carrier. The linebacker was so intent on tackling the running back that he never saw 88 bearing in. 88 bolted toward him and unloaded such a vicious hit that it knocked his opponent's helmet right off. This gave the running back enough room to spring ahead. He tried to get out of bounds to stop the clock but he was brought down by another defender. It was a nice gain of fifteen yards, but the clock was still ticking. The quarterback desperately yelled for everyone to get up to the line. They got into formation and got the play off, but by the time the quarterback could throw the ball out of bounds to stop the clock, the clock had dwindled to five seconds.

Now they were close enough for their signature play. Everyone knew they were going to number 88. He lived for these moments. He could almost feel himself conjure up a razor-sharp concentration and unmatched ability, where nothing in the world could stop him. If the ball were thrown anywhere near him, he knew he would catch it.

The quarterback just had to get him the ball. Dan Logan was an average passer at best and his accuracy sometimes faltered. But on this play it wouldn't matter. He only needed to get the ball close. His intended target was huge with the arms of an octopus.

The huddle broke again and number 88 lined up to the right. The defense knew what was coming, so they put two guys on him, with a safety in the area as well. Number 88 smiled and before he put in his mouthpiece he said, "Hey, boys! Want to go for a run?" and got ready. He stood up tall, his left leg forward and his right back. With his arms hanging down, he cocked his head to the left, watching the quarterback and waiting for the signal. Dan Logan yelled, "Red 16! Red 16! HUT!" Number 88 hitched right, but the defenders didn't take the bait. They knew he was headed for the end zone. He bolted toward the center of the field, angling toward the goal line. The defenders followed closely. 88 knew it was going to be a difficult play between three defenders, but he had the size advantage and his terrific hands.

The quarterback faded back to pass, but a defensive lineman broke through the scrum to his left and forced him to run out of the pocket to his right. He spotted 88 and launched a pass deep toward the back of the end zone. As the football flew out of his hands, however, even *he* knew it wasn't a good pass. The momentum was forcing the ball to the right. Number 88 and his three defenders were moving to the left toward the goal posts. But the massive receiver picked up the flight of the ball before the others. He was looking over his left shoulder and saw the ball was headed just behind his path. *Jesus!* 88 thought and he instantly twisted his body counterclockwise. He reached back with his incredibly long left arm and was barely able to tip the ball up in the air. With that, he swung his hips around 180 degrees, dancing his legs around so he could reach the ball without so much as breaking his stride. After tipping the ball up, it arced away so he now had to dive for it. With outstretched arms, he got his fingertips on the ball as he lay almost horizontally in midair, and was finally able to pull it into his body, with his toes just inside the line. Securing it to his chest, he finally fell out of bounds.

It was the most spectacular catch anyone had ever seen. The home crowd was stunned into silence and lost among the pandemonium of the Charger faithful. The loyal fans jumped and screamed, raising their arms in the air and hugging each other while the players and coaches of the Chargers ran onto the field. They all wore expressions of pure amazement and joy. Pom-poms and popcorn flew toward the sky and shrieks of incredulous glee rang all around.

Number 88 was swarmed by his teammates. They tried to lift him on their backs, but he was just too big. He took off his helmet and yelled, "Yeah, Baby! Woo-Hoo!" surprising many of the Treemont crowd. For this massive warrior, this huge, dominant unstoppable force was none other than a freckle-faced teenage boy.

As he bounced away with his teammates, the crowd began to disperse. The bleachers thinned out, leaving only a handful of remaining spectators. Among them were two middle-aged men seated apart, yet both with the same expression of wonder. Each one was thinking the same thing: that they had discovered some sort of hidden treasure. They took out their pens and began to write. The scout from Florida State University wrote, "Incredibly talented and poised for a 17-year-old. Great size and speed. We could use him." The one from Notre Dame simply noted, "Scholarship material. High priority" and closed his file.

The only other person in the stands after the two men left was an attractive young woman with bleached blonde hair, a small nose, and light freckles. Her eyes were very clear and her pupils were largely dilated. She sniffed, rubbed her nose, and moved her gaze from the exiting Charger players to a picture in her hand. It was a team photo of the Chargers, and there, circled in the group of young athletes with his wide boyish grin, was number 88, Tommie O'Leary.

* * *

That evening, Tommie was running around trying to get dressed. His hair was still wet from the shower, and with only his pants and socks on, he was rummaging through his closet looking for a suitable shirt. His ride was about to show up, so he was in no mood for distraction. But his older brother was being a pain in the ass.

"Forget it, Mick," he said, "you're not coming."

Mickey was leaning in the doorway. He appeared to be relaxed and nonchalant, but his appearance belied his true feelings. "Why not?" he laughed uneasily. "What's the big deal? Your friends all love me."

Tommie paused in his hunt for the perfect ensemble and frowned. "Don't you have your own friends?" he said. "Why all of a sudden do you want to hang out with us?" He took a shirt out of the closet, sniffed it under the arms, shrugged, and began to put it on.

"What's wrong with spending some quality time with my kid brother?" said Mickey. He looked down the hall as if to see if anyone else was listening and then leaned forward to speak quietly. "Don't worry," he said, "whatever happens at the party stays between you and me. Shit, after that catch you made today, you deserve a few beers."

Tommie was now sitting on his bed, bent over tying his shoes. "Thanks, bro," he said without looking up, "but seriously, I just want to hang out with my friends tonight. Alone."

Mickey was starting to feel anxious. "Well at least let me drive you there."

Tommie sat up abruptly, his cheeks flushed. "What's wrong with you? You've been acting weird all week. Every time I look up, you're in my face. It's like you're following me around and it's starting to creep me out."

They both stood there for a moment looking at each

other until a car horn sounded from the front of the house. Tommie grabbed his jacket and started for the hallway. As he passed his older brother in the doorway, Mickey grabbed him by the arm. "Come on, Tom. Don't be like that. Listen, I'm sorry. I know I should be giving you your space. It's just that I don't want you to get into any trouble right now. One little mistake can screw up your entire life. Believe me, I know."

"What are you talking about?" Tommie said. "Oh, that's it. You think I'm gonna screw up and ruin my football career. Like what happened to you with basketball? That ski accident?"

"Well...sort of."

"Don't worry. I can take care of myself. And besides, it's just a party. I'm not going skiing."

"But that's just the thing. It all can fall apart any time, any place. *Especially* at parties. Believe me, I know from experience. People get drunk and stupid. I just want to make sure it doesn't happen to you."

A glimmer of appreciation and amusement lit up Tommie's face. "Look, thanks, Mick, but I can't live my life with my big brother up my ass all the time."

The horn honked again and Tommie said, "I gotta go."

With that, Mickey pulled his younger brother to him, closed his eyes, and hugged him tightly. When he spoke, his voice came out rough and unsteady. "I can't tell you how proud I am of you."

Tommie hesitated and then hugged him back, somewhat startled by his brother's sudden affection. "Thanks." He laughed, a little embarrassed, and started down the hall. He got halfway to the stairs when he paused and looked back at his brother. "So what are you gonna do tonight, then?" he asked

"Who, me? Don't worry about me. I'll figure out something... but thanks."

"Why don't you go drinking with your friends or something?"

Mickey smiled, grateful for his brother's concern. "I probably will."

Tommie's gaze shifted between the floor and Mickey several times before he said, "You know it's got nothing to do with you, right, Mick? You know I think you're the best."

"Sure."

"I just want some space."

Mickey swallowed and managed a bittersweet smile. His arms crossed, but he raised his right fist and said in a voice that was barely above a whisper, "Go get em', kiddo."

The horn honked once again, this time in a prolonged blast. Tommie said, "Gotta go! See you later!" and bolted out of the house. Once he was out of sight, Mickey's chest tightened and he went into action. He took out his cell phone and made a quick call. Shane picked up immediately. Mickey said, "I'm not driving him. We gotta go with Plan B."

"You got it, Mick," Shane said. "Same as before, 'cept Tommie goes with Danny and Matt."

"Right. I'll ride with you once they take off. Everything in place?"

"Yep."

Mickey approached the front door and looked out. He saw Tommie get in Dan Logan's car, which idled for a few moments before leaving. That gave the lead car time enough to pull out in front of them and head toward the party.

Dan's instructions were to keep a close distance between them and the lead car, as well as going slow enough for the rest of them to follow. It seemed easy enough, kind of like driving in a funeral procession, but keeping Tommie oblivious to everything wasn't going to be easy. He was as observant as they came.

They drove for fifteen minutes until they came to the town of Treemont, where earlier that day Tommie had made his game-winning catch. It had become a tradition over the years that the team hosting the football game also hosted a party that night. Since the parents had gotten wise to the tradition, it had become harder to find a suitable venue, so the kids looked for anyone they could to host the parties.

This year, the event was being hosted by a preppy kid named Winchester Harrington III. He was better known as Chester around the school and was in high social standing, in no small part because he typically had the best drugs available. He attorney father and anesthesiologist mother were prominent members of Treemont's elite and had the house to show for it.

The weekend of the party, Chester's parents were on vacation; his mother with her boy toy in the French Riviera and his father gambling and boozing with high society hookers in Las Vegas. The loose arrangement between Mr. and Mrs. Harrington made for a comfortable relationship between the two of them, but it made for a toxic one with young Chester. Despite his limitless trust fund, he was growing up apathetic and bitter. Their little separate vacations were going to cost them a lot more than they expected this time. He was going to trash the house just for fun. Maybe, he thought, that would finally get their attention.

The security procession for Tommie arrived at the party around 9:30. Cars were parking up and down the street as scads of high school kids emerged carrying cases of beer up toward the house. Dan Logan, Tommie, and Patrick parked and followed the rest of the kids up to the bash. Danny and Patrick were on alert, scanning the crowd for anything unusual. They had been briefed over and over again by Mickey and Shane; they knew how much was at stake. Tommie had been their friend for as long as they could remember, and the idea of anything happening to him was almost as horrible as it was to Mickey. It was also a chance for them to make a huge contribution to The Shamrocks and build up their reputation within the gang.

Mickey and Shane pulled up shortly after and watched the three of them disappear into the house. Both got out of Shane's blue Mustang, with Shane speaking into his walkie-talkie to position his men and Mickey lighting up a cigarette and leaning on the car.

Mickey assessed the sprawling house in front of him and was reminded of the mansion owned by Salazar. He couldn't believe Frankie had been murdered. He had asked Shane if a hit had been ordered, but Gallagher had assured him that The Shamrocks hadn't been involved. Shane would never have made such a big move without consulting Mickey, anyway. And it wouldn't even have made sense to kill off Malone because it would only serve to make matters worse.

Victor Salazar was nothing if not vindictive.

So it remained a mystery.

Frankie's death confounded Mickey to no end. It raised

so many questions. If The Shamrocks didn't kill him, then who did? Was there another war going on between Salazar and someone else? Was Salazar angry enough at Frankie's failures to kill him himself? Or could it have been some sort of personal vendetta taken upon Frankie by someone unknown?

But most importantly now, how did it affect Tommie's safety?

Whatever the case, Frankie was dead and many of the people in Soundview believed it was the work of The Shamrocks. Would Salazar think that as well? If he bought the media's speculations, then he too would likely have thought Mickey was responsible. Mickey shivered at the thought. If that was the case, there was no limit to what Salazar might do.

Mickey took a drag from his cigarette and breathed out shakily. He hadn't eaten a good meal in days and a complete lack of sleep was putting him on edge. Every night the past week he had lain awake in bed, tossing and turning, until giving up on sleep altogether, binged on coke until dawn. It was in this manic state that he had devised all his ideas for protecting Tommie, but he had still yet to figure out how to deal with Salazar. He decided to have a talk with Jack. Jack was always good at solving problems.

CHAPTER 27

A NIGHT OF STARS AND STROBE LIGHTS

Saturday Night, October 28

That evening, Jack drove to pick up Tessa for a night of dinner and dancing. They had been speaking on the phone all week, telling each about their secrets, their hopes and dreams. They had long conversations, often lasting until the wee hours of the morning, and usually they hung up unawares they had been on the phone so long. It was like their connection was limitless, immune to the constraints of time, whisking them both away to a place where only their own rules applied. And it was there, they wanted to stay. They joked about how the time flew when they spoke, and were both looking forward to the weekend, when they could actually spend some time together.

By the time Jack headed out, it had gotten much colder. And as the dusk faded, chasing the daylight away, the stars began to glitter like streaks of diamond dust spanning across the sky.

When Jack arrived, Tessa was once again waiting for him on the front porch. She was standing in the shadows, and he couldn't help but notice her charming silhouette. She had on a dark woolen coat this time, fitting just like her leather jacket; tied firmly around her waist with the edges flared stylishly over her hips. And she wore dark leggings with calf high, black suede boots.

She ran down to the sidewalk, a hint of a smile on her face and got in the car. As she sat down and closed the door behind her, she grinned and said, "Hey!" But before he could decide how to greet her, she simply leaned over and kissed him on the lips. He was both startled and thrilled. Not only did he love the feeling of her mouth against his, but the mere fact that she kissed him in such a familiar way solidified the idea that they were now indeed a couple. Or at least on their way to being one. He wished he had been ready for the kiss, but aware it was now permissible, was already anticipating the next opportunity. It was difficult to hold back a grin.

"Hey," Jack said, "You hungry?"

"Famished." Tessa said. "Where we going?"

"I figured we'd stay local this time. There's a Chinese place down near the dance club. You like Chinese food?"

"Sure, I could go for that."

"Yeah this place is nice. It's quiet and the food's pretty good."

"Which one?"

"Tang's."

"Oh, I know that one. The one with the green sign. They have great sesame chicken."

Jack looked at her with mocked suspicion. "You reading my mind?"

Tessa laughed. "Yes, I have zoned in on your frequencies." She widened her eyes, wiggled her fingers at him like a sorceress and said in a deep, accented voice, "You are now under my power. You will buy me lots of expensive things." She then burst out laughing.

Jack gave her an amused, mocking glance and said, "Well…..maybe around the holidays."

"Great," Tessa said back in her normal voice. "I like jewelry."

"I'll keep that in mind."

Jack drove to Tang's and found a parking spot. He got out and opened Tessa's door with one thing in mind: to get closer. Taking her by the hand, he guided her out of the car and closed the door behind her. She was pleasantly surprised by this gesture and they walked arm in arm all the way to the restaurant. Inside, they were greeted by a young Chinese girl who took two menus and brought them to a booth. Nearby was an artificial koi pond, equipped with its own automatic waterfall. The restaurant was both welcoming and warm, with *Guzheng* music playing softly from speakers all around.

On the walls were traditional Chinese murals, a menagerie of tigers, dragons, and sword-wielding warriors on horses. At tables heaped with aromatic dishes, families enjoyed their dinners respectfully and quietly, their conversations weaving together into a trance inducing murmur.

The hostess said someone would soon take their orders, and handed each a menu. Moments after she left, a bus boy came to pour them both a glass of water and some hot tea. A skinny, middle aged Chinese man with a bad comb-over came to take their drink orders. He had a heavy Chinese accent and wore black horn-rimmed glasses. They both opted for cokes, Jack having a regular and Tessa, a diet.

After the waiter left for their beverages, Tessa looked around and said, "I always liked this place. It's kinda cozy."

"Yep," Jack agreed, "Food's good too. So, what are you havin'?"

"How about the sesame chicken?"

"Okay. What else?"'

"Well I picked something," Tessa said, "now your turn."

"Hmmm, okay. How about some garlic shrimp?"

Tessa nodded. "Yeah, good idea. Compliments the sweetness of the chicken."

"Listen to you," Jack said, "Miss connoisseur of dining."

"Nope," she said, "Just reading your mind again."

"Oh, right. *The sorceress.* I better guard my thoughts better."

"Um, not gonna happen."

They both chuckled and the waiter returned with their drinks. His English was basic and his accent was strong. He said, "Your order?" But it sounded more like "Yaw awdah?"

They requested their entrees, along with a side of roast

pork low mein and a couple of wonton soups. The soups came in no time and they immediately dug in. The broth was hot and salty and the wontons were meaty and tasty. It warmed their insides.

"So," Jack said, "How did the mid-terms go?"

Tessa crinkled her nose. "Ugh, I'm so glad they're over. If I had to study for even one more exam, I'd pull my hair out."

"That would be kinda painful."

Tessa laughed at that, and Jack stole a moment to admire the disarming color of her pale blue eyes. Her complexion was smooth, with a tinge of cream, and the bemused, inquisitive expression of her eyebrows added to her appeal. She was wearing a light blue and black plaid skirt, with a tight, black long-sleeved sweater that was cut in a low arc, revealing just a hint of cleavage. The only jewelry she wore were tiny, silver lightning bolts that dangled lightly from her ears. He suddenly realized he was staring at her and cleared his throat. "So you think you did okay?" he asked.

"Yeah, I think so. I mean, I don't want to sound conceited or anything, but I know most of this stuff already. Remember, I had lots of experience helping with my Dad. I used to go on-line and read up on nursing, so I kinda have a head start on all the other students."

"I'm sure you did great. Good luck with the results."

"Thanks. So how was your week? Have you been giving mid-terms yourself?"

"Yeah, it is that time of year for us too. I'm hoping my students did well. I collected a bunch yesterday, but didn't grade them yet. I'll go through them tomorrow night."

"I always get most of my work done on Sunday nights too. Not much goin' on, so why not be productive?"

"Yeah, Sunday nights are weird. Everyone's just sitting around waiting for the week to begin. It's like we need that break to recharge. A sort of limbo, you know?"

"You got that right, kiddo!"

Jack smiled, but then it faded and he looked away. Tessa noticed the sudden change in his demeanor. "You okay?" she asked.

Jack looked back at her, a little embarrassed. "Oh, yeah," he said. "Sorry, I was just thinking about my best friend. He calls people "kiddo" all the time and you reminded me of him. He's going through a rough time right now."

"Is he the guy who you were with at the pool tournament? At The Live Wire?"

"Yeah, his name is Mickey. Really good guy. We go all the way back to elementary school. Twenty-something years, you know? You can make new friends all the time, but the ones that stick with you your whole life? There's just no comparison."

"The closest person I have like that is my cousin Ashley."

Jack smiled. "The one that nearly kicked the crap out of Sticks Favors?"

"Yep, that's my Ash! She's very protective of me."

"Yeah, I kinda noticed that at the hospital."

"Oh that's *right*! I forgot about that! Don't worry. She's cool now. I've been keeping her up to date on you. She knows you're behaving."

The waiter took their empty soup bowls and delivered the main courses, announcing each dish as he placed them on the table. They weren't disappointed. The pieces of sesame chicken were tender and juicy, sautéed to a golden brown and doused in a honey glaze. The shrimp were large and smothered in a spicy brown sauce and tossed with chopped broccoli, onions, and mushrooms. They served each other and also took a healthy helping of roast pork lo mein, the side dish of tasty, long brown noodles.

"So what's going on with your friend? Is he sick or something?" Tessa asked.

Jack looked at her while chewing and considered how much she should know. She was so sensitive and considerate that it had become harder and harder to keep her in the dark. He decided to fill her in. "No, nothing like that. But it's kinda scary. Some pretty dangerous people have been threatening his family and he's got to figure his way out of it."

Tessa's eyes widened. "Threatening? How so?"

Jack sighed. "I'll tell you, but you *cannot* tell a soul. It's a very tense situation. I'm not sure how to handle it myself."

She showed him the palm of her hand and said, "Scout's honor, lips are sealed and all that."

Jack smiled. "Okay, remember those punks that were causing all that trouble at Ma's?"

"Uh, yee-ah. I kinda recall one holding me in a bear hug."

Jack leaned forward and gestured for her to come close. He smelled her perfume as she leaned in toward him.

"Well," he said quietly, "you know that drug dealer I was telling you about the other day? They work for him. In a gang called The Power. Bunch of idiotic goons. They've been harassing store owners for money, selling drugs to kids and kidnapping young girls, most likely for sex slavery."

They both sat back slowly, Tessa frowning as she thought

it over. Jack looked around to see if anyone was listening. Finally, Tessa spoke quietly. "But what does this have to do with Mickey?"

Jack nodded. "A while back Mickey and a bunch of guys formed this sorta vigilante gang to keep Soundview safe. The cops weren't doing anything about The Power and Mickey thought he could help. It's been working well for a while. Now this, this creep wants to control Soundview more than anything, and he's trying to force Mickey into convincing his gang to join forces with The Power. The problem is, there's no way in hell Mickey's gang would go for it. They're protecting their families for God's sake. And Mickey would never do it anyway."

He reached for his soda and took a sip. "So now this guy's threatening Mickey's family and it's turning into an all-out war."

Tessa was intrigued. It amazed her that such a struggle of power could be taking place right here in her own town. She frowned as she tried to picture the scene from Ma's. "I don't remember much about what happened on Sunday. It all happened so fast. But there were two guys who helped us at the diner. One of them threw a pot of coffee. And he had a tattoo on his arm. A four-leafed clover, actually. I saw it. Are they in Mickey's gang?" She was visibly excited now and seemed extremely eager for his answer.

Jack nodded. "Yeah I know those guys. They're members of Mickey's gang.

Tessa gasped. "You mean Mickey started *The Shamrocks*?"

He scanned the restaurant once again for any listeners. He looked back at her, widened his eyes, and nodded again.

Tessa shot forward, slapped her hands on the table, and exclaimed, "Holy shit!" The noise drew some attention and when Jack shot her a reproachful look, her face reddened. She lowered her voice. "Sorry about that." She scanned the restaurant herself before saying, "*The Shamrocks*? I mean, wow. Those guys are like heroes. I wasn't even sure they existed. I've heard stories but…wow, that's just unbelievable." She fell silent for a moment and then gave a Jack a suspicious look. "So are you in The Shamrocks too?"

"Not my thing," Jack said. "I mean I'll always be there for Mick, and I'm not afraid to fight, it's just…I'd rather not make it a habit."

Tessa gave him a bemused smile. "Well you certainly punched that guy's lights out at Ma's."

"Let's just say the idea of some sleaze bag abusing you gets me all riled up."

"I'll say," Tessa said, "You really came through for me." She frowned for a moment. "So what about going to the police?" she asked, "Couldn't they do anything about it?"

"Highly doubt it." Jack said. "You've seen what's been going on around here, right? More crimes taking place than ever. Notice any cops around? It's like they're all on a permanent vacation."

Tessa said, "And I bet this drug dealer is paying for it."

"Seems that way."

"So what's Mickey gonna do?"

"I'm not sure. He seems to have a plan, but I'm concerned about his state of mind." He paused, but before he could stop himself he blurted it out. "He kinda has a bit of a drug problem."

"Really? With what?"

Jack hesitated but it was too late. He rolled his eyes up to the ceiling and sighed. "Sorry, Mick," he said. He then looked back at her and said, "It's cocaine."

"That's the stuff that screwed up my sister." Tessa shifted uncomfortably in her seat. "What about you? I mean, you must spend a lot of time with Mickey. Do you do coke too?"

Jack raised his eyebrows. "Me? Nah. I mean, I tried it a few times a while back but I'll never do it again. It feels good at first, but it seems like once you start, you never have enough. Then it takes control of you. I never liked that. I could never let a white powder consume my life." He shook his head and thought of Mickey in one of his manic states. "And it makes people crazy. They start doing it every day, blowing all their money and then when they can't buy anymore, they start stealing money from their families."

"I remember all of that with my sister."

"But the worst thing of all is it can kill you. Cocaine addicts die of heart attacks all the time. Makes you wonder why so many people do it."

"I know, Jack, but addiction dulls the senses. People are rarely rational when they need to get that high."

"I guess you're right. I wish I could help Mickey but he has an extremely strong personality. He's as stubborn as you get, and when he doesn't want help, there's no convincing him."

"Wow, he's got a lot to deal with right now. No wonder you seemed distracted."

"The drug problem's been going on for a while. It's this new thing with Salazar that I'm worried about."

"Salazar's the drug dealer?"

Jack rolled his eyes, getting increasingly frustrated with

himself. "Jeez, I'm telling you too much." He smiled at her and reprimanded, "Stop being so easy to talk to!"

Tessa laughed. "Sorry. Ashley says I shoulda been a psychiatrist."

"Probably! Anyway, please. We never had this conversation. For your own safety, mention this to no one." He paused for a moment, not sure whether to say more, then decided to press on. "Yes, that *is* the guy's name. Listen, I know Mickey and The Shamrocks can beat this guy. But I'm worried that in his current state, he could be making bad decisions. It's hard enough for *anyone* to hold it together in a time like this, let alone someone hooked on drugs. I'm just afraid someone's gonna end up getting hurt."

"Have you tried to help him?"

"Yeah, but he wants me to stay out of it. Usually I would be fine with that. I never got too involved in the gang thing. I was always kind of an advisor. You know, like Robert Duvall in The Godfather?"

Tessa smiled. "Yeah, Tom Hagen. The consigliere."

Once again, she surprised him.

Tessa pointed to herself with both index fingers. "Come on, with a last name like Dori? I used to watch The Godfather movies with my dad all the time."

"Sorry," Jack said, "none of the girls I've dated ever watched The Godfather."

"Don't tell me. They only liked sappy romantic comedies, right?"

"Yep. Too funny. Anyway, he's been really stubborn about me staying out of it. He doesn't want me to get involved."

"Well, how persistent have you been?"

"It hasn't been easy…and he hasn't exactly been playing fair."

"What do you mean?"

"He keeps telling me not to waste my time with his problems… and to spend more time with you instead."

Tessa was visibly moved. "I think I like this guy," she said almost to herself. "Yeah, I think like him a lot."

"He's a likeable guy. I just wish I could do something for him; to make this all go away."

Tessa said, "Wouldn't it be awesome if we could just snap our fingers and everything went back to normal? Like I Dream of Jeanie? I actually used to pretend I was a genie when I was a little girl." She started to play with her napkin. "Too bad it my wishes rarely came true."

Jack thought for a moment and then said, "Life can be so overwhelming, you know? I mean, every decision you make, every action you take changes things. Hopefully you make the right choices most of the time, but it's the bad ones that really get to you in the end. And you could even have the best of intentions with your decisions and *still* end up spending the rest of your life with regrets."

"Absolutely."

Jack contemplated something then asked, "Tessa, do you ever dream?"

"Hmm, yeah, sometimes. But I usually forget about them when I wake up. How about you?"

"I have the wildest dreams all the time. Must be my over active imagination. I should keep a pen and paper next to my bed because some of the things that happen in my dreams are the wackiest things ever."

"Tell me about one."

"Well the other night I dreamed I was looking for my car and couldn't find it. Then I saw it parked by the curb. When I approached, it took off backwards, really fast. Like it had somehow become possessed and no longer wanted any part of me. It just kept darting all over the place, you know, like a phantom? So bizarre. Then I'm searching around for all my friends and I can't find a soul. Another car pulls up in front of me and they're inside. They're all laughing and making fun of me. Just having a blast. Then they motion for me to get in."

"Okay…"

"But then I notice they're all pale and grey and not breathing. Sorta like cartoons. I hesitate and they become exasperated. They tell me to stop being a wimp and try to convince me to get in. They say being dead is the best thing ever. They can do anything and never get hurt. Eat anything and never get fat. Have sex and never worry about getting someone pregnant or catching VD. There's no accountability. No regrets. No consequences."

"Yeah, but Jack. You would be dead."

"I know, but the idea of being worry-free just seems extremely appealing to me right now."

"It usually does."

"It *sucks* having to carry our problems with us our entire lives. They build up and it's like we're dragging around this huge bag on our shoulders that just gets bigger and bigger until it finally weighs us all down."

"Well, yeah. A lot of people have trouble handling their problems. But most of us figure out *some* way to deal with it."

"Well what do *you* recommend?" Jack asked.

"Find people to help carry your bags."

That gave Jack pause. "Huh…well when you put it that way, it all sounds so easy. Just help each other out. Could it just be as simple as that?"

"Yeah, I think so."

"I'm not so sure. It sounds good, but it really only works if you have good people around you. That's not always the case. And you also have to be willing to *let* them help you."

"That's true."

"If only it *were* that simple. I mean, I know there are great people out there. It just sometimes seems impossible to find them, and people end up only having themselves to rely on. Paul McCartney once said, 'Boy, you gotta carry that weight, carry that weight a long time.'"

"I know," Tessa said. "But John Lennon said, 'All you need is love.'"

And smiling, she reached out to take his hand.

* * *

They ordered ice cream for dessert. Jack suggested one of them have vanilla and the other have orange sherbet so they could split it up into a mix. They both enjoyed the way the citrus of the sherbet cleansed through the creaminess of the vanilla.

They opened up their fortune cookies and Jack suggested they read their own out loud and add "in bed" to the end of each one. Tessa was skeptical, but after Jack insisted she joined in. Tessa's fortune read "You will soon meet the President of the United States," and Jack's said, "You will climb high mountains and explore deep crevices".

It was too hard for them to keep a straight face. By the time they paid their bill and made their way outside, the maitre'd, two waiters, a waitress and several diners thought them both mad. As they walked through the parking lot, tears were rolling down their faces and their stomachs began to hurt. It was an old, familiar sensation, laughing out of control, and both of them felt out of practice.

When they got to the car, Jack leaned back on the passenger door and pulled Tessa to him. He took her by the hands, pulled her close, and put his arms around her waist. Their hips met and she put her hands around his neck. Their faces came close, but Jack held back, just briefly to take in the moment. Then he moved his hands up her back to move her closer. He gently brushed his lips up against hers, feeling the heat of her firm, young body, and then they kissed. They drank each other in as if to quench a thirst that had been denied for far too long. It was as if they wanted to devour each other right there in the parking lot.

The door to the restaurant opened and a family with children came out. Tessa pulled away and cleared her throat, somewhat disarmed by her own passion. She stepped back, but kept Jack's hands in hers. She breathed in deeply and then as she exhaled said, "Okay! Why don't we go check out that dance club?"

Jack laughed and said, "Yeah, that was the plan, wasn't it?"

Tessa smiled and looked at him askance. "Yeah, let's try to stick to the plan. The night's still young." She looked up at the sky and said, "Why don't we walk? It's a nice night. You think you can keep your car here?"

"Yeah," Jack said, "they won't chain me in."

So they walked down the street, hand in hand in the direction of the club. Jack's gait was a little awkward at first, the result of their little heated interaction, but he dealt with it as best he could, hoping Tessa wouldn't notice. *The things guys have to deal with*, he thought.

Tessa, meanwhile, was captivated by the sky. "Look at all the stars!" she said. "I don't remember seeing so many before!"

Jack had noticed too. "Yeah, it reminds me of all the times I went camping when I was a kid. I used to lie on my back in front of my tent long after everyone else went to sleep. Sometimes I would actually fall asleep there and everyone would wake me up in the morning thinking I was crazy."

"Too funny."

"Yeah, the mosquitos loved it when I came around!"

Tessa continued to look up as they walked. "So many of them! My God, it's so hard to believe that the sky is so endless. You ever think about those things? That we are so insignificant in the grand scheme of it all? I mean, we are so tiny compared to the rest of the universe and our time here is just…just like a zillionth of a second compared to all eternity."

Jack was amused. "This sounds like the kind of conversation you have when you're stoned," he said.

"Well, maybe. But it's still true. Doesn't it make all of our problems seem so insignificant?"

"Yep. Sometimes I wonder what it's all about. You know, what's the point of our being here?"

"You mean the meaning of life and all that?"

"Kinda. I've thought about it a lot and there seems to be only one thing that makes sense to me."

"What's that?"

"Well, whether or not we like it, the fact is we're all born to live and die. We all came from the same place, we're all here together and we're all going back to the same place when we die. Just at different times. Whether or not birth is the beginning and death is the end is a matter of opinion. I don't know much, but I do believe the only thing we can *really* control is our own behavior. Sometimes that can make the biggest difference of all."

"You may have a point."

"I'm starting to think so. It feels like the only way we can really make a difference is by somehow making world a better place." He noticed Tessa's expression and he cleared his throat self-consciously. "Yeah, I know it sounds like something a beauty queen might say, but it's true. And I never said it was easy. Some people you really want to avoid. But it *is* possible. Just put a smile on someone's face and you've made a difference. I don't know, call me crazy."

Tessa stopped walking, moved in front of him, and took both his hands. "Well you know what Jack?" she said.

"What?"

"You make a difference to me."

* * *

By the time they finished their after-dinner stroll, it was nearly ten o'clock. They had walked slowly through the town, stopping in the soda shops and candy stores that stayed open late on the weekends hoping to lure in patrons for dessert. Jack and Tessa got a kick out of all the Halloween decorations in the windows and even contemplated trying the holiday pumpkin flavor that was featured at the ice cream parlor. Wisely, they abstained and continued on to their destination.

The dance club they were going to was called "Pulse". It was known for its '80s New Wave music and for their DJs, who spun a lot of underground industrial music on Saturday nights. The place drew all sorts of people, from groups of young kids looking for fun, to whacked-out social misfits. All kinds were welcome there and it was often worth the trip just to see what kind of strange characters funneled in.

I took fifteen minutes for Jack and Tessa to get inside the club. Standing in the cold, Jack wrapped his arms around Tessa's waist and nuzzled her neck, while she leaned back into him for bodily warmth. He was so caught up in her, he took no notice of the group of young girls smoking cigarettes near the doors. He remembered all the times when he had stood on lines for the movies or concerts, feeling bereft as he gazed at all the adorable young girls surrounding him, wondering why he was always alone. But now it was happening to him. He was with the cutest girl around. And he prayed it would never end.

Once they got past the door and paid the cover, they headed for the bar and sat down at two stools. As the bartenders served some of the other guests, Jack said, "You ever try firewater?"

Tessa pondered this for a moment and then said, "No...I don't think I've ever had the pleasure. What the hell is firewater?"

"Oh, you're gonna like it. It's cinnamon schnapps. Let's do a chilled shot. It'll give us a head start."

Tessa looked at him with the amused suspicion that

they had been playfully exchanging all night. "Is this gonna knock me on my ass?" she said.

"Trust me. Nothing like that. But it's got a great kick. We can chase it with a beer."

"Sure."

A muscular bartender with bleached blonde hair and wearing a tight black T-shirt eventually took their orders. The aspiring mixologist took a dark, burgundy-colored bottle and poured the liqueur into a silver shaker containing ice and covered it with a strainer. He shook it a few times to chill the shots and poured them out.

They raised their glasses in a silent toast and then downed the shots in one quick gulp. The drink was aptly named: the cinnamon flavor was strong and spicy, burning their throats as the liquid slid down toward their stomachs. Tessa shuddered playfully after the shot but assured Jack she enjoyed it. The cold beer was a perfect chaser and cooled their throats pleasantly.

They each put a foot on the other's footrest and looked around, taking in the scene. Across from the bar were a few cocktail tables separated from the sunken dance floor by a railing. The floor itself was made of granite and there were large square support beams throughout, painted and molded for décor. The crowd was sparse, still early for a Saturday night, and the dance area was practically empty.

Five or six people were scattered on the floor, dancing by themselves. Each one was more bizarre than the rest. It seemed like they were all in their own world, acting out some sort of secret drama that only they could know. And yet there they were, putting on a show for everyone else to see. Whether or not they cared anyone was watching, no one knew. But it seemed to give them a cathartic outlet to express some inner passion or eternal grudge that had been stored up their entire lives, and was now being put on display, on the dance floor for everyone else to see.

One young man was dressed head to toe in black leather, including his jacket, pants, and boots. Silver chains hung on the boots, on his jacket, and out of his pockets. He had a silver nose ring and his hair had been coiffed in the form of rising black flames. He danced violently to the music, swiveling his torso in opposite directions as he lunged forward with high knee kicks. It was as if he were sparring to the music, giving some particular person a beating in his mind.

Several feet away from him was a skinny woman in a long tight, floral dress. She appeared to be in her late thirties and was wearing heavy makeup. She was twirling her body around in an unusual way, performing some horrible rendition of a ballet that only she knew. It was as if she were living in the past, holding desperately onto some failed, dream-crushing audition that she thought she had won.

The other dancers were all living out equally bizarre scenarios, like some group of circus sideshow acts, keeping everyone entertained until the crowd finally filed in. Jack couldn't help but be reminded of "The Peanuts" kids when they all got up and danced to Schroeder's piano, one style more amusing than the next.

After watching for a few minutes, Tessa slowly turned back to Jack, her eyes wide with amazement. She smiled and shook her head. "What's with these people?"

"I don't know," Jack said, "but they sure put on a show."

More people began to filter in and they decided to walk

around. The music started getting better and when George Michael's "Freedom" came on Tessa took Jack by the hand and led him onto the floor. More dancers followed and instantly the atmosphere became more festive.

It was the first time they ever danced together and it seemed a little awkward at first. But after a few moments and guided by the music, it got easier for both of them to move their bodies to the rhythm. Tessa flowed more naturally, gracefully following the beat, rolling her shoulders and hips in subtly suggestive ways. Jack just followed along, hoping he could dance well enough to blend in. Tessa grinned as he moved with her and then it all became second nature. Soon, they got lost in the familiar music, leaning in and singing the lyrics to each other and laughing the whole time. One great '80s anthem followed another. Adam Ant's "Goody Two Shoes," U2's "I Will Follow," the Go-Go's' "We Got the Beat," The Cure's "Just Like Heaven," and New Order's "Blue Monday." As they danced, Jack and Tessa mimed each other, trying out new moves for fun, and when they failed miserably, the charade dissolved into a fit of laugher. And all around them, the Pulse's eccentric patrons performed their own strange dances, to the amusement of the young couple.

Finally, they had to take a break. Tessa went to the ladies room and Jack went to get more beers. He couldn't remember having such a good time. He looked around the bar as he waited for the drinks and wondered how Mickey was doing. He vowed to call him the next day to catch up and tell him how well it was going with Tessa.

He gazed over toward the ladies room and caught a glimpse of her in the distance. She seemed to stand out amongst the rest of the people, like a shining beacon in a tumultuous sea. Everything seemed to pale in color around her and as she approached, he assured himself that he'd never seen such a smile.

She sat down and Jack handed over her beer. She had merely taken one sip when the beginning of Marilyn Manson's "The Beautiful People" began to play on the system. A huge roar rose up from the crowd and Tessa's eyes grew large. With the beer in her mouth, she murmured, "MMM!" Then she swallowed and said, "We have to dance to this!" She took Jack's hand and they ran down to the floor.

The excited dancers began acting out the song in their own individual ways. Not like the isolated outcasts who were out there before, but in an interactive way, having fun with friends. The song had a powerful way of building a crowd into a frenzy and that night it was no different. Marilyn Manson began screeching over the heavy industrial sound and the song's unbridled energy suddenly exploded.

Ba DAH de DAH DAH….Ba DAH de DAH DAH…. Ba DAH DAH…….Ba DAH de DAH DAH….Ba DAH de DAH DAH…Ba DAH DAH. The crowd moved in unison, throbbing like a pulsating organism with its limbs flying in different directions. Everyone seemed to be jumping and bobbing up and down at the same time. Then the lights went out and the strobes came on, causing the crowd to erupt into reckless abandon. With every flash of light, the moment was captured in a series of black and white snapshots of people caught in peculiar positions.

Jack watched Tessa closely. She was moving her body in a sexy rapture, feeling the music, as if she was in the throes of some primal ritual. She closed her eyes and swung her head back and forth, her hair flying this way and that while moving her hands up and down her body in a sensual tease; a tantalizing picture show that drove Jack wild. They continued to dance, reveling in the euphoria of the moment, forgetting everything else, all their worries, all their outside concerns.

But as Jack and Tessa immersed themselves in their rapture, something was watching them, roiling with resentment that churned deep inside. He knew deep in his heart he would never experience the joy Jack and Tessa were feeling. He wasn't good enough for people like them. He wasn't smart enough for people like them. They laughed at him. Ridiculed him. And God knew he was a freak. They all knew. They told him so and he now believed them. Hope had abandoned him long ago, and his pain had finally festered into a whirlwind of malevolence. Now no one was safe.

He watched them have their fun, resenting them for his alienation. He began to lose his restraint and drew nearer to them, his powder-white face flickering in the strobe lights among the crowd. His body tensed as he readied himself to attack, when the song ended suddenly, jolting him from his trance. He realized he was way too close, and he ducked away, knowing his moment would come soon. He glanced back at Jack and Tessa bitterly and headed for the door.

Marylyn Manson had left everyone giddy. The next song was a ballad by Depeche Mode, its smooth, ethereal melody sweeping them away into a dreamy, amorous reverie.

Both Jack and Tessa were breathing heavily from exertion. Each one looked around, a little self-conscious about their reckless abandon, but Tessa almost instantly began to move to the new song. It was called "Policy of Truth," a tune Jack didn't know, but it didn't matter. Her familiarity with the song somehow made it more appealing to him. As she danced, she moved close to him, flirting suggestively with her body until he could no longer help himself. She turned her back to him and leaned into his chest, causing him to almost reflexively reach around her waist and pull her to him. Thus, they swayed together, his left hand on her thigh, her left hand on top of it and her other arm on the one around her waist. He nuzzled her neck, which exuded a hint of strawberries, while she gasped at the sensation of his warm breath.

She spun around and, while moving to the beat as one, they embraced each other, this time face to face. For the moment, their eyes were closed, taking in the pleasure of each other's body. But then, almost at the same time, they opened their eyes. They gazed at each other with a look of startled realization, when vague thoughts and abstract feelings are coalescing into truth. And a notion that had been in the process of forming, but had yet to be completely acknowledged, finally materialized. It was both alarming and powerful, but it was real. And it unnerved them both. For at that very moment, moving to the romantic flow of Depeche Mode, Jack and Tessa fell in love.

After they danced for a while, Tessa whispered something in Jack's ear and he stiffened. He suddenly sobered, processed the significance of her words, and then looked directly into her eyes to see if she was serious. Once satisfied by her sincerity, he guided her off the dance floor, led her to the coat room, and out the door.

Hand in hand, they hurried back to Jack's car, and he

nearly left tire tracks peeling out of the parking lot. Tessa put on the radio and tried not to look ashamed about her forwardness. Jack paid attention to the road and tried to lighten the atmosphere by talking excitedly about Pulse and what a great time it was. In his mind, he tried not to speculate about what was to happen next, because he was superstitious, and didn't want anything, specifically his expectations, to ruin what might soon be the best night of his life.

CHAPTER 28

MINIMAL RESISTANCE

When they got to his place, Tessa was already out of the car before he could open her door. They walked quickly to his front porch and Jack almost lost the handle of his keys as he fumbled for the right one. Once inside, he took Tessa's jacket and she rubbed her hands together. "Nice place!" she said, "A little chilly though."

Jack took their coats to the closet. "Oh, sorry about that." he said, "I'll turn the heat up. It's been much warmer lately." He smiled mischievously to himself as he pretended to adjust the thermostat. He had deliberately left the house cool that evening because he thought there might be a possibility he'd be bringing Tessa home and, whenever it was cold, women were more likely to snuggle for some "shared bodily warmth". He led her into the den, where he offered her a seat, and put on some music. A special CD had also been placed in the stereo before the night began. He left the light dim. "You want something to drink?" he asked. "Some wine?"

"Sure, wine sounds great."

He went into the kitchen and Tessa heard his rummaging. She got up and started to inspect the book case. "So do you live alone?" she called to him.

"Yeah," Jack said from the kitchen.

"Wow, that must be nice, having a place like this all to yourself."

He arrived back with two wine glasses in one hand and a chilled bottle of white in the other. "You ever try German wine?"

"Riesling?" Tessa asked.

Jack smiled at her broad expanse of knowledge. "Yep. First time I tried it was at a vineyard in Frankfurt. Tasted awesome. Even bought a case of it to bring back home. Drank two whole bottles by myself that night on a river cruise on the Rhine. Great wine. Love the name too." He showed her the label which depicted a terrified black cat standing sideways, the hair of its back sticking straight up in the air. Underneath the picture were the German words "Schwarze Katz".

Tessa got a kick out of it. "Oh my God, I love it! Schwarze Katz. Too funny."

"I know," Jack said, "Isn't that awesome? Love the

expression on the cat's face." He took out a cork screw and began to peel the foil away from the top of the bottle. "So how do you know so much about wine? Not too many people drink Riesling."

"From my Dad. Though it wasn't good for him, he was really into fine wines. We often had a glass or two with dinner, with my father telling us stories about their origins. I know now most of the stories were made up, just to entertain me and my sister, but it was always a lot of fun. Riesling happens to be one of my favorites."

"Huh! Your dad sounds like a really interesting guy. I wish I could have met him."

Tessa smiled at Jack with gratitude. "Yeah, I think you two would have gotten along quite well." He had no idea how much his last comment had meant to her.

Jack opened the bottle and poured them each a glass. They toasted with a clink, then sipped the wine, savoring the tart and fruity flavor as it swirled around their mouths. "Your Love Is King" by Sade came on the stereo and Tessa said, "I like this singer. Who is she?"

Jack told her she was a popular jazz singer from the '80s and was about to expound upon the romantic allure of her music when Tessa put down her glass, came over and kissed him.

He chuckled and drew her body near while, at the same time still holding onto his glass. He wanted both of his hands on her, however, so he broke for just a second to put it down. Now they swayed together to the music, without distraction, solely focused on one another. Jack held her close as they kissed, tasting the wine on her lips, and then on her tongue. He ran his hands all over her back and shoulders, then on her waist and over her ass. Through her clothes, Jack could feel her body was firm, further fueling his desires.

He explored her mouth with his tongue, then, delicately kissed her lower lip. He nuzzled her cool, smooth cheek, caressing it with his lips and his nose, lingering there in bliss. He pressed again into her, feeling her breasts against his chest and gently forcing his thigh between her legs. It was getting heated, and Jack knew they were getting to a critical stage. Should he try to push further or wait for Tessa to give him a sign?

She gave it to him. She took him by the hand, and fell back onto the couch, pulling him on top of her. There, they kissed passionately, all at once embracing and fondling, pressing into each other and feeling each other's body. Without resistance, Jack got his hips between Tessa's legs and their heat met, sending a feverish thrill through them both. They simulated sex for a while, undulating full dressed, until Jack finally made a decision.

He pulled away, looked into Tessa's eyes, and said quietly, "Let's go upstairs."

She didn't hesitate. "Okay," she said.

"Grab your wine," Jack said, and took her by the hand into his bedroom. She sat on his bed and took off her shoes. Jack put music on again and took another sip of wine. In the dim light, he looked at her, not quite believing that this beautiful young girl, with her pale blue eyes glowing in the dark, was waiting for him on his bed, ready for him to do almost anything he wanted. It was like a dream he had been having for as long as he could remember and it wasn't quite sinking in.

He had waited long enough.

In three quick strides he closed the space between them and joined Tessa on the bed.

And it was even better than he ever could have imagined.

* * *

Afterwards, when all their passions and energies were utterly spent, they lay there in the dark, bathing in the afterglow, neither one wanting, nor able, to speak. Music was playing softly in the room; songs Jack had handpicked for such an intimate moment. "Mercy Street" by Peter Gabriel, "Angel" by Sarah McLachlan, "Something So Right" by Paul Simon, and "Night Vision" by Suzanne Vega were just a few of the soothing lullabies that whispered to the young lovers as they drifted in and out of consciousness, lost in quiet serenity.

Both were overwhelmed with emotion, never having experienced such a combination of physical and emotional bliss. It was as if they were afraid to break the spell, wanting to linger there together for as long as they possibly could.

After a while, Jack stirred, rousing Tessa out of her comfortable doze. She was on his left side, her head on his chest and her limbs draped comfortably around him. Her eyes were closed, and she was smiling to herself.

"Mmmmm," she said and squeezed Jack in a gesture of intimacy. "That was nice."

"Nice?" Jack said. "That's an understatement." He was lying on his back, staring at the ceiling, only for the first time in as long as he could remember, he wasn't yearning for anything. He was exactly where he wanted to be. In his mind he had finally fulfilled a dream he had for almost his entire life: to lay within the arms of his soul mate.

It almost felt too good to last. Or even be real. He didn't have any delusions of living happily ever after. God knew everything thrilling and exciting in his life had had a very short existence. Something always happened to bring him back down to earth.

But here he was, lying naked in the dark with the most exquisite girl he had ever known. "That was way more than nice," he said. "That was...more like nirvana."

Tessa lifted her head up to look at his face. "Really?" she said. "I thought more like Pearl Jam."

Jack chuckled and gave her a quick squeeze on her side, which made her jump and laugh at the sensation of being tickled. "Wise-ass," he said.

When their giggling finally settled down, Jack said, "Tess, you ever feel like you're reaching for something, like trying to get a hold of some sort of special feeling that could never be beat?"

"What do you mean?"

"Well, there have been a few times in my life where everything seemed...I don't know, kinda unreal? Like at a party or a carnival or some kind of unplanned spontaneous event with good friends but also with a whole bunch of new and interesting people...and all sorts of things were happening like fireworks and live music and great food. I'm trying to think of the word for it. Escapade, maybe?"

"Could be."

"The funny thing is, there always seemed to be a girl involved. Some new and mysterious girl whom I had become instantly and completely infatuated with."

"Why am I not surprised?" Tessa said.

"Well, I feel like I've always been looking for experiences like that because…because to me, it's like living life the way it was meant to be."

"Huh," Tessa said, considering the concept. "So why did you bring that up?"

He lay silent for a moment, prompting Tessa to lift her head off his chest and look in his eyes. Through the dimness, she thought she saw a tear streaming down his cheek.

When he could finally speak he whispered, "Tess… you're my escapade."

* * *

Outside, Sticks Favors sat in his car watching Jack's house. He was leaning forward, his hands gripped tightly on the steering wheel and his emerald eyes peering wildly through the windshield. He was desperately watching for any signs of movement in Jack's bedroom window and he wasn't going to move until he did. He had remained frozen in that position for almost two hours, in a sort of trance, the kind that happens to predators while waiting to pounce on their unsuspecting prey.

What was happening here was wrong. *He* was the one who was supposed to have everything. Not that guy Banks. Banks was the one who made him look like a fool. Banks was the one who dared to defeat him in the pool tournament and then knock him out and leave him there for the cops to arrest him. And now Banks was alone with the girl. The type of girl who should belong to Sticks more than anyone. But things were about to change. Now Sticks had the *power*. He could do anything he wanted now. He could make *anything happen*. It was *his* world and if anyone got in his way, well...they'd just get what was coming to them, wouldn't they? That's right, get what's coming to them... get what's coming to them...get what's coming to them... get what's coming to them...

CHAPTER 29

THE ANGEL OF DARKNESS

Earlier that same night…..

I nside the Harrington residence, Tommie was with Dan and Patrick in an enormous kitchen, filling sixteen ounce, red plastic cups from a keg full of beer. The house was filling up with high school kids from both Treemont and Soundview High. The mix of strangers and familiar faces made the party comfortable yet exciting, especially the prospect of checking out the girls from the other school. For some reason they always seemed to be better looking.

Several of the Tiger football players came up behind them. A few of them crossed their arms on their chests and glowered with hostility. One of them began to punch his fist in his hand. Soon, the rest followed along in unison. They were mostly huge, muscular athletes, and while Tommie was clearly the biggest, the three Chargers were largely outnumbered.

One particularly animated aggressor was wearing a dark blue Treemont baseball cap and had bright yellowish hair which flowed out from beneath it. He was thin, if not somewhat lanky, and didn't appear wide enough to be a football player. Even so, almost in a way to compensate for his lack of size, he seemed to exaggerate his threatening posture, and in an extreme display of intimidation, stepped forward and said, "You guys are from Soundview, aren't ya?" He smugly evaluated Tommie from head to toe.

Tommie just continued to fill his cup and answered without looking up. "That's right." he said, "You got a problem with that?"

The leader looked around at his friends and smirked. "You Chargers got a lot of nerve showing up here." That elicited some more grumbling and challenging gestures from his crew. One of them bit into his plastic cup and began tearing it to shreds.

Patrick grabbed Dan's sleeve and gave him a wide-eyed look. He was reaching inside his jacket for a weapon, but Dan grabbed his arm and shook his head.

"You're that receiver, aren't you?" the blonde-haired kid said with a sneer.

Tommie took a sip of beer and gave back a challenging look. "Yeah, what of it?"

Silence suspended for what seemed like an eternity. Then suddenly the yellow haired kid broke out into a wide grin and said, "That was some fuckin' catch, bro!" And the rest of the kitchen erupted with laughter. "Let me shake your hand, man," he said, "Call me Chester. This is my house. Hope you have a blast." Then all the Treemont players then came up and congratulated Tommie, shaking their heads and swearing they had never seen a game winning catch like that in their lives.

Patrick, who had worked up a sweat during the brief tension, took a huge breath and exhaled so hard his cheeks puffed out. The quarterback just laughed with the rest and reassured his partner. "Stay cool, Pat," he said. "I'll let you know if anything's up."

As the blonde-haired kid and his friends showered Tommie with adulation, the wide receiver tried to remain modest. But it wasn't easy. He loved the attention. Especially from the girls, who were sending him curious glances. It all caused a strange and wonderful feeling, this recognition; an ecstatic surge of adrenaline that floated up from his chest and shined out through his broad, boyish grin. It was how a person feels when he realizes he's becoming a celebrity. The world was opening up for him and everything he had ever dreamed of was coming true.

After bullshitting about football and drinking lots of beers, the guys shifted their attention toward getting laid. Tommie came back to Dan and Patrick, whose eyes never left him the whole time. "Let's take a look around," he said.

They edged their way through the crowd into a spacious living area. A huge fireplace was built into a stone covered wall that ran the entire length of the room. It was nice to look at, but for the moment was obsolete. Heat permeated the atmosphere. Everyone was young and vibrant; alive with the excitement of the world unveiling itself before their very eyes. After a long childhood kept under restraints, a party like this gave them an exhilarating new freedom to explore their desires and test their own boundaries. Their bodies were now hard and strong, with torrents of hormones streaming through their veins. And something extraordinary, come hell or high water, was going to happen soon.

Lynyrd Skynyrd's "That Smell" was playing on the stereo, a warning about living too hard and pushing beyond the limits of caution. Reckless abandon could ruin you, it preached, no matter how indestructible you thought you were.

> Whiskey bottles and brand new cars, oak tree you're in my way
> There's too much coke and too much smoke, look what's goin' on inside you
> Ooh ooh, that smell, can't you smell that smell
> Ooh ooh, that smell, the smell that's around you
>
> Now the Angel of Darkness is upon you
> Stuck a needle in your arm (you fool, you)
> So take another toke, have a blow for your nose
> One more drink, fool, will drown you...

But the kids were just reveling in the joy of experimenting with anything that looked exciting and new. The girls were dressed in tight, revealing clothing, calling attention to their sexy young bodies. They wore snug, low cut, bell-bottom jeans with loose, silky blouses or tight, form-fitting tops.

They had done all they could to look their best and it was working.

When Danny, Patrick, and Tommie moved into the room, their eyes nearly popped out of their heads.

Young couples were dancing slowly to the music, their arms all over each other and their hips moving back and forth in time. Others were lying on top of each other on couches and love seats, making love with their clothes on. Joints were passed around, filling the air with an aromatic herbal scent, while bottles of hard liquor were swigged like they were jugs of water. The seats were set around a large coffee table that was covered with beer bottles, red plastic cups filled with strong mixed drinks, ash trays, and half-eaten bowls of chips and dips.

Tommie and his friends perceived a difference in the girls here. They were more mature and confident, more exotic even, than what the boys were used to. They seemed like young women, rather than high school co-eds, as they strutted around with a self-assured sensuality, knowing their moves aroused the lustful gaze of every boy in the room. These girls knew they were in control because they had what was in demand, an irresistible, sizzling sexuality.

The younger girls looked on with veiled jealousy, somehow knowing it would be impossible to compete with them. These were women who knew what they were doing. The funny thing was, no one knew who they were. The Treemont kids thought they were from Soundview, and the Soundview kids thought they were from Treemont. Either way, it didn't matter. They fit in just the same.

And they were all extremely aware of Tommie. Without being too obvious, each one made eye contact with him and smiled as they pretended to be involved with something else. One poured a drink. The other flirted with another guy. One began dancing. But each one was, in her own seductive way, trying to get the attention of the young star football player.

Tommie was in a daze. The excitement of the room short-circuited his consciousness. For a moment he looked back over his shoulder to see where all these girls were looking. This new celebrity was strange indeed, but just like any person with a pulse, he was loving it. Even Dan, a kid who could probably have had any girl at Soundview High, and may have already, was in shock. He nudged Tommie on the arm and said, "You see what I'm seein'?"

Tommie nodded slowly, a look of awe on his face. "Oh yeah."

Dan said in a voice of wonder, "Soundview parties ain't like this." And they both started laughing.

Patrick wasn't laughing. His eyes darted left and right, ready for chaos to erupt at any second. His fingers gripped his concealed gun. He hadn't felt comfortable since they arrived.

Tommie glanced around the room until his gaze finally rested upon a girl with hair the color of ivory. She was wearing a white silk button down blouse over a cotton halter-top of the same color. The sleeves of the blouse reached down to the middle of her forearms where they split apart, revealing creamy smooth skin. Her skirt was jade green and cross-hatched with a white and black pattern, and shiny white leather boots showed off her long firm legs which she crossed with a confident poise as she sat comfortably on the couch. She had been in an animated conversation with a skinny, acne-scarred boy with braces and disproportionately large glasses. The lenses magnified his eyes. He seemed younger than most of the kids, but there he sat in the middle of the couch, visible from all corners of the room, gaining the attention of the sexiest girl at the party. He was in over his head and he knew it, so all he could do was laugh like a donkey and agree with everything she said. Not knowing what to do with his hands, he laced them firmly together in his lap, desperate to hide the erection growing in his pants.

Every few moments, the blonde girl would glance over at Tommie, give him an almost imperceptible smile, and then quickly look away again. Finally she got up, placed her hand on the inner thigh of the geek, gave it a squeeze, and said she'd be right back. His back arched a bit, he shuddered for a moment, and then melted back into the couch. Seconds later, completely mortified, he slinked quickly out of the room, praying no one would notice the new wet stain on his pants.

The girl, however, had her sights set on Tommie. In one graceful motion, she rose, got off an adolescent without appearing to notice, picked up her drink, and made her way over to Tommie. His eyes never left her. At her full height of 5'10", it became evident that she had both the body and legs of a dancer. And she moved like one. With her short skirt and leather boots, she appeared to glide rather than walk. She coasted right into him and looked directly in his eyes.

"You're that football player, right?" she said.

"Which football player?" Tommie said, smiling wryly.

"Oh, we're gonna play that game? Okay, I'll bite. You know, the one that all the college scouts are talking about?

The one all my *girlfriends* are talking about?" Her voice was getting louder and more animated as she spoke.

Tommie tried to suppress his grin. He let her go on.

"The wide receiver who made that crazy catch? The wide receiver who almost *single-handedly* kicked our ass on our own field?"

"Oh, *that* one!" Tommie finally said. "I guess that would be me."

"Uh huh," she said while assessing him with a mischievous smile. She nodded with her mouth slightly ajar, as she touched her upper left molars with the tip of her tongue. "Yeah, I thought so."

Now that she was close, Tommie got a better look at her. She had eyes the color of silver, which seemed to take on a sparkle all their own. Two small diamond studs glittered on the edge of her left eyebrow, and the very bottom of her blonde bob was dyed jet black, giving it the shape of a horseshoe that surrounded her neck. Yet Tommie noticed that while beautiful, her face was beginning to show lines that would not be seen on faces of girls his age. And when she smiled, the skin around her eyes twitched, as if she were fighting with some dark secret that lay hidden there. A voice of caution whispered, weak and frail, but quickly faded in the distance, until it was completely silenced.

Lines or no lines, twitches or no twitches, he wanted this girl. He wanted her regardless.

She offered her hand. "Name's Krys with a K."

He took her hand and she leaned her head down, giving him an upward, almost timid glance. Her hand was soft and moist and cold. *Very cold.* He barely noticed. "Is that short for Kristin?" he asked.

"Nope, it's Krystal."

"Oh, gotcha. Name's Tommie with a T."

"Is that short for Thomas?"

"Nope. Long for Tom."

They both got a chuckle from that. Meanwhile, Dan and Patrick looked on with amazement. A moment later, a girl behind them said, "This music sucks" and went over to the stereo, took a CD out of her bag, and put it on. It was Beyoncé's "Single Ladies," and the instant it came through the speakers, practically every girl in the room got up to dance.

Two other girls jumped up to dance with the one who put on the music. Instantly the three of them began to move together, synchronizing their bodies to the rhythm, as if they had done it before hundreds of times. They alternately smiled at one another and then to themselves as they bathed in the glow of admiration from all the younger girls. They twisted and turned together, spinning, stomping, and undulating as if they were on stage.

Dan was mesmerized. He started to move toward the center of the room to get a closer look when Patrick grabbed his arm. Dan looked back with a frown and growled, "What?!" Patrick opened his eyes wide and nodded his head backward toward Tommie. Dan watched briefly as Krystal's flirtation became even more obvious. She was leaning into Tommie now and he was grinning, his right arm settling on her lower back.

Dan shrugged, moved close to Patrick's ear, and said, "What? She's hot. Give the dude a little space, for God's sake."

"But—" Patrick said.

"But what?" Dan said. "What's she gonna do, fuck him to death? Come on, these chicks are hot!"

He moved out closer to the girls putting on the show, and Patrick, after an anxious glance back at Tommie, reluctantly followed. Dan moved quickly in on the girl in the middle. She was tinier than the other two and had the deep, brown eyes of a fawn. She was wearing tight, low-cut torn up jeans, her flat midriff bare below perky breasts held firmly to her chest by a purple tube top. She spun and turned with more agility than the other two, her long hair swishing this way and that. Once she saw Dan, she broke off from the other two and moved close to him. One of the other two girls, a redhead wearing a black headband, took Patrick by the hand and began dancing with him. She put her arms in the air, thrust out her chest toward him, and fought with determination to get his attention. He moved around her to get a better view of Tommie but his view was instantly blocked by the third girl, who had dark blue eyes and a dirty blonde ponytail. The pony tail swung all over the place as she jumped around and he had to bob and weave in order to maintain his view. The redhead spun him around and said, "Hey, I'm over here!" She gave him her best smile, which finally melted his resolve and he smiled back. He noticed her body for the first time, stirring in him a suppressed desire. She put her arms around his shoulders and said, "You like me?"

Patrick swallowed. "Um, sure."

"I'm Trixie!" she said, putting his hands on her hips. She nodded toward the blonde. "And this is Lacey."

"Oh, I'm Patrick."

She moved in closer and said, "Wow, you feel strong. Are you a football player too? I like football players."

She began to press her body into his. She then looked back in the direction of Tommie and Krystal. The tall girl with the ivory hair was leaning her back into him and searching the middle of the room. When Krystal finally saw Trixie, she raised her eyebrows and nodded.

She then turned toward Tommie, stood on her tiptoes, and said something into his ear. He smiled his boyish grin, nodded, and let himself be taken by the hand out of the room. Dan and Patrick remained in the crowd, euphorically distracted by the girls. When the song finally ended, Dan went to kiss the tiny brunette, who deftly moved her head to the side just in time. Patrick, though, in a surge of dismay, suddenly remembered Tommie and looked toward where the couple had been standing only a moment ago.

But they were gone.

"Dan!" Patrick yelled and grabbed his friend's arm.

"What?!" Dan said.

Patrick jabbed his finger toward the wall. "Where's Tommie?" He began searching the room with his wild eyes.

"Come on!" Danny said, and they took off in Tommie's direction. "Hey!" the redhead said, and the brunette added, "Where you going?" Both tried to hold onto their guy's arms. The boys shook them off, but the brunette and the redhead glanced at each other and followed. Dan led Patrick out of the living room, sliding through the crowd. He was about to go down a long hallway when Patrick said, "Dan!" and pointed up a wide carpeted stairway that led to the second floor. There, being led by the hand up the stairs was Tommie.

"HEY TOM!!" both of his friends yelled almost simultaneously.

Startled, Tommie turned around at once, with a confused expression on his face. Having had plenty to drink already, he almost lost his balance, spilling some of his beer in the process. Krystal steadied him as best she could and he reached out to grab the banister. When he saw his teammates, he smiled and said, "Dudes! Great party, huh?"

"Yeah, awesome. Where you going?" Dan said.

Krystal looked at Dan warily as she stood next to Tommie. The young wide receiver put his arm around her waist and said, "Nowhere special. What are you guys up to?"

Dan said, "Not much. Umm…you guys want to get another beer?" He pointed his thumb behind him toward the kitchen.

The two on the stairs looked down at their mostly filled cups and held them out to Dan. "Um, no. We're good," Tommie said.

"You want to get something to eat?" Patrick said.

Tommie looked at Krystal, who shrugged and smiled. She ran a hand up the back of his shirt and began rubbing his muscles. It felt incredible.

"Hello? Food?" Dan said.

Krystal then took a chance. She pulled her hand away and said, "Maybe you should go with your friends. They seem to need your company."

Tommie's expression of bliss shattered. "I don't think so. They'll be fine without me." He turned to them. "Right guys?" he said through gritted teeth. "You'll be fine without me?"

"But Tom," said Dan, "don't you—"

"You crazy guys!" Tommie laughed. "I love you guys!" He turned to Krystal and said with a nervous smile, "Just give me a minute," then descended the few steps to reach his friends. Krystal sat down on the steps and sighed dramatically. She then put her elbows on her knees and her face in her hands.

Tommie put his massive arms around his teammates' necks and pulled them back down the stairs with him. It was as if they were in one of their fourth quarter huddles, but this time Tommie clenched them harder. Quietly, he said, "You guys are *killin'* me. Do you see this girl? You see how hot she is? I'm getting under that skirt if it's the last thing I do. Now don't fuck this up for me. Go back into the party and find some girls of your own! Okay?"

Both of them writhed under his painful grasp and said, "Okay! Okay!" as they struggled to pull away.

"Good!" Tommie said and pushed them away. "Good." He gave a nervous chuckle as he caught Krystal's eye. She beamed as he walked back up the stairs. "They're going back to the party," he said.

Danny headed back to the living room rubbing his neck while the couple ascended the steps. Patrick lingered there, watching his friend disappear onto the second floor, a miserable whine rising on his throat.

* * *

Once on the landing, Tommie and Krystal turned the corner to look for some privacy. Krystal pushed Tommie up against the wall, a mischievous look in her eyes. Behind her, overhanging the stairway was a huge chandelier with hundreds of glittering shapes of glass. It framed Krystal's beauty, giving her a shimmering essence, and Tommie fought the urge to rub his eyes. It all felt like a fantasy. Like some adolescent dream.

She gazed at him in a curious way, smiling inquisitively. She nodded back over her shoulder and said, "Those guys pretty much do what you tell them, don't they?"

Tommie tried to play it cool, but his pride leaked out. "Yeah, I can handle them. I've known them practically my whole life. Great guys, but sometimes they can be kinda dense."

She laughed, looked deep into his eyes, and for a brief moment she seemed to be admiring him, almost really liking him. But just as quickly she became distracted, as if a distant thought began to gnaw at her. Her smile faded ever so slightly and she looked at his chest. Her voice deepened a bit and she said, "So you're the captain of the team then, right?"

"I guess you could say that."

"Leader of the pack?"

"King of the castle."

She looked back up at him, ready for action. "Okay, Admiral. Let's go see what floats your boat."

"Let's," Tommie said.

She led him down the hall to the front of the house where there were two opened double doors. A couple of teenage boys were taking off their jackets and throwing them on a mound of clothing piled high on a king-sized bed. Heading back toward the stairs, they almost bumped into Tommie and Krystal. As they continued down the hall, both of them spun around and walked backwards to catch another look at the girl. Their eyes bulged and, grinning back at each other, they both shook their heads and said, "Holy shit!" One of them then said, "This is gonna be a sick party…Unbelievable."

Once inside the master bedroom, Tommie looked around. The large room was adorned with original paintings, mostly landscapes of sleepy harbors dotted with anchored sailboats of all shapes and sizes. On the wall opposite the bed was a huge flat screen TV above a fireplace made of pale chiseled stones, and the furniture positioned neatly around the room gleamed a blended gray and white. The bed was made up with pink and blue pastel linens and the floor was a light polished oak, disrupted only by a plush area rug in front of the bed.

"Amazing," Tommie said and sat down on the bed next to the coats. Krystal closed and locked the doors and went over to the bed. "Let's tidy up a bit," she said, and tossed the coats unceremoniously on the floor. Tommie helped her with them, playfully throwing some of them at her in the process.

"Come here," she said and pushed him onto the bed. She climbed on top of him, straddling his waist and leaned down to kiss him hard. She jammed her tongue into his mouth while she grinded her hips into him. Then she sat up and began to take off her top. When she looked at the headboard, she cocked her head to the side and said, "Huh!" It reached way up to the ceiling with recessed lighting and shelves holding several vases, propped up crystalline platters, imported ornaments, and large picture frames with photos of the Harringtons. "I love these things," she said. "It kinda turns the bed into a stage, doesn't it?"

"Why, are you a good performer?" Tommie said.

She looked back down at him, amused. "You have no idea."

"Oh yeah? Then show me."

"Okay, you asked for it." She looked around the room and spotted the stereo. She went over to it and found suitable music on the radio. Tommie moved to the foot of the bed, where he watched her mischievously and seductively strip down to satin, silver lingerie. Once all her outer garments had been discarded, she climbed upon his lap and began to kiss him playfully, and rub him with her hands, arms, and other parts of her body. She moved with a familiar sensuality and grace, and by the time the song changed, she had Tommie almost completely under her spell.

She got off of him and went over to her purse. "Let's have some fun," she said. She rummaged inside it for a moment while Tommie looked on with curiosity. "Where is it?...where is it?...Oh! There you are!" she said as she pulled out a small vial. It contained a white powder that she held up for Tommie to see, and she smiled naughtily. "This will make it even better."

Tommie stared at the vial, his mouth parted slightly and a faraway look in his eyes. Then the light came back into them. "Is that what I think it is?" he said.

"Yep, only the best." She moved closer and whispered, "I have *connections*."

Tommie paused for a moment, something deep inside imploring him to beware. It was a small voice, barely a whisper, but it was loud enough for him to hesitate, or at least think about what was happening. He remembered Mickey earlier that evening, begging him to be careful. But Mickey had done his own share of partying over the years, hadn't he? He had always seemed to come out okay too. So why was Mickey the only one allowed to have fun?

Still, Tommie was uncertain. He had never done cocaine before. He tilted his chin up a bit and gave her a suspicious but playful look. "What will it do to me?"

Krystal's eyebrows rose. "First time?"

He nodded slowly.

She gasped with excitement and took his face in her hands. "Oh, how adorable! A virgin! You're gonna love it." She took out a small mirror and a razor blade and pushed away a stained glass lamp to make room for them on the night table. Then, with the delicate expertise of someone who had done this many times before, she unscrewed the vial and tapped out some coke onto the mirror. With the razor, she pushed the powder into two thick lines and then rolled up two dollar bills into straws. She handed one to Tommie.

He looked dubiously at the straw in his hand and then at the coke. "No, seriously. What's gonna happen?"

She smiled, stepped back, stuck out her hip, and put her hand on it. "Baby, it's just about the best feeling in the world. Bliss, joy…ecstasy…like you've never had before."

"I don't know…"

"Come on, honey. Trust me. I do it all the time and look at me." She tilted her head down and gazed up at him with a smile that made his heart skip a beat. "Don't I look healthy to you?"

He nodded nervously but still didn't move.

She rolled her eyes and sighed. "Okay, let me give you a little incentive." Reaching behind her back, she undid the clasps of her silver satin bra and let it slowly fall, revealing her full firm breasts. Tommie swallowed and made a move toward her. She held up her left hand and waggled a finger at him. "Uh, uh, uh....ah," she sang. "Not unless you join me. Just do one line with me, and I'm all yours."

He looked over at the drugs on the night table and then back at her.

She nodded enthusiastically. "I promise you, it'll be the *ultimate* experience."

A few more times he looked between the night table and her.

"Come on, big boy, what do you say?"

Finally, Tommie said, "Oh, what the hell!" and turned toward the night table.

Krystal clapped her hands and squealed, "Yay!" She followed him over and showed him what to do. "Okay, ready?" Tommie nodded enthusiastically. They both leaned over, put the dollar straw in their noses, held the other nostril closed with their fingers, and sucked up the white powder. It made a vacuuming sound like the tubes dentists use to suck the saliva out of your mouth.

They both stood up and looked at each other. Krystal sniffed back again and inhaled deeply as if she were breathing in fresh mountain air. "You see? Doesn't that feel great?"

But just as soon as Tommie began to nod, Krystal's smile suddenly faded and was replaced by an expression of fear. A pinkish foam began to drip from her nostril and she let out a series of high-pitched gasps. Her eyes then rolled up and she suddenly collapsed to the floor, her arms and legs splayed out in impossible angles, like a discarded marionette.

Tommie bent over to help her but suddenly felt a

terrifying pain impale his heart. In a reflex, he shot back up and reached for his chest. He tried to breath but struggled to fill his lungs with air. Another massive pain gripped him, feeling like his ribs were cracking, and his chest then caved in upon itself like a dry ceramic vase, crumbling apart. He gave one last desperate attempt to breathe, but to no avail. Helplessly he wheezed and swallowed, tears beginning to form at the edges of his eyes. The light began to disappear in front of him, the darkness coming like a growing shadow, a blinding ring that progressively thickened until at last he was fully engulfed in black. Flailing his arms as he fell backward, he slammed into the night table and knocked the bed lamp onto the floor with a crash, shattering it into a million pieces. There he sat motionless, his empty gaze staring questioningly into space. And as the tingling in his fingers began to fade, the last thought Tommie O'Leary ever had was, "Wait..."

* * *

Outside the bedroom, Patrick shot to his feet with a start. Unbeknownst to Tommie, he had been sitting against the wall next to the doors, suspicious of anyone who came near, his hand sweating around the .38 revolver he was hiding in his sweatshirt. He had heard a bump, then a louder thud followed by an ugly crash, which set off the blare of a fire alarm in his head. While keeping the gun hidden, he reached for the doorknob and tentatively said, "Tom? Everything okay?" The question was met with silence. Fear pooled inside him. "Tom?" he said a little more urgently and knocked lightly on the door. When no response came, he knocked even louder. "Come on, Tommie. Quit jokin' around. What's going on in there?"

"Fuck!" he exclaimed. Unsure of what to do, and he bolted toward the top of the steps. Below, he could see Dan still flirting with the little brunette who was laughing with her friend Trixie. "DAN!" Patrick yelled, and the practiced smile of the quarterback disappeared. Exasperated, Dan looked up the steps, held out his arms, and said, "What!?!?"

"IT'S TOMMIE!" Patrick yelled, and the terror in his voice told Dan all he needed to know. He sprinted up the steps three at a time and ran past Patrick yelling, "What the hell happened?!"

"I don't know!" Patrick said miserably, running alongside him. "I was sitting outside the room and it sounded like someone fell. Someone *big*."

The girls, following them cautiously up the stairs, paused at the landing and listened from a distance. At the bedroom door, Dan anxiously looked back at Patrick, his eyes now wide and his body stiffening. He took his own .38 out from behind his waist and knocked on the door. "Tom, you okay?" he said, "Come on, buddy, you're making us nervous out here." He waited a couple of seconds, looking at Patrick and shaking his head. "Just tell us to go fuck ourselves and we'll leave." When there was again no response, he shook his head, said "Dammit!" The quarterback then stepped back, and kicked in the door.

When he saw what had happened he cried out, "JESUS!!" and ran inside.

The brunette ordered Trixie to stay and slinked quickly toward the door, like a spy trying to stay out of sight. When she finally got there, the calamity of the scene was unreal.

Tommie was sitting motionless, his upper body wedged in the corner between the night table and the bed, his head hanging listlessly to one side. His mouth hung sickeningly open and pinkish foam was dripping out of his nose. Dan sobbed as he pressed his head to Tommie's chest in a desperate effort to find a heartbeat.

She raised her hand to her mouth to stifle a gasp.

Patrick was bent over at the waist, his hands on his knees, chanting "Oh my God, Oh My God! OH MY GOD!" like a mantra.

The girl moved slowly through the door while Dan yelled, "Someone call 911! Someone call 911!" and began pleading to Tommie's lifeless form in his arms. "Come on, Tommie, come on, big guy, wake up. Come on, WAKE UP! SOMEBODY CALL 911!"

The brunette turned to the right and suddenly felt like someone had punched her in the gut. Her right hand flew to her mouth again, but this time nothing could hold back her high-pitched gasp. She bent forward slightly, wrapped her left hand around her waist, and moved to get a closer look at her best friend Krystal, whose lifeless form now lay staring at the ceiling. The same pinkish foam was running down her cheek. For a horrifying moment the tiny brunette stood frozen, staring at the corpse until her body began to shake. She slowly backed up and turned toward the night table, where she instantly noticed the coke and the mirror.

Patrick was pacing around the room, still weeping his "Oh My Gods" when Dan said, "Pat, you gotta call Mickey."

Patrick froze. The color drained from his face. He began shaking his head vigorously and said, "Oh, no. Oh, no. You do it. I can't. I can't!"

While this exchange was taking place, the brunette swiped the vial and slipped out of the room, quickly disappearing into the crowd of kids who were now curiously climbing the stairs. She pressed through them, her head bent forward, sobbing with fear and grief. When she got to Trixie, she grabbed her by the hand and said, "Let's go."

Trixie looked back toward the bedroom. "Why, what happened?!" she said, a gnawing dread growing in her stomach.

"Come on!" the brunette cried. "I'll tell you outside."

"But what about Krystal? Where is she?"

The brunette jerked Trixie's arm down so their noses were an inch apart. "Shut up!" she harshly whispered, "We don't know her, you understand me? Now, we have to get out of here. Don't ask any more questions. Come on!" She pulled the redhead along with her down the stairs, dodging what seemed to be the entire party coming the other way.

As they neared the bottom, Trixie was in tears. "You're hurting me!" she cried.

"Pull it together!" the brunette said and began searching the crowd on the first floor "Where's Lacey?"

"I don't know!" Trixie whined and looked back up the stairs anxiously

The brunette searched through the crowd, craning her head this way and that while wiping away her own tears with her wrist. "Come on, where are you?" she said urgently. "Lacey!? LACEY!?"

Finally someone answered.

"Over here!" a voice yelled and they turned to the left where the girl with the dirty blonde ponytail was waving to them from the hallway. She then turned back to the boy she was flirting with and began laughing at what he was saying.

The brunette came up to her, took her by the hand and said, "Get your stuff, we're leaving."

Lacey's smile faded. "Why, what happened?"

"This party's fucked up." she said. "Let's go." She began pulling the blonde away, but after a few steps, Lacey threw the brunette's hand off of her. "What's your problem?" she demanded, "What's going on? Did something happen upstairs?"

Just then, a tall, terrified-looking man burst through the front door, knocking people aside with furious desperation. He nearly ran over the girls before he darted up the stairs. Another young man, a little thicker, with a green skull cap and black beard followed. In his quick movements, he scanned the crowd, his intense blue eyes briefly locking in on the brunette. For a moment, a fleeting look of recognition appeared on his face, and just like that it was gone. He continued up the stairs yelling, "Mick! Wait!" and disappeared. More angry young men began jostling through the crowd, all armed with some sort of weapon. Some had guns, some had switchblades, and others had pipes and bats. Their faces contorted with alarm, they sprinted up the steps, throwing anyone aside who was in their way.

The crowd erupted into chaos as the girls started screaming and the guys ducked hastily out of the way, all of them running over each other to get out of the house. The front door became log-jammed with people straining to escape the pandemonium.

The brunette grabbed both girls by the shirt and said,

"*Let's get the fuck out of here.*" They nodded at her soberly and she said, "Follow me."

They moved rapidly toward the living room, grabbed their belongings, and followed the brunette out the back of the house. Once in the yard the tiny dancer whispered, "Come on!" and ran with a crouch over to a group of hedges, hidden in shadow. The other girls followed suit and when they arrived, the brunette was already planning their next move. She strained to see what was going on out front.

"What are you three hiding from?" said a suspicious male voice behind them.

The girls all shrieked and turned around, their hearts racing with fear. A young man wearing a green bandana and suspicious expression stepped out of the gloom.

The brunette quickly said, "There's a bunch of crazy guys in there running around with guns for starters."

"Yeah," he said, "well one of our friends is dead upstairs, along with a blonde named Krystal. You know her?"

Lacey gasped, "Krystal!" and his eyes jerked toward her. The brunette suddenly took out a can of mace and sprayed the guy in the face. He let out a howl and began reaching for them blindly. The girls shrieked again, jumping away as he flailed his arms.

"Hey!" someone shouted from the second floor window. It was the man with the green skull cap and beard. He pointed at them and said, "Grab those girls!" Petrified, the girls sprinted to the front of the house, following the brunette toward her car. When they got there, she desperately rummaged for her keys in her bag. The girls cried and pleaded for her to hurry until she finally found them. With a shaking hand she managed to open the door, just as Shane Gallagher was emerging from the house.

He ran toward the car, but it peeled away before he realized his mistake, and he had to run all the way back to his own car fifty yards in the other direction. "Somebody follow that car!" he yelled, but nobody heard. All of the Shamrocks had run inside and no one was near a car. And he knew by the time he could give chase, the girls would be long gone.

Salazar's girls.

* * *

While Tommie was being seduced by Krystal, Mickey was back at his car debating whether or not to involve the police. He still hadn't made a decision when the call came. The ring tone pierced through his brain like a skewer, paralyzing him so that he could barely move. He looked down toward the pocket where he kept his phone.

Shane looked at him and said, "You gonna answer that?"

That seemed to break the spell and he reached for it, his hand trembling. He flipped it open, but it slipped out of his hand and fell to the ground. An agitated, horrified voice then blared from the receiver.. "MICK? YOU THERE? MICK, YOU GOTTA GET IN HERE. IT'S TOMMIE!"

A thousand chips of ice exploded in Mickey's chest. He lunged for the phone and picked up. "WHAT HAPPENED?!" he cried.

Dan shouted miserably, "I don't know, he's not moving! Come quick! Upstairs. Master bedroom."

The world seemed to rush past Mickey's face as if he were tied to the front of a speeding train. Before he knew it,

413

he was racing toward the house, his arms and legs pumping with such fury no one dared get in his way. His mind was in a whirlwind. Tommie, no, please, this can't be happening, please don't let this be happening. Please God, let him be okay, please, oh God, Jesus, let him be okay, please, please, PLEASE!

He burst through the door and had to fight his way up the stairs through a crowd that was straining to see inside a bedroom. One of the double doors was hanging loosely by its hinges, and as he peered into the room he spotted Dan tending to Tommie, who was sitting unconscious next to the bed.

Dan stood up, his arms outstretched toward the floor, pleading, "Mick, I don't know what happened. He met this girl and…"

Mickey shoved him aside, took one look at his little brother, and felt his heart shatter. He fell to his knees and put his head on Tommie's chest and desperately listened for a heartbeat. He heard none. He looked up at the other football players and yelled "CALL 911!" Dan and Patrick answered miserably that they had.

Mickey turned back to his brother and gazed sorrowfully at him, up and down, and then began to touch him tentatively, caressing his hands, his arms, chest, and face. It was as if he knew this was it, the last time he would ever see the child he practically raised himself in this world. "Tom? You okay?" he choked out. "Tom, come on, we gotta go. We got a big game coming up. You know, the one with the scouts? Gonna go to Notre Dame, right? Make Pop proud, the way we always said, right? Come on, kiddo. Wake up. Wake up, please…" And, wracked with sobs, he simply buried his head in his little brother's chest and let the grief overtake him.

Shane stood frozen at the doorway, unable to process the devastation in front of him. He looked back and forth between the two lifeless bodies in the room, the incapacitated football players and then the drug paraphernalia on the night table. He inspected the mirror and the rolled up dollar bills. When he asked Logan about it, the teenager said, "Not sure what happened. The girl must've had it."

With that, a howl of pain sounded from outside the bedroom window. He ran to it and saw three girls, one of them spraying a Shamrock in the face with a can of mace. He yelled, "Hey!" and the girls looked up at him with fright. He had seen them on the way up the stairs, and it finally occurred to him who they might be. The little brunette. The girl they had saved from getting kidnapped a few years back. The stripper who had been Jack's girlfriend. The one who worked for Salazar.

And they had now poisoned Tommie.

"Stop those girls!" he yelled and bolted back out of the room. But the damage had already been done.

CHAPTER 30

ENOUGH IS ENOUGH

Gretta drove with frantic speed, racing through stops signs, ignoring red lights, and nearly avoiding several accidents. The other girls held on for dear life and pleaded for her to slow down, but in her frenzy she just kept going, making loops and sharp turns until she was sure they weren't being pursued. On one dark block with large overhanging trees, she turned the headlights off and cruised to a stop underneath the shadow of a massive oak.

She turned off the engine and swung around in her

seat. In the passenger seat, Lacey glared at her while Trixie shrunk back in the rear seat, crying hysterically.

"It's okay now, Trix. Calm down," Gretta said. Her chest was heaving hard. All of the ugliness that she had seen in her life, the abuse, the violence, the exhausting hours of emptiness, and now the senseless death of Krystal ran her over like an avalanche. Her face, that of a brown-eyed angel, twisted into a countenance of despair and she finally broke down and cried.

The other two girls came forward for a miserable embrace. Thus, the three prostitutes lingered, grieving the loss of their friend, lamenting their own broken lives, and worrying about the future to come.

When they finally pulled away from each other, wiping their tears, Lacey said, "Is it true, Gretta? About Krystal? You absolutely *sure*?"

Gretta just nodded, her face threatening to crumble again.

"How do you know?" Trixie managed.

Gretta sighed, emotionally exhausted. "Because I saw her."

"What do you mean?" Lacey said.

"I've seen that look before, Lace. Remember what happened to Vanessa a couple of years ago? When we found her in her car? That's what Krystal looked like. Frozen, staring into space, and that pink stuff coming out of her nose. It was horrible!" Her hands flew to her face and she broke down once again.

When she finally composed herself, Lacey asked, "So she OD'd? The kid too? But we didn't have that much coke!"

Gretta suddenly punched the dashboard. "That fuck!" she said. "He gave us all bad shit. Poison. To kill the kid!"

Trixie sat back hard in her seat and began weeping quietly to herself.

Lacey was at a loss. "But it was supposed to be just a *little* bit of coke. You know, just to let O'Leary know we could get to his brother? It wasn't supposed to *kill* him. At the worst get him hooked!"

Gretta spoke with bitterness. "What, you don't think Victor's capable of this? He's as cold-blooded as it gets! He'd kill anyone to get a point across. Even innocent people. The bastard sent us to do his dirty work and now Krystal's dead. It could have been any one of us."

Lacey opened her purse and pulled out her vial of coke. Then Gretta took out hers and Krystal's. She told Trixie to take out hers as well.

"Give them to me," Gretta said. "We have to get rid of them." The other girls handed over the vials and she stared at the white powder, shaking her head in questioning remorse. "Two young, beautiful people dead. Lives wiped out by this little white stuff." She rolled down the window and was about to throw them out when she hesitated, looked down at the tiny glass bottles, and put them back in her purse.

"No," she said, "I have a better idea."

Lacey gasped. "What are you talking about? We have to get rid of those. The cops are gonna think we killed them!"

"We need them."

"Why!?"

Gretta stared through the windshield into the darkness and a whole series of events, many of them traumatic, danced across her eyes. Barely noticeably she flinched and then shuddered while Lacey waited for an answer. The tiny dancer with the liquid brown eyes finally turned back to her remaining friends and said, "It's time."

"What's time?"

"How many times have you guys wished you could just go home? To be done with all this abuse? To get away from all these sadistic maniacs?" She paused and put her hand over her mouth. "I can't even remember what it's like to not be afraid."

In the back seat, Trixie managed to pull herself together and asked, "So you think we should take off? Just leave?"

"No," Gretta said, "I say we take him down."

Lacey leaned forward, her eyes raging with disbelief. "Are you *crazy*?" she said. "What? Testify against Victor Salazar? They'll find us all in a dumpster, not to mention our families! What are you thinking? You know how many witnesses he's killed over the years?" She reached for Gretta's bag. "Give me those!"

"HEY!" Gretta said, and jerked her bag away. Lacey continued to try for the bag, but Gretta spun around and fought back. Although she was small, she was more firmly built than the lithe Lacey. Gretta quickly shoved her back into her seat. "Knock it off!" she said, her eyes wide and her chest heaving, "You didn't see Krystal back there! I did!" She glared back and forth between the other two girls. "She's dead! And it could have been any one of us!" She lowered her voice and looked soberly into the eyes of her friends. "How long do you think it's gonna be before the rest of us end up like her? Victor doesn't care about us. We're just money-making slaves who he can fuck any time he wants to."

She sat back and looked down at her hands and her voice got very quiet. "I don't know who I am anymore. No family. No real purpose." She looked up with a rueful smile. "The only man I ever loved thinks I'm a whore."

"That's fine, Gretta," Lacey said. "We'll all pretty much in the same boat. We've all been shit on, but I still don't want to die."

Gretta wiped her eyes with her hands and dried them on her thighs. "Well if you stay with him, you're going to. Sooner or later he will suck you dry and you'll have no life left in you. As for me? I'm done. I'm not going back there."

Trixie came forward from the darkness of the back seat. She gave Gretta an empathetic look while wiping away tears with the cuffs of her sweatshirt. She sniffled and said, "I'm done too, Grets. Whatever you want to do, I'm with you."

Lacey said, "What? You two are out of you mind!"

Gretta gave Lacey a familiar glance. She cocked her head to the side and looked deeply into her friend's eyes. "Come on, Lace, you know me. You know I'm not stupid. You know I'd never do anything this risky without thinking it through."

Lacey made quotation marks with her hands and said, "So what's this 'brilliant' idea you have that's gonna get us all killed?"

Gretta nodded to herself, like she could see all the pieces fitting together. "We need to call George."

CHAPTER 31

MCGAVIN HAS A CHANGE OF HEART

Captain George McGavin parked his car halfway up the block from his apartment, in the darkest corner of the street. He shut off the ignition and sat there quietly, his senses on high alert. Having determined for the moment that there was no clear and present danger, he grabbed his KFC takeout with one hand, and got out of the car with his Colt 45 in the other. He shoved the door closed with his butt, looked around once more, and moved as swiftly as his portly body could toward his home.

McGavin's living arrangements were a perfect example

of how Victor Salazar could single-handedly ruin a person's life. To Salazar, it was purely business. If he needed someone's services, all he had to do was zero in the person's weakness, offer up a little bait, and set the trap.

It was the perfect formula.

McGavin's lust for sports gambling had always been a problem. And it was a problem that had played right into Salazar's hands. The mob boss had been looking for someone on the inside of the police department, someone well liked and with a lot of connections. When one of Salazar's bookies had informed him of a cop with some sizeable losses, Salazar went into action. He offered McGavin an unlimited line of credit, enabling the gambler to slowly sink deeper and deeper into a quagmire of debt. Salazar then befriended the gambler, forgave his debt, and offered him anything he wanted: expensive dinners, tickets to big concerts, sporting events, girls…and even cocaine.

He just had to do Salazar some "favors." Favors like shaking down smaller drug dealers. Like having evidence disappear when some of his men got themselves arrested. And favors like introducing him to other members of the police force. High standing members of the police force.

It seemed clear to George now, that Salazar had simply used him to forge powerful connections in his precinct. Though these relationships had facilitated his promotion to captain, it was now evident that he had become obsolete. And with a criminal like Salazar, if you knew too much, you were considered a loose end. A liability. A hazard to the trade. After Salazar had cut him off, McGavin felt like his life was in danger. Especially after Frankie was killed. And now his paranoia was starting to get the best of him.

So it was to his dingy one-bedroom condo, that, McGavin slinked through the darkness. When he finally reached his back door, he held up his gun, put the KFC bag in his mouth, and inserted the key in the lock. As he pushed it open, a fire truck horn blared fiercely. With his hairs standing on end, he fell to one knee and desperately pointed his gun around in every possible direction, ready for the imminent gunfire

When nothing happened for several moments, he blinked, clumsily got back to his feet, and went over to disengage the alarm. He then proceeded to check every nook and cranny for some unwelcomed intruder. Once satisfied, he breathed a deep sigh of relief, made sure every door and window was locked, and drew down every shade. Only then was he able to spend his Saturday night in peace.

McGavin couldn't believe Frankie was dead. The investigation into his murder had revealed little so far, but that was of no surprise. It appeared to be a professional hit, and in such cases evidence was rarely left behind. McGavin had his own suspicions for sure, fully aware of the tension between the O'Leary kid and Salazar. *But did Mickey have the balls to pull off the execution of such a high ranking thug?* Maybe the balls, he thought, but it didn't seem likely that Mickey would make such a drastic move against cold-hearted killer like Victor Salazar. The more probable scenario was that Salazar had seen enough of Frankie's nonsense and decided to send a ruthless wake-up call to the rest of his crew.

It *was* kind of troubling that Frankie's "girlfriend" Maria was missing. It crossed his mind that she had something to do with it, but shrugged it off. She probably just took off after hearing what had happened to Frankie, wanting no part of whatever turf war was being waged at the moment.

McGavin put his fried chicken dinner on the kitchen counter and went into his bedroom to undress. His took a hot shower and let the stress of the past week drain from his body. After drying himself off, he put on a pair of boxer shorts, one of his purple silk robes, white sweat socks that he pulled up over his calves and his favorite Nike flip-flops. He went to the refrigerator, retrieved the plastic gallon of milk and took a pull from it, holding it like a lumberjack would a jug of brandy. After several gulps, he exhaled deeply and then belched so loud it vibrated the picture frames on his wall. He then farted and scratched his ass before grabbing the ten-piece Tub-O-Chicken, and lugging it over to his favorite La-Z-Boy chair, the one thing he was allowed to take after Madge had thrown him out.

He placed the food onto a snack table in front of him, grabbed the remote and turned on the TV. The World Series had played an afternoon matinee game, so the only other interesting sporting event that night was the Islander game. By the time McGavin found the channel, the Islanders were already down 3-0. And it was only five minutes into the first period.

"Jesus Christ!" he yelled, waving a chicken leg at the TV. He then closed his eyes and groaned, realizing the highlight of his evening had been ruined before it even began. He shook his head in disbelief, took another bite of chicken, and bellowed, "Fuckin' SUCK!", spraying particles of food everywhere. *How could a professional sports team be so bad for so long?* For over 25 years since the team had won an unprecedented four Stanley Cups in a row, the organization had been a complete and utter disaster. If he heard another Islander broadcaster say that the Islanders were "getting younger" or "in a rebuilding mode," he was going to toss the whole greasy bucket of the Colonel's finest through the TV.

After he gobbled down the chicken, he retrieved his plaid-patterned shaving kit, sat back, unzipped it, and pulled out his coke and marijuana stash. First he was gonna "roll a fattie" and have a smoke to "help digest." Then he'd do a couple of lines just to pick up his mood. Hey, it was Saturday night and it had been a long week.

While the nightly news droned on in the background, he smoked his joint, sucking in the fragrant, spicy vapor and letting it linger in his lungs to get the full effect. After a moment, he breathed it back out with a moan of satisfaction that would turn the head of a sleeping cat. Once burned down to the roach, he tossed it in the ashtray and then tapped out some coke.

After sucking up two particularly wide lines, he suddenly jerked his head up, with both his eyes threatening to shoot out of his head. Anchor Maria Chavez, whom George had watched deliver the news professionally for over ten years, had just announced a shocking news bulletin. Thomas O'Leary, the star wide receiver of Soundview High School and an unidentified female between the ages of 18 and 30, were pronounced dead at Lady of Our Lords hospital earlier that evening. Sources believe the deaths were a result of a drug overdose, most likely cocaine laced with a powerful toxin...

McGavin listened to the rest of the story, stiff as a mannequin. When the newscast broke for commercial, he got up slowly and walked into the bathroom. In the sickly yellow light of the incandescent bulbs above the mirror, he examined his reflection. His eyes had become shriveled raisins, receding back into their sockets, and swimming in clear liquid. And his cheeks, both oily and flaccid, sagged somewhat below his jaw, his skin the texture of a moldering, rubber mask.

He stood there over the sink, wheezing rhythmically and gazing stupidly at his reflection, contempt slowly but surely creeping into his face. "What have you become?" he whispered, and lowered his head and wept.

* * *

The phone rang and roused him out of his pitiful state of self-loathing. He dried his left eye with his arm and with a balled-up clump of toilet paper he wiped the rest of his bloated face. He sniffed once, took a deep breath, and went into the living room. On the fourth ring he picked up the phone with a quivering hand.

"McGavin" he croaked.

A young girl said, "George?" Her voice sounded urgent.

His mind began to race and he stood up straight. He frowned and cleared his throat. "Yeah. Who is this?"

"Oh my God. Thank God I got you. It's Gretta."

McGavin put hand over his other ear and went to turn down the volume on the TV. "Gretta?" he said, "you okay? What's going on?"

"We're in trouble here, George and we...we don't know what to do." Her voice caught and she paused, fighting back the tears that were trying so hard to break free. "We need someone we can trust and there's nobody else. Can we trust you, George?"

His mind was whirling. "Gretta, what's happening? Who's we?"

"I'm with Lacey and Trix and something bad's happened. Krystal...oh my God, Krystal..."

"Jesus Christ, Gretta. Please don't tell me...was she... the girl they found at that party over in treemont?"

When he only heard weeping on the other end, he lowered his head and fell back on the couch. One hand was holding the phone to his ear, while the other one kept rubbing his forehead. His voice came out dry and hoarse. "Are *you* three okay? Are you safe?"

Gretta regained her composure. "Yeah, we're fine right now but we need to talk."

"Did he do this, Gretta?"

There was silence on the other end for an impossibly long moment.

"Gretta?"

When she spoke, her voice was low but fueled with defiance and strength. "Meet me at the Apollo diner in one hour."

McGavin looked at his watch and began to move. "Okay, I'll be there."

"And George?"

"Yeah?"

"If anything happens to me, you'll be hearing from the FBI."

* * *

McGavin arrived at the diner fifteen minutes early and found Gretta sitting in a booth furthest away from the window. She was staring into a steaming cup of coffee. Her hair was back in a ponytail but her bangs were still hanging low over her cocoa-colored eyes. When she sensed him approach, she lifted her head up and shook her hair from her face in a reflexive motion that, to McGavin, had become so charmingly familiar. She motioned for him to sit down.

He noticed she was pale, her eyes weary with sadness and her cheeks stained with dried tracks of mascara. "You hear about it on the news?" she asked, nodding toward the TV at the counter.

"Yeah, I did," he said. "The O'Leary kid." He swallowed and gazed off into the distance. Almost to himself he said, "I can't believe he did it. A high school kid. An innocent kid." He looked back at Gretta. "So Krystal was the girl they found?"

Gretta's face threatened to crumble but she fought it back. She nodded and when she spoke, her voice quivered with controlled rage. "George, it could have been any one of us. Me, Trixie, Lacey. It didn't matter to him if any of us lived or died. All he wanted was for one of us to get the kid to do some coke and the job was done. What's another dead whore to him?"

"But that's pretty risky, isn't it?" said McGavin. "Even for him. What if you guys decided to do the coke before the kid?"

"Victor was very specific when he spoke to us. He said he had mixed up a very special batch for the kid to try. He said it was unbelievable stuff and it was sure to get the kid hooked. He said we could do it too, but only after the kid did it. He was very clear on that. He said if he found out any of us did it before the kid, we would be sorry. It just turned out the kid liked Krystal the best, so she ended up with him. Sucks for her, right?"

A waitress in her forties with long dark hair tied in a bun appeared and looked expectantly at McGavin. She wore a white button down shirt, black vest, black skirt, and white sneakers. She took a pencil out of her hair and said, "What can I get you, honey?" He looked at the menus sitting on the table, then back at the waitress with an embarrassed smile. "Sorry, haven't had the chance to look. Um, just coffee for now."

The waitress gave him a warm smile and looked back and forth between him and Gretta. "Like daughter, like father," she said. "Take your time. I'll be right back with your coffee."

McGavin watched her leave and turned back to Gretta. "Like father?"

A hint of a smile appeared on her face. "I gave her your description before, told her to bring you back here when you arrived. She gave me this look like 'Why are you meeting an older man by yourself in a diner late at night?' So I gave my usual response which was 'he's my father.'"

"Oh," McGavin said and looked back over his shoulder at the waitress. She was smiling to herself while pouring his coffee, but when she noticed him glancing at her, she quickly looked away.

Gretta sat back and put her knee up, the holes in her frayed jeans spreading apart to reveal smooth, mocha skin. She scratched her knee and said, "She's totally checking you out, you know."

He frowned. "Who, *her*? No! You think so?"

"Trust me, I'm a woman. I can tell." But then her smile

429

faded and she sat forward. "George, I need to know. Can we trust you? I mean, we're kinda screwed here. The cops want us for questioning in a double homicide, Victor couldn't care if we were alive or dead, probably better off dead for him, and if The Shamrocks get ahold of us, God knows what they'll do." She wrapped her hands around the still-steaming coffee, gazed over his shoulder, and then searched his eyes. "We're putting our lives in your hands, George. What's it gonna be?"

McGavin gazed at her for a moment. They had been together on and off in the past, sometimes in a business transaction and then one time after Jack, when she was desperately lonely, in a spontaneous tryst. Salazar had never found out about it or it would have cost both of them. There had actually been a special bond between them; McGavin admiring her independent strength and she enjoying his goofy sense of humor. She could have been his lover or his daughter and fit each role equally well. In either scenario, he liked her. Liked her a lot. And she had been precariously close to death. She and the other girls. None of them had deserved such a precarious way of life. Whether or not they had chosen the lives they led, they were still people and no one, not even Victor Salazar, had the right to render them expendable.

"What do you need?"

"I need a reason to trust you."

He nodded and said, "I got ya. I understand. God knows my track record ain't all it's cracked up to be. Okay, how about this? You could be wearing a wire now, right? You get me to say something to incriminate myself or Salazar and I'm screwed, right? So here is what I'll say. Last week

I heard Victor Salazar say to Mickey O'Leary that if he didn't merge The Shamrocks with The Power, he'd hurt his brother Tommie. I saw Mickey freak out, saw him tased by Frankie Malone and then dragged out of the room, unconscious. I could have done something. I could have acted like a cop. But what did that do? Nothing. Now two people are dead. One, from what I understand, was a terrific kid with a tremendous future. The other, a misguided young girl who should have had a better fate. And I coulda stopped it from happening."

He slid his hand up over his bald head, the palmsof his hands running through the rusty-colored hair that grew in over his ears. "I'm done looking the other way. Enough is enough."

Gretta studied his face for dishonesty and found none. A decision had to be made. "Okay," she said and waved to someone over his shoulder. He turned around and recognized Trixie, the sensitive redhead, and Lacey, the fun one with the dirty blonde hair. He moved over to allow Lacey a seat and Trixie moved in beside Gretta.

Trixie questioningly looked at Gretta, who said, "It's okay. Give it to him." She opened her purse, took out a white plastic bag, and handed it over to McGavin. It made a light clinking sound as he took it.

He raised his eyebrows, and in succession looked at Gretta, Trixie, Lacey, and then back to Gretta. "What's this? he asked.

Gretta said, "Just look inside."

He opened the bag, glanced inside, and smiled in understanding. "So this is all of it?"

"Yep, we each had one. You can check it out, right? See if it's poison?" said Gretta.

"Yeah," McGavin said in a daze. "Yeah, I can do that."

"So that can put him in jail?" Trixie said.

"Maybe, Trix, but it's much more complicated than that. This is just stuff in some tiny jars. Even if his fingerprints on the bottles, and I doubt they are, it's still a flimsy case. He wasn't at the party, right? So how do I prove he had anything to do with this?'

Gretta said, "Well you heard him threaten Tommie O'Leary, didn't you?"

"Yeah, but he's got good lawyers. They could make me look like a dirty cop who fell out of favor with a mobster and was looking for revenge."

"Well," Gretta said, "what if you had more witnesses?"

"Yeah," Trixie said excitedly. "*Three* more witnesses."

McGavin glanced around at the girls, astonished. "You'd *all* testify?"

Gretta said, "What are our choices? We can't go back to Salazar. He thinks our lives are worthless. He'll probably try to hunt us down because we all know too much. And we can't stay on the streets. The Shamrocks are looking for us all over." She glanced anxiously toward the front of the diner. "We're taking a risk just being here right now." Fire flashed behind her eyes. "The only chance we have is to fight. We have nothing left to lose."

Trixie said, "That's right," and Lacey nodded somberly.

And in an awestruck voice, almost entirely to himself, Detective George McGavin of Soundview said, "*No shit.*"

CHAPTER 32

SALAZAR GOES FOR A RIDE

Two days later a battalion of police cruisers and unmarked cars arrived at Victor Salazar's estate with their sirens blaring and proceeded up the wooded drive to his house. There were also six cops on motorcycles wearing the requisite regalia, reminiscent of the patrolman from The Village People. A loud rhythmic hum ebbed and flowed from the sky as two police helicopters circled above the vast front lawn. The patrol cars pulled up near a dark blue limousine that was parked by the marble porch.

Then Victor Salazar made his appearance. He strolled

out onto his porch with the grin of a movie star, his veneers sparkling in the morning sun, delighting in all the commotion he had caused. He slipped into his Armani sports jacket and made a production out of pulling his shirt cuffs through his sleeves. One of the helicopters zoomed by again and he threw his arms up into the sky, pacing around, nodding in self-satisfaction like only the Roman emperors had once done.

While Salazar was basking in his own glory, Detective George McGavin emerged from his black sedan and wearily approached him on the veranda. Nikos Moustakas was in his postition, crossing his meaty arms across his chest and looking defiant behind a pair of mirrored aviators.

"You guys are early," Salazar said, half-squinting in the sunlight. "Didn't have time to floss." He made a sharp sucking sound with his tongue, the sound one makes when trying to dislodge a piece of food that's stuck between his teeth. "So you gonna read me my rights?"

McGavin put his hand in his pockets, tilted his head back, and looked as if he was holding back what he really wanted to say. Finally, he said, "Can we get this over with? You're not under arrest. There isn't even a warrant. Like I told you on the phone, this is just a formality. You come in, answer some questions, and everything will be taken care of."

Salazar stuck out his chin, nodded, and looked at Nikos. He then pointed his thumb at the detective and said, "You hear that Nikos? He's gonna take care of everything."

The bodyguard simply stared ahead, frozen like a statue wearing sunglasses.

Salazar turned back to McGavin with a suspicious glare. "You sure I don't need Shapiro?"

"Nope. But that's up to you."

Salazar looked past the detective at the other patrolmen and considered it for a moment, "Maybe I should have him meet us there…or maybe not." He leaned over to McGavin and said quietly, "Fucker charges five thousand an hour.." He shook his head in mock lamentation. "Lawyers. Now *they're* the ones that should be arrested. Greedy bastards." He stood back and studied McGavin for a moment. "Nah, fuck him," he said. "You say I don't need him, I don't need him. Like you said, we've been through this before. I'll call him away from his golf game if I need him." Grinning, he clapped his hands loudly, rubbed them together vigorously, and said, "So Georgie, just like old times, huh? I love it."

"I guess so," McGavin said. "But seriously, you needed all this?" He gestured toward the patrolmen.

Salazar put out his arms and said, "Maybe not *all* of it. But it couldn't hurt to be too careful, you know? No need to take any chances with O'Leary on the warpath. I bet he thinks I had something to do with his brother's stupidity and I'm not about to let my guard down. You know I had nothing to do with it, right?"

McGavin shrugged. "Not my business."

Salazar's smile widened and he said, "I wouldn't want to be a victim of any kind of misunderstanding, if you know what I mean. So, thanks for your cooperation."

"Happy to be of service."

"Right! And what service it is! Gotta love these escorts!" He looked up at the sky and took in a deep breath. "Let's have our little parade."

He moved forward, put his left arm around McGavin, and directed him toward the limo.

"I'm going with you?" McGavin said.

Salazar nodded and patted McGavin on the chest. "Yessiree! We've got a few things to iron out."

"Then hold on a second." He extricated himself from Salazar, went over to his car, and leaned inside. He pulled out a plastic bag, went over to a nearby plainclothes officer, and handed him his keys. He then came back to the limo. A chauffer ceremoniously ushered Salazar, Nikos, and McGavin inside and finally the procession started off.

Inside the limo, the cabin was dark with soft velvet seats, plush carpeting, and plenty of leg room. The bar was stocked with top shelf liquor, ice, juices, fresh fruit, bagels, and all sorts of spreads. McGavin could even smell the freshly brewed coffee from a set of secured urns on the shelf.

"Nice spread," McGavin said.

"We spare no expense," said Salazar. "Especially on a day like this. Would you like a mimosa?"

"No thanks. Too early for me."

Salazar's eyebrows rose. "Really? That's not the McGavin *I* know." He sat back, spread both his arms out on the top of his seat, and examined the detective. "You don't look so good, my friend."

McGavin stifled a yawn. "Haven't been getting much sleep lately."

Salazar held up his hands and circled them in opposite directions. "Working your magic for me?" He let out a loud guffaw, then leaned forward and clapped the detective on the shoulder. "Wow, that must be exhausting. Have some coffee, it won't spill." He lean forward again and whispered,

"Car purrs like a cat. Never feel a bump." He looked around the limo with genuine pride. "Shit, this thing could hit a two-foot pot hole and you wouldn't know it. Ingenious design, don't you think?"

"Feels nice."

"So, you want some?"

"What?"

Salazar looked at Nikos, who simply stared at McGavin with an expressionless face carved out of granite. Seeing nothing worth noting there, Salazar looked back at McGavin and said, "The coffee, numbnuts, what do you think?"

"Oh," McGavin said, and ran a hand over his worn face. "Yeah, sure."

Nikos, as if now miraculously brought to life, said, "How you want it?"

"Milk and sugar, I guess."

"Milk and sugar, you guess." He went over to the urns and prepared the detective's coffee.

One of the helicopters passed overhead and Salazar opened the roof to take a look. The aircraft glided by under a canvas of bright blue, slashed with brushstrokes of white fire. The chopper flew on like a giant prehistoric insect. "Love those things," he said. "So cool the way they can hover, go up, down, back and forth. Gotta get me one of those."

Once McGavin had tried his coffee, Salazar said, "How is it?"

"Not bad. Thanks."

"Not at all. But now, if you don't mind, you need to put it down for a second." He gave Nikos a signal and the body builder went over to McGavin. "Hands up. Just

want to make sure we can talk. Don't want any surprises."
He scrunched up his face and whispered, "Can never be
too careful with you corrupt types." He shook his head
emphatically. "Nope. Don't like recordings. I mean, how
can you lie about anything later if you're on tape, hmm?"

Nikos checked the detective for any kind of recording
device and returned to his seat satisfied. "Clean." He
muttered and resumed his empty stare.

"So, let's talk," Salazar said. "The sluts came to you after
this, this, how should I put it…tragedy?"

"That's right," McGavin said. "They were all hysterical
and didn't know what to do. Guess they thought I could
help them."

"And they're claiming I was behind all this?"

"Correct. They said you gave them each some laced
coke with the instructions to find and seduce the O'Leary
kid and get him to do it."

"Huh! Unbelievable. Stupid girls. None of them will
ever have a peaceful night's sleep again." He looked out the
window and watched one of the motorcycle cops wave a
pedestrian out of the way. "So how do they intend to prove
I had anything to do with this?"

"They're all willing to testify in court that it was your
plan and they had no idea the coke was laced." He winced
and said, "Obviously Krystal had no idea."

"Yes, well, she never was too swift, that one."

McGavin reluctantly nodded. "Anyway, it would be
tough to convince a jury you were guilty if it were just your
word against theirs."

"That's promising. Why's that?"

"Well, they could have gotten the coke anywhere. And

they're prostitutes. Known con artists. It's not out of the realm of possibility they could be trying to frame you."

Salazar gave a mock gasp and pressed his fingers on his chest. "You really think they could be holding a grudge against me? After all I've done for them?"

"Anything's possible, but like I said, their word against yours doesn't make a case."

"So then there's no problem?"

"Well, it does get a little more complicated, but nothing we couldn't handle." He then handed over the plastic sack he had removed from his car just before they left.

As Salazar took the bag, it made a soft, clinking sound inside the rustle of the plastic. When he saw what was inside, a cold light appeared in his eyes.

McGavin said, "Gretta gave me those as long as I promised to protect her and the other girls."

The drug lord studied McGavin for a long while, searching for any hint of deception. He then closed the sky roof and quickly reached down between his legs. He lifted up a piece of carpeting, took his set of keys out, and opened a small safe in the floor. He dropped the bag in, closed the safe and replaced the carpeting.

"This limo leaves once we get to the precinct, you got it?"

"That's the idea."

Salazar drummed his fingers on his thigh. "A little risky giving it to me now, don't you think?"

Beads of sweat started to form on the detective's upper lip. "Just wanted to show you I'm on your side. I guess I coulda told you I had it somewhere but I thought it would be best to give it to you. Get rid of it yourself." He shrugged and looked out the window. "Doesn't matter anyway. You got nothing to worry about. Last thing anyone wants is you on trial for murder. Too many important people are tied up with you and nobody wants to be exposed. Don't worry. We'll make it go away."

Salazar nodded. He seemed to relax a bit. "So where are the girls?"

McGavin went to reach inside his jacket pocket but then hesitated. He looked to where his hand was and then down at the floor, his eyes moistening with sorrow. He then made a decision and took out a small piece of paper, holding it out to Salazar. "This is where they're staying."

Salazar leaned over and took it. He examined the note, jutted out his chin, and nodded. "I got to tell you, I'm impressed with your loyalty." He handed the note to Nikos and told him, "Make sure this gets taken care of." He removed a cigarette and lit it with a shiny gold Zippo, then blew out a cloud of smoke that filled the entire compartment. "But there's one thing I don't get, Georgie. Last week I threw you out of my house, insulted you, and said I never wanted to see you again. I would think you'd be thrilled to see me go down. Why are you in such a rush to help me now?"

McGavin swallowed, his pride at an all-time low. "The truth? The fact is I'm busted. My bank accounts are cleaned out. My paycheck goes almost entirely to my bitch of an ex-wife and my kids who I never get to see think I'm a loser. I live in a shitty one-bedroom apartment in a lousy neighborhood and my life is in the toilet. So what can I do? I got no choice. I need money." He swallowed dryly and looked pleadingly at the powerful mobster who had controlled him for the past ten-odd years. "I want back in, Vic."

"I don't know. Seems to me you been slippin'"

McGavin leaned forward, rested his elbows on his knees, and held his hands out. He glanced at Nikos' granite face and then back to Salazar. "Listen, I know I fucked up with this whole Shamrock thing, but I figured maybe I could make it right with you right now. I can make this case go away, I know it. And after this is all over, I can do even more for you. What do you say?"

Salazar just gazed at him, giving away nothing.

"Come on, Victor. I got nothing without you."

Salazar considered this for a while, taking long slow drags of his cigarette while alternately glaring at him and gazing out the window. Finally, he said, "So that's all you want for this? To get back in my good graces?"

McGavin looked back, a clear icy expression on his face. "I didn't say that."

Salazar raised his eyebrows. "Really? What then?"

"I want Frankie's job."

Silence hung in the air as the limousine hummed along. Salazar turned his head to look Nikos, still inscrutable in his petrified pose. Finally he turned back to McGavin and said, "If you can get his whole thing to go away, you can have what you want. But let me tell you something, and listen very carefully. If anything goes wrong and I have to spend even one day in jail, I will *bury* you. You'll never see your kids alive again."

McGavin blinked and on several occasions opened his mouth as if to say something, *anything* to assure Salazar that it would never come to that. *Could* never come to that.

But the words never left his mouth. All he could do was look out the window and watch the world pass by. Salazar, meanwhile, was enjoying inflicting such discomfort.

But as they rode on and the time passed silently between them, McGavin gradually switched his gaze back to the drug lord and his demeanor changed from uncertain submission, to a more confident composure, and then ultimately to a smug satisfaction.

"What the hell are you smirking at?" Salazar said.

The smile dropped from McGavin's face instantly, as if he didn't realize it was there. He then seemed angry at himself for allowing it to happen. "I just gotta ask you something, Vic," he said

"Yeah, what's that?"

"Was it really necessary? A high school kid? I mean, kinda low even for you."

"Watch it, McGavin," Nikos said.

Salazar put an arm on his bodyguard's arm and said, "It's okay, Nick." He assessed McGavin in his typical smug manner. "I don't have to explain myself, Georgie, but since you asked, I'll say this. O'Leary was in my way. A stubborn, reckless kid. He fucked up my shit once too many times. I tried to work with him but he decided to thumb his nose at me. And that was after I gave him a warning. He knew what was at stake and opted for a battle. Killing Frankie was the final straw."

"You sure Mickey had him killed?" McGavin said.

"Sure enough for me."

McGavin nodded, then said, "What about Krystal?"

Salazar held out his arms. "What about her?"

"All she was doing was carrying out your orders. Why did she have to die too?"

"The O'Leary kid was too well protected. I had to use the girls. And none of them would've gone through with it if they knew what they were doing." He chuckled and shook his head. "Gotta hand it to the dumb blonde, though. Did a great job. I'm actually quite pleased with her performance."

McGavin felt ice water run up and down his spine. He fought back a shudder. He looked down and swallowed. When he spoke, his voice sounded like a car wheel rolling over gravel. "Krystal was a good kid," he said.

Salazar shrugged. "She was a whore. Expendable. Plenty more where that came from." He pulled a piece of lint off his suit. "She won't be missed."

As the limousine pulled up to the precinct, a throng of reporters was roped off along the walkway that led up to the front of the building. Salazar put on his sunglasses, grinned the widest grin he ever would, and said, "Come on, guys. We're gonna be on TV."

The driver put the limo in park and opened up their door. McGavin got out first and made a signal with his hands. Once Salazar and Nikos were on the sidewalk, every officer, uniformed and plainclothes alike, drew his gun and rushed forward.

Pandemonium exploded.

Like a wave, the cops surged forward bellowing "FREEZE! DON'T MOVE! HANDS IN THE AIR!" and shoved Salazar, Nikos, and the limo driver up against the car. They frisked and cuffed the three of them while Salazar pleaded his case of entrapment and proclaimed his innocence to the media personnel, who were already foaming at the mouth.

McGavin, who had the pleasure of hand-cuffing Salazar himself, then announced loudly enough for the media to hear, "Victor Salazar, you're under arrest for the murder of Tommie O'Leary and Krystal White. You have the right to remain silent. Anything you say can and will be used against you in a court of law…"

The group of reporters erupted into a frenzy, taking photos and volleying forth a desperate bevy of questions. When McGavin finally asked Salazar if he understood his Miranda rights, the drug dealer simply glared at him. His expression told the detective all he needed to know.

McGavin said, "I repeat. Do you understand these rights I just read you?

Salazar just looked deeply into his eyes and said, "You're gonna regret this someday."

McGavin smiled easily. A soothing feeling cradled his scalp and he felt a lightness in his chest. It was the most genuine feeling he could remember. He beamed, shook his head, and said three words:

"No, I won't."

* * *

Captain McGavin signaled over two plainclothes officers, who took Salazar forcibly by the arms and ushered him briskly inside. With indignation, the mobster loudly proclaimed his innocence and assured the media that before it was all over, he would be a free man, suing the department for defamation of character.

Once inside the station house, everything stopped.

Conversations halted mid-sentence. People froze in their tracks. And everyone stared slack-jawed as one of the most notorious gangsters of their time was brought in.

To all who were involved in the process, it was a remarkable sight to see. Victor Salazar was booked, fingerprinted and photographed, as if he were merely a street punk being detained for drug possession. He was ordered to strip, removed of his clothes and personal effects, and sent in for a cold shower. He was then given an orange jump suit with convict numbers printed across the back, shackled around his wrists and ankles, and escorted rather hostilely to a remote wing, where he was to be secluded from the general population for his own protection.

They took him down a few flights of steps and proceeded along several dimly lit hallways that echoed their footsteps among dreary silence. By the time Victor Salazar was sitting on the hard, concrete floor in the space the size of a closet, he was furious. No matter what happened, George McGavin was now his mortal enemy. And amidst the stench of urine, the suffocating darkness, and the scream of scurrying rats, he conceived of his plans for revenge.

* * *

Two days later Victor Salazar heard a loud buzz at the end of the hall and the sound of a heavy door unlatching and rolling open. He listened as footsteps and the voices of two men approached his cell. The steps stopped in front of his door and a set of keys jingled. The lock was turned and the door flung open. A blinding light burned into his eyes and he jerked away from it, ducking back into the gloom of his tiny cell.

The guards plunged in and grabbed him by the arms and dragged him into the hallway. "Stand up!" one of the men demanded and they held him up between them.

Salazar's eyes slowly adjusted and he began to recognize the two men with him. One was tall and skinny with dark hair and a mustache. The other was a little shorter, with a short crew cut and a baby face. "Hanson, Billings, what the hell is going on? What is this bullshit?! You people are gonna pay for this!"

The stocky guy with the crew cut pulled Salazar's arm down so they were face to face. "Shut up!" he said through clenched teeth. "If you know what's good for you, you'll keep your mouth shut."

"But what—"

"Save your questions for McGavin," the other cop said, and they pulled him along, his cuffed ankles limiting him to tiny steps along the floor.

After about fifteen minutes of walking they got to a heavy metal door. It had a vertical rectangular glass window embedded with wire mesh. Hanson, the tall cop with the mustache, unlocked the door and they went inside. Salazar saw McGavin sitting at a table wearing a light blue button down shirt with the sleeves rolled up, his collar open, and a navy blue tie loosened around his neck. A pair of half eye reading glasses rested on the end of his nose and he appeared to be studying an open file while scribbling on a yellow note pad. He looked up briefly, saw the three of them, and smiled. "Ahhh! Our guest has arrived!" he said cheerily. "Come, have a seat." He gestured to the chair in front of the desk and went back to his reading. Hanson and Billings pushed Salazar forward and sat him down. They removed the cuffs from his wrists and ankles and used them to cuff each wrist into a fortified slot in the table. They then returned to the back of the room where they stood at attention on either side of the door.

After about a minute of watching the detective taking notes, Salazar said, "What the fuck is—"

Without looking up, McGavin held up a finger and said, "Shhhhhhh!" as he finished reading one last sentence. He put down his pencil, took off his glasses, and sat back in his chair. He examined the man across the table, the man who for so many years had insulted and belittled him. The man whom he allowed to beat and abuse others at a whim, ruin innocent lives just because he could, and kill without impunity because no one dared got in his way.

But there he sat, looking older than he ever had, his hair a tangled mess, his cheeks sunken and streaked with grime, and his eyes blazing with a frustration he had never felt before. "I want to speak to my fucking lawyer," he said.

"Really? You got a lawyer?"

"Yeah, McGavin. Stop with the bullshit. I want Shapiro here, now!"

"Oh yeah, Shapiro. Well, uh, he called us, seeing that you've been incarcerated, and he wanted us to let you know that, uh…" He lifted up a couple of sheets of the yellow pad to read something and then said, "his slate's full."

"What the fuck does that mean, 'his slate's full'? I pay him more than any of his other clients put together. Okay, fuck him, I'll get a better lawyer. Give me a phone. All I gotta do is find another big time defense lawyer and he'll eat you guys for lunch." He turned to look at the cops behind him and then back at McGavin. "Between the entrapment, the brutality, and withholding of my rights, you can all kiss your badges goodbye."

"So you're gonna find a better lawyer?"

"That's right."

"Perhaps one of those big time criminal lawyers on Park Avenue?"

"Maybe."

"One of those Harvard types who are so good only rich crooks like you can afford them?"

"Whatever! Just get me my fucking phone call!"

"Okay," McGavin said, "but I wouldn't waste my time calling an attorney that actually charges for defense."

"What the fuck are you talking about?"

"Well, the fact is, Vic, you can't *afford* a lawyer."

Salazar gritted his teeth together. "I'm telling you, McGavin, you better stop fucking around."

The detective reached down into a briefcase and pulled out several computer discs bound together by rubber bands. He separated them and began reading the labels off each one of them as he placed them on the table. "Geneva. Lucerne. San Jose. Buenos Aires. Cayman Islands."

Salazar began to tremble and his right eye began to twitch. "What the hell are those?"

"Oh, these? These were all your bank accounts. Actually they're still your accounts. They're just empty." He laced his fingers, put his forearms on the table, and whispered, "I had a little talk with Sheldon."

"YOU'RE LYING!" Salazar roared and futilely lunged at the detective, the handcuffs holding his wrists firmly to the desk.

McGavin sat back and yawned. "Yeah, Shelly gave you

up pretty easily once I threatened to turn him over to the IRS. They kinda frown upon money laundering in Washington. Especially in this economy. But don't worry, we'll find you a real good lawyer down at the public defender's office." He lifted another few pages of the yellow note pad. "Where is it? What was his name? Oh yeah, here it is. Trevor Gumb. He'll be defending you. Not much of a track record, but he did pass the bar on his third try. He'll be down to meet you tomorrow."

He reached down into his briefcase and pulled out the bag of vials he gave to Salazar in the limo. "You know, Vic. I gotta tell you. You are one cocky fuck. To think you could come down to the station house, so confident you'd get off from a double homicide, it's just mind-boggling."

"I didn't kill nobody."

"Yeah, well, a few days ago I might have believed that was possible. And I had to find out for myself if there was any chance, any chance at all that you weren't behind it all. But when you took these from me in the limo and also the address of where the girls were staying, that said it all. So now we have the motive, the method, witnesses willing to testify against you, and the poison itself. And everything points back to you. So I got one word of advice for you, Vic. *Confess.*"

Salazar said two words back to him clearly and emphatically. "Fuck you."

McGavin sat back and held his arms out. "Okay, have it your way. But we're talking capital murder here, Vic. Life without parole. And God knows what can happen to guys like you in the joint. Guys who have built up enemies over the years and have no money left to buy protection? You'll be someone's girlfriend before you know it. And when you're washed up, they'll find ways to torture you until you wished you confessed while you had the chance."

Salazar wouldn't give up. He held onto his arrogance despite his dire circumstances and reached desperately for leverage. "I got something on all of you corrupt motherfuckers and if I go down, I'm taking every single one of you with me."

"I'd be careful what you say here, Vic," McGavin said, "Look where you are. Chained and locked down by people who want nothing more than to see you go away forever."

"Yeah, well, I ain't goin' down without a fight. Get me Joe Cassidy. Tell him if he ain't here in two hours, all the secrets are out."

McGavin stared at him, watching the fallen man flounder in denial. He sighed and said, "Okay, you want him, you got him." He pressed down an intercom button and said, "Chief, you hear him?"

A metallic voice responded, "Yeah, be right there."

Salazar's eyes widened. "He's here already?"

"You don't think I'd be bringing you down without clearing it with him first, did you?"

A loud buzz sounded and the door behind McGavin opened. A man with short cropped grey hair entered the room. He was well built for his age, not looking a day over fifty, though his sixty-fifth birthday and retirement were fewer than eight months away. He had a firm, square jaw, sparkling blue eyes, and a space between his teeth that gave his smile a charming, yet odd effect. It made it almost impossible to know whether he was calculating or genuine. Police Chief Joseph Ryan Cassidy was wearing a black sports jacket over a tight, white crew neck that proudly accentuated the muscles of his chest. He had his hands in his pockets and began to pace behind where McGavin was sitting, his head tilted downward, seemingly deep in thought. Every few moments he peered over at Salazar and then back down to the floor.

The fallen crime lord watched him for a few moments and finally said, "Cassidy, what the fuck?" He held out his wrists as far as they could go, the chains straining against their limits. He gazed at the handcuffs in disbelief and then back at the police chief, a pleading look upon his face.

Cassidy held out a silencing hand and went back to pacing. Again, every once in a while he raised an eyebrow and glanced over to Salazar, but then shook his head in disappointment and walked on. Finally he approached McGavin's desk, leaned both hands on the surface, and said to Salazar, "What the fuck were you thinking?"

"What do you mean?"

"What do I mean? Jesus, Vic, you're even more of a psycho than I thought. You're poisoning *civilians* now? You really think we'd stand by and let you kill innocent kids?"

"I don't know what you're talking about."

"Cut the crap, Vic," Cassidy said, "Don't start pretending you didn't do this." He then started to count out on his fingers. "We got witnesses, three of your own girls for that matter, we got the murder weapon, which you took with intent to destroy, you accepted an address of where you thought the witnesses were in order to silence them, and we have a pretty damn good account of how this whole thing was conceived of and executed by you."

"From who? This corrupt piece of shit over here?"

451

McGavin said, "Keep talking, asshole. You're in no place to be throwing insults. But just in case you were wondering… Without breaking eye contact he removed his tie clip and placed in on the table. "Guess what this is, genius," McGavin said.

"Looks like an ugly tie holder to hold your ugly tie." Salazar said.

McGavin's eye sparkled. "It's a recording device, dumbass. Wireless. Everything you said in the limo is on record. Apparently your new head of security hasn't kept up with new technology. Big mistake relying on that muscle head Moustakas. It's a shame, really. It never would have gotten by Frankie."

For a moment Salazar looked truly afraid. His eyes darted all over the place, but then stopped and a subtle, evil sneer then appeared on his face. He sat back smugly, "You guys really think you have me here? You forget all the shit I did for you over the years? You think I'm gonna go quietly? Think again."

Cassidy pulled a chair over, sat down, and pointed a finger at Salazar. "You have no idea what you've done, have you? I got some bad news for you, asshole. Barney O'Leary is a friend of mine."

Salazar's stomach cramped. He started to say, "How was I supposed to—"

"I don't give a shit what you knew or know or didn't know. The fact is you killed an honor student who was on his way to being a star at Notre Dame. That's right, Vic, the news came out today that he was getting offered a scholarship for next year."

"O'Leary killed Frankie. I couldn't sit by and let that go."

"The fact is, asshole, you couldn't get to Mickey, so you had to go after his family. Well, you pissed off the wrong people this time, Vic. The wrong people. Were you even aware you were sending the girls to kill him at Chester Harrington's house? The Chester Harrington who is next in line to become county judge?"

Salazar just looked back blankly.

"I thought so," Cassidy said, "He wasn't too happy to find out you had two kids murdered in his own bedroom." He sat back and examined his fingernails. Then he looked up at the ceiling and shook his head. "The whore maybe we could live with, but the kid?" He looked back at Salazar. "Nobody in this town has ever seen anyone play like him before. People loved to watch him. He was a terrific kid with a terrific future ahead of him and you ended it. For what? Ego? Power? Revenge? Sure, you ruined Mickey. He'll probably never have a good night's sleep for the rest of his life. Does that make you happy? Does that make you feel all at one with the world? I hope it does, because that's going to be the last bit of satisfaction you will ever feel." The police chief swallowed, his eyes glistening now with tears. "It's funny. The one thing you didn't count on was everyone's love for football. This whole town? We *live* for football. Those kids mean the world to us. And Tommie? He was going to be the best thing that ever came out of Soundview. And you had him killed."

Salazar's face had turned ashen. But then an evil light began to glow within his eyes and he sat up straighter. "Yeah, well, I've always been more of a baseball fan anyway."

Cassidy reached over the table and smacked him in the

face. "You think this is a joke? You've fucked up way too many ways this time, Vic, and I'm through helping you."

Salazar's face was turned to the side by the impact of the slap, but he showed no pain and slowly turned his face back to the police chief again. "No you're not. You *will* help me. Whether or not you like it. The both of you. I got more on the two of you than you can ever imagine so you better start acting like it."

Cassidy clapped his hands and began to laugh. "You think you own us, do you? You think that's why we've looked the other way while you ran around here dealing drugs, shaking down people, selling girls? Let me tell you something, my friend, you never owned us. We own *you*. We've *always* owned you."

"Be that as it may," Salazar said, "I still have contacts and money." He looked at McGavin. "What, you think I'd tell Sheldon where *all* my money was? How stupid do you think I am? I'll get the right lawyers and before all this is done, you guys will be doing more time than me." He attempted to cross his arms, but the handcuffs held him back. "I know my rights. I want my phone call."

"Fuck your rights," McGavin said.

The two officers just sat there and glared at him. Sweat began to appear on Salazar's forehead and upper lip. Finally he yelled at the top of his lungs, "HELP! I WANT MY LAWYER! I'M BEING OPPRESSED! HELP!"

When he finally realized no one was coming to help him, Salazar looked directly into Cassidy's eyes and said, "I killed for you."

The police captain kept Salazar's gaze and stood up. He scratched his head and began to pace again. He ended up by the door and leaned back against it, crossing his arms. He looked at Hanson and Billings, who just stood expressionless by the back door. He wasn't worried about them. They were in the middle of it all as well. "That may be," he said, "but it was only guys who had it coming to them. Not young girls or high school kids. Sorry, Vic, like I said before, you really fucked up this time and you're gonna have to take the fall. Too many important people want you gone."

"Then I'm just gonna have to talk to the feds now, won't I?"

McGavin, who was staring intently at Salazar, pushed his chair back from the table and looked back at Cassidy. "I told you he was gonna say that," he said.

The police chief said, "You did indeed, George."

"Well it probably works out best this way, Joe. We kinda owe the kid something."

Joe Cassidy continued to gaze at Salazar. "We do indeed, George. We do indeed."

CHAPTER 33

DECONSTRUCTING A MONSTER

The following night, not long after midnight, Hanson and Billings dragged Salazar back to the same room and handcuffed him to the same table. He resisted all the way there. Throughout the struggle, Salazar first pleaded with, insulted, then threatened the two cops until he sat chained and helpless, except for his barbed tongue. After he was secured, he glowered at the two of them and said, "Your lives ain't worth a load of shit right now. See you boys on the outside."

Hanson just chuckled and said, "I doubt it. You'll never see the light of day again."

"Fuck you," Salazar shot back, and spit on his badge. Hanson went to punch him, but Billings held him back, and at that moment the front door to the room opened up. McGavin came in and said, "Now, now boys, play nice."

Billings said, "Take it easy, Ray. Asshole's gonna get what's coming to him."

Hanson shrugged off his partner and said, "Can't happen soon enough."

"Just take these cuffs off, tough guy, and we'll see who's got what's coming to him," Salazar said.

Hanson started at him again, but this time McGavin stepped in front of him and said, "Take it easy, Ray. Don't let him get to you. All he's got left is his mouth. Soon he won't even have that. Come on." He motioned for the two cops to follow him out the door and out of sight.

Salazar sat there for a few minutes listening intently to what was going on outside the room. He heard a muffled conversation but was unable to make out what was being said. "Hey!" he yelled. "This is bullshit, you know! I still haven't gotten my phone call! And I want my fucking lawyer, you bastards!" When there was no response, he leaned his body toward the door to try to see what was going on. In a weaker, more confused voice, he said, "Hey, I'm not kidding! I'm an American citizen and I demand my rights!"

He strained to listen and began to pick up pieces of the conversation. He heard "So he's really coming?" and "That's what he said" and "Shit, I'd do the same thing if it were me."

While Salazar was trying to figure out what exactly they

were talking about, he heard a buzzing sound, a door clank open, and footsteps approaching the room.

"He's in there?" someone asked.

"Yeah, he's there," said McGavin. "You okay?"

"Yeah."

"You sure you want to do this?" McGavin said.

"I *have* to do this."

"Okay then, he's yours."

* * *

Salazar saw a shadow chase some of the light away from under the door and the knob turned. He heard a click, the door swung ajar and a young man entered the room. He was tall and lean, with long, wavy brown hair and sad brown eyes, laden with regret. He wore a faded denim jacket, blue jeans, and black high top Converse sneakers. He tossed a gym bag on the table, and without looking up, he unzipped the bag and began to lay out its contents on the table. A pair of dental pliers. A blow torch. A college sports magazine. A football jersey. And several other items that didn't seem to make sense. By the time Mickey had taken out a Taser, Salazar's eyes seemed ready to shoot out of his head. "HEY!" he directed to the door. "YOU CAN'T LEAVE ME IN HERE WITH HIM! LET ME OUTTA HERE! HEY!!!"

He continued to yell and bang his fists on the table until Mickey stepped around the table and shoved a sock in his mouth. It was an athletic sock that was clearly soiled, caked with mud and hardened with dried sweat. The only noise that came from Salazar's mouth was "MMMFFFFFF!!" as Mickey pushed it deeper into his mouth. Mickey then said,

"If you bang your fists again, I'm gonna dig my fingers into your eyes. Nod if you understand me."

Salazar saw that he wasn't kidding and nodded.

"Good," Mickey said and went back to the other side of the table and sat down. He stared at the killer of his brother with so many mixed emotions, he didn't know how to sort them all out. All he knew was that the distress, the grief, and the guilt had abated, if only for the time being, and only for the fact that justice was now in his hands. "How's it taste?" he asked.

Salazar's head jerked forward and he made a gagging sound.

"The sock's from his last game. Haven't gotten around to washing it. What with him dying and the funeral and all. Glad to get some more use out of it though.

Mickey smiled and looked toward the ceiling. "We got him, kiddo. What'd you think I should do with him now?" He looked back at his brother's killer with a sparkle in his eyes. "Think he'll give me a sign?"

He lowered his gaze, the smile fading from his face and shook his head. "Such a good kid," he said. "Quick learner too. Did you know, I taught him everything he knew about football? That's right. We used to toss the ball around all the time. Both loved the game. But he was the one with the skills. Man, I wish I had his hands. Basketball was more my game. Was pretty good myself. But I kinda lost interest. Got hurt and then just lost interest. Not Tommie, though. He had big plans for himself. Yep, he was gonna make it big."

He took a football out of the bag and stood up. Began to flip it around, spinning it in tight spirals in the air. "You should have seen the catch he made last weekend. It was incredible. Down with the clock running out, no time outs left. Made a ridiculous adjustment while the ball was in the air." He took a few steps and reenacted the movements of the catch with a blissful look on his face. He tossed the ball in the air, jumped, twisted his body, tipped the ball, and caught it. Then he shook his head in amazement. "How he got his feet in bounds I'll never know."

Mickey stood motionless for a moment, staring into space as if he were replaying the whole scene in his mind. He blinked, then swallowed, and went back over to the table. He looked at the football in his hands, spun it a few more times, and then put it back in the bag. He sat down, put his elbows on the table and his face in his hands. His body tensed and heaved. When he took his hands away, his eyes and cheeks were wet. "Look at me. Such a pussy," he said, wiping away his tears with the sleeve of his denim jacket. His eyes were red and he needed to blow his nose. For a while, he just sat there in a daze, replaying a series of precious memories in his mind.

Finally, he just sighed and shook his head in disbelief. "Jesus," he said.

He then took notice of Salazar, whose cheeks were puffing in and out, like a fish out of water. Part of Mickey almost felt bad for the murderer, as helpless as he was at the moment. But the feeling passed swiftly and Mickey's heart hardened. The fury returned to his eyes and he reached over and yanked Tommie's dirty sock out of his mouth.

Salazar coughed and sputtered, gasping for air. He spat on the floor and glared at Mickey. "So this is how it's gonna be? You gonna kill me while I'm chained up like a dog?"

Mickey said, "As far as I'm concerned you're less than a

dog. You're the lowest life form I could imagine. A slug has more dignity than you."

"Yeah, well, you bastards'll never get away with this. I know my rights."

Mickey smirked. "*Your rights*. Unbelievable. Fuck your rights. It amazes me that people like you think you've got rights. Only human beings get rights. You're not human. The moment you sent those girls after Tommie, you lost all your rights."

"That's not what the law says."

"Yeah, well apparently the law doesn't apply to you."

They sat there, staring at each other for a while, the clock ticking away in the early hours of the morning. Mickey clenched his fists and his breath came hard and deep. His shoulders shook. He then spoke in slow measured words. "You ripped my family apart," he said.

Salazar tilted his head back, a defiant look on his face. "You killed Frankie. Now we're even."

"I DIDN'T FUCKING KILL FRANKIE!"

Salazar flinched, but his arrogance remained. "So you say."

Mickey's throat began to close on him. "It's fucking true, you asshole!" he choked out. "Tell me that's not why my brother is dead. Tell me!" He reached out and grabbed Salazar by the shirt and pleaded with him. "Tell me you didn't kill Tommie because you guessed wrong!"

Salazar just looked at Mickey for a moment, considered his demand, then said, "You had your chance, tough guy. I gave you a choice and *you* chose wrong. You and your foolish pride. You should have known it would end up like this."

Mickey let go of his shirt and shoved him back in the

chair. "You better watch what you say, fuckface. I got a million ways to make you suffer right now." He patted the heavy gym bag. "You don't want to make me feel like this was all my fault."

"Wasn't it?"

Mickey reached for the black Taser. Salazar's eyes widened and he tried to pull away, but was held in place by the handcuffs. Mickey swung the device up under Salazar's chin and jammed the electrodes into his throat. There was a buzzing sound and the older man let out an "AAAAAAHHHHHH!!!!!" His body shook and convulsed violently, as his feet tap-danced spasmodically on the floor. When Mickey stopped, Salazar slumped forward, his head collapsing on the table with a BANG!

Mickey leaned over and growled in his ear, "I'd lose that shitty attitude of yours if I were you. You're kinda out of your element."

Mickey grabbed a pitcher of water that was on the table and dumpsome of it on Salazar, who groaned, his head still on the table. Mickey picked his head up by the hair. His eyes were rolling back in their sockets. "Wake up!" Mickey said. "We're just getting started. I want some answers from you."

"Fuck...you," Salazar croaked between gasps.

"Okay," Mickey said and picked up the Taser again.

"WAIT! WAIT! Okay! Okay! Whatever you want! Just put that away!"

The powerful Victor Salazar at my mercy, Mickey thought. A hint of satisfaction appeared on his face. "Kinda sucks to be in you now, doesn't it?"

The killer said nothing as he tried to catch his breath.

Mickey stared at him hard, his eyes seething with

hatred. "What makes a man like you? What turns someone into something so cold that he has no respect for someone else's life? Can you tell me that?"

When Salazar didn't answer, Mickey punched him lightly in the chest. It resulted in a loud moan, but he still didn't answer.

"ANSWER ME!"

"Okay, just... just give me a second!" Salazar wheezed, "Can I...can I have some water? I'll tell you what you want...just gimme some water."

Mickey poured a glass and held it up to the older man's mouth. He drank deeply, the water spilling out the sides of his mouth until he had his fill. Mickey took the glass away and sat on the table. When Salazar composed himself, he finally spoke. "When a man's in a business like mine, it's kill or be killed. The moment you let your guard down, the moment people stop fearing you, that's the moment when someone kills *you*. So you *can't* show any mercy. You have to be a hard ass. And you can't give a shit about anyone else's life but your own. Survival of the fittest. Simple as that."

As Mickey considered this answer, his face twisted in revulsion, his eyes shut tight . "Yeah, so you kill your rivals or to keep people in fear, but why kill a kid? Someone who never did anything wrong in his life, never threatened you or anyone you know?"

"I couldn't get through to you. You were too stubborn, so I had to resort to more drastic measures."

Mickey shook his head incredulously. "You are one devious fuck."

Salazar just shrugged. "I had to let everyone know that if you fuck with me you're gonna regret it."

"How did I fuck with you so badly that you had to kill my kid brother?"

"Like I said before, you killed Frankie."

"Stop saying that, asshole. I already told you I didn't kill him."

Salazar closed his eyes and stretched his neck around from side to side. He cleared his throat and looked back with his familiar cold gaze. "Okay, O'Leary. Let's say you *didn't* kill Frankie. You say that like you would never kill a man. But we both know better, don't we?"

Mickey's stomach felt cold and his body stiffened. "What are you talking about?"

"Stop with the bullshit already, kid. We both know why you left The Shamrocks to begin with. You had the smarts and skills, but when you finally had to kill someone, you had a meltdown."

Mickey just stared at him in a trance.

Salazar nodded. "What, you didn't think it would get around? You thought you'd be able to hide it the rest of your life?"

Mickey swallowed. "I don't know what you're talking about."

"Lenny Morales, Mickey. Lenny Morales. The kid you knifed in the gut in that alleyway. What, you don't remember?"

Mickey slid down off the table and looked warily at the door. He put a hand to his mouth and closed his eyes.

"That's right, Mick," Salazar said, gaining momentum, "You're a murderer just like me. So don't get all high and mighty about how precious life is. You're no better than me."

Mickey was in a confused state, somehow trying to

make sense of his past. Envisioning the very scene that took place so long ago, he reached out a hand with the palm up, as if to stop this unsubstantiated accusation. "The girl was fifteen," he pleaded, "She was screaming at the top of her lungs. Nobody was around. I, I was the only one who could help her." He winced at the memory. "He was raping her. Beating her. And *molesting* her."

"Still doesn't change the fact that you're a murderer."

"I pulled him off of her and he had a knife. He came at me, but, but…"

"But you were quicker than him. Better with a knife. So you gutted him. *Murdered* him."

"It was self-defense."

"Whatever…"

"No, it was different. It wasn't murder. I was helping that girl and he came at me."

Salazar laughed. "It still makes you a killer."

"Not like you. You plotted and planned to kill an innocent kid out of revenge. Out of spite, you evil fuck. I'm not like you at all."

"Yes, you are."

Mickey lunged at him and grabbed him by the throat. Salazar's eyes bulged out of his head and he let out a "NNNGUNKK!" His face turned beet red and it seemed that Mickey would kill him right there, but he relaxed his grip and let go. As Salazar gasped for air, Mickey went over to the bag and pulled out a set of keys. "I'm not gonna kill you like that," he said. "I want to see what you got." He freed Salazar's left wrist and then went to work on the right.

In his haste, however, instead of unlocking the cuff attached to Salazar's right wrist, he unlocked the cuff that was fastened to the table. The sadistic killer then seized his opportunity while he could. He jerked back and swung the handcuff that was still on his right wrist. It caught Mickey just above his left eye, and when he tried to protect his face, Salazar side-kicked him in the stomach. Mickey doubled over and fell to his knees. Salazar then roared and began peppering him with a flurry of punches.

But the prisoner had been weakened by several days of poor nutrition and restless nights on a cement floor. His punches only seemed to infuriate Mickey, who got his wind back and threw his shoulder into his assailant. He practically carried Salazar across the room and slammed him into the far wall. They fell to the ground together, Mickey on top of the older man. Salazar held him close, knowing that if he let go, Mickey would pound him into submission. He opened his mouth and bit down on Mickey's left ear with all his might. Blood spouted everywhere and Mickey screamed in agony. He pulled away, giving Salazar just enough room to bring his knee up into Mickey's crotch. Mickey let out an "OOOFFFFF!" and Salazar got a foot on his chest and shoved him back across the room. He then came at Mickey, swinging the handcuff this way and that, like a pair of nunchucks. He caught Mickey once again on the top of the head, and though the pain was excruciating, it only served to anger Mickey more. The old Shamrock in Mickey then awakened. His instincts took over, and suddenly it was as if he were back on the streets fighting in some brawl. In one swift motion, with all the strength he could muster, Mickey ducked down, grabbed Salazar over the shoulder with his left arm and between the legs with his right, lifted him up in the air and body slammed him onto the floor.

Salazar let out a grunt and then lay in a motionless heap. Mickey got to his feet, his chest heaving. Blood was oozing out of his ear and the wounds on his head. He poured himself a glass of water and drank deep while Salazar lay still on the floor. His balls ached and he reached for them and winced. After a moment, he went over to Salazar and lifted him back into the chair. He went to re-cuff his hands back to the table when Salazar suddenly screamed and grabbed Mickey's face. He dug his thumbs into Mickey's eyes and pressed in as hard as he could. Mickey howled in pain. He jerked his arms up in defense, knocking Salazar's hands away. He then grabbed the killer of his little brother and again threw him to the floor. Taking his mortal enemy by the hair, Mickey proceeded to bash his head against the floor with all his might, one blow after the next; the misogynist, the murderer, the torturer, the fiend, wailing in agony and fear until the sound of his own torture became a whimper, then no sound at all, except for the wet, battering sound of his face getting mashed to a bloody pulp.

When Mickey finally felt no life left in Victor Salazar, no heartbeat, no pulse, he finally let go and weakly stood up. He took off his shirt and leaned his head against the wall, wiping the blood off his face and neck. He was utterly physically and emotionally spent. After one long moment, he walked slowly over to the table, put everything back in the bag, and took it to the door. He rapped softly and McGavin, Cassidy, Hanson, and Billings came in.

McGavin said, "You okay, kid?"

"You better call the morgue," Mickey said.

McGavin looked at the bloody heap that was once

Victor Salazar and nodded. "I figured we'd need one." He looked at Hanson and Billings and said, "Boys, get a mop."

Hanson said to Billings, "He couldn't have just strangled him?"

CHAPTER 34

BLOWN FUSES

By the time Mickey got home, the shadows of the night were beginning to lift. As if on cue, the resident mockingbird began his daily song, signifying that another night had passed and a new day had begun. From dawn until dusk he would call, never faltering in his solitary symphony, providing the ongoing score to the routine day.

To Mickey it only meant one thing. He had once again been out until morning, defiling what was left of his tattered soul while the rest of the world was asleep. Since his bloodied hands were shaking, now more than they had been of late, it took him longer than usual to unlock his door. Finally the key slid home and he let himself in. He moved slowly, his body aching in so many places it felt as if he had been hit by a train. With his shoulders slouched, he made his way to the bathroom and relieved himself with his eyes closed, for fear he would catch his reflection in the mirror, the last thing on earth he wanted to do. He so badly wanted to go to sleep, but the idea that Victor Salazar's blood was still upon him, drove him to scrub himself so vigorously in the shower that it left his skin red and sore. When he had finally dried off, he literally fell onto his bed and slumbered away into the depths of unconsciousness.

It seemed like he had been asleep for barely a few minutes when he heard loud knocking on his outside door. He awoke with a start and rubbed his eyes. The morning light was creeping in around the window shades of his bedroom. He looked at the clock to see it was nearly noon.

The knocking began again in more earnest. "Mick? You up?" It was a young man's voice, eager, curious, and impatient. "Mick, come on. I know you're in there." The knocking continued on, this time in sync with the words, "COME! ON! WAKE! UP!"

"Okay, okay," Mickey croaked. He cleared his throat. "Be right there!" He was wearing a white tee-shirt, light blue boxer shorts, and white sweat socks. He slowly got up and put on his bathrobe and leather slippers. His head felt like a nail had been hammered through it. "Oooooooh…" he muttered and put a palm over his left eye. The knocking switched to banging now, causing the door to strain at the hinges. Mickey said, "Hold on! I'm coming!" He took a few steps, yawning, and then mumbled, "Quit that racket." He shuffled over to the door and leaned his shoulder against it, with his head down and his eyes closed. "Who is it?"

"Who do you think it is, dumbass? It's me, Tommie. Now open up!"

Mickey froze. His eyes shot open and he stood there in a daze. He stepped back and frowned, shifting his eyes in all different directions, from the door to the window to the floor and back to the door again. "Tommie?" he said and moved to peer around the shades.

"Yeah, it's me! Come on already. It's gorgeous out here!"

Mickey tried to make out the form that was standing at his doorstep, but the glare was too great for him to see. The figure was tall and muscular, about the size of his younger brother, but...could it really be? He stepped back and opened the door.

Clear as day, Tommie brushed past him into his apartment with the vigor and exuberance found only in the youth. He had his football with him, flipping it up in the air with a tight spiral and catching it on the way down. The door was left ajar and as Mickey stared incredulously at Tommie, the sunlight seemed to surround his younger brother with an otherworldly glow.

"Come on," Tommie said, "help me out. I'm catching everything in sight, but my sideline technique is terrible. I keep stepping out of bounds. Coach says I need to work on my footing." He reached out and took Mickey by the hand. "Come *on*," he pleaded. "It's a stellar day. Throw me some passes."

Mickey didn't move. He resisted the urge to rub his eyes with his knuckles. "Tommie? Kid? That really you?"

The teenager frowned. "Who the hell do you think it is? Jesus, Mick, what's *wrong* with you?"

Mickey suddenly broke out in a grin and said, "Nothing! Nothing's wrong with me. Everything's awesome. Just give me a sec. Have a seat and I'll be right with ya. Just gotta get dressed. Have a seat!"

Tommie looked at Mickey's moldering couch and cluttered coffee table. He decided to remain standing. "You ever clean this place? Mom would never let me keep my room this way."

Mickey poked his head out the doorway of his bedroom. "What's that?"

"I said, you need a maid!"

"Oh, oh yeah, that. Well, uh, yeah, I'll get one soon."

Tommie shook his head and tossed the football again. He went to look out the window and frowned. "I haven't seen anyone around for a while," he said, confused. "Nobody to practice with."

Mickey appeared in a tee-shirt and shorts and holding his high top Converse sneakers. He was beaming, thrilled that it had all been a bad dream. It *must* have been, because here Tommie was, in the flesh, and he was about to throw passes to him once again. And Mickey was going to savor it like never before.

Tommie was still frowning. "Where's Danny and Pat been? I haven't seen them in like forever."

Mickey finished tying his shoes and went over to Tommie. He took him by the shoulders and smiled broadly. "We're gonna have a great day, kiddo. Just you and me." He then hugged him tightly, probably tighter than he ever had before. "Nothing's gonna hurt you, kiddo. I'm gonna see to it if it's the last thing I do."

Tommie just stood there, staring off into the distance. "Where's Mom and Pop? Katie and Meg? The boys? They're all gone."

Mickey still clung to his brother. He lingered in the embrace, but then felt something cold and wet on his shoulder. His smile faded and he stepped back to see what it was. He wiped his shoulder with his hand and it came away with a white, pinkish foam. He looked at Tommie, who was now agitated, the foamy mixture dripping from his left nostril. It oozed over his lip as he spoke.

"Why can't I find anybody?" he whined. "Nobody's here! No practice, no games! Where *is* everyone, Mick? I'm all alone!" The pinkish liquid was now coming out of both nostrils and dripping over his chin. He began to cry and the foam started streaming from his eyes.

Mickey's hand flew to his mouth in horror and he slowly began to back up. "No, no, no, no, NO, NO, NO!"

The foam began to coalesce into a thick black liquid, the texture of dark, crude oil. It now began to pour out of his mouth. Deep sallow rings formed under his eyes and his cheeks began to sink inward, his complexion fading to a ghastly white. "You did this to me!" he gurgled. "You and your foolish pride!"

Mickey was now sobbing. "No! It wasn't my fault!"

"Yes, it was! I was gonna be a star and you fucked it all up!" He began to walk stiffly toward Mickey, his face a black and white abomination, twisted with resentment and fury.

Mickey backed into his room and fell back onto his bed. "No! You're not Tommie! Stay away from me!"

The thing kept moving closer, just a few feet away. "I'll never forgive you for this, Mickey. Never. NEVER!"

Tommie O'Leary's apparition fell upon Mickey and groped for his neck. Mickey couldn't move, couldn't do anything to fight back. The thing got its hands around Mickey's throat and began to squeeze, choking the life out of him while the black ooze dripped onto his face.

Suddenly, Mickey shot up in bed, gasping for breath. His heart was racing. He looked around and saw that he was alone. He then felt for his ear and found it in shreds. His eyebrows were cut, his face was swollen, and crusty scabs were beginning to form on his scalp. Realizing what was still so horribly real, the misery came on like a tidal wave and mercilessly washed him away.

* * *

He fell into dark abyss, a blackness where there was no pain, no fear, no despair. He was simply elsewhere, suspended in an unfeeling world without thought and regret. It was what he needed: relief from his grief and his unbearable remorse.

By the time Mickey was roused by running footfalls above his bedroom, it was nearly noon. The family had been gathering at the house every day, for the past week and a half since Tommie's death, and while it was comforting for everyone else, Mickey was finding it more and more difficult to be around them. His guilt was eating away at his increasingly fragile soul and he was beginning to feel like a snitch among thieves. He felt like an outsider.

Nonetheless, he knew they would be calling for him sooner or later, so he dragged himself out of bed and shuffled toward the bathroom. His cuts and bruises screamed and throbbed as he moved, and he once again avoided the mirror before getting into the shower. There, for the second time in eight hours, he scrubbed his body thoroughly, making sure not a speck of Salazar's blood remained. He then toweled off and slowly got dressed, wincing with every stretch of his aching limbs.

It was at this time that he finally dared to look in his bathroom mirror. He was immediately sorry he did. He had the appearance of a battered boxer. His eyes were so swollen he could hardly see their color, the brown irises barely visible through meager slits between the lids. The wound above his left eye, where Salazar had hit him with the open handcuff, was caked and scabbed, and his ear was a mangled mess. He groaned, put both hands on the sink, and lowered his head.

Suddenly he heard knocking at the door at the top of his staircase, the one leading to the house above. A young boy's voice called out to him. It was Donnie. "Mickey, Ma wants you! Come on, get up!"

Mickey continued looking down at the bathroom floor as he called out, "Okay! Be right there!" When he finally got the courage to look in the mirror again, he gingerly probed his face. He decided the best he could do for now, was to wear a skull cap to cover the damages to both his head and ear, and sunglasses to hide his eyes.

He made his way upstairs, threw the bolt, and opened the door. As usual, the boys were playing in the living room, but the atmosphere was now subdued. Rather than running around, playing tag and wrestling like they normally did, the boys sat quietly on the couch playing video games, with looks of anxiety and confusion on their faces.

Meg came out from the kitchen, little Shannon in her arms, her head resting in the crook of her mother's neck. She had a pacifier in her mouth and her eyes were wide and melancholy. Meg frowned at him. "What's with the disguise?" she asked.

Mickey cleared his throat. "I have a migraine. And the light hurts my eyes."

"A headache, huh? Your face is all swollen too. What *really* happened to you?"

Mickey swallowed. He could never put one over on Meg. She was too sharp and never let anything go. "Okay, you really want to know?" he said quietly, "I got into a fight last night."

Meg stepped back. "A fight? What's *wrong* with you?" she said bitterly, "Isn't it enough what we're going through with Tommie? Now Ma's gotta see you like that?" Shannon began to whine.

Meg stared at her brother for a moment, seeing him differently for the first time in her life. "You know, there's been talk," she said.

"What do you mean 'talk'?"

"People been saying…"

"What? Saying what?"

She hesitated once again but decided to say it. "People been sayin' that you were in some gang and you were in some kinda war with this guy Salazar."

Mickey felt his stomach drop a foot. He couldn't say a word and just waited to hear out his sister.

"They say he poisoned Tommie to get even with you." Her voice dropped to a choked whisper. "Is it true, Mickey?

Is it really true? Is Tommie gone because of some kind of… *stupid turf war of yours?*"

Mickey was aghast. "No, Meg. You got it all wrong. It… it wasn't like that."

Meg gasped and her hand shot to her mouth. "Oh my God, Mickey. Oh my God!" Little Shannon began to cry through her pacifier, getting louder as her mother became more distraught.

"No, wait, you don't understand!" Mickey pleaded. "This guy was bad news. He was dealing drugs to kids, he, he was kidnapping women, stealing from everyone."

"So? What did that have to do with you? Why'd you have to get involved? Look what it cost us!"

Mickey just stared at her, realizing the pain she was going through, the pain he had caused everyone. He just bowed his head and said mostly to himself, "Someone had to do something."

Meg's face twisted with rage. "*Someone?* You? Why not let the police do their job? What, were you some kind of half-assed vigilante? Playing some kind of game so you can be a hero? And now Tommie's gone? Well, shame on you, Mickey. Shame on you. This is all your fault! I'll *never* forgive you for this!" And she ran up the stairs with Shannon screaming in her arms.

Mary O'Leary called out from the kitchen. "Meg!"

Mickey looked toward the kitchen and made his way over. Now more than at any other time in his life, he needed his mother. When he got to the doorway, he saw her with his nephew Ryan sitting on her lap coloring with crayons. The little boy must have sought comfort with his Granma, while Megan flew into her indignant rage. Mary O'Leary

477

looked up, saw the state Mickey was in, and quietly told her grandson to go back to the living room.. "Come," she said to Mickey and pulled the chair out next to her.

He moved slowly to her side, sat down, and reached out to her. She took him in her arms where he quietly wept, his body wracked with sobs. When he had finally composed himself, he sat back, somewhat embarrassed. Mary then handed him a box of tissues, nearly empty, having been drained of its contents over the last few miserable days. Mickey awkwardly wiped his eyes under his sunglasses, still not wanting his mom to see his face. He felt his throat closing in on him. He could barely speak. "This is so hard," he managed. "How the hell are we gonna get through this?"

Mary O'Leary had tears on her face as well, but she was more composed than Mickey. "We do it together, Mickey. We do it together."

"But it hurts so much. And she's right, Ma. It *is* my fault. If I didn't…I didn't…oh Jesus Christ…" He began to cry again and once more sought comfort in his mother's arms.

"Shhhhh," she said. "It's okay, Mickey. Don't beat yourself up. I know you're a good boy. Meg's wrong. She's just upset. I know you would never do anything to hurt anyone."

"It's not true. You don't know…"

She took him by the shoulders and held him back so that he could look into her eyes. "Listen to me," she said, "I know you more than anyone else in this world. I watched you as a boy and watched as you grew into a decent young man. You would never intentionally hurt anyone. *I just know it.* This just…this just happened."

At that moment, Barney O'Leary entered the kitchen.

Mary looked up and Mickey could see a hint of anxiety come over her face. His father shot him a look of disgust he had never seen from him before. Instead of greeting his son, Barney walked over to the fridge, took out a can of Heineken, and cracked it open. He leaned against the fridge and took several deep gulps while looking at the ceiling.

Mary said, "A little early for a beer, isn't it?"

Barney stifled a belch, wiped his mouth with his wrist and then drank some more. When he had his fill, he said, "Not today." He glowered at Mickey. "What's with the shades, boy? Don't ya have the decency to take them off in front of your ma?"

"It's okay, Barney," Mary said.

"No, it's not okay. Take them off, boy. And yer stupid hat too!"

"Barney!"

Mickey looked at his dad, the man he had so desperately wanted to please his entire life, and all he could do was obey. He slowly took off the hat and sunglasses, revealing the cuts on his head, his face, his swollen eyes, and the abomination of his ear.

Mary gasped, then said, "Oh my dear sweet Jesus!"

Barney's face registered surprise, then anger. "What the hell happened t'yer face??"

"I got into a fight."

"What's that?! Got in t'anoh-ther fight?" his father said, lapsing into a quick, agitated Brogue, "Drinkin' and carrying on again with those hooligan friends of yers?! And your brother not yet two weeks in the ground? Have you no respect?"

Mickey just hung his head.

Barney continued his assault. "You know I always had high hopes for ya, Mickey. You shoulda been able tah doo somethin with yer life." He paused for a moment and looked at the floor. "Maybe t'was my fault. I knew yah were up to no good with those bums 'til all hours of the night." He returned his disapproving glare at his son. "But I figgered after a while you'd grow up and someday learn howda be a man. Oh-viously I was wrong."

Mickey said, "I was only trying..."

"DON'T INTERRUPT ME, BOY! NOT IN MY HOUSE!"

"Barney!" Mary said.

"Quiet, woman! I'm not finished." He pointed his finger at Mickey. "What on earth were yah thinking? Gangs? Everything we ever had was our family and you...you...put it all at risk!" He sucked in air and puffed out his chest, then, in profound resignation he concluded, "You're a *poonk*."

"Barney!" Mary yelled. "Don't talk to him that way!"

He held up a hand to her, his eyes continuing to bore fiercely into Mickey. "You're no longer a son to me. I want yah outa the house immed-yately."

"No!" Mary pleaded.

Mickey slowly got up and took a deep breath. He touched his mother's arm and said, "No, he's right. I'm leaving. I'm no good to anyone here anymore."

And with that, in the deepest state of despair he would ever know, Mickey descended the stairs, took whatever he needed, and left his house for the very last time.

CHAPTER 35

A PHANTOM IN THE MIST

The weeks passed by as autumn faded into November, the warmth of the sun receding to the south. And as the afternoon drifted toward dusk, a chill took hold, turning Tessa's breath into a fine mist. She sat on a set of swings in the middle of Cunningham Park, wearing a navy hoodie under a vest of powder blue. Below her waist she wore bell bottom jeans and Puma track shoes. A woolen cap was pulled down over her ears, pushing down her bangs that parted flatly over her forehead. In the coolness of the early evening air, her cheeks were shaded pink and her pale eyes glistened as she laughed, for poor Jack kept missing one free throw after another.

"Come on, lame-ass," she called. "You couldn't hit the side of a barn!"

Jack just flashed her an exasperated smile. "Okay, here goes," he said. "Gonna hit ten in a row, now. Watch." But even after being together for over a month now, he was still unnerved by her natural charm. He tried to impress her any chance he could, but usually failed miserably in the process. Whenever he was around her, his brain somehow short-circuited, rendering him clumsy and dysfunctional. He attempted another shot, but the ball never even made it to the rim.

Tessa giggled, relishing the effect she had on him. She knew how disarming she was to him and it felt good to feel his deep affection for her. Not only did it give her a great sense of emotional security in their relationship, but the fact was, she was in love with him.

"Air ball!" she chanted, and Jack just groaned and ran after the ball.

The sky had thickened with a drab blanket of clouds, giving the late afternoon an eerie glow; a silvery kind of light that seemed to warp the world into an odd replica of itself. It was as if the familiar had been turned inside out, rotating a full one hundred and eighty degrees, creating a mirror image of everything and revealing a dreamscape that had been ever-present, just hidden beneath the surface.

"Come on, Jack!" Tessa called. "You promised to push me!"

Jack retrieved the ball and ran back, bouncing it with a Ping! Ping! Ping! that echoed throughout the stark empty playground. As he approached, he felt uplifted by her smile. "Guess I lost my touch somewhere along the way," he said.

"No, you didn't," she said and knocked the ball out of his hands. "At least not an hour ago."

He laughed and grabbed the chains just above her hands and leaned into her. The swing swayed back and upward, causing Tessa to rise above the ground. When she was at just the right height, he pressed his lips into hers and she wrapped her legs around his waist. There, they lingered in a kiss. Not just any kiss, but *their* kiss. A kiss that could never lose its magic, its *electricity*. And when their lips stopped moving, they stayed there, their faces resting on one another in a moment so natural and easy; a state of bliss neither had ever known before.

After a time, Jack pulled back to look at her. She kept her eyes closed, an expression of rapture on her angelic, heart-shaped face. He gazed at her with awe, straining to contemplate such beauty. It was as if he had stumbled upon a precious jewel that had somehow miraculously brought meaning back into his solitary life. And it wasn't just her beauty that had him captivated. It was her personality; her easy going charisma. She had such a sweet disposition that it made him feel good all the time. When he was down, all he had to do was see her face and he knew everything would be alright. She was a smile waiting to happen.

He gently caressed her cheek with his knuckles, until she opened his hand and held it flat on her face. He then put his other hand on her face and leaned forward so that their foreheads touched.

Somewhere behind them another basketball began bouncing off the pavement. Jack turned to look, but Tessa wouldn't let him, turning his face back to her and rubbing her lips on his.

"I love being with you," she said. "You make me happy."

Jack closed his eyes and smiled. "Say that again."

"You heard me."

"I know. I just want to hear it one more time."

Her eyes sparkled. "Well stick around, buster, and you just might."

The echo of the bouncing basketball continued behind them, along with the sound of missed shots careening off the rim. The errant tosses were followed by aggravated mutterings, and as they embraced, the air kept filling with PING PING PING...CLANG!...FUCK! Over and over again.

"*Is that my ball?*" Jack said as he glanced behind him, but Tessa turned his face back once more. He gave in to her again, powerless under her spell.

After a moment they stopped kissing, satisfied to rest in their embrace. The noise of the basketball suddenly stopped and Jack stepped back, letting Tessa and her swing lower back down to the ground. His smile suddenly faded and he winced, as if a painful thought had just occurred to him, and he once again glanced back over his shoulder. Across the basketball court, he saw his ball, lying abandoned against the fence. No one else was in sight. He turned back to Tessa. "You see who was there?"

She shrugged and shook her head.

"Strange," he said, and scanned the park, now barren and silent. He sat down on the swing next to her and withdrew, studying the ground, deep in thought. Every few seconds he looked up and craned his head around as if he were searching for something. But then he caught Tessa looking at him and turned away.

She frowned at him. "Looking for something?"

"No, not really."

"*Not really?*"

He gazed at her briefly, uncertain of what to say, but finally pointed beyond the basketball court. "See that old factory over there?" he said.

She followed his finger. "Yeah?"

"That's where The Shamrocks hang out. I've been trying to get a hold of Mickey ever since Tommie's funeral. He won't return my calls. His family said he left home weeks ago and never came back. Apparently he got into a fight with his dad, and from what I've heard, he's now a basket case. He's got himself holed up in a room inside that old brewery there and won't see anyone except his friend Shane. He's even given Shane specific orders not to let me in. He's got this weird idea that he's bad luck and doesn't want to ruin anyone else's life. *Especially mine.*" He swallowed and shook his head. "He's taking this all very hard."

Tessa's blue eyes grew wide with sympathy. "Wow, sounds like he's really depressed."

"I know. I gotta find some way to talk to him. I really think I can help him. The problem is, I can't get to him while he's in that building. He's got all the gang members guarding it."

"So what are we doing here if he never comes out?"

"Well, I spoke to Shane the other day and he agreed that Mickey could really use my help. He told me Mickey only leaves the club house on Friday nights around five-thirty to go to confession. The church is just a few blocks away, so he walks." He looked at his watch. "It's a little after five now. I'm hoping I can catch him tonight."

"Oh, okay."

"I hope you don't mind that I brought you. I'm not really sure why I did. I guess I just wanted your company in case he didn't come out." He smiled sadly. "It's tough seeing a friend go through something like this."

She nudged his thighs with her own and smiled. "No problem, Jack. I want to be here for you. I enjoy being in your life, even in the hard times." She looked over toward the old Gallagher brewery. "I actually feel pretty bad for Mickey. Maybe I can help."

"I don't know, Tess. He doesn't want to talk to anyone. From what I've been told, he thinks his family blames him for his brother's death."

"How could he be responsible? Didn't Tommie overdose on bad coke? Coke from Victor Salazar?"

"Yes, but if The Shamrocks never took on The Power, Salazar never would have even known about Mickey...or Tommie."

"If that's the case, Mickey *must* blame himself. How awful!"

Jack felt a headache coming on and pinched the bone between his eyes, sighing deeply. "What a fucking disaster. This whole thing. I know Mickey only meant well, but he took a big risk by getting involved. I mean, it took a lot of courage, taking on a guy like Salazar. But he didn't see the big picture. A psycho like Salazar? He's capable of anything. Even your family is fair game. That's what happened with Tommie. Mickey just couldn't stop it."

He stood up and stretched his back, moaning in the

process. He closed his eyes and shook his head. "I think it was the coke that did it."

"What?"

"The coke. I told you Mickey does a lot of it. It made him delusional. Giddy. I don't know, manic I guess. It's what drugs do. It can make you impulsive, distracting you from the broader sense of things. He made lots of hasty decisions while he was on it and I just *knew* there was gonna be trouble. I tried to talk sense into him but he wouldn't listen. I know he had good intentions but…eventually it all caught up to him."

He sat back down heavily on the swing. A cold wind stirred out of the northwest, brushing past them with a chilling finger. Tessa shuddered and crossed her arms. "Hope he comes out soon. It's freezing out here."

Jack stood up and took her hand. "C'mere," he said and drew her toward him. He turned her around and held her from behind, warming them both in the process. "Shared bodily warmth," he said smiling, and kissed her neck.

They both rocked there for a moment, watching the last few yellow leaves fly away in the November breeze. Somewhere in the neighborhood a fireplace was being put to use, and the smell of burning wood filled the early evening air. The blast of a train horn rang out, announcing the arrival of thousands of daily commuters returning home. Jack took Tessa by the hand and brought her over to a bench. They sat down together and she put her legs over his and leaned into him. "I always wondered why people did drugs," Tessa said, "What is it that makes people that way?"

"I don't know. It makes them feel good I guess."

"I know, but what is it that drives us towards that kind of…artificial pleasure?"

"What do you mean?"

"Well you're a biologist, right? You studied Evolution. Biochemistry. Natural Selection. Why did our brains evolve to feel that kind of stimulation? What is it that drives us to do these drugs?"

"Good question."

"It's called *euphoria*, right? I mean, we don't really feel euphoria naturally. The kind of pleasure that one feels doing, let's say, heroin. So why can we do that? How did that benefit us as we evolved? What does it do for us now, except get us all addicted?"

"All good questions. I don't know. The brain is so complicated we can't even begin to understand how complex it is. People are emotional creatures, and I'm pretty sure those pleasure centers that are stimulated by drugs have something to do with emotions. Primitive people experimented and explored by instinct. Discovery actually did have many advantages for us. But over the years, there's no doubt that primitive man came across these drugs in nature. Opiates came from poppy plants. Technology just purified them and made them stronger. Maybe *that's* the problem. We made the drugs so potent, addicts just want them more and more." He shook his head sadly. "I don't know, maybe there are parts of the brain better left alone. It would sure eliminate a lot of heartache." He looked at his watch and sighed.

Tessa considered this explanation. "It kinda makes sense, Jack. But somehow I think there's more to it."

"Well, yeah," Jack said, "Believe me, with all that's

happened to Mickey I've thought about it a lot. Sometimes I think it has nothing to do with nature."

"What do you mean?"

"Well, some people, religious leaders for example, might say that it has something to do with temptation and discipline. They say we're all supposed to live moral lives, and for good reason. Look what happens to people with vices. Gambling, sex and drugs, they all lead to bad decisions. Sometimes even, as we saw with Tommie, death. All these things give us excitement and pleasure at first, but in the end can leave people sick, empty and lost. Who knows, maybe that's why gambling, prostitution, and drugs are illegal. Those things can ruin lives. And maybe that's why certain religions call them sins."

"You're saying this is God working in mysterious ways? Tempting us with sins to test our resolve?"

"Maybe that *is* it. Built in desires for pleasure *can* be overwhelming for a lot of people. God knows we all want that immediate gratification. It's the people who can resist these things, people with discipline, who usually are the ones rewarded with happiness and contentment."

Tessa nuzzled into his chest. "It all seems so complicated. Maybe we should just keep it simple."

"How do we do that?" Jack asked.

Tessa chuckled quietly. "Fall in love, appreciate all life has to offer, and try to make the world a better place."

Jack raised an eyebrow and glanced down at her. "If it were only that easy."

* * *

They sat there together for a while, both silently

reviewing the events of the past few weeks and considering Mickey's grim scenario. All at once, Tessa sat up with a start. She frantically pointed across the park and cried, "Jack! Look!"

Roused suddenly from his own reverie, Jack moved Tessa aside and bolted upright. Through the chain-link fence and across the street, Jack saw a skinny young man with his head bowed down, moving purposely along the sidewalk. His hands were thrust deep in the pockets of his tight worn jeans. He had wavy brown hair and was wearing a denim jacket and black Converse sneakers.

Jack turned to Tessa, an urgent look in his soft hazel eyes. "Give me a minute," he said and took off toward the opening in the fence. Tessa took a few steps after him, but then stopped, fraught with curiosity and concern. She decided to watch from a distance.

Jack ran toward the briskly walking man and when he was within twenty yards or so, cried, "Mick!"

Mickey seemed not to hear at first and appeared to be muttering to himself as he moved on his way. As Jack closed in, he slowed down, the last of his footfalls slapping heavily on the pavement. "Mick, Mick! WAIT UP!" he called out and went to reach for his friend's arm.

Mickey suddenly spun on his heels and backed up in a defensive stance, his eyes wild with fear. He took his hand out of his pocket and flashed his blade, ready to use it at any moment.

"GET THE FUCK AWAY!" he yelled and bluffed a stab Jack's way.

Jack darted back and cried "Mick! It's me! Jack!"

Mickey's face transformed from fury, to confusion, and

then finally recognition. He stared at Jack for a moment, looked frenetically around for others, and then put the knife away.

"What the fuck, Mick!? What's wrong with you!?" Jack said.

"Leave me alone," Mickey said and began to walk away.

Jack ran around him but gave him a wide berth. Once in front, Jack held out his hand and said, "Come on, Mick. Talk to me. I've been waiting around in the freakin cold for an hour."

Finally Mickey slowed down, an exasperated look on his face. "What are you doing here?"

"What am I doing here? You disappear off the face of the earth, you don't answer my phone calls, and your folks told me you took off weeks ago. What gives?"

Mickey swallowed. "You talked to them, huh?"

"Yeah, they're concerned about you and quite frankly so are a lot of people. Including me."

"Yeah, well, don't let them fool you. My family doesn't give a shit about me anymore."

"What? What are you talking about? Families don't just stop caring."

"Mine did, Jack. Trust me. They blame me for Tommie."

"No, they don't."

"Yeah, they do, Jack. My sisters can't stand to be around me, my mom pities me, and Pop practically threw me out the door. Believe me. They don't want any part of me." He started to walk again, but Jack grabbed his arm. Mickey jerked it back and Jack jumped away.

"Relax, Mick. I'm not here to hurt you. Just…leave the knife alone."

Mickey looked at him for a moment. A new sadness fell upon his face and he sighed deeply. "I don't know what to do, Jack. I have nothing now. Everything I loved is gone. Tommie…" He swallowed hard. "Jesus Christ, Jack. Tommie's dead. Gone. Never gonna see him again. The dreams we all had. Busted, like glass. All 'cause of me."

"No, Mick. It wasn't you. Salazar—"

"Don't tell me it wasn't me! You *know* if I didn't get in his way none of this woulda happened. It was me and my stupid ego. JESUS! What was I thinking? My father was right. I put my whole family at risk by getting involved in this shit."

"But you did it for all the right reasons, Mick. You did it for the town when the cops wouldn't do anything. You did it for everyone here. The stores that were getting robbed, the girls who were getting raped, the kids who were getting drugs. And as much as it's hard to believe now, you did it for your family."

Mickey just shook his head and motioned Jack to stop. "What? Are you crazy? My family is ruined because of me."

"But your heart was in the right place. It may not seem like it now, but at the time you were looking out for everyone."

"No, Jack. I was looking out for my own glory."

Jack studied at him long and hard. "Mick, you're telling me that when you decided to stop Salazar, you weren't thinking of protecting your little brothers, your niece and nephews? Come on, Mick. I was there. You might have liked the idea of being a hero, but you were doing it for all of us. You put your own neck on the line for the whole town."

Mickey just looked down and shook his head. "It doesn't make a difference now anyway."

"What do you mean it doesn't make a difference? Salazar is gone now. No one's afraid anymore. No more drugs to kids. No more sex slaves. And store owners can now make a living without worrying about some punk coming to them for money. You cleaned the streets up for us, Bro."

Mickey looked miserable. "You know why Salazar's gone, Jack?"

"Because of you, Mick. He lost his cool. He thought you killed Frankie and did something stupid. He got cocky and got caught."

Mickey shook his head. "That's not what I meant, Jack. You know why he's *gone*?"

Jack stood back, not sure where this was going.

Mickey leaned in close and said, "He's gone because I killed him. With my bare hands. These hands. I took his head and mashed it into the ground." He paused for effect. "So there you have it. I'm a murderer too. And it wasn't the first time. Remember Lenny Morales? The kid some girl claimed was killed by a stranger after he tried to rape her? That was me, Jack. I caught him raping this girl so I stabbed him. Murdered him in cold blood. That's why I got out of The Shamrocks in the first place. I wanted to get away from all this shit."

As they spoke, the evening air began to thicken. The cloud cover above seemed to collapse under its own weight, lowering a cool mist toward the ground. It left a clammy dampness all around.

The two of them heard a noise and looked back. Tessa was leaning on a car several yards away. She was biting one of her fingernails and listening intently. Neither of the boys knew how long she had been there.

Jack just nodded at her and motioned that all was okay and she should stay where she was. He turned back to Mickey. "Sorry about that. She's with me," he said.

Mickey peered over toward her, wary of her presence. "Is that Tessa?"

"Yeah, we've been together for a little while now."

Mickey turned his head this way and that, scanning around for anyone else who might be close by. "You shouldn't have brought her here."

"She's no threat, Mick."

"I told you, no one should be around me. Nothing but bad shit happens to people around me."

"Mickey, that's ridiculous."

"Right, ridiculous. Tommie's gone, Jack. *Gone.* Because of me. You can say all you want about why it is or what it is. The fact is he's no longer here." He began to choke up. "Nothing matters anymore, Jack. There's nothing for me now. I have no family, no job, no money, and I'm living with the weight of guilt so heavy on my head I can barely breathe. I can't sleep because I have nothing but nightmares and whatever sleep I get is not enough because I dread waking up in the morning."

"Mick, things will get better. You just need a little time."

"No, Jack. You have no idea what I'm going through here. My life is shit."

"Let me help you, Mick."

Despondently, Mickey peered over Jack's shoulder to catch of glimpse of Tessa. A single tear ran down her cheek.

He looked back at Jack and said, "There's nothing you

can do for me, anymore. I'm lost. Take care of your own life." He turned and moved quickly away.

"Mick!" Jack cried and took a few steps toward him.

"Leave me ALONE!" he cried, and ran off in a sprint.

Jack turned to Tessa and said, "Wait here!" and took off after him.

Tessa wasn't sure what to do. As the heavy mist moved in, she watched the boys disappear around the corner and sighed. She jumped up on the hood of a car and rested her head in her hands. *Jack knows what he's doing*, she thought, *I'll give him a few minutes.*

* * *

It wasn't easy keeping up with Mickey. He was a fast runner. His legs were longer than Jack's and he was moving further away by the moment. Jack had to strain to see Mickey's form, and with every second, it was getting harder and harder to see. The darkness was settling in now, the fog becoming a pearly veil, swallowing everything up in its murky silence.

With his eyes peering toward the end of the block, Jack watched in frustration as Mickey turned the corner and disappeared from sight. He then redoubled his efforts, pressing on with even more desperation. He chased Mickey with reckless abandon now, nearly losing his footing around the corners, as the mists coated the streets with a slick dampness. An oppressive silence now hung in the air, the only sounds being his heavy breaths and the wet echo of his shoes clattering on the pavement.

But as he turned the next corner, Jack wasn't remotely prepared for what he was about to see. Halfway down the block, Mickey had fallen and was struggling to get back on his feet. He was holding the side of his neck, which was now spraying a steady stream of blood from between his fingers. Over and over he attempted to stand, only to stumble a few steps then drop back to the ground.

"MICK!" Jack yelled and haphazardly ran to his friend, who no longer had the power to stand on his own. He skidded clumsily toward Mickey's prone body, his feet nearly coming out from under him. In a deep state of dismay, Jack turned him over. Mickey writhed in both pain and confusion as Jack watched his blood flow copiously out of a deep gash, which ran clear across the side of his neck.

Jack clutched his friend to his chest and pleaded, "MICK! What the fuck happened?!" He searched Mickey's face for an answer, but he was barely conscious. *Had he run into some fence wire? It didn't make sense.* "HELP! SOMEBODY CALL 911!" Jack yelled to anyone who could hear. He searched the area in desperation, but saw and heard nothing, enveloped by a dense shroud of gloom. "Jesus Christ, Mick, hang in there, man. Don't worry, we'll get you to a hospital. Just stay with me, buddy. *Please!* Don't you die on me now. SOMEONE HELP!!"

Mickey reached out and touched his arm. Jack noticed that the fear in his expression had softened into weary acceptance. Mickey then shook his head and Jack thought he caught a hint of a smile on his face. He pulled Jack down by the collar, bringing his lips to his ear. He then whispered something which caused Jack to clench his eyes in sorrow. He pulled back and looked into Mickey's imploring eyes. "I will, Mick," he said, "I will. I promise. Don't worry.

You'll be there to see it. Now just relax. We'll get you an ambulance."

All at once, Mickey clutched Jack's jacket tightly, seemed to tense up, then fell listless in Jack's arms, the light fading from his eyes like the dying embers of a once mighty blaze.

"Jesus Christ, Mick! MICK!" Jack cried, and was about to attempt CPR, when all at once he felt a sudden jolt, a faint ringing sound, and a blinding flash of light.

And then nothing...

* * *

Tessa's curiosity was getting the better of her. Not only was she afraid of what might happen between Jack and Mickey, but she was getting creeped out being alone on the streets on a silent, foggy night. She jumped down from the car and headed quickly in the boys' direction, the way she knew led toward the church. She felt bad ignoring Jack's request but thought maybe she could somehow help out in the matter. She could calm Mickey down or at the very least be there for Jack. She began a slow run.

As she reached the second block, she heard Jack cry out in panic and her heart nearly stopped. "CALL 911!" he yelled, and she broke into a frantic sprint, making small whining noises as she ran.

Heart pounding, she turned onto Bay Street. On the right, the poorly lit street was lined with brooding warehouses, seafood storage facilities housing the bass and bluefish that were brought in by fishermen every day. Each night, the sea creatures lay on their icy graves, waiting to be picked up by delivery trucks the following morning.

To the left was the Sound. Tessa couldn't see it, but she

felt its presence nonetheless. The restless voice of the water filled the air with the invisible shrieks of angry seagulls and the incessant lapping of the tide against the wharves, as if it were tasting the world, wanting to know what it could consume next.

And the fog lay on top of it all, growing and pulsating, spilling over the docks and blanketing the streets with gloom. Tessa stopped, her chest heaving for air as she frantically searched for Jack. She was about to call out when she first caught a glimpse of the most grotesque scene she would ever see.

Two lifeless forms lay in the middle of the street, one on top of the other. Instantly she knew who they were. Her hand flew to her mouth and she gasped, unable to breathe. She suddenly felt very cold, as if icy fingers were caressing her heart.

She was about to run toward them when a strange-looking form suddenly appeared out of the shadows, stopping her in her tracks. He was in black, from neck to toe, with dark gloves covering his hands and a turtleneck up to his chin. The black of his clothes in the darkness made his body practically invisible, save for his white, shiny head, which seemed to float above the ground as he moved.

The head approached the bodies speaking to itself, assessing the situation and nodding. It then peered around suspiciously, making sure it was alone. When it turned her way, Tessa ducked behind a car and froze, vulnerable and alone. She waited until it was safe to look again.

After a few seconds she slowly peeked around the car. She couldn't believe her eyes. The head was now hovering over the bodies, which now appeared to be moving on their own. The head muttered and snapped and giggled to itself as Jack's body was pulled off of Mickey.

Then Tessa then saw the blood. They were covered with it. "JACK!" she cried and moved away from the car.

The head suddenly shot toward her and snarled. "What do YOU want!?" it demanded. The voice sounded deep and shrill, like that of a withered old hag. It glowered at her hatefully.

"What happened? What are you doing to them?!" she cried, her voice wracked with fear.

"None of your business!" Sticks Favors yelled. "Now go away!"

"Leave them alone!" Tessa begged.

Sticks just looked back, smug and defiant. "You're not the boss of me!" he said. "Who do you think you are?" You people think you're so special. Yeah, too cool for school, all of you. So much better than everyone else. Well I'm the one in charge now. Just try to stop me."

Tessa stared incredulously. *What the hell was he talking about?* "What do you mean 'better than you'? I don't even know you!"

Sticks grinned sinisterly. "Oh yes, you do," he mocked, and reached down to pick up what looked like an elongated pole. He pointed it at her. "Remember this?"

Tessa's breath caught in her throat. She reached for her forehead where he had hit her at The Live Wire so many weeks ago.

"Now stay back and be quiet!" Sticks said. "You're ruining my moment!"

He bent down and rolled Jack on his back, then sat down on his chest and unzipped Jack's jacket. In one motion he ripped Jack's shirt open, the buttons popping off and flying in all directions.

Almost reflexively, Tessa cried, "GET OFF HIM!" and took a run at the glowing head.

But Sticks was fast. Before she got too close, he reached down, pulled the top half off the pool stick, and jabbed it in her direction. At the end of the stick was a sharpened metal spear stained red with sticky blood. "STAY AWAY!" he screeched, and she skidded to a halt.

She looked around desperately. She was utterly powerless. Not knowing what to do, she balled up her fists, pulled her arms to her sides, and doubled over. "HELP! SOMEONE HELP US! PLEASE!" she cried. But her pleas went unanswered, save for the lapping of the cold, unfeeling sea.

Sticks decided to ignore her. He had to move fast if he was to finish what he started, and he had no time to chase down the little slut. He looked down at Jack's peaceful face and was instantly nauseated. "Banks," he said, "*Mr. Entitled.* Thought I'd forget about you, didn't you? Think you're so much better than me? 'Fuck off, you freak,' huh? In front of all those people? Think I'd take that lightly? Well you were wrong, big shot! This is *my world*! I am in charge now. And it's time for you to go!"

Tessa had to do something. But what? She took off her gloves and began to circle behind him. She had to stop him somehow.

Sticks closed his eyes and raised his face to the sky. He breathed in deeply, held it for a moment, and exhaled as if in a blissful trance. He then raised the pool stick above his head, the sharp end pointed perilously down at Jack. Grinning malevolently, he opened his eyes. "REDEMPTION!" he yelled ferociously and went to plunge the dagger down into Jack's chest.

"NOOOOOO!" Tessa screamed as she lunged forward. From behind Sticks, she grabbed the butt end of the stick and held on for dear life.

"GET OFF!" Sticks yelled and tried in vain to thrust the weapon down. Tessa twisted around and got the stick under her arms and close to her body. Sticks was in an awkward position. His back was to Tessa, his body was extended, and his arms were up in the air.

"LET GO!" he yelled and tried one more time to pull the stick down.

But the cue was slick with the dampness of the air and the sweat from his hands. He pulled down in one last ditch effort, but Tessa jerked back with all her might. The wider end of the pool stick held fast in her hands, and to Sticks' horror, the pool cue slid up out of his hands, slicing deep gashes into his palms.

Ribbons of excruciating pain shot up Sticks' arms. He cried out and gazed in horror as his hands bled and cramped up into hideous claws. He stumbled off of Jack and shrieked with rage, stomping around in spasms of agony.

"GIVE THAT TO ME! IT'S MINE!" he yelled, eyeing Tessa with an animalistic enmity.

Tessa stood her ground, her left hand gripping the middle of the stick and her right on its rubber base. "NO!" she yelled. "GO AWAY!" She tried to sound intimidating, but she was unable to stop her crying.

"YOU'RE GONNA BE IN TROUBLE!" he said.

"I DON'T CARE!" Tessa yelled.

A faint police siren then began to ring out in the distance. A flicker of hope registered on Tessa's face. "*You're* the one who's gonna be in trouble if you don't get out of here."

Sticks raised his head, looked off into the distance, and listened to the approaching sirens. He then let out a high-pitched wail and began punching his thighs and stomping his feet. Finally, he glared hideously at Tessa. "YOU LITTLE BITCH! YOU RUINED EVERYTHING! NOW GIVE THAT TO ME!"

He ran at her and she took several steps back in fright, all the time holding the weapon up in defense. He launched himself at her and she tripped backward over Mickey's prone body. As Sticks was upon her, in a cry of terror, she thrust the spear up into the underside of his jaw, through his mouth and into the base of his brain. It made a sound like CHHHHCCKK! and he fell down on top of her, convulsing, blood spurting everywhere.

Tessa shrieked with revulsion. With a grunt, she shoved him off and watched in horror as his arms and legs jerked in spasm until he was finally still.

* * *

When she finally felt it was safe, Tessa shuddered and quickly turned to Jack. Kneeling by his side, she saw with dread that he had suffered some sort of blunt trauma to his head. Thick oozing blood covered his face and his hair was matted down and sticky. Frozen by panic, she could do nothing but sob and lovingly caress his face.

"Jack? Hon?" she barely managed. "Are you okay? Can you hear me?" When he didn't respond, she clenched her eyes shut and lay her head upon his chest. She could feel his breathing as she wept, but it was labored and weak. The nurse in her awoke and she became more and more worried about the blood loss. There was just so much of it. She began to think coma, brain damage, death.

The sirens were approaching in the distance, but *what the hell was taking so long*? "Jack, wake up," she said to him. "Please. Don't do this to me! I need you!" She started to shake him more forcefully. "Jack! Wake up! Don't leave me!" When he still didn't move, she finally stopped shaking him, overwhelmed with grief. She then closed her eyes, lowered her head above his face, and whispered, "Please, God. Don't take him from me…I love him."

Her tears came heavy now and streamed down to the edge of her chin. She was too distraught to notice them collecting there, and rather than wiping them off, she allowed them to pool and drip onto his face.

He stirred.

Tessa gasped and said, "Jack! Oh my God! Are you alright?!"

He moaned and opened his eyes for a moment. He tried to sit up, but a sledgehammer of pain slammed into the side of his head and he moaned in agony. His face contorted into a grimace and he said, "What happened? Where am I?"

"Everything's okay, Jack. Do you know who I am?"

He was able to open his eyes briefly and look at her. He closed his eyes and managed a groggy smile. "Of course. You're my guardian angel." He heard the sirens approaching. "Am I dead?" he asked with his eyes still closed.

"No, you are most definitely not dead, Jack…thank God. Do you remember anything?"

Jack lay still for a moment and frowned. "Not sure. I was chasing after Mickey and then…I don't know. It's a blur." He licked his lips and then cleared his throat. "What happened?"

"That crazy guys Sticks attacked you, Jack. He was gonna kill you, for sure."

He blinked. "So Mickey stopped him?"

Tessa gasped. In all her concern for Jack, she had forgotten about Mickey. She shook her head.

Jack began to sit up again despite the pain in his head. "Where is Mickey?"

Two patrol cars screeched to a halt twenty feet away, their red, blue, and white lights circling the scene like swarms of fireflies. Four cops spilled out of the cars, pointing their weapons at Tessa and Jack.

"Put your hands where we can see them!" one of the officers yelled and the two of them complied.

"We're okay!" Tessa yelled. "We were attacked!"

The cops hurried toward them. "By who?" the same officer asked.

"Him," Tessa said, pointing to the bald-headed corpse with the spear sticking out of his throat.

The cop looked at Sticks and then back at Jack. "You did this, sir?"

Though it hurt like hell, Jack shook his head. "Nope."

"I did it, sir," Tessa said. "He was about to kill my boyfriend."

One of the officers spoke into his radio. "We're gonna need an ambulance at the wharf. STAT!"

Jack looked at Tessa, dumbfounded. "*You did that*? I thought Mickey…where is Mickey?"

Tessa looked back at Jack soberly. She shook her head.

"Tess, where is he!?"

Slowly, she pointed to his left. He turned and his heart suddenly shrank. There, in a deepening puddle of blood lay his best friend, motionless, with a vacant, empty stare. It was clear that Mickey was gone.

Jack froze.

"Are you two okay?" another officer asked. "Can you stand up, sir?"

The lights began to swim in front of him. He felt a crippling nausea. A ball of bile shot up his throat and he caught the bitter, acidic substance in his mouth. He didn't want anyone to see him throw up, so he crawled away and was somehow able to make it to the dock. He stuck his head over the water and it all came out.

"Jack!" Tessa cried and went after him. He retched and retched as Tessa put her hand on his back and comforted him as best she could. When he was done, he turned and sat down, leaning on his left hand for support, his left foot out and his right foot flat, knee in the air. He spit and wiped his mouth with his sleeve. "Sorry," he muttered, his head still swirling and throbbing. He sat there, bewildered, for the next few moments.

The cops just stood there, waiting to see what would happen next.

"Any you guys got water?" Tessa asked, and the youngest officer, as if roused from a trance, ran to one of the cars and brought back a small bottle of Poland Spring. He couldn't have been much older than Tommie. Looked a little like him too.

"Thanks," Tessa said, without little disgust and handed

the bottle to Jack. After he took a drink, awareness took hold of him. He glanced over toward Mickey's body, where one of the cops was checking for a pulse.

"NO!" he yelled and got to his feet. He stumbled over as quickly as he could.

The officer stood up and held out his hand. "Sir, you need to stay back."

Jack's voice was hoarse. "He's my best friend, asshole!"

The officer kept his hand up and looked at the others for guidance. His partner then said in a sad voice, "Leave him alone, Bill. The ambulance is on its way."

The cop stepped aside and Jack moved around him. When he looked down, his chest wrenched into a knot of ice.

Mickey was dead. It was starting to sink in. Jack would never watch football with him again. Never hear his stupid jokes or see his shit-eating grin again. Never play golf or poker or talk about girls with him again. He was gone. It was all starting to sink in, yes. But it never would, *ever could* make sense to Jack.

Ever.

Mickey lay on his back in a pool of blood, his eyes gazing blankly up to the sky. A strange expression was on his face, an expression that would perhaps be on his face for all eternity. It mesmerized Jack because it wasn't the agonized frown he had seen on Mickey earlier that day. It was a look of enlightenment, salvation, as if all the weight of his miserable life had finally been lifted away. And he was now free.

The thought seemed to comfort Jack for a moment, but then he realized how much he was going to miss his dear friend and he dropped to his knees. He gazed sorrowfully down at Mickey and shook his head in disbelief. When he spoke, his voice came out in a harsh whisper. "It wasn't for nothing, pal. It wasn't for nothing."

Tessa came over and took one of his hands in both of hers. "Jack," she said.

He looked at her, searched her eyes for an answer, and pulled her close. He shut his eyes hard and tears quietly fell. Then they got up together and Tessa began to lead him away.

But as they started, Jack glanced back and was once more stricken by Mickey's expression. He stopped Tessa and lingered, trying to somehow decipher his face, and for the first time also took notice of Sticks Favors. His body, too, was lying in a pool of blood. And his bloodied hands held fast to the stake that stuck out of his throat. But it was his expression too, that Jack now noticed. For the both of them, Mickey and Favors, gazed gently toward the heavens in a state of eternal bliss, free of the pain that would have haunted them for the rest of their lives.

He frowned, trying once again to understand what no one had ever understood in the history of man.

Enlightenment.

"C'mon," Tessa said gently. "Now let's go get *your* head fixed."

Epilogue

A Complete Circuit

It was a Saturday morning, the second week of May, and as noon approached, the sun rose into an expanse of radiant, resplendent blue. Around it, the sky was unbroken save for randomly painted wisps of white, which hung like various shapes of pulled cotton, floating across the atmosphere. Here and there, trails of plane vapors crisscrossed, leaving a patchwork of grey-white streams soaring high into the heavens.

The mid-spring morning was alive, the Japanese cherry blossoms blooming in explosions of pink, while the dogwood stood fragrant with clumps of white flowers decorating its branches. Little grey sparrows chattered and danced excitedly through puddles while the red, dignified cardinal whistled its early spring song.

Much had changed in Cunningham Park over the past six months, and if anyone had been away in that time, they never would have recognized it upon their return. Most of the concrete had been removed and replaced by lawns of well-watered green. New handball and basketball courts had been built and a sizable fountain had been constructed in the middle of the park.

It was promising to be a warm and pleasant day, and many people had already arrived to enjoy the beautiful weather. Kids were playing games on the courts, posturing, trash-talking, and laughing. And young couples sat around the fountain, eating sandwiches and bathing in the sun.

Jack and Tessa entered the park walking hand in hand, each holding a bouquet of flowers. Tessa held a dozen roses, their deep red bursting with color, their fragrance both familiar and fine. But Jack's was a more striking arrangement that looked as if a lot of thought had been put into it. There were huge pink stargazer lilies, bearded irises, and pink and peach Gerbera daisies nestled beside purple liatris, peach snapdragons, and lots of purple statice. A couple of large yellow chrysanthemums completed it all.

Tessa was wearing a yellow sundress printed with large blue and white flowers. On her feet she wore comfortable sandals and her toenails were painted new. Her short hair was held back from her face by a carefully placed barrette. She had an anxious look upon her face, and every once in a while she glanced uneasily at Jack.

When he felt her squeeze his hand, he almost reflexively lifted hers and pressed it to his lips. He then rubbed it on the side of his cheek and turned to her. His normally serene, amber colored eyes seemed unusually unsettled that morning. He smiled nervously at Tessa and put her hand on his chest.

"Jeez," Tessa said, "your heart's racing!"

"Is it?" Jack said and pulled her hand away. He looked anxiously over his right shoulder.

Tessa reached up and brushed Jack's loose blonde hair away from his eyes. "We can do this, Jack," she said. "You *need* to do this." She gave him an understanding smile.

Jack took in her face again: the genuine sympathy and profound affection of her features. He blinked, smiled uneasily, and took a shakey breath. "Yeah," he said, "I think I can do this."

He took her hand again and they proceeded down the path between the cherry blossoms and the dogwoods, past people on benches, young mothers holding babies and intellectuals reading books. Once they got to the other side of the fountain, they stopped and looked up at a newly erected statue.

Jack froze, seeing it for the first time.

"Wow," he said. "They did an amazing job."

Tessa nodded in wonder. "Looks just like him."

The likeness of Mickey O'Leary had been commissioned by the local government and funded by an anonymous group of dignitaries to be erected in Cunningham Park. Word had leaked that the group included, among others, Barney O'Leary, Fire Chief Artie Connor, Commissioner Joe Cassidy, and The Honorable Winchester Harrington, the newly appointed county judge, in whose bedroom Tommie's body was found.

The sculptor had consulted with Jack on how to do the job. Jack was delighted to be involved and was extremely enthusiastic about the idea. But when he learned that the project had been completed, he had become too nervous to see the result. He was afraid that the statue would somehow be unflattering, a mockery of his best friend on display for years on end.

But it was sight to behold. There, standing ten feet tall in front of them was Mickey, larger than life, a sober expression of undying gratitude, an encouraging smile upon his face. He was leaning back against a wall, one foot up against it and his left arm across his waist. His left arm held his right elbow and his right hand made a fist, telling anyone gazing upon him, I love you, man. *Go kick some ass.*

Tessa walked over to the base of the statue and placed the roses there. The stone was etched with Mickey's birth and death dates and words by which to remember him.

Tessa read it out loud. "This statue commemorates Soundview's own true hero, Mickey O'Leary. For years, Mickey's courage, toughness, and sense of fairness helped protect our streets when all else failed. Founder of the legendary vigilante gang, The Shamrocks, Mickey risked and lost everything to keep us all safe. He will be forever remembered with love, admiration, and gratitude"

"That's beautiful, Jack," Tessa said. "You really wrote that?"

He just nodded silently, gazing up at the statue until a lone tear fell from his eye. "Good," he choked out, "good." He then smiled and said, "It's time, bro."

Tessa looked puzzled. "What's time?" she said.

Jack just looked at her and smiled nervously.

"Jack, what's time?"

"Nothing."

He just kept looking at her with a stupid frozen smile.

Tessa frowned and looked at the other people around them, waiting for the punch line. "Um, Jack? You're acting weird. You want to sit down?"

He cleared his throat and said, "No, I want to stay here."

"Are you gonna put the flowers down by Mickey?"

"No."

"You want me to put the flowers down for you?"

"No."

"Okay, then what do you want to do?"

Jack looked at Mickey and said, "Here goes." Finally, despite the agitation in his stomach, Jack said to her, "The flowers aren't for Mickey."

"Really? I thought…"

"They're for you."

Her face flushed, the rosiness highlighting the blueness of her eyes. She drew in a breath and then grinned, "Wow, that's so sweet!" She reached up and hugged him. "You're the best."

When she stepped back, she took the flowers and pulled them to her face. "Mmmm, they smell so good. But what's the occasion?"

He took one of her hands and gazed at her like the explorer who just discovered Victoria Falls, the Grand Canyon, or the Aurora Borealis. To Jack, she was as majestic as one of the seven the natural wonders of the world. She was the wonder of *his* world.

"You see…" he began, but his voice failed him in her presence once again, and it came out in a croak.

Tessa giggled. She was used to it. "Jeremiah was a bullfrog," she sang, causing Jack to smile and poke her in her side.

Her cleared his throat and started again. "You see all this?"

Confused, Tessa looked around. "The park?"

"Not just the park. The trees, the blossoms, the birds singing." He looked up at the sky and raised his hands to it. "This sky. This fucking gorgeous day."

"Um, yeah?"

"This all means nothing to me without you. I could win a million dollars today and it wouldn't mean a thing without you, Tess." He looked back at Mickey and then reached into his pocket and took out a small black velvet box.

Tessa's hand shot to her mouth and she gasped. "Oh my God!" she whispered.

"Tessa, when I'm with you I never want to be anywhere else. I'm drawn to you. I'm *fascinated* with you and I want to learn so much more about you. You are the color in my life. You are the sanity in my world when nothing else makes sense. From the deepest part of my heart, I love you."

He knelt down and opened up the box to reveal a 1.25-carat, round-cut diamond ring that glittered and shimmered in the radiant sun. It almost blinded Tessa as she looked at it.

"Will you marry me, Tessa Dori?"

Her hand dropped to her chest, but her smile faded and changed into a look of disbelief. Tears welled up in her eyes and she couldn't speak. When she held out her hand, Jack slipped on the ring. It was a perfect fit. He then took her in her arms in an embrace they would share many times for years to come.

Applause rose up from the onlookers. When Tessa heard this, she laughed through her tears, the giggling expressing a whirlwind of shyness, gratitude, and joy. Too aware of everyone watching, she took Jack by the hand and drew him over to a bench.

Jack beamed. He bent to look in her eyes and chuckled. "You okay?"

Tessa wiped at her tears and punched him in the arm.

"Ow!" he said and laughed again.

"So why today?" she asked. "What was so special about today?"

Jack looked back at the statue of Mickey. "That night. The one when Mickey died? After my head injury, I really couldn't remember much. Everything came back to me in pieces, but I never could put it all together. Then last week, I'm not sure if it was in a dream or if it really happened, but…"

"What?"

"I remember Mickey saying something to me before he died."

"Really?"

He looked at her and nodded soberly. "Tess, I knew from early on you were the one for me. I just could sense it deep inside. I knew I could never feel for anyone the way I feel for you. But Mickey knew this too. And he kept me out of all the problems with Salazar and Tommie because he wanted me to be with you."

He looked at the ground and then back at Tessa.

"Mickey's dying wish was for me to propose to you. I promised him he'd be there to see it. After he passed, this was the closest thing to making it happen.

Tessa said nothing but slowly got up and walked over to Mickey's statue. She looked up into his eyes for a long time, saying nothing, doing nothing. Finally she said, "Thank you." She then bent down, kissed her hand, and pressed it to the plaque. Then she walked back over to Jack.

"This is amazing," she said, shaking her head. She gazed at her new diamond ring in disbelief. "This must have been so *expensive*. Where did you get the money from?"

He just looked at his new fiancée and said, "Remember the night we met? The night of the pool tournament?"

Her hand reflexively reached for the scar above her left eye. "Yeah, how could I forget?"

"Well, that night I won two prizes."

"There were two prizes?"

"Yeah, the first one was five grand. That's how I paid for the ring."

"Oh. And the other prize?"

"That was you."

THE END

We are all artists. We alone paint our own canvasses. We alone write our own songs. And as the palettes shift and the melodies rearrange, we must choose wisely. For in the end, only the strongest voices remain, echoing, with the undying resilience of the eternal spirit.

J.M. Abrahams